Shetland Library
Tom Holt

Fal**ling** sideways

25

D0319659

FALLING SIDEWAYS

FALLING SIDEWAYS

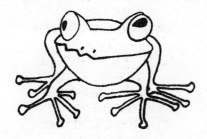

Tom Holt

www.orbitbooks.co.uk

SHETLAND LIBRARY

An *Orbit* Book

First published in Great Britain by Orbit 2002

Copyright © Tom Holt 2002

The moral right of the author has been asserted.

Interior illustrations by Ben Sharpe

*All characters in this publication are fictitious and any resemblance
to real persons, living or dead, is purely coincidental.*

All rights reserved.
No part of this publication may be reproduced,
stored in a retrieval system, or transmitted, in any form
or by any means, without the prior permission in writing of the
publisher, nor be otherwise circulated in any form of binding
or cover other than that in which it is published and
without a similar condition, including this condition,
being imposed on the subsequent purchaser.

A CIP catalogue record for this book
is available from the British Library.

ISBN 1 84149 087 3

Typeset in Plantin by M Rules
Printed and bound in Great Britain
by Clays Ltd, St Ives plc

Orbit
A Division of
Little, Brown and Company (UK)
Brettenham House
Lancaster Place
London WC2E 7EN

In memory of

DAVID GRANT POTTER

(1947 – 2001)

– And thanks for all the fish.

CHAPTER ONE

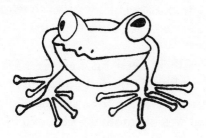

Her name was Philippa Levens, fifth marchioness of Ipswich; and as she smiled at him, her eyes were as clear and bright and brown as they'd been on the day she died, wearing her fire like a bridal veil, on the seventeenth of June 1602. She knew him better than anyone, he was convinced of that, and if only he could reach out and pull her through the glass—

He felt the rope brush against his knee, and pulled himself together. A few millimetres further and he'd have set off the alarm, again; and after the last time, he didn't want to do that. He took a long step back – it felt like a betrayal – and looked up at her again, but somehow the closeness between them had dissipated. She was disappointed in him.

(A middle-aged couple walked up behind him and stopped to look at the painting. He didn't want to resent them, but he did. English people seem to have difficulty telling the difference between art galleries and zoos; they don't often try to feed the pictures with bananas, but only because they know it wouldn't be allowed. English people are only comfortable in the presence of unruly, uncivilised things like animals or art if they know there's a sheet of toughened glass in the way, to stop the predators from getting out. The idea that they're the ones in the cage, or the frame, doesn't seem to have occurred to them yet.)

Ironically, it had been his mother ('David, isn't it about time you found yourself a nice girl . . . ?') who'd introduced them, twenty-one years ago, on his twelfth birthday. That was his mother's idea of a birthday treat; dragging round some dreary old art gallery, followed by tea and stale Black Forest gateau in the gallery café. They'd only stopped in front of Philippa because Mum wanted to get a bit of gravel out of her shoe.

'That's a nice one,' he'd said.

'What?' Mum had looked up, a shoe in her hand. 'Yes, dear. Willem de Stuivens, Dutch school. Quite derivative, of course.'

He'd neither known nor cared what she'd meant by that. He'd been too busy staring at the perfect heart-shaped face of the young girl in the picture. It wasn't a very good painting; the enormous dress was flat and unconvincing, giving him the impression of one of those fairground stalls where you have your photograph taken sticking your head and hands through a big plywood cut-out of the Fat Lady. She – the girl – seemed to think so too, or at least her smile, or grin, or smirk, suggested that she knew perfectly well that her body had come out two-dimensional, and that the joke was on Willem de Whatsisname, not her.

And then she'd stuck her tongue out at him.

It had happened just as he was turning away, and he'd only caught a fleeting glimpse of it out of the corner of his eye. He'd frozen and burned with shame – he had, after all, only that day turned twelve and had just fallen in love for the first time – and he hadn't dared look back; and then Mum had put her shoe back on and said they'd better be getting a move on, they still had rooms fifteen to twenty-six to do before lunch, and they'd been parted, before he'd even had a chance to look at the label on the wall and find out her name.

So, here he was again, twenty-one birthdays later, and here she still was. She was exactly the same, of course; he wasn't. He was very self-conscious about that. It was his thirty-third birthday and already he had a bald spot on the top of his head and a little round tummy like a hobbit, and a quiet voice at the back of his mind was pointing out (sounding ever so faintly like his mother) that it wasn't fair to expect her to wait for him for ever . . . His birthday, traditionally the point in the year when he should be taking stock of his life, considering the path he'd come by and the road ahead; also, by a coincidence so huge it blotted out the sun, the day when a lock of hair, reputed to be that of the notorious seventeenth-century witch Pippa Levens, was due to go under the hammer at Larraby's, five hundred yards down the road from the gallery.

So: he took a step forward, as close to the rope and the invisible infra-red barrier as he dared to go, and looked her squarely in the eye.

'Shall I?' he asked.

She grinned at him. It's well known that some paintings have eyes that follow you round the room. Pippa Levens had a grin that followed him everywhere, like a butcher's dog, and it was never the same grin twice.

'Well?' he said, feeling just a little annoyed. The guard by the door turned her head and looked at him.

Of course, he should have known better than to expect a straight answer. He looked away and, as he did so, noticed something for the first time. It was curious, maybe just a trick of the light or a fluke of incidence and refraction, but the painting to the left of Pippa was clearly reflected in the glass of the big display cabinet in the middle of the room, and so was the big, heavy battle scene to her right. He could make out quite a lot of fine detail in both reflections – the horses and the cannon of the battle, the little squashed-looking bird on the hand of the chubby baroness – but Pippa wasn't there, just her frame and a gleaming, smeary blue glow.

He turned round and looked at her one more time. Now her grin was mocking him, telling him that she'd known all along that he didn't have the nerve for a stunt like this; that it was all right, she understood, because it'd be a pretty wild thing to do. Remarkable, this ability she had to burn him up with embarrassment and shame; maybe because, in all his thirty-three years, he'd never found such an accurate mirror as Pippa's glass

He had, of course, made his decision.

Bloody nerve, he thought. Even if she is over four hundred years old, a witch and quite definitively dead, she's got no right to go smirking at me like that, like I'm something small and wriggly she found in a rock-pool.

Now she was laughing at him for getting upset. That was the trouble with her knowing him so well: she could read him at a glance. The one thing he'd never been able to figure out, after all these years and all these visits, was whether she actually liked him.

There was only one way to find that out; and if he hung around here much longer, that one opportunity could easily be gone for ever. What if someone else got the lock of hair – some American, or a museum? Short of burglary (he wasn't cut out for burglary) he'd never have this chance again. At the very least, he had to buy the hair; once he'd got it, safely and permanently his, he could make up his mind about the rest of it later.

He looked up at the painting. Just for once, was she actually smiling now, with approval? He couldn't really see for looking. 'Just stay there,' he said, 'I'll be back.'

It cost him twelve thousand, seven hundred and fifty pounds, exclusive of buyer's premium and VAT. Just as he'd feared, there had been an American, *and* a museum, and they'd clung on like piranhas. It was the first time he'd bought anything in an auction. Probably the worst two hours of his life.

It was just as well that he'd got the necessary money (plus buyer's premium and VAT). Fortunately, one side effect of having fallen hopelessly in love with a dead witch at the age of twelve was that he'd never bothered with girls, parties, people his own age, a life or any of that stuff, which only left work and sleep. He'd got into computers simply because he seemed to have an affinity with bright things on the other side of a pane of glass, and now for the first time in his life he'd actually wanted something, and he'd been able to buy it. So that was all right.

Apparently, you couldn't just pick up what you'd bought and go home with it. You had to wait till the whole auction was over, though you were allowed to leave before the end. The man who'd come over and taken his credit details told him they'd probably all be through by four; that left him with two hours to kill. For some reason he didn't feel like going back to the gallery. He knew he'd feel embarrassed facing her. She'd grin at him ('You spent fifteen thousand pounds on a few bits of old hair? You must be . . .') and he couldn't bear the thought of that. Crazy as a barrelful of ferrets, he muttered to himself, and went for a beer.

The nearest pub to Larraby's was the Blue Boar in New Row. He sat down at a table under the window; through the glass he could see the back door of Larraby's in one direction, and the roof of the building two doors down from the gallery in the other. The beer was authentic, had a silly name, and tasted as if something leprous had died in it several years earlier. He looked at his watch.

'Excuse me.' He lifted his head. A man had slid into the seat opposite, and was looking at him. It was an odd way of looking, inquiring but familiar; as if he was an exhibit of some kind.

'Excuse me,' the man repeated, 'but I believe you were at the sale just now. You were bidding on that lock of hair.'

The man was in his mid-fifties, very dark, with a big nose and a pointed chin; David had an idea that he looked Russian, though he'd never met a Russian in his life. The most noticeable thing about him was the big, ugly scar where his left eye should have been. It was the kind of disfigurement you couldn't help staring at, however hard you tried. These days, of course, there was no excuse for leaving messes like that lying about where they might disturb sensitive people. The man's hair was unconventionally long, and there was a light dusting of dandruff on the collar of his suit jacket; but the suit itself looked very new and extremely expensive. David wasn't terribly good at accents, so he couldn't place this one. It was very faint, in any event. If forced to hazard a guess, David would have said it was either Turkish, Portuguese, Australian or Newcastle.

David really didn't want to talk to this person, but he couldn't see how he could avoid it; the strange man was looking straight at him and smiling pleasantly. They were the only two people in the bar.

'Um,' David said. 'Yes, that's right.'

'Did you get it? I had to leave halfway through.'

David nodded.

'Ah, well done. I saw that Dr Weiss was bidding against you, and I noticed Neil Kovacs from the Sluys Collection had the lot highlighted and ringed in green in his catalogue, so I guess he was after it too. Did they give you a hard time?'

David shrugged. 'Par for the course, I expect,' he said. 'I don't go to auctions, you see.'

'Very wise.' The man's smile widened. He had very white teeth, rather crooked. 'I'm glad you got it, anyway. Or at least, I'm glad Weiss didn't; he belongs to the Alcatraz school of art appreciation – lock it away in a dark place and throw away the key. I'm not sure I follow the logic behind that; presumably it's to teach all those pesky paintings a lesson they won't forget in a hurry. The Sluys Collection isn't quite so bad; at least it's an open prison. Actually, I'm not sure that's any better, but then, I don't really like museums. They always make me think of old-fashioned lunatic asylums, where people could pay to go in and look at the freaks. So; you collect seventeenth-century memorabilia?'

'No,' David said.

'Oh. Well, presumably you collect something, or you wouldn't have outbid Barracuda Weiss for a few strands of hair. So what's your speciality? I imagine there's a theme to your collection, rather than just a magpie's fondness for shiny objects. Curiosities of Old Suffolk? Sorceriana? Bits of dead people?'

There was an intensity in the strange man's one eye that David didn't like one bit; but he was still smiling in a thoroughly pleasant, friendly way. Despite David's rapidly growing panic, he couldn't help thinking that the stranger reminded him of someone.

'I'm sorry,' the man said, leaning back, 'I'm being most offensively nosy. It's a fault of mine. My name's Dean, by the way. Oliver Dean.'

David smiled feebly. 'David Perkins,' he replied. Looking at the man from a very slightly different angle (as he leaned back, the light from the window changed its emphasis just a little) he realised that he instinctively knew two things. One, Oliver Dean wasn't the man's real name. Two, the someone the stranger reminded him of – the resemblance was actually little short of startling – was Pippa Levens. The same chin, the same delicacy about the tapering at the bridge of the nose; the stranger could quite easily have been her father. No, belay that, obviously. The man could quite easily have been her thirteen-greats-grandson, except that she'd died childless – without siblings, too. Aristocracy, David said to himself; all those aristocratic families were related to each other, so it's quite possible that this bloke really could be a distant relative. (Only someone with blue blood sloshing up and down his veins would dare to act so weird in public, so that fitted, too.) Not that that gave him the right to go around terrifying innocent people in pubs; but it might explain why he was so interested in the hair. Maybe the strange man wanted it because of some family connection, and was going to try and buy it from him. He sincerely hoped not; David hated saying 'No' to people, not because he was unusually compassionate or soft-hearted but because it was so embarrassing, especially if they got upset. Fortunately, there had been very few occasions in his life where he'd had anything anybody could conceivably want.

'Maybe you noticed,' the man went on. 'There's a family resemblance, isn't there?'

David thought before answering. 'Sorry?'

And the man had her smile. One of her smiles, anyway. 'Between me and Marchioness Levens,' he said. 'Not surprising – we're related. Distantly. In the past.' He twitched his nose, like a rabbit. 'Actually,' he went on, 'I think I've seen you in the gallery, looking at her picture. Is that it?'

David said nothing. For some reason he was feeling profoundly guilty, as if this man had just caught him with his teenage daughter behind the blackberry bushes.

'It's an absolutely fascinating painting, of course,' the man went on, leaning back slightly. (Letting him off the hook? No, not really; just playing out the line a little.) 'And with a quite remarkable history. Did you know it's been stolen no less than thirteen times?'

No, David hadn't known that.

'And the really curious part is,' the man went on, 'every time it's been returned, a few months or a year later. No attempt to sell it, no ransom demand, no explanation, even: it's just turned up on the doorstep of the place it was stolen from, intact and undamaged. Except for the last time but one, of course; in 1977, I think it was. That time, when it came back, the painting was untouched, as usual, but someone had nailed bars across the frame.'

David breathed in slowly. 'Really,' he said.

'The police reckoned it was something to do with how they planned to smuggle it out of the country; built into something, like a pallet or a crate. Well, it was the only rational explanation anybody could come up with. And Philippa herself,' the man went on. 'Such an amazing career.'

'Is that right?'

'Astonishing,' the man said, 'especially when you bear in mind that she was only nineteen when she died. Hardly more than a child. Except,' he added, producing a small cigar and lighting it, 'that now she's been nineteen for nearly four hundred years. Personally, I'd have hated that. Twelve months of being nineteen nearly finished me off. Mind you, I've heard it said that some people just sort of stick at a certain age – mentally, I mean, like a default setting. Excuse me, I'm rambling. Can I buy you a drink?'

'No, thanks,' David said, very quickly. 'I'm, um, driving.'

'Ah. Very sensible attitude. Heaven knows, there's enough mind-freezingly terrible danger in the world without going out and actively looking for it. Could you tell me the time, please?'

David remembered that there was a clock on the bar directly behind him, plainly visible from where the man was sitting. 'Certainly,' he said, glancing at his watch. 'It's a quarter to five.'

(Was it? Watch must be wrong; it'd been just after two when he came in here.)

'Thanks. I'd better be going. I'm supposed to be retired, you know, but it feels like I'm busier than ever. So nice to have met you. Goodbye.'

The man breathed out a thick cloud of cigar smoke as he stood up; by the time it had cleared, he'd gone. Once he was sure of that, David spun round and looked at the clock on the bar. It said a quarter to five.

Doesn't time fly when you're having fun?

He picked up his glass and put it down again. Maybe, he thought, I should take this as a timely warning; I'm not cut out for weird stuff, I can't handle it, so maybe it wouldn't be entirely sensible of me to go out looking for it. Maybe I'd be better off going home and doing some work for a change.

He remembered something else about the strange man. He'd lit a cigar and drawn on it a few times, enough to produce an awful lot of smoke; but there was no ash in the ashtray, or on the table or the floor, and the damn thing hadn't got any shorter.

Weird indeed. What kind of god talks to you from out of a burning cigar? An unhealthy one, presumably, you'd recognise him instantly when he spoke to you on the road to Damascus because he'd be coughing all the time. More important, why should he choose to talk to me?

David sighed and stood up. He'd been around computers long enough to realise that there are a great many strange, terrible, inexplicable forces loose in the world, and not all of them (the vast majority, yes, but not all) come from the Microsoft corporation. But he'd found that if you ignored them and replaced the motherboard once they'd gone, they tended not to leave behind any lasting, damaging traces; they peered at you through the glass, grinned scornfully, and went away to pick on someone their own size. That was one of the advantages of being very small and insignificant – they only trod on you by accident, not on purpose.

Once he was outside the pub, away from the cigar smoke and the general ambience of weirdness, he felt much better. He checked the time once more by a clock in a shop window – it really was a quarter to five; maybe he'd fallen asleep in there, and the strange man had been a dream – and walked round to Larraby's to pick up his lock of hair.

They were impressively efficient and polite about it, and fairly soon afterwards he was sitting in a Tube train heading west. He was being hustled towards a decision; he could stay on the train till it reached Ealing Broadway, where he'd get off and go home and promise to be good for ever after, or he could jump the train at Ravenscourt Park and go in search of destiny, darkness and danger (assuming he could find it, with only the directions he'd been given over the phone to guide him).

Another coincidence; that, two days after he'd seen the short paragraph in the newspaper about the lock of hair coming up for auction, he'd been coming home from town on the Underground and had been struck down by a desperate need for a pee, in the long, slow haul through the desert between Hammersmith and Acton Town. If he'd caught the Piccadilly rather than the District Line, of course, none of this would have happened, since the Piccadilly didn't stop at the funny little stations in between, he'd have had to dig deep into his inner reservoir of stoicism and held his water as far as Acton. But it hadn't panned out that way; instead, he'd bounded off the train at Ravenscourt Park (wonderfully evocative name, that; until you've actually been there, you can't help conjuring up mental images of Gothic castles, forked lightning and gargoyles) and sprinted painfully out of the station in search of a public bog or a shady, unfrequented section of wall.

Successive governments have ignored the aspirations of Ravenscourt Parkers in the area of communal widdling; as David found on that memorable occasion, there aren't any public bogs within awkward hobbling distance of the railhead. But there are walls and corners and nooks where the wild flowers grow, and it was after he'd found one of these and was beginning to feel a whole lot better that he saw the sign. It was quite some way away in the distance and he couldn't really spare a hand to fish his glasses out of his top pocket; but what he'd thought it said was:

[HONEST JOHN'S HOUSE OF CLONES]

– except that it couldn't really say that, what it probably said was 'clowns' or 'cones' (Honest John's House of Crones? A cosy cottage built by the Three Little Pigs, using the latest in geodetic technology?) or something equally prosaic and mundane. Not clones, though. Surely not.

Once he'd done up his zip and made sure nobody had been watching, he snuck across the road and took a closer look:

[HONEST JOHN'S HOUSE OF CLONES]

– just as he'd thought; and under the big block letters, in fancy italic signwriting,

[*Because everybody needs somebody*]

– and a phone number. The building itself didn't look all that promising: a tatty timber-frame lock-up with the paint peeling off in leaf-sized flakes, the double doors padlocked, a pool of oil soaked away into dust and grime out front. Back when David had owned a car, he'd been to quite a few backstreet garages that looked just like this.

Just then, for some reason, he thought about the lock of hair.

Absolute nonsense, of course. For a start, cloning people was pure science fiction – all right, they could do sheep, but people weren't a bit like sheep (except once every five years or so) and the technology simply didn't exist. And if it had existed, it would have needed to be a huge multibillion-dollar laboratory, and even if it wouldn't have, there'd have been all sorts of laws against it. And even if there hadn't been, even if you could have just strolled into some private establishment and said, 'I'd like half a dozen Mrs Williamsons, please, and can you have them ready by Friday?', nobody in his right mind would have given his custom to an outfit calling itself Honest John's.

And then the little voice spoke to him; not the one that sounded just like his mother, the other one, the quiet, sweet one that he'd suspected for a long, long time belonged to Pippa Levens. Fair enough, the little voice had said to him, somewhere inside his ears, if it's all nonsense and completely impossible, what harm would it do, just writing down the phone number? Just writing it down, you wouldn't actually have to call it. But you'd know it was there.

He'd looked up. And the writing on the door still said:

[HONEST JOHN'S HOUSE OF CLONES]

– just like it had when he first saw it. But this time he had a pencil in his hand, and the back of an envelope.

And sure, simply having the phone number in his possession didn't mean that he was ever going to use it. He'd put the envelope down beside the telephone in the hall. Next time he tidied up (he liked everything nice and neat, because clutter grew in the dark like mushrooms, and next thing you knew you had to climb up on the kitchen table to reach the sink) he'd have forgotten what it signified and he'd throw it away. Nothing was going to happen. It'd all be all right.

Three whole days had passed, and every time he'd passed the phone he'd picked up the envelope and stared at the number, as if hoping it'd mysteriously vanished since the last time he'd looked. On the fourth day he must have been thinking about something else, because by the time he realised what he was doing, he'd already dialled the number.

'Honest John's,' said a voice at the other end of the line.

Even then, he could have slammed the phone down and left the country for a week or so. But he hadn't; contact had been established, and it was *rude* to put the phone down on people (said the little his-mother's-voice). So he'd coughed, and said, 'Honest John's House of, um, Clones?'

'Yeah.'

'Ah.' He hadn't got the faintest idea what to say next.

'Can I help you?' The voice at the other end sounded bored, mostly, as if it had had conversations like this before. That only increased the embarrassment, which in turn increased the pressure on him to say something. Anything . . .

'Do you, er, clone things?' he'd asked.

'Yes, that's right,' said the voice; and he could imagine the man at the other end of the wire, slumping his shoulders, thinking, Oh great, another bloody time-waster. 'You want something cloned, then, do you?'

The correct answer, of course, would have been 'No'. 'Yes,' he replied. 'So you can do that, can you?'

'Depends,' the voice had replied, 'on what it is.'

'Ah. Right.'

'What was it,' the voice asked patiently, 'you had in mind?'

(Bizarre, he'd thought; here I am, talking to a self-proclaimed clone artist called Honest John, and I'm the one feeling embarrassed because I'm afraid I'm sounding like a fruitcake.)

'I've got this lock of hair,' he'd heard himself say. 'Well, I haven't got it yet, actually, but I might be getting it quite soon. Fairly soon. Nothing definite,' he'd added, 'but it's a possibility.'

'I see. Human hair, is this?'

'No. Well, yes.'

Short, excruciating pause. (What's he up to? Is he calling the police on the other line?)

'Are we talking fresh,' the voice said, 'or frozen?'

'Neither.' It occurred to David that he might just possibly get out of this in one piece if the project turned out to be too difficult; if Honest John said, Sorry, no, can't help you there, try NASA or someone like that. 'Actually, it's very old.'

'Right.' Another pause. 'How old, roughly?'

'Centuries,' David said, with a touch of desperation. 'Four hundred years. At least.'

'Mphm.'

'That's much too old,' he said hopefully. 'Isn't it?'

'Not necessarily,' the voice replied. 'I mean, there's your second-hand old, your antique old and your *Jurassic Park* old, if you get my meaning. It all depends on the linear degradation.'

'Ah.'

'I mean,' the voice continued, 'they done all sorts of old things, they done simple mosses from the Late Cretaceous, they done mammoths. Mind you,' the voice added, 'that was the Yanks, they'll do any bloody thing. And the Russians – well, you haven't got a clue what *they* were up to, towards the end. And, 'course, the mammoths were frozen.'

'Well, quite,' David said crazily. 'They would be, wouldn't they?'

'Four hundred years,' the voice went on, 'look at it one way, that's practically yesterday. Or it might be completely fucked, you just don't know.'

'Because of the linear degradation?'

'There's that, and other stuff. Not cheap, either,' the voice went on. 'Not dear, the way these things go, but not cheap, if you know what I mean.'

'Oh, quite,' David said. 'Sort of how much . . . ?'

(He had no idea what had possessed him to ask that. It just seemed called for, by the shape and general drift of the conversation.)

'Well,' replied the voice, 'now you're asking me something. Like, it all depends. Don't even know if we can do the job, let alone give you a firm quote.'

'Ah, right. I quite understand—'

'Definitely not more than fifty, though. Seventy-five, top whack.'

'Seventy-five?'

'At the most. And then there's your vat, of course.'

'VAT?'

'No,' replied the voice wearily, 'your vat. That's another fifteen on top. Not going to see much change out of a hundred, anyway.'

'I see,' David said. 'A hundred thousand pounds.'

This time, the voice sounded bewildered. 'No,' it had said, 'a hundred quid. And there's your gel, of course, call that another ten. Soon mounts up, doesn't it?'

'A hundred and ten pounds? For a clone?'

From the other end of the line, a sigh. 'Bloody dreadful, isn't it? And that's shaving my margins right back, I got to make a living too. No wonder this business is dead on its feet.'

'Thank you,' David had said, in a little, lost voice. 'I'll think about it and get back to you.'

– And now here he was, with his small, crisp curl of hair in its plastic envelope in his pocket, lurching towards Ravenscourt Park to be born. I don't have to do this, he muttered to himself, like a mantra; but the soft, sweet voice was drowning him out, saying, A hundred and ten pounds, it's an absolute bargain. You couldn't buy a decent suit for that. For some reason, he found that argument quite irresistible.

The doors slid open. Through them (as if through

the frame of a picture) he saw the words *Ravenscourt Park*. You Are Here, he thought, and stood up.

There was a very real possibility, so real that with encouragement, support and some Lottery funding it could easily morph into a virtual certainty, that Honest John's wouldn't be there any more. After all, the banshee wailed for perfectly legitimate, straightforward, socially useful businesses every day; strolling through the local industrial estate was like a tour of a utilitarian version of the Valley of the Kings, surrounded on all sides by gauntly looming mausolea of dead enterprises. A backstreet clone shop in the Ravenscourt Park badlands – something like that would probably come and go so fast that it wouldn't even show up in stop-motion photography. In which case, he could forget all about the idea and go home.

Honest John's was still there.

Ah yes, but that didn't necessarily mean it was still in business; and even if it was, the odds against anybody being there and willing to talk to him were comfortingly long. The last time he'd been here, hadn't it been all padlocked up and dark?

Even as the thought crossed his mind, the doors opened. Well, he was still a free man. He could carry on walking past, as if he had nothing more extreme on his mind than whether or not to have curry sauce on his saveloy and chips.

'Evening,' said the man in the doorway.

'Hello,' David replied (and compared to him, one of Pavlov's dogs was an anarchist). 'Are you Honest John?'

The man looked at him with a cold, searching eye. The right one, its counterpart being distressingly conspicuous by its absence. 'That's me,' he said. 'Do something for you?'

David yelped out loud and took a step back. As well as the gruesomely missing left eye, the other points of resemblance between this character and the loony who'd cornered him in the pub were: hair length and colour, nose shape, the Levens chin. This one was scruffier, wearing an Albert Steptoe-exclusive cardigan with holes in the elbows, and he didn't have a cigar. Otherwise they could've been twins.

'Just nipped outside for a smoke,' said Honest John, producing a packet of small cigars. He pointed them at David, either offering him one or threatening him with them (the gesture was ambiguous).

'No, thanks,' David said, in a very quiet voice. 'Excuse me, but have we met before?'

Honest John laughed. 'Nah,' he said. 'I'd remember you. Only, your voice sounds familiar. Did you ring me up a few days ago?'

David admitted that he had.

'Thought so,' said Honest John, breathing out smoke through his nose like a dragon. 'You're that bloke with the bit of hair, right?'

'That's me,' David whispered. It was the same voice that he'd used twenty-five years ago, when owning up in front of the whole class. 'You remind me of someone,' he added.

Honest John looked down at the ground for a moment. 'You must've met my brother Joe,' he said. 'Looks a bit like me. He's an art dealer in Town. Right ponce, but there you are, can't choose your family. Except in my line of work,' he added, with a new variant of the Levens grin, 'and even that's just adding to it, not getting rid of the bloody embarrassing ones. You got your bit of hair, then?'

Lying to this person was impossible; David wanted to, but his brain and voice had forgotten how, and there wasn't time to consult the manual.

'Right, so we're in business. Come inside. Kettle's just on.'

He pinched out his cigar – not that it was any shorter than it had been – and pottered through the double doors. David followed.

Inside, the workshop looked just like one of those garages. The floor was concrete; there were patches of something dark and sticky spilt on it and partially soaked up by sawdust. The walls were lined with tools and empty spaces for tools. The roof was high and rested on I-section girders. There was something that looked a bit like a car-inspection pit, but slightly different in some respects he couldn't quite make out. The main difference between this place and the ordinary backstreet garage was the line of glass boxes, like overgrown tropical-fish tanks, up against the far wall. They were filled with something green. And they all glowed.

CHAPTER TWO

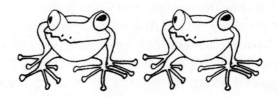

'I'll need just the one hair,' said Honest John, wrapping a filthy handkerchief round the handle of a battered kettle and tilting it over two mugs.

His voice was interesting; the same accent, more or less, as his brother's, but spliced with something else. He wasn't the same man that David had met earlier in the Blue Boar.

'OK,' David replied apprehensively (for one thing, each of the hairs in the little curl had cost him something over five hundred pounds; for another – well, that really didn't bear thinking about). He took the plastic envelope from his pocket and handed it over. Honest John was squeezing a tea bag against the rim of a mug with the end of a biro.

'Yup, human all right,' he said, glancing casually at the envelope. 'Who's this when he's at home, then? Somebody old, you said.'

David nodded.

'Anybody I'd have heard of?'

Once again he tried to lie, and found he couldn't. 'Philippa Levens,' he whimpered. 'You may have . . .'

Honest John laughed. 'Here,' he said, 'you didn't buy this off of my brother Joe, did you? Bloody hell,' he went on with a chuckle.

'I don't think so,' David replied, realising that he didn't have a clue who the seller had been. 'It was an auction, they didn't say who it had belonged to.'

Another variant of the Levens grin appeared on Honest John's face; at least fifty-seven varieties, like Heinz beans. 'My brother Joe likes to tell people we're descended from the aristocracy,' he said. 'Usually just before he sells them something. You don't mind me asking, how much did you give for this?'

David shrugged awkwardly. 'Fifteen,' he muttered.

'Fifteen quid? Oh boy.' Honest John chuckled again. 'Still, it's your money, you do what the hell you want to with it. Right, let's see. There's number six, that's empty. Scrubbed it out last week, as it happens, so it's all ready to go. Unless the cat's been in it, of course.' He slurped some tea and handed David the other mug. By the looks of it, the last time it had been washed England had still been a Catholic country. 'Right,' Honest John went on, 'let the dog see the rabbit.' He put his cup down on top of a bench vice, took a pair of tweezers from his top pocket and fished out a single Levens hair. It was probably just David's imagination, but it seemed to squirm a little, like a worm on a hook. Four identical cats jumped down from a high window ledge and walked past, their tails stuck up in the air at precisely the same angle.

'Looks all right to me,' Honest John muttered,

handing back the plastic envelope containing the rest of the hairs. 'But you can't really tell just by looking. No good fartarsing about, let's bung this under the spectrometer and take some readings.'

The spectrometer turned out to be something like a salon hair-dryer, with grubby matt-green paint peeling off the cowl. Honest John put the hair on some kind of slide and flipped a switch. Cruelly bright blue-white light, like a welding arc, flared up all round the slide, and David looked away, though not quickly enough to avoid having a hole burned through the central point of his field of vision that persisted for some minutes afterwards. Honest John didn't seem bothered by it in the slightest.

'Nah, that's all right,' he said. 'Got a bit chewy in places, or else she had split ends, but no more'n point nought-nought-one-one-five cellular detail loss. Worst-case scenario, she could come out the tank with a *really* blank expression on her face, but not enough to worry about.' He flipped an 'off' switch, and the machine went quiet. 'So,' he said, 'what d'you want to do?'

Now that was a really good question, and the first answer that came into David's mind was 'wake up'. One thing he was fairly sure he didn't want to do was to carry on with this lunatic scheme of cloning a dead witch. Unfortunately, he couldn't think offhand of a way of saying so without making a total and irrecoverable fool of himself.

'You think you can do it, then?' he said.

Honest John shrugged. 'Give it a go, anyway. I mean, the very worst that can happen is, you end up with a hundred and twenty quid's worth of green, slimy cat-food. You got a cat?'

Trying not to shudder too visibly, David said no, he hadn't.

'I have,' replied Honest John. 'I got *loads* of cats; like, you know how they leave their hairs all over everything? It'd cost a fortune feeding 'em, if it wasn't for the occasional – well, you know, in the end it all comes down to your quality control, doesn't it?'

David had already come to the conclusion that he didn't like Honest John terribly much. He hadn't liked his brother, either. The thought that even the best possible outcome to this escapade would result in these people being his in-laws was almost enough to give him the courage to run away.

'Right,' said Honest John, picking the hair off the slide with his tweezers before David could say anything else. 'Off we go, then. I'll heat up number six and we'll be away.'

So that was that: so little thought, so little consideration of the implications, before bringing another life into the world. Just allowing oneself to be carried away by a moment's impulse, the urge not to give offence by saying no, the irresistible force of a good idea at the time. In other words, pretty much normal behaviour, for a human being.

'Um,' David said. 'How long does it take, usually?'

'Depends,' replied Honest John, as he fiddled with some controls. 'I mean, there's all sorts of things, like your gel consistency, your pick-up speed and response time, your thread density. It can vary a hell of a lot.'

'Ah.'

'Could be as little as four and a half hours,' Honest John went on, 'could be as long as seven, you just can't tell. Now then,' he added, pressing a button. The tank lit up, like a frogspawn-green light bulb. 'There you go. Just got to wait and see.'

Now, David thought, would most definitely be a good time to wake up. Please?

'So,' Honest John continued, 'you can hang around here if you really want to, or you can bugger off somewhere and I'll let you know when it's done.'

David nodded. 'I'll do that, then,' he said. 'Um, do I pay you now, or . . . ?'

Honest John picked up his mug, saw that it was empty and put it down again. 'Half now,' he said, 'half when we slop it out. Cash preferred,' he added.

'Ah. I've just realised, I haven't got that much cash on me. I can give you a cheque—'

Honest John gave him a scornful look, as if David was standing on his doorstep at nine a.m. on a Sunday morning trying to interest him in The Gospel According to the Easter Bunny. 'How much have you got on you, then?'

David pulled out his wallet. 'Forty pounds,' he said. 'Oh, just a moment, I've got some change . . .' Finally, counting in all the fivepences and tuppences and pennies, he was able to make up forty-six pounds, seventeen pence. Honest John wrote him a receipt on the back of a vintage Chinese takeaway rice-carton lid – *recd on a/c 1 cloan £46-17*, and the date, and a squiggle like the edited highlights of a tachograph chart. Clearly they didn't call him Honest John for nothing.

David took the rectangle of card and put it solemnly in his inside pocket. 'Well,' he said, 'thank you very much. It's been—'

'Hang on,' Honest John interrupted. 'What about your phone number, then? So I can let you know when she's done?'

'Oh,' David said. 'Sorry.'

Once again, here was an opportunity for escape: partial escape only, true enough, but if he wrote down a false phone number, how would Honest John ever find him again? He could just walk through the door into the night air, forget any of this had ever happened; it would still be his fault, but he probably wouldn't get the blame.

Someone else could probably have brought himself to do that – someone, for example, with half a brain, or ten per cent more backbone than a pint of custard – but not David. Telling lies is a bit like tiling bathrooms – if you don't know how to do it properly, it's best not to try. He pulled out the carton lid, wrote his number down on a corner, tore it off and handed it over. 'I'll be hearing from you, then,' he said.

'Yup.'

I'll just go home and wait, then, shall I? (he wanted to say). And when you phone, I'll drop by and collect my brand new artificially synthesised human being – actually, 'human' is probably pushing it a bit, or at the very least it's a grey area; but that's OK. While I'm waiting I can watch a video, or maybe make a start on my quarterly VAT return—

'Okay,' David said. 'Well, thanks for everything.'

Honest John shrugged and turned a shoulder towards him, implying that he'd now become a slight nuisance and this wasn't a waiting room or a bus shelter. David smiled feebly, thought about waving, decided not to, and walked out.

Outside – in a way it was like waking up out of a dream, the moment when the screwy dream logic melts and falls away and you realise that none of that weird stuff could ever possibly have happened. He walked thirty yards down the street, stopped, and reached inside his jacket. Under the amber light of the street lamp, the writing on the carton lid still said *recd on a/c 1 cloan £46-17*; and today's date, and a squiggle. He very much wanted to throw it away; but he came from a society and a culture that throws away receipts about as often as it drowns unwanted kittens in steaming cauldrons of mulled yoghurt. He put it back in his pocket and walked to the Tube station.

The train was unusually slow, both in arriving and in taking David home. He stopped at the Kentucky Fried Chicken place on his way back to the flat. On the door-mat he found a bank statement, an invitation to join the Aerospace Design Book Club, a postcard of the Gettysburg battlefield from his friends Steven and Tamsin (he hadn't even realised they'd gone abroad) and a road fund licence-renewal form for the car he'd sold seven years ago. He put the bank statement in the shoebox marked 'Bank Statements' and binned the rest.

There were six messages on his answering machine. Five of them were just clicks and buzzes. The sixth was from his unbearable cousin Alex, the lawyer, instruct-ing David to meet him for lunch tomorrow. David sighed. He'd known and hated Alex since he was six and Alex was eight, and had been trying to get rid of him for as long as he could remember. But, for some reason, Alex seemed to like him and made a point of staying in touch, no matter how hard David tried to elude him. This tenacity always made him think of a cat his mother had owned at one stage, who had insisted on bringing its newly slain prey into the house and depositing the corpses in places where they'd be sure to be found eventually – behind sofa cushions or inside slippers. No amount of reasoning, yelling or violence had ever managed to persuade this cat that its contributions to the household economy were neither necessary nor welcome. What made it worse, of course, was that Alex was a successful, well-paid, highly respected lawyer with a junior partnership in a prestigious West End firm and parents who were proud of him, whereas David was still just a successful, well-paid, highly respected computer geek whose mother told her friends he stacked shelves in Safeways for a living because she couldn't bring herself to admit to the shameful reality. Alex was also blue-eyed, curly-haired, good-looking in a Hugh Grant sort of way, and a Tall Bastard. Everything else was forgivable, assuming a proper level of sincere contrition. The height thing, on the other hand, went way beyond casual thoughtlessness and into actual malice.

He switched off the machine and looked round. In a little over six hours, I could be bringing Philippa Levens back to this, he panicked. Welcome to the twenty-first century; things are a little different here. He hurried through into the kitchen and looked in the freezer; he could defrost her a Waitrose lasagne, or he could phone out for a pizza.

But of course that wasn't going to happen, because none of it had happened . . . He sat down on the sofa, fidgety and tense, feeling almost as if he'd just taken a life rather than bespoken one. (How about the other clone joints, the better-class ones? Did they deliver? Did they take Visa? Assuming Honest John was down at the opposite end of the spectrum, did that make him a clone

shark? Which reminded him, he'd have to find a cash-
point at some stage.) Sitting down proved to be torture,
so he got up and paced, an activity that the architect
who'd designed his home had left at the bottom of his
list of priorities. Seven paces brought him up sharp
against the kitchen sink. He stopped and turned round,
monarch of what little he surveyed. On the very few
occasions when he'd brought girls home to his flat,
they'd appeared either disconcerted, amused or both (as
if they'd broken down on a lonely road at night, and
there'd been a blinding light in the sky, and suddenly
they were on an alien ship, and the aliens had turned out
to be the Teletubbies) and they hadn't stayed very long.
Perhaps he should clean the kitchen floor. There'd be
time.

He looked again. A clean kitchen floor probably
wasn't going to solve his problems. The feeling of being
about to be submerged up to the chin in very deep
trouble closed in all around him. Perhaps, after all, the
most sensible thing would be to read a book or watch
something. Was that how people passed the time on
Death Row, he wondered, when the point came when
it no longer mattered? Strange way of thinking. He
walked across to his desk. The obvious thing to do was
work, but he knew he'd have no chance of concentrat-
ing to the level his kind of work required. He stood up
again and put the kettle on. When all else fails, make
tea.

What have I done? he asked himself, as the watched
pot took its own sweet time coming to the boil.
Everything was happening in deadly slow motion, even
perfectly straightforward things like making a cup of
tea. Not a good omen, really. Nothing had actually

happened yet, and already he was stressed out, his mind chasing up and down strange avenues of thought, speculation and downright craziness. Were real expectant fathers as wound up and twitchy as this, he wondered?

At some point he must have sat down, just for a moment; because he woke up in his worn-out old armchair, and the phone was ringing. He jumped up like a cat, and tripped over his feet with a degree of athletic clumsiness that Charlie Chaplin could've learned a thing or two from, before reaching the phone and picking it up.

'Hello?'

'Hello, dear. So you're not dead or anything, then. Only it's been so long since you phoned, I was beginning to wonder.'

Oh, for God's sake. 'Mum . . .'

'Yes, I know, you can't talk now. Probably expecting a vitally important call any minute now, just like you always seem to be, though I can't really think of any vitally important people who're going to ring you this late in the evening – obviously *I* don't fit in that category, I'm only your mother . . .'

He closed his eyes, took the phone away from his ear and counted up to ten before putting it back.

'. . . At least he's got the decency to phone his mother from time to time, even if he is in prison and wears a ring through his upper lip. But you might as well be living on the Moon, actually that'd be better, at least I'd know where you were and what you're up to.'

'Yes, Mum,' David said. 'Look, this time I really am waiting for a very important—'

'This time,' said his mother. 'I see. So you admit that all those other times . . .'

Inspiration. When all else fails, tell the truth. Part of the truth, anyhow.

'Actually,' he said, 'there's this girl—'

'Oh.' Two seconds of complete, golden silence. 'So, what's she like? What's her name? Has she got hair? Only so many of the girls you see these days, either it's bright purple or they've shaved it all off right down to the scalp; sometimes I wonder if young people these days are even human. She's not one of those, is she?'

'She's got lovely hair,' David replied accurately. 'Sort of reddish auburn.'

'Really? You sure it's not out of a bottle? Mind you, even that'd be better than shocking pink. Marcia Crebbins's daughter came home the other day with one side pink and the other side green. Marcia said she took one look at it and ran upstairs screaming, though of course she was always a bit hysterical. How old is she? I know you said 'girl', but—'

'I'm not sure, actually,' David replied slowly. Properly speaking, she's at least four hundred, but she was only nineteen when she died, he reminded himself. 'Mid-twenties, probably. Look, I really don't want to be rude but she said she'd ring around now, and—'

'All right, all right. Though you want to be careful, I mean, you're a bit old to be waiting by the phone like this, it's not like you're still a teenager. I wouldn't like to think of you going all to pieces just because . . .'

'Yes, Mum. I'll call you back tomorrow, only—'

He knew it wouldn't be as easy as that. 'So what's her name? Is she pretty?'

'Philippa,' David replied. 'And yes. Very.'

'Really. Then – I'm not being nasty or anything, but

you've got to think about these things – if she's so very young and pretty—'

'What the hell does she see in me? Honestly, Mum. I haven't got a clue. My guess is, she's probably only around because of my money. Call you later. 'Bye.'

He put the receiver down, screwed his eyes shut and clenched his fists till they hurt. Usually, this alleviated the worst of the pain within five to eight seconds. This time, it took a little longer. He'd just got his breathing back under control when the phone went again.

'Hello?'

'All done,' said an unmistakable voice. 'You coming over to collect tonight, or do you want me to stick her in the freezer till the morning?'

'No! I mean, no, that's fine, I'll be right over.'

'Don't forget the rest of the money.'

'I won't, I promise. And, um, thank you—'

The line went dead; either Honest John had no stomach for such displays of raw emotion, or he kept an eye on his phone bill. David gently replaced the receiver, as if he was afraid of waking it, then took a long, deep breath and tried to relax. Some hope.

Just for once, he decided, he'd get a taxi. Normally he wouldn't dream of doing such a wickedly indulgent thing (if God had intended us to take taxis, he wouldn't have authorised the Devil to create London Transport) but this was something of a special case.

Luckily, the bank was only a few hundred yards from the cab rank, opposite the station, and there was a taxi waiting. Of course, he didn't know the name of the street, so he said 'Ravenscourt Park Tube' and hopped in. The driver looked at him, as if to say that people who took a taxi to get from one Tube stop to another were the reason why the country was going to hell in a handbasket, and drove off.

The journey took longer than he'd anticipated, partly due to a plague of municipal moles that obliged the driver to take a detour, apparently by way of York and Kiev. That didn't help David's nerves very much – what if Honest John got fed up with waiting for him, or assumed he'd decided to leave it till the morning after all, and gone home? It had been bad enough enduring the last few hours. Trying to keep his head from exploding till nine a.m. the following morning would probably turn out to be downright impossible.

Just when he'd reached the conclusion that the taxi driver was the Flying Dutchman, the cab slowed down and stopped. He could see the lights of a Tube station dead ahead. He paid the driver the price of a small communications satellite, and clambered out into the night air.

[HONEST JOHN'S HOUSE OF CLONES]

It occurred to him to wonder whether the sign, or indeed the whole building, was there when he wasn't; whether it was some kind of miracle, vision or practical joke that only he could see; or whether there were lookouts posted all around to give notice of his approach, whereupon dozens of mischievous pranksters scurried round furiously assembling the shed and carefully arranging the props so that it'd all be ready as soon as he came within visual range. He could almost have believed in something like that, except that he knew he was too unimportant to warrant so much trouble and expense.

The door opened before he could knock. 'You're here, then,' said Honest John.

'Yes.'

'Well, you'd better come in.'

So he came in; and there were the glowing green tanks, and the many cats, and the workbench cluttered with tools (what did a clonefounder need with two angle grinders, a cutting torch and four big lump hammers? *Really* don't need to know that), and the empty coffee mugs, some of them with dust-clogged spiders' webs spanning their rims; and there he was, and there was Honest John. Other than that—

'Um,' he asked nervously, 'how did it go?'

'Hm? Oh, fine, no problems. Well, the neutrino collimator had a funny five minutes, and an earwig managed to get inside the Kluth diffractor, which means it's going to be interesting working in here after dark for the next week or two. But you got to take stuff like that in your stride in this business.'

David waited for a second or so, while Honest John bit off a hangnail. 'So,' David ventured cautiously, 'is she, um, ready?'

''Course.'

'Great. So can I, er—?'

Honest John looked at him quizzically. 'Can you what?'

Not for the first time in his life, David felt as if he'd missed last week's episode. 'Um, can I see her, please? If that's all right, I mean.'

'You want to look at her?'

'If that's all right.'

Honest John shrugged. 'Don't see why not.' He beckoned, and crossed over to the row of glowing green tanks. 'I've written out an invoice,' he said over his shoulder.

'Ah, right. Thank you.'

''S no problem.'

They were standing beside one of the tanks. The sides were misted up, but David reckoned he could just make out a shape that could conceivably be that of a reclining humanoid. 'In there?'

Honest John nodded. 'All yours, mate,' he grunted. 'Soon as I get the balance, of course.'

For a moment David couldn't think what he meant. Further adjustments needed to the clone's inner-ear mechanism? One leg slightly longer than the other, just hold on a mo' while I fetch the oxy torch?

'The rest of the money,' John explained.

'Ah, right, that sort of . . . Here.' He took the cash-point-crisp notes from his top pocket and thrust them at Honest John like a fencer. The clonewright looked at them.

'Don't suppose you got the right money, have you?' he said. 'Only I'm a bit short on change. You want to hang around a few minutes, I can nip up the Spar shop and get 'em to change a tenner—'

'Don't worry about that,' David said. 'Please.'

Honest John shrugged. 'Suit yourself,' he said. 'All right, if you're ready, I'll wake her up.'

David had thought about this moment, of course; ever since the idea had first crawled, wet-furred and muddy-pawed, through the cat flap of his imagination. And, not unreasonably, the thought had presented itself to him in various conventional, archetypal images: Sleeping Beauty (the Disney version); Pygmalion and Galatea; Brynhild kissed awake by Siegfried on the fire-curtained mountain; Aphrodite, rising from the white foam; even (in a dream, after a toasted Edam sandwich and a strong black coffee) Frankenstein's monster, wreathed in lightning. Above all he'd imagined her eyes opening, her lips parting—

'Yurghsptttt!' said a voice from inside the tank, followed by frantic splashing noises. A glob of luminous green snot the size of a snowball shot out over the rim and hit David in the face. It tasted like iron filings in rancid egg white.

'All right, all right, hold your bloody water,' sighed Honest John, taking a long stride over to the tank and reaching inside it. David heard another wild spluttering shriek, followed by a glub-glub noise. Two green feet rose out of the end of the tank, like lobsters crawling out of a saucepan, and kicked ferociously, spraying more of the green stuff in all directions. One of the feet (humanoid, but disconcertingly green) caught Honest John neatly under the chin; he made a grunting noise and sat down on the concrete floor, looking distinctly cross-eyed.

'YURGHSPTTTTGNURGYTTCH!' yelled the voice inside the tank. It was unmistakably female, probably human and definitely unhappy about something. 'YNGMMPTCHOO!' it added, and David ducked just in time to avoid another massive green glob hurtling from the tank. Whatever it was in that tank, it was fairly safe to assume it wasn't a morning person.

'Shut it, you!' snapped Honest John, scrambling to his feet and reaching for a broom that stood propped up against the workbench. 'Sorry about this,' he added in David's general direction. 'Some of 'em take it a bit funny, you just can't tell. It'll be better when the language centres kick in.'

Holding the broom over his head like Neptune wielding his trident, Honest John advanced on the tank, sidestepped a flailing green leg and jabbed down with the broom-head. There was a shriek of pure rage; then something grabbed hold of the broom and pulled sharply, dragging Honest John up sharp against the glass; whereupon a naked female humanoid sprang almost vertically out of the tank, broadcasting green slime like a wet dog shaking off water, and kicked him Bruce Lee-fashion on the chin before dropping to the ground on all fours. David jumped back about a yard and groped instinctively for one of the lump hammers. Between this, he decided, and the equivalent scene in *Sleeping Beauty*, there were a number of rather crucial differences.

'Yaaagplutchk!' shrieked the female creature, springing backwards and using Honest John's chest as a bouncy castle. 'Mmpluj ykkk! Splut!'

(Admirable motor skills and coordination, though. And absolutely nothing whatsoever wrong with her lungs or vocal cords.)

'Splut?' She was staring at David, pointing to herself, then him. 'Spluffle splut? *Splut?*'

From one perspective, she was a raging monster, an inhuman, savage harpie. She was also, nevertheless, a girl he'd only just met. Accordingly, David felt himself go pink and couldn't think of anything to say.

Just then, Honest John crept up behind her with a heavy-duty paper sack in his hands and popped it neatly over her head. Before she could claw her way out of it, he produced a hypodermic. A moment later, she was peacefully asleep on the floor in a little pool of green slime, like some nouvelle cuisine recipe.

Honest John cautiously felt his jaw, and winced. 'All yours,' he said.

Clearly, David's thoughts were lucidly reflected in his face, because Honest John sighed and said, 'You got anything to take her home in?'

David shook his head. The thought hadn't occurred to him, and the situation was obviously way, way beyond carrier bags.

'All right,' said Honest John wearily, 'I'll see what I can do. Properly speaking, I ought to charge extra. Let's have a look over here.'

'Over here' turned out to be a big cardboard box containing black plastic dustbin-liners and raggedy old hessian sacks. 'Where are you parked?' Honest John asked, as he sorted through the heap.

'Actually,' David whimpered, 'I came in a taxi.'

Honest John looked up at him. 'Marvellous,' he muttered. 'All right, I'll keep her under while you go back and get your motor.'

'I, um, don't drive.'

'You don't drive,' Honest John repeated. 'Fine. Well, I'll tell you this for nothing, you won't find a cab round here at this time of night.'

'Oh.'

It was one of those moments that made you believe in telepathy, because as David and Honest John looked at each other, it was apparent that they were sharing the same mental image: of David trying to get a fighting, squirming, green-slime-flecked girl in a potato sack back home on the District Line. 'Bugger it,' said Honest John, in a very sad voice. 'Whereabouts do you live?'

'Ealing Broadway,' David replied.

'Fine,' said Honest John, with a nothing-surprises-me-any-more look. 'I'll drive you.'

David breathed out hard through his nose. 'Thanks,' he said, just about managing to keep from bursting into tears of gratitude. 'That's really—'

'Give me a hand with this lot,' Honest John interrupted. 'Come on, you take the feet. I got to be home by midnight.'

So David took the feet. They were hard to get a grip on, because of the slime, and because David had never touched a girl's foot in his life before, let alone a bare one, let alone a *green* bare one belonging to a creature he was responsible for bringing into the world. He averted his eyes, which didn't do a lot for his ability to navigate—

'Look where you're going, for crying out loud,' John muttered, as they nearly knocked over the pillar drill.

'Sorry.'

They had to dump her on the pavement while John opened the back doors of his old, ex-British Telecom Bedford van. It was the most conspicuous moment of David's life, and he felt like he'd just committed a murder. (Illogical, since he'd just done the exact opposite. That set him thinking: the law recognised a variety of different forms of unlawful killing, but were there equivalent gradations of unlawfully bringing to life? Probably.)

'Right,' John said, wiping his hands on a bit of old cloth before turning the ignition key. 'Ealing Broadway, you said?'

'Just off Warwick Road,' David replied. 'You know it?'

John shook his head. 'But you do,' he replied, 'so that's all right.'

They drove in silence for a while, until David managed to save up his courage allowance and ask: 'Excuse me, but the, um, colour—'

'What?'

'The colour of her skin.' Dear God, he sounded like the Ku Klux Klan. 'Is it meant to be like that? Green? Not that I mind,' he added quickly, 'I mean, brown, yellow, green, it really doesn't matter to me one little bit, I was just wondering—'

'It wears off,' John said wearily. 'Quicker in daylight. It's your basic photosynthesis.'

'Ah.'

He turned left at the very last possible moment, sending David cannoning into the door. 'Because basically,' he went on, 'what you got there at the moment is a plant.'

'I see,' David said, as truthfully as a politician. 'A plant.'

'That's right. Definitely the vegetable kingdom. Physiomimetic fungoid algae. Bloody wonderful stuff, couldn't do a thing without it.'

David closed his eyes for a moment. 'You're saying,' he murmured, 'that the thing in the back, the *girl*, she's a *fungus*?'

John shrugged. 'It's a grey area,' he said. 'See, there's this goo. It's what's in the tanks. Give it like a template to copy, and it'll grow into anything you like. That's just for starters, mind. Treat it and feed it like a human, pretty soon – a day or so – all the plant cells get replaced with human ones and it becomes *really* human. Just like you and me.'

'Ah.'

John nodded. 'All there is to it. 'Course, that's the

only reason I can do cloning, with the law how it is. Because technically, see, it's not human, it's a plant. You can buy and sell it, keep it, sling it out, you could slice it up thin and make toasted sandwiches if you wanted to. No red tape, no bullshit: it's as if I was growing roses. Or turnips. And by the time it turns human, of course, it's nothing to do with me.'

'I understand,' David said, in a tiny voice.

John laughed. 'That shocked you, didn't it?'

'Um, no. Not really.'

'Liar. Anyhow, bottom line is, this time tomorrow it should be talking, most of the green should be gone – chest, stomach and groin stay green longest. Like I said, if you want you can speed it up by parking it outdoors or shoving it under one of those sunray lamps. Or a greenhouse.'

David felt both nauseated and fascinated, as if he'd just eaten a spellbinding earthworm. 'And will it – *she* – will *she* know who she is?'

John nodded. 'In a day or so. Only up to the moment the hair got cut off, of course. Everything after that, you're going to have to tell her.'

Marvellous, David thought. On top of all the other tricky explanations, he was going to have to find a tactful way of letting her know she'd been burned as a witch four hundred years earlier. ('Oh, and by the way . . .') 'But she'll be able to talk? And understand what I say?'

'Sure. Well,' John added, 'sort of. They talked different in her day. Like Shakespeare and stuff. I saw that *Henry the Fifth* on the telly once. With, you know, Kenneth Wassname. That kind of thing. Like, a cross between the Bible and Monty Python.'

Oh boy (David thought), it gets better and better. As befits a computer scientist, he'd spent English periods at school drawing circuit diagrams and little spaceships on the cover of his exercise book, and looking out of the window. Still, he had an idea she'd find a way to communicate, sooner or later; for example, sticking her head out of a window and screaming 'Help! Summon thou the watch!' as soon as she'd figured out what had been done to her. He had little doubt that his neighbours would get the gist of it easily enough.

(Whereupon, as the police battered down his door and pinned him to the floor, all he'd have to do was explain that it was all right, she was only a rather precocious form of pondweed, and of course they'd apologise and let him go. Absolutely. No worries on that score.)

''Scuse me asking,' John said suddenly, 'but why her? Why not – oh, I dunno, Michelle Pfeiffer? Or that big blonde on EastEnders? You could get a bit of hair easy enough, just go round the bins.'

David looked out of the window. 'It's hard to explain,' he said. 'You see, when I was twelve, my mum took me to see this painting of her, in a gallery in London. And ever since—'

'Whatever.' John shrugged. 'None of my business. You don't ask questions in this game.'

And that was odd too, since patently he did, because he just had. For some reason, David had the impression that he'd just been checked out, positively vetted; immensely subtly, of course, by a highly skilled and experienced judge of human nature. (Honest John? Are you *sure* about that?)

'It's all right,' he said quickly. 'It was just—'

'Yeah.'

'Yes.'

'Left here?'

'That's fine. Or right, you can go either way. But left's quicker. A bit.'

Honest John turned left; and fairly soon they were in David's road, and the awful moment when he'd be alone with her, it, that *thing* in the back, couldn't be put off any longer. 'Just pull in here,' David said. 'Actually, it's three doors further down, but this is the nearest space.'

John grunted and parked the van. 'You better go and unlock the door first,' he said.

'Yes, right.'

Outside again, in the night air. Nobody on the street. (But anybody could be watching from a darkened window or behind a curtain. What if somebody knew? What if the police had been tapping his phone, and they were coiled like snakes waiting to spring out at him from behind Number Thirty-four's privet hedge?) He tried walking normally from the kerb to his front door, and succeeded in looking like Norman Wisdom doing Olivier's Richard III with a stone in his left shoe. His keys tried to hide inside his handkerchief, which had wrapped itself round his loose change in his pocket. He couldn't find the keyhole for quite some time.

Once he'd finally managed to cajole the door open, he went back (*Now is the winter of our discontent*, shuffle-shuffle, hur-hur) to the van, where Honest John had just lit a cigar.

'There you are,' John said. 'Wondered where you'd got to.'

The cloud of smoke caught and diffracted the orange light of the street lamp, so that it glowed like a nebula. 'I was just opening the door,' David replied.

'Really? Oh well.' John balanced his cigar on the van roof. 'Catch hold of the ankles, I'll go round the other side and push.'

'All right,' David replied unhappily. 'Here, are you sure she's not going to wake up?'

'Pretty sure. Gave her a shot that'd cripple an elephant.'

Heigh-ho, David thought, and reached for a green ankle, as if putting his hand in a jar full of carnivorous earwigs. One small grab for a man . . . he pulled gently, but he felt no movement other than a slight stretching of the ankle joint. He wondered if he'd dislocated anything, maybe crippled the poor creature for life.

'Well, pull, then,' John muttered from inside the van. 'Haven't got all bleeding night.'

'But— All right,' David said, tightening his grip. 'I'm pulling.'

'Then pull harder.'

So he pulled harder. For the first two seconds, nothing carried on happening. Then he got movement. A lot of it. 'Ouch!' he yelped, as one of the feet shot out and connected forcefully with his nose.

'Bugger,' John's voice, slightly distorted by the acoustics inside the van. 'Now look what you've—'

The heel of the other foot jabbed him in the mouth. Contrary to what you might have been led to expect, human heel doesn't taste in the least like chicken.

'Stop fooling about, for God's sake,' John's voice boomed at him. 'Come on, get a bloody grip.'

Something told David that this might not be the best advice going, but he was too put out to think for himself, so he did as he was told. It was at that point that the clone started screaming.

Absolutely nothing wrong with the lungs. First-class workmanship.

'Hold on,' John bellowed, just audible over the screams. 'Don't let it get away, whatever you do. There,' he added a few very long seconds later (just after the kicking and screaming suddenly stopped, as if a plug had just been pulled out). 'I doubled the dose, that'll keep it under for hours. Now then, let's get it inside before some nosy sod calls the law.'

Too late for that, surely. By now, they'd already have dug the SWAT teams out of bed and scrambled the black helicopters. Considering the volume and intensity of the screams, if the police *hadn't* been called then it was a sad comment on public apathy. He grabbed the ankles as if they were wheelbarrow handles and tugged as hard as he could. The clone shot backwards, sending him staggering into the gutter, and flumped down on the base of her spine.

'You're not very good at this sort of thing,' John said.

'No practice,' David explained.

John scooped the clone up, hands under her armpits, dragged her round through 180 degrees and trotted backwards, lugging her behind him. As soon as he was through the front door, he let go. 'Now you're on your own,' he grunted, pressing his hands to his back as he straightened up. 'Bloody good luck to you, and all.'

'Yes, but—' David said to the door, as it closed firmly in his face.

A few moments later, he heard the van start and drive away. He looked back at the clone, slopped at the foot of the stairs like a pile of unironed laundry. Pygmalion and Galatea, he thought. Yeah, right.

This is the moment I've been waiting for all my life.

CHAPTER THREE

Two options. Either David could try and drag the clone up the stairs, or he could leave her there till she woke up and see if he could persuade her to walk up of her own accord.

Well, option one was definitely possible. He thought of the great engineering feats of prehistory – Stonehenge, the pyramids, the seamless walls of Macchu Picchu. He was as human as the men who'd built them. By nearly every criterion he was way ahead of them, in knowledge, nutrition, easy access to equipment and materials. For example: he could nip up to his flat, get on the Net, do a search and download the schematics for an A-frame and a block and tackle. Four thousand years of technology and ingenuity were right behind him, only a mouse-click away. Highly unlikely that this was the first time in four millennia that a man had been faced with the problem of how to shift a sleeping girl from the bottom of a stair-case to the top; and as someone once said, anything that'd been done once could be done again. Think of Archimedes, he told himself. Think of Isambard Kingdom Brunel.

He kneeled down beside her and prodded her tentatively on the point of the shoulder. 'Excuse me,' he said. 'Excuse me, but would you mind very much waking up?'

No reply. Of course, he was used to girls ignoring him, it was one of the main default settings in his life, but just for once it would've been nice to have been pleasantly surprised. He sat down on the floor and looked at his watch. Almost midnight; and today was Tuesday. That meant Terry and Joanne, from the flat above his, would be back any minute from wherever it was they went on Tuesday nights. He reconsidered his options and found a third one he'd somehow overlooked. Flight.

Nothing simpler: go upstairs, double-lock the door and leave all the lights off. Stay like that for a couple of days, so people would assume he'd gone away for a while. One thing he was fairly sure of, nobody who knew him would think of his name in the context of abandoned nude girls. It was the obvious, sensible thing to do. Someone would call the police or the social services or whoever dealt with cases like this; they'd come and collect her, take her to a hospital or something of the sort, she'd get the finest medical treatment the Health Service could provide, followed by expert psychiatric care—

Well, quite. She'd wake up and start demanding explanations in perfect Elizabethan English. She'd tell them she was Philippa Levens, Marchioness of Ipswich. When they didn't believe her, she'd probably lose her rag and threaten to turn them into frogs. It didn't take much in the way of imagination to figure out where she'd end up after that. But that wasn't his problem, or at least it didn't have to be, because, unlike her, he had the option to run away. Dammit, it wasn't even his last chance; he still had several dozen hairs left from the lock, there was nothing to stop him doing it all over again, having given a little more thought to basic logistics and having made suitable preparations.

Indeed.

'*Please* wake up,' David hissed, prodding her shoulder quite hard this time. Still nothing. Might as well prod a sofa cushion (except that sofa cushions didn't bruise).

He stood up and straightened his back. The truth was that he only had one option.

First things first. He grabbed her ankles – throughout, it should be borne in mind, he was at all times painfully aware that she wasn't wearing anything apart from a few smears of green slime – and wheeled her round so that her head and shoulders were resting on the bottom stair. That was hard enough work in itself for someone who wasn't used to lifting anything heavier than a computer monitor. Then, trying to remember the angles and handholds he'd seen Honest John using, he hopped up a few stairs, turned round, crouched down and very tentatively slipped his hands under her armpits. The feel of her skin against his was very strange and disconcerting; partly because of the slime, partly because of other factors he really didn't want to stop and think about at that particular time.

In fact, she wasn't quite as heavy as he'd anticipated: he could just about manage, one stair at a time. He'd never had any use for his physical strength before, what there was of it. He was, after all, a creature of intellect rather than brute muscle, a thinker, a dreamer, proud to be weedy. There had always been men in overalls to deal with this sort of thing, and his part in the order of things was to provide employment for the poor, unreasoning creatures. He could've used a couple of them right now (except, of course, that he couldn't have) but there weren't any around when he really needed them, so he had no choice but to find a way of managing. Amazingly, he managed.

Piece of cake, really.

His back foot slipped, and suddenly he was heading downstairs again on his bum, covering distance considerably faster than he'd been able to the last time he passed that way. He let go with one hand and grabbed for a banister rail. The tug on his shoulder nearly dislocated his arm, but at least they'd stopped going bump-bump-bump like Winnie the Pooh. That was, however, the best that could be said of their situation. Single-handed, he couldn't haul her back up even one step. If he let go of the banister, he'd be headed for the bottom of the stairs at warp speed. To summarise, (always a great talent of his, getting straight to the heart of the problem) it was one minute to midnight on his birthday and he was stuck.

Having no better way to pass the time, David traced the slender thread of causality that connected him to the relatively carefree young idiot who'd woken up that morning and decided to screw up his entire life beyond all possible hope of recovery. At every stage, he realised, he'd peeled off and discarded whole handfuls of options, second chances, possible means of salvation, until he'd arrived here, halfway up his own stairs, with a banister rail in one hand and a naked clone in the other. One minute to midnight, on the first day of a new year in his life. Having no choice in the matter, he stayed as still as he could and waited for it to become Wednesday. 'Happy birthday to me', he sang quietly under his breath; but in his heart he knew it was fairly unlikely.

'Hello,' said a voice behind him. 'Mind if I squeeze past?'

It was only pure instinct that stopped David from letting go of the banister. He tried to turn his head so as to get a look at whoever it was, but his neck wouldn't unscrew far enough.

'Oh,' the voice went on, 'I see, you're a bit stuck, aren't you? Hold still, I'll see what I can do.'

Two hands like mole wrenches clamped on to his shoulders and he felt himself rising a short way into the air, like a Harrier; then he was sitting securely on a stair instead of dangling by one rapidly fading wrist; one of the wrenches let go of his shoulder and an arm in grey worsted brushed past his face, pushing it gently to one side. 'There you go,' the voice said, and he realised he could get his hand back under the clone's armpit.

'Thank you,' he said automatically (good manners are like Russian vine, you can never quite get rid of them); then he looked up.

The man was wearing a smart business suit, crisp white shirt and shiny black brogues. His hair was short, pepper-and-salt, with a distinct curl just above the collar. There was a nasty mess like a pink fried egg where his left eye should have been. The voice was different.

'I don't think we've met,' the man went on. 'I'm Bill Van Oppen, I've just moved into the flat above yours. It was quite sudden,' he added, with a smile that (for some reason) turned David's stomach. 'I'm in computers.'

Recovery time improves with practice. 'Have you got a brother?' David asked.

'Several,' replied Mr Van Oppen. 'Look, I don't want to intrude, but do you need a hand with that?'

Well, it was an option; nevertheless, David had an overwhelming sensation of being about to sign something he hadn't been given a chance to read. But—

'Yes, please,' he said. 'If you don't mind.'

'Pleasure,' said Mr Van Oppen. He was obviously stronger than he looked, or else he'd been professionally trained. One fluent bending motion and he had the clone in his arms, like Snow White being gathered up by her prince. 'If you wouldn't mind going on ahead and getting the door open?'

While he did as he was told, David was thinking: So if you're Mr Van Oppen, and the other one was Mr Dean; and I don't know what Honest John's surname is, but I'm guessing it's not Dean or Van Oppen . . . How many more of you are there, for crying out loud? He reached for the light switch, then thought better of it.

'There you are,' Mr Van Oppen said cheerfully, walking past David to the sofa and putting down his burden with a light, careful touch. 'Mind if I use your bathroom? My hands are a bit slimy.'

He knew where the bathroom was without asking, just as he'd found the sofa in the dark, without even seeming to look. David heard the taps shooshing.

'My God, is that the time?' Mr Van Oppen rematerialised in the doorway, silhouetted against the light. 'I'd better be cutting along, I'm late enough as it is. I expect I'll be seeing you about the place from time to time. Nice to have met you.'

The door closed behind him, and David waited for

five seconds before putting his back to the wall and sliding down it until he was crouched on his heels in the dark. He listened, but all he could hear was breathing; his own, and a steady purring from the sofa. Sooner or later she was going to wake up (unless he killed her, smothered her with a cushion; after all, nobody even knew she existed, and wouldn't it save a lot of fuss, in the long run? No, not even close to being an option) and once she was awake, one way or another his life was going to be extremely fraught for a while. But, at least for now, he had a brief interlude of peace and quiet, enough time to think of some way out of this mess—

Well, he could tell her the truth (assuming the language barrier wasn't insuperable). He *could* tell her the truth, sure; he could also run himself a nice bath and jump into it while holding the switched-on toaster. Fortunately, he didn't have to do either. Instead, he could create a rather less provocative alternative, and who would there be to contradict him?

I was walking through the park, near the pond, and I heard this splash . . . So I ran over and there you were in the water, floundering about in that stagnant bit at the end, where it's so deep. I think you must've bashed your head when you fell in; that's probably why you can't remember. Sorry, I looked but I couldn't see your clothes anywhere. So why did I bring you all the way up here, instead of calling an ambulance? Well . . .

He shook his head and thumbed the 'reset' button on his imagination.

I was just about to get into bed when I heard this awful thump out there on the landing. So I opened the door and there you were, lying on the floor. Sorry, no idea what happened to your clothes. The green slime? Search me . . .

He frowned. At a pinch, it might just do, depending on how well he put it across. But surely he could do better.

. . . So I looked out and there was this amazingly bright light up in the sky, and this big silvery dish thing was sort of hanging in the air; and a flap opened in the underside, and this dazzling blue beam . . .

. . . For God's sake, it's bad enough being burgled, at least you could have the common decency to put some clothes on when you break into someone's flat. All right, yes, so I crept up behind you and smashed the goldfish bowl over your head; what was I expected to do, finding someone creeping round in the middle of the night . . . ?

. . . Excuse me, but have you got any idea what's going on? No, I just woke up myself. Never seen this place before in my life. God, my head hurts, I guess someone bashed me . . .

. . . Oh boy. Doesn't Nigel throw the wildest parties . . . ?

He thought about all of them and swept them into his mental trash. That just left the truth. All right, so let's just run through that and see if it sounds any better.

. . . I've been in love with you ever since I was a kid, even though you've been dead for four hundred years, so I cloned you from a lock of your hair. Hope that's OK.

. . . You were dead. I brought you back to life. And here's me thinking you might be just a little bit grateful . . .

. . . Hey, you know what? You're even cuter than you look in your portrait. Will you marry me?

Slowly he shook his head. The fact had to be faced: all

Mr Blair's horses and all Mr Blair's men couldn't get a decent spin on this one. He stood up and plodded into the bathroom, looking for his towelling robe. It might just help if she had something to drape round herself.

When he came back, she was sitting up on the sofa. And the light was on.

'But . . .' he said. She looked at him.

'Date,' she said.

So that was what she sounded like. Of course, he could tell she was having a bit of trouble with her voice; she spoke like you do when you've been to the dentist, and half your face is dead and feels like it's been blown up with a bicycle pump. But there was enough voice there to give a fairly good idea; lower than he'd expected, and *gorgeous* . . .

'Date,' she repeated angrily.

Date. Date. *Date*, for pity's sake. Could mean the kind of date you eat; possibly a rather direct way of asking him if he fancied dinner or a movie sometime, but he doubted that. Date. Oh, right, yes, *date*—

'It's, um.' He glanced at his watch. 'Wednesday, thirteenth of March.'

She scowled impatiently. 'Year.'

'2002.'

'Wussat?'

'2002.'

She paused for a moment, thinking. (He knew the feeling: brain clogged up with little wispy strands of sleep.) Then she grinned. 'Yippee!' she said.

'Yippee?'

'Good,' she explained, beaming, and hopped to her feet. She staggered. 'Much better,' she added. 'Gimme.'

'Gimme?'

'That.' She reached out, slightly unsteady on her feet, and grabbed the robe from his hands. 'Get lost,' she added.

'Ah. Right.'

'Now.'

'Um. All right, then. I'll be in the—'

'*Now.*'

'Right. Sure.' He turned round (he could feel his face burning, like a bombed oilfield) and strode into the bathroom, straight-legged like John Cleese. He shut the door behind him and leaned against it.

Huh? he thought.

Well. From one perspective at least, it had all gone much, much better than he'd dared to expect. From another— He thought about Mr Dean, and Honest John, and Mr Van Oppen. Was it just conceivably possible that someone was taking him for a mug?

'Hairbrush!'

He opened the door just a little. 'Sorry?'

'*Hairbrush!*'

A frown folded his face. 'Sorry,' he repeated, 'would you like me to get you a—?'

'Forget it.' She wrenched the door from his grip. She was wearing his bathrobe, and a smile you could have poured on strawberries. 'Bath first. Go away.'

The door closed, with her on the inside, and once again he heard the sound of whooshing taps, followed by an angel singing:

> 'My old man's a dustman,
> 'He wears a dustman's hat—'

David nearly fell over. The voice: unmistakable. And, if

he wasn't mistaken, he'd heard that voice in his dreams since he was a kid—

(No, *really*. He had this recurring dream where he'd died and gone to heaven, and there was this incredibly lovely angel who just happened to look like the girl in the painting, and she was singing – *exactly* that voice – and then, just as he realised he wasn't wearing any trousers, a huge silver trombone snuck up beside him and ate him, whereupon he woke up. A few years ago, when it was really bad, he'd been to see a shrink about it. The shrink had asked him a few questions about his personal life and relationships with women, looked at him in silence for about thirty seconds and advised him to stop drinking strong black coffee last thing at night.)

She'd known what the light switch was for; and 'My Old Man's A Dustman' was an old song, sure, but not *that* old. Explanations, please? Well, the easiest one was that the lock of hair he'd paid so much money for wasn't a genuine relic of the early seventeenth century but rather a snipping that some cunning bastard had picked up off a hairdresser's floor a week ago last Tuesday; in which case, the voice and the total similarity between the clone and the girl in the painting was just a coincidence—

Yeah, right. It was still a damn' sight easier to believe than any of the alternative versions—

The bathroom door opened and she came out, still wearing his robe and now with a towel wound round her hair. As David stared at her she looked like the newly born Aphrodite, assuming that the Olympian gods shopped for bathroom accessories at Marks & Sparks.

'That's better,' she said. Her face was slightly pink,

and a single moist curl was sneaking out onto her forehead from under the towel. 'You must be Derek.'

'David.'

'Hmm? Oh, yes. Pleased to meet you. I'm Philippa Levens.'

She held out her hand, as if she was interviewing him for a job. He shook it. She had a grip like a bench vice.

'Sorry for darting off like that,' she said, crossing the room and flumping down on the sofa, 'but you know how it is when you haven't had a bath for simply ages. Well, unless you count that horrid green stuff as a bath. Could I be awfully pushy and get you to pour me a drink?'

It took David three seconds to remember to breathe. 'What? Oh, yes, sure. Um. What would you like?'

'Large whisky, please. Glenlivet if you've got any; if not, any old single malt'll do. No ice, just a splash of Evian.'

'Coming right up.' David shifted towards the kitchen, then stopped. Apart from the stuff that came out of the tap he had a dozen tea bags, a quarter of a jar of Gold Blend and two cans of lager, left over from his birthday before last. 'Actually,' he said, 'I haven't got anything like that.'

'Oh.' She frowned, ever so slightly. 'I don't suppose you'd fancy nipping out and getting some. If it's no bother.'

'Of course,' David replied immediately. 'Except it's sort of after midnight. I don't think there's anywhere open.'

'Bother.' She scratched the tip of her nose with her little finger. 'So how are things on the food front? Or would it be easier if I went and had a look for myself?'

'Please, help yourself.' The voice David could hear was his own, no question about that, but he couldn't remember having chosen the words or made the decision to utter them. It was as if someone else was operating him by remote control. 'It's, um, through there.'

'Yes,' she said, as she hopped off the sofa and vanished into the kitchen. She moved very fast, though without appearing to move at all. 'Poo,' she said, as she opened the fridge door (and, yes, she had a point; it didn't smell particularly nice in there at the best of times, which this wasn't). 'There doesn't seem to be a whole lot in here,' she went on, examining a packet of half-fat Cheddar and putting it back.

'No,' David replied. 'Sorry. I didn't think—'

'Never mind,' she sad, 'I expect I can last till morning. Just a few Ritz crackers and some Normandy butter would tide me over just fine.'

'There's some ginger-nuts,' David suggested helplessly. 'Somewhere.'

Philippa Levens breathed out slowly through her nose. 'Doesn't matter,' she said. 'The shops'll be open in, what, seven hours. I don't suppose I'll actually starve to death between then and now. Talking of which, could I be an awful bore and get you to turn the heating up just a trifle? It's a bit chilly sitting here in nothing but a towel.'

David nodded, trying very hard to remember how the heating worked. He'd been there six years and never bothered with it, preferring to regulate his immediate environment by putting on or taking off sweaters. After a minute or so he found a knob on the side of the radiator and managed to get it to turn.

'Thanks,' she said as he emerged from under the window, his knees grey with dust. 'And now, would it be terribly rude of me if I said goodnight?' She yawned exquisitely. 'I know I've only been awake for a few minutes, but somehow it isn't really proper sleep in those tank things, if you know what I mean. Don't bother making the bed,' she added, 'I'll be asleep as soon as I hit the pillow.' A moment later she was in the bedroom. 'Well,' she called out, 'actually, if there's a spare pillowslip handy—'

Fortunately, David knew *precisely* where to find a clean pillowslip. It was still in its cellophane, pristine from the shop. He pulled off the little card. ('For David, happy birthday, love, Mummy'), ripped off the wrapping at the third attempt and took it through into the bedroom. Philippa Levens was looking round with a curious expression on her face, like a child at the zoo peering into the chimpanzee cage. He changed the pillowslip.

'Thanks ever so much,' she said, with a heart-melting you-can-go-away-now smile. 'See you in the morning.'

Lying awkwardly on the sofa (the headrest bit into his neck like a shire-horse's collar) he stared up at the ceiling and tried to figure at least some of it out. It was like trying to make up a composite jigsaw out of leftover pieces from four entirely different sets, blindfold, wearing thick woolly mittens: some bits seemed to slot together, but no amount of ingenuity or imagination would get them to connect with anything else. Not that it seemed to matter any more; it was as if he'd walked barefoot across the desert and climbed the mountain on his knees to reach the cave of the Prophet, only to be told to go away and come back in half an hour after the Master had finished watching *Neighbours*. He grabbed the cushion and stabbed it a couple of times with his elbow, but that didn't seem to make it any softer.

There's bound to be a perfectly simple explanation . . . He thought about that for a moment. Yes, there was one extremely simple explanation that would account for pretty well everything he'd seen, done or had done to him in the last twenty-four hours: at last, after years of teetering on the brink of delusional insanity, he'd finally taken that one small step. Accept that – and everything else slotted neatly into place. Try and work round it, and he faced the impossible task of cooking up a theory that explained Honest John and his serendipitous kinsmen, the light being on in the sitting room, Philippa Levens's perfect command of modern idiomatic English (and she'd known his name, too – sort of). Couldn't be done, even if you widened the parameters to include reincarnation and witchcraft. Trouble was, he didn't feel particularly crazy. (Ah yes, pointed out his inner voice, but the really crazy ones never do. By the way, are you aware that you've started hearing voices in your head? Told you . . .)

Of course, with all this strange and terrible stuff swirling round in his head like lint in a Dyson vacuum cleaner, there was absolutely no danger of him falling asleep—

He opened his eyes and immediately assumed he was dreaming; but when a whole second passed and still the huge silver trombone hadn't sidled up to him and eaten him, he opened his mind to other possibilities—

'I said, excuse me,' Philippa Levens repeated, shaking him rather more vigorously by the shoulder. 'Ah, you're awake. Look, I'm dreadfully sorry to disturb you, but it's gone a quarter to seven.'

A quarter to seven. Six-forty-five a.m.

As far as the first ten hours of each day were concerned, David was a convinced agnostic; he was prepared to accept that they might very well exist, in some form, in a dark and neglected corner of space-time, but he had so little personal experience of them that he didn't feel justified in forming a coherent opinion on the matter. 'Really?' he groaned.

"Yes. So if you're going to be waiting outside the Spar shop when it opens, don't you think you ought to be getting up?'

Why the hell would I want to be—? He remembered; something about Ritz crackers and Normandy butter. 'Good idea,' he heard himself say. 'Right, I'll do that, then.'

'Splendid. And while you're there, there're a few other things you could get. I've made a list.'

She shoved a piece of paper under his nose. It was shorter than the Old Testament, though the handwriting was so small that physical size was a misleading criterion. As it flashed by, he caught sight of a few words and phrases; *gruyère* was one, and *fresh asparagus* and *plovers eggs* and *smoked salmon paté, irish* not *scottish*. Expensive stuff like that. There was more on the back, but he didn't get a chance to take a close look before it was whisked away.

'That ought to tide us over for now,' she was saying, 'at least till Sainsbury's opens. We can leave the clothes and stuff till after lunch.'

He blinked twice. 'How do you know about Sainsbury's?' he asked.

She smiled at him. 'While you're out,' she said, 'would it be all right if I use the phone? Just local calls,' she added. 'Mostly.'

'Of course, help yourself,' he replied. 'Well, I'd better be going, then.'

''Bye.'

As his front door closed behind him, he couldn't help remembering the last time he'd passed that way. In a sense, it had all come together far, far better than he could possibly have expected. He hadn't been arrested. He wasn't lying in a heap on the floor, with a shattered jaw and three broken ribs. He'd actually talked to the girl of his dreams. Furthermore, she'd actually smiled at him and allowed him to run errands for her. This time yesterday, he'd have sold his soul for that.

(Why did he have an uncomfortable feeling that that was precisely what had just happened?)

Anyhow, all the seemingly insurmountable problems had melted away like chocolate in a blast furnace; and if they'd been replaced by other, subtler problems, wasn't that the nature of things, with the proviso that a change is always as good as a rest? High time he stopped cribbing and acknowledged his good fortune—

'Morning,' said a voice behind him; and Mr Van Oppen, his new neighbour, hurried past him down the stairs and vanished through the front door before he had a chance to reply. In his haste to pursue, David very nearly tripped over his feet and broke his neck.

By the time he had the front door open, there was no sign of Mr Van Oppen. He took a deep breath and headed up the road to the shop—

(Indeed. How did she know there was a Spar shop five minutes' walk away?)

As he'd anticipated, they didn't have most of the things on the list she'd given him. (Bizarrely, they *did* have fromage frais and Parma ham.) While he was at it, he slung a carton of milk and a sliced Hovis in the basket for himself. He didn't have enough cash on him to pay for the stuff, but luckily they accepted cheques for twenty-five pounds or over, so that was all right.

On the way home he noticed that he was walking more slowly than usual. Curious: the girl of his dreams was waiting for him, but he was trudging along like someone on his way to a meeting at the tax office. He thought about that for a moment; then, as the implications started to seep through, he made a conscious decision not to think about it any more, and turned his attention to other aspects of the situation, in particular the matter of the John brothers. Now, then: pigeon-holing for a moment the I've-gone-crazy hypothesis, was it possible to put together an explanation for what was going on that accounted for the three of them plus the girl?

Try this. Brother A (Mr Dean), having seen him hanging around the gallery gawping at the painting, had checked him out and discovered that he had a certain amount of money; so he planted a spurious lock of hair belonging to a female accomplice (his daughter, say) in the auction, knowing that he, David, would buy it and take it to Brother B (Honest John) to be cloned. Meanwhile Brother C (Mr Van Oppen) rented the flat above so as to be in a position to gather photographs and other materials necessary for effective blackmail.

Well, there were loopholes in the story, but no more than you'd find in the average made-for-TV movie, and if it wasn't one hundred per cent right, maybe it was along the right lines; it would explain why the girl knew so much about the twenty-first century, the neighbour-hood and him, and why the Brothers John—

He froze, at the junction of Warwick Road and Elm Drive. The Brothers John: three men who looked almost but not quite identical, the differences being mostly such things as length and colour of hair. Maybe they were triplets, born the old-fashioned way; or maybe they'd all come out of a vat of green gumbo under the railway arches at Ravenscourt Park. In which case, it was better than even money that they weren't the only copies of that particular original floating around the place—

Close, he suspected, but no cigar; even if the Brothers John really were somehow related to the late Philippa Levens, marchioness of Ipswich (who died childless, remember, in her nineteenth year), was it likely that they'd be able to find anybody, even his/their offspring, who just happened to be an identical, peas-in-a-pod match for the girl in the portrait? Not just a similarity, or even a striking resemblance. *Identical* (and he should know, since every detail of the face in the picture was ingrained into his mind to the point where it acted as his mental screen-saver, immediately there every time he closed his eyes or allowed his attention to wander). In order to get round that one, you'd have to prise the goal-posts another furlong or so apart and find a way to fit mind-altering drugs into the scenario, something that'd make him imagine that the female plant (to coin a phrase) looked like the girl in the painting, when in fact she looked completely different—

Of course, he could always quit speculating and ask her.

Or – rather more practical? – he could get a jemmy or a big screwdriver and bust his way into the flat upstairs, now supposedly the home of the enigmatic Mr Van

Oppen, and poke about until he found the obvious clue, the letter or file or document. That was what they did in movies.

(And he'd always wondered about that. For example, if he was the bad guy in a film and the hero and his sidekick burgled his flat, they wouldn't have a lawyer's chance in Heaven of finding anything. After all, he lived there and he spent hours vainly looking for letters and bills and stuff that weren't even hidden.)

More to the point, he didn't have a big screwdriver, let alone a jemmy. True, you're supposed to be able to open locks with a credit card, but David had a fairly shrewd idea that if he were to try that, he'd end up standing outside a locked door holding a sliver of terminally bent plastic. Kicking the door in was probably way beyond his physical abilities, shooting the lock off would require a gun, and it was the Lottery jackpot to a bent pfennig that Mr Van Oppen didn't leave a spare key under the mat. Assuming, of course, that he'd been telling the truth when he'd said he was the new tenant; David only had his word for that, and right now he wouldn't be inclined to believe Mr Van Oppen if he told him that snow was white.

Or he could just ask the girl.

Yes, it was theoretically possible, like so many things: world peace, an end to famine in Africa, England winning the World Cup. All it would take was a certain amount of courage, strength of character, determination. He knew at least a dozen people – people very like him in many ways – who'd do it like a shot without a moment's hesitation. 'See here,' they'd say (his cousin Norman, for example, or his aunt Sheila), 'what the bloody hell's going on here, and who are those three identical jokers? And while you're at it, buy your own sodding plovers' eggs.'

He considered the position. They probably sold big screwdrivers in Halfords, which was only a few doors down from Sainsbury's; or there was that big ironmongers across the road from the library (or had it closed down? He couldn't remember offhand). There was probably a knack to it, you'd have to get in behind the latch and force it back in—

David looked up, and saw his front door. He prayed to any gods who happened to be listening that she wouldn't be too upset about the lack of smoked-salmon pâté, and let himself in.

She was on the phone as he walked up the stairs; her voice carried (it was exquisitely lovely, like a shaft of bright sunlight in a dark and dusty attic or the high, clear note of the lark on the moors in summer; but you could hear it quite distinctly right the way down the hall) and he had no difficulty making out the words—

'Mr Snaithe, please. No, that's fine, I'll hold. Yes, that's right, I called about ten minutes ago. Yes, I'm sure you do.'

Snaithe: as in his loathsome aunt Mary Snaithe and her revolting son Alex, the lawyer. What the hell was she doing calling him?

He walked up a few more steps, then hesitated. Eavesdropping on someone else's phone conversation was the sort of mean, tricksy behaviour he most despised. Eavesdropping on the girl he loved with all his heart was—

—Was probably the only way he was likely to find out what was going on, since he was too chicken to ask her outright. Besides, he desperately needed to know why she was ringing Alex Snaithe, of all people, and where she'd got the number from. He leaned against the door-frame and held his breath.

Silence, for a very long time. Then she said, 'Yes, please, I'll carry on holding.'

(My phone bill, he caught himself thinking. Of course, he suppressed the unworthy thought immediately, but nevertheless: his phone bill . . .)

More silence; and in the meantime, the carrier bags hanging from his hands weren't getting any lighter, nor their handles any less sharp where they were cutting into his fingers. Dropping the bags with an audible crash might well put her on notice that he was outside, ear-wigging (see above under mean, tricksy behaviour). Bursting in on her while she was making this secret, probably highly personal call would quite likely register somewhere between embarrassing and unforgivable. Of course, it would all resolve itself quite satisfactorily if only that bastard Alex would get off the other line and talk to her—

(Of course: it was all Alex's fault. Now that he'd figured that out, everything dropped neatly into place. The only question was how come it had taken him so long to realise.)

'Lost your key?'

Miraculously, he didn't drop the shopping bags with a deafening crash (only because his foot was between the bag and the concrete, shielding the impact). He secured them, then turned round.

'I said,' repeated Mr Van Oppen, 'have you lost your key?'

'What?' It was, David realised, a perfectly civil

question. 'Oh, no. Thanks all the same. I was just, um, resting.'

'Ah, right. Cheers, then.'

And away Mr Van Oppen trotted down the stairs, blithe as Christopher Robin; and with him went an opportunity—

(You could ask him; he probably knows. Yes, but if he knows, he might tell you, and maybe you won't like what you hear—)

'Just a moment,' David heard himself call out. 'Please.'

CHAPTER FOUR

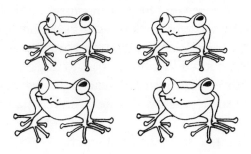

Mr Van Oppen stopped and looked up at him. 'Yes?' he asked.

I've done it again, David chided himself, committed myself to a course of action. Must stop doing that . . . 'Excuse me,' he said, keeping his voice down, 'but have you got a minute?'

'What?'

David hesitated for a moment, then tiptoed down to join him. 'Have you got a minute?' he repeated. 'Only there's something I'd like to ask you.'

'Sure,' Mr Van Oppen replied amiably. 'Fire away.'

David opened his mouth, but nothing came out. Of course he knew exactly what he wanted to ask, but it wasn't the sort of question that went easily into words. *What the hell's going on?* Too vague. *Who are you, and who's the girl in my flat?* Too direct, too toe-curlingly embarrassing if Mr Van Oppen replied with a blank stare and a polite enquiry as to what he'd been smoking lately.

'Excuse me,' David said, 'but could I borrow a cup of sugar?'

'No problem,' Mr Van Oppen replied. 'Follow me.'

He wasn't sure what he'd been expecting to see when Mr Van Oppen turned the key and pushed open the door: something bizarre, certainly, because that was the way his life had suddenly decided to go, and the most disconcerting thing he could imagine running into at this stage was normality. But he definitely hadn't anticipated—

'Here you go,' said Mr Van Oppen.

—Bare whitewashed walls, nude floorboards, uncurtained windows, a total absence of furniture, not even a doormat or a lampshade. Nothing at all, except for a single packet of Tate & Lyall granulated sugar in the exact centre of the living-room floor, and next to it a plain white cup, of the sort you get in old-fashioned cafés and railway-station buffets. Mr Van Oppen bent down, picked up the packet, opened it and poured sugar into the cup. 'Will that be enough?' he asked.

David nodded. 'Thanks,' he whispered. 'I'll let you have it back tomorrow.'

'No hurry.'

(Needless to say, he couldn't think of a rational explanation. But he did know what was going on: someone was taking the mickey, and not being desperately subtle about it, either.)

'While I'm here.' David took a deep breath. 'Would it be all right if I asked you a personal question?'

Mr Van Oppen smiled. 'That depends on what it is,' he said.

'All right.' David looked at the sugar in the cup. Just sugar. 'Do you know a lawyer by the name of Alex Snaithe?'

'Alex? Sure.' Mr Van Oppen nodded vigorously. 'He does a lot of work for my company. Nice enough chap, for a lawyer, though if you ask me he's so far up himself he can see out of his ears. Still, I think that's par for the course if you're a high-powered lawyer these days.'

'Ah,' David said. 'He's my cousin.'

'Really?' Mr Van Oppen hoisted an eyebrow, Spockwise. 'Small world.'

Indeed. Any smaller and you could use it as a ball-bearing. 'Right,' David said. 'Well, thanks a lot for the sugar.'

'My pleasure. Oh, by the way,' Mr Van Oppen added, 'I almost forgot. I've got a message for you.'

'For me?'

Mr Van Oppen nodded. 'From my brother,' he said. 'Apparently you left your briefcase at his workshop yesterday. No rush about collecting it; when you're next passing, he says.'

'Your brother.'

'John.'

'Ah,' David said. '*That* brother.'

Now I know, David reflected, how a cue ball feels. He took a deep breath. 'That's something else I'd like to talk to you about,' he said. 'If that's all right with you.'

Mr Van Oppen twitched his nose, like a rabbit. 'OK,' he said. 'But I'll have to be getting along in a minute or so, or I'll miss my flight.'

David nodded. 'Your flat,' he said. 'It's a bit—'

'Sparse?'

'Yes, sparse. I was wondering—'

Mr Van Oppen shrugged. 'Typical of my rotten luck when it comes to moving,' he said. 'Mix-up with the vans, or something like that. I phoned the removals people this morning, and they called me back and told me my stuff's in Durham, of all places. Apparently it's going to take a week to get it back. They didn't explain why – I've got this startlingly vivid mental image of all my socks lined up in a row, like the Osmonds, singing 'I'm gonna leave old Durham town', but I don't suppose it's anything as anthropomorphic as that. Fortuitously, I'm just off to Ulan Bator for a week on business, so it's not going to be fatally inconvenient. Actually,' he added, his face lighting up like a small floodlit cathedral, 'you could do me a tremendous favour, if you wouldn't mind. If I give you the key, could you let the removal men in when they do finally show up? Otherwise, I can just picture me coming home and finding all my worldly goods stacked into a barricade on the landing, like the defence of Rorke's Drift.'

'Sure,' David said automatically.

'That's extremely kind of you,' said Mr Van Oppen, handing him a keyring. It had an eight-legged pewter horse for a key fob and one solitary key.

(And nobody, *nobody* in the whole world had just one key on his keyring.)

'My pleasure,' David said. 'And I'll be sure to get some sugar.'

'What? Oh, yes, right. Look, sorry if this sounds rude but I really do have to fly.'

Mr Van Oppen trotted away down the stairs, his footsteps inaudible (and that was strange, too: the communal stairs had a tendency to creak like the special effects in a radio ghost story), and David put the key in his top pocket. It was time he went back to his own flat and faced up to his heart's desire.

He paused outside his front door and listened; he couldn't hear her voice. So he let himself in.

'There you are!' Once again he was knocked completely off balance by the sheer beauty of her voice. 'You've been ever such a long time.'

She was wearing a pair of his jogging pants (he'd never jogged in his life, needless to say) and a dark blue sweatshirt given to him a long time ago by someone who didn't know him very well. She looked like an angel.

'Sorry,' he replied. 'But I bumped into my new neighbour, the man who's moved into the flat upstairs, and—'

In the most graceful and attractive way possible, she wrenched the carrier bag from his hand. 'Danish butter,' she said, wrinkling her nose ever so very slightly. 'Oh.'

'They didn't have Normandy,' David explained.

'Really?' She seemed genuinely shocked, disappointed, as if she was five years old and someone had just shown her irrefutable proof that there was no Santa Claus. 'Oh, well,' she said, sadly but with a degree of genuine compassion for the world. 'Just have to make do, that's all. Where's the gruyère? In the other bag?'

'They didn't have any of that, either.'

Just briefly, a little flicker of fire sparkled in her eyes; small and fast as a spark plug, or the divine flame passing between fingertips in Michelangelo's painting. It faded immediately, but it left a burned patch in the middle of David's vision, as if he'd watched somebody arc-welding. 'Never mind,' she said. 'We'll just have to get a couple of spare pats when we go to Sainsbury's. Which reminds me; if we leave now, we'll get there just as they open.'

'Before we do that—' The sound of his own voice amazed him. That was no way to speak to a lovely young woman, especially a lost, frightened, vulnerable one who'd only just—

She looked at him. It wasn't even a frown, let alone a scowl. Compared with some of the looks he'd been on the sharp end of over the years, it was pretty innocuous, simply a polite warning intended to put him on notice that there were unexploded scowls hidden in the vicinity. But it hit him like a rake in the grass.

And, most remarkable of all, he kept on going, like the Light Brigade charging the wrong way down a one-way street. 'Before we do that,' he repeated, 'maybe we should talk about a few things.'

'Can't we do that on the way? Only I'm starving, and I thought we could grab something to eat in that little café next to the railway station – you know, the one that does the Danish pastries with the yellow custard in the middle—'

'How the hell do you know about that?'

Silence; the quality of silence that follows the moment when the waiter drops a towering pile of trays on the tiled floor. 'Excuse me?' she said.

'How the hell do you know about little cafés in Ealing Broadway?' David demanded. (Either that or there was a ventriloquist hiding behind the sofa; he still couldn't believe he was actually saying the words, and in such an aggressive tone of voice.) 'You can't know about that. Dammit, you're less than twelve hours old.'

'What on earth are you talking about?'

The penny dropping, like a shooting star, streaked his mental skyline with agonising red fire. The only surprising thing was that he hadn't thought of it before–

He only had Honest John's word for it that she was a clone. All he knew for certain was that she'd jumped up out of an overgrown fishbowl, covered in green slime. The one didn't necessarily follow on from the other. Wasn't it far more likely that she wasn't a clone at all, just some perfectly normal female who for some reason had been curled up asleep with no clothes on in a tank full of green yuck? Improbable, yes, but a stone-cold certainty compared with the odds of her being a construct extrapolated from the hair of a centuries-dead witch in a shed in Ravenscourt Park by a man who called himself Honest John. 'Excuse me,' David asked, very quietly, 'but who exactly are you? And what are you doing here?'

Another look from those starlike eyes. They left David feel like a clumsy Jedi Knight who'd been cleaning his lightsabre when it went off. 'Are you feeling all right?' she asked.

'Could you answer the question?' David pleaded. 'Please?'

'Sure.' She was looking at him with wide, round eyes. 'My name is Philippa Levens—'

'You're certain about that?'

'Don't be silly. My name's Philippa Levens, and I'm in my first year at Exeter University, reading chemistry, and Uncle John said I could earn some holiday money working for him in his factory.'

'Factory,' David repeated.

'All right, it's a bit small for that. Call it a workshop, then. Anyway—'

'Your uncle,' David interrupted. 'Honest John?'

She giggled. 'I think he meant it as a joke to start with,' she said, 'and then it sort of stuck, somehow.

Anyway, I think it's got a sort of ring to it: "Honest John's House of Cones".'

'Cones?'

'Cones. You know, the plastic pointy things they stick in the road. Like orange-and-white witches' hats. He makes them.'

'Ah. I see.'

'Oh good. Anyway, there I was helping him clean out the polymer vats – that's the tanks where he mixes up the chemicals – and I slipped on a damp patch, and next thing I knew—'

'You fell in the vat.'

She nodded. 'You know all this already,' she said. 'I mean, obviously you know all this, if you're an old friend of Uncle John's.'

He frowned. 'I'm an old friend of your Uncle John's?'

'Well, that's what he told me. Aren't you?'

David shrugged. 'Anything's possible. Look, sorry to wander off the subject, but have you got an Uncle Bill?'

She smiled. 'Of course I have. Why else would I be here?'

He thought about taking her up on that, but decided to let it ride for a moment or so. 'How about an Uncle Oliver? Have you got one of those?'

She shook her head. 'Of course not, silly,' she said. 'Oliver's my dad's name.'

David shook his head. 'I don't think so,' he said. 'When I met him, he said his name was Oliver Dean.

'Of course it is.'

'Then why aren't you Philippa Dean?'

Not anger in her eyes, not yet; just irritability, the sparkle of the fuse rather than the flare of the blasting charge itself. 'You know perfectly well why.' She sighed.

'Because when my mum and dad split up, my mum made me take her maiden name. All right? Really, all these questions. If I pass, do I get a badge or something?'

David took a long, deep breath. 'All right,' he said. 'Can we just wind back a bit? You said something about me being a good friend of your Uncle John? I'd never even seen him before yesterday.'

Just for a split second, the time it takes for a cell to divide or a lawyer to earn sixpence, she looked nonplussed, as if she'd been caught out in a careless mistake. 'Mutual friend's what I meant, of course. I know you don't know Uncle John, or Uncle Bill; but your best friend is their best friend. But that's a real mouthful to say, so—'

'My best friend? I haven't got a—' He stopped short, like a swallow flying into a plate-glass window. 'You mean Alex,' he said. 'Alex Snaithe.'

'Of course I do.' She smiled as she said the name. 'Oh, come on, you're not trying to tell me he's never mentioned me.'

The feeling that swept through David's body, invading every part of it simultaneously, was pure horror. 'No, he hasn't. Why would he mention you?'

'But he was going to—' She stopped and looked at him. 'All right,' she said, 'I suppose I'd better tell you. Alex and I are getting married.'

The fact that he'd intuitively anticipated it by a couple of seconds didn't make the blow any less painful. Those few seconds had been the time between seeing the other car pull out of the side turning in front of you without looking, and the actual moment of impact. 'You're going to marry Alex Snaithe,' he said.

'That's right. He was supposed to ask you if you'd be his best man, but obviously he didn't get round to it. Honestly, there are times when – anyway, that's between him and me.' She paused and frowned slightly. 'You're supposed to say "Congratulations".'

'What? Oh, right. Congratulations.'

'Thank you.'

David took a step back and a deep breath. 'That still doesn't explain—'

'Doesn't it? Oh dear. Look, can we talk about whatever it is you want to talk about on the way to the shops? I really don't want to be a nuisance, but I'm rather hungry and I'd quite like to get some clothes. Not that your things aren't really nice, in their own way, but these were the only ones I could find that were even *remotely* clean, and they aren't even my colour.'

At another time he'd have disputed that. Dressed in his shapeless old clothes she looked like a fairy-tale princess wearing someone else's shapeless old clothes. Even now, with all the confusion and strange connections ringing bells in his synapses and running away, he found it very difficult indeed to get past the fact that she was the most beautiful creature he'd ever seen in his life. But he managed it, just about.

'All right,' he said. 'But you've got to promise—'

'I promise, I promise. Come on.'

He followed her down the stairs and into the street, where she stopped and looked round.

'Which one of these is your car?' she asked.

'None of them. I haven't got a car.'

'You haven't— Oh. Right.' She broke off eye contact, as if he'd replied to some tactless remark of hers by confessing he had leprosy. What the hell was it about not owning a motor vehicle that made people look at you like that? 'Doesn't matter,' she went on, just a little too briskly. 'We can walk. Or we could get a bus,' she added, making it sound like some kind of mythical or fabulous beast that no grown-up could seriously be expected to believe in.

'That's a good idea,' he replied. 'And while we're waiting, you can explain a few things. For a start—'

'Where's the bus place? You know, where you get on them.'

That was a good question; David hadn't been on a bus for nearly ten years. But he seemed to remember seeing a bus-stop sign in Freemantle Avenue. 'This way,' he said, turning left. 'Now, then—'

'Are you sure it's this way?'

'Yes. Now, I hear what you say about your Uncle John and falling in the vat, but in that case, what are you doing here?'

She looked away for a moment. 'I explained all that,' she said. 'You're Alex's cousin and best friend, and he's Uncle John's lawyer, and Uncle Bill's too, and Uncle Bill's just moved into the flat above yours—'

'Yes, all right,' David persisted. 'But it still doesn't really explain anything, does it? I mean, if I had a niece and she fell in a tank full of chemicals, I don't think my first reaction would be *My God, I'd better get her over to my lawyer's best friend, quick.* I'd be thinking more along the lines of pulling her out, and towels.'

He could feel her uncertainty; it was like standing next to a fire that had suddenly turned icy cold. 'You're missing the point, silly,' she said. 'I fell in the tank—'

'Yes. And?'

'And you happened to be there, and I needed

somewhere to have a shower, get all those horrid chemicals off me. There aren't any showers at Uncle John's workshop.'

David nodded. 'I can see that there wouldn't be. But why didn't you just go home?'

She frowned. 'I live in Ipswich,' she said. 'Your flat was just a little bit closer.'

'All right,' David said, 'why didn't your Uncle John take you back to his house? He has got one, hasn't he?'

Her uncertainty was growing. 'No, as a matter of fact he hasn't, he sleeps in the workshop. He had to sell his house to set up the business.'

David shook his head. He could see a tiny crack opening, just wide enough to get the tip of a wedge in. 'I see,' he said. 'That still doesn't explain why your Uncle John brought you here,' he said. 'Why didn't he take you to Alex's flat, for instance? He's nearer to Ravenscourt Park than me, and I expect he's got an absolutely fantastic state-of-the-art shower.'

'Yes, but it's broken.' She started walking a little faster. He had no trouble keeping up. 'There was a leak, water was going everywhere. And the plumber's busy, can't come and look at it till Friday. Honestly, sometimes I think it'd be easier getting a private audience with the Pope.'

'All right,' David said. 'Let's suppose for a moment that it's all true, what you've been telling me. So why don't I remember it that way?'

She looked at him. 'I was trying to be polite,' she said. 'But, if you insist. You're the one who's acting really strange, if you must know. But Uncle John said that's only to be expected. Because of the fumes.'

'Fumes?'

'The fumes from the polymer tank. You breathed in rather a lot of them, and it's a well-known fact that they can have a funny effect on people who aren't used to them. Temporary amnesia. Delusions, even. It's all right, the effects go away within forty-eight hours.'

'So why aren't you—?'

'I'm used to them,' she said quickly. 'Chemistry student, remember? And besides, I've been hanging round Uncle's workshop since I was little. You build up a tolerance.'

They'd reached the bus stop. She made a show of reading the timetables.

'That's all very well,' David persisted. 'But it still doesn't explain—'

'Wrong bus,' she interrupted. 'We need a number seven. Or a number thirty-three.'

'That still doesn't explain two things,' David ground on, feeling as though he was wading through hip-deep snow. 'One, why you need a whole new wardrobe—'

She laughed. 'You obviously don't know what that stuff does to clothes. Fzzzz. all gone.'

'And you haven't got a change of clothes where you're staying?'

'No, as a matter of fact I haven't. I only came down to visit, I didn't bring a bag or anything.'

He could feel the snow getting thicker and stiffer; but it was still all false, it had no right being there. 'All right,' he said. 'Number two. If all this is true, what you've been telling me, how come you look exactly like the portrait of a seventeenth-century witch in the National Gallery?'

She stared at him, then giggled. 'Say that again,' she said.

'There's a painting in the National Gallery that looks exactly like you,' David said grimly. 'Absolutely identical. Care to explain that?'

'How absolutely fascinating!' She smiled. 'So, do tell. Who's it a painting of? Anybody famous?'

'I just told you, a seventeenth-century witch. Her name was Philippa Levens—'

Her smile broadened a little; and now he wasn't wading through snow, he was a snowman, and the sun had just come out. He could feel everything he'd always thought he was melting away.

'Ah, right,' she said. 'That painting. Yes, I suppose I *do* look a bit like her. After all, she's my – what, great-great-great-several-more-greats-aunt. Mummy always said I've got the family nose (which sounds rather revolting if you ask me).' She shrugged her slender shoulders. 'There's a slight resemblance, I'll give you that. Sorry, you threw me off track there by saying the picture looks just like me, that's why the penny didn't drop for a second.' Her stare was cutting into him like a plasma torch. 'So,' she said, 'was that your Big Deal Number Two?'

He nodded.

'Fine.' She was silent for a moment, then added, 'I'm sorry if I sounded a bit snappy just then, I didn't mean to. I should be more sympathetic, because I do know, it can feel really strange sometimes when you've breathed in those fumes.'

'The poly whatsit?' He fumbled for the right word, but it slipped away. 'The green stuff in the tank?'

'That's right, yes. But it does go away, I promise. No harmful effects.'

'Ah. Right. So in a few hours it'll all be back to

normal and I should start remembering all this stuff you've told me. It'll all start making sense, I mean.'

'That's it. You'll be just fine, you wait and see.' She looked over his shoulder. 'Gosh, look, isn't that the bus coming down the road?' She stood on tiptoe and waved at it, for all the world as if it was a ship and she'd spent the last ten years marooned on a desert island. 'Would it be all right if we ride up on the top deck, at the front? We've only got single-decker buses where I come from.'

Another curious thing: the bus was a Number 17 and the sign on the front said it was going to Ruislip. Once they boarded it, however, it seemed to undergo a road-to-Damascus conversion, abandoning its misguided intentions and taking them to the Broadway non-stop. 'Now then,' she announced, heading for the Bentalls centre like an iron filing drawn by a magnet, 'we'll start with Principles and take it from there. After all, I'm not really in any position to be fussy. A potato sack with three holes cut in it would probably do me, right now. Tell you what,' she went on, 'I'll be taking a look round while you just nip over to Sainsbury's and get the food shopping. I'll meet you back here in, say, an hour and a half. By then I should've found a few things I could bear to be seen dead in, and you can buy them for me.'

At various times in his life, David had thought how great it would be to find a nice old-fashioned girl. When he staggered back from the supermarket ninety minutes later, his arms feeling as if they'd stretched two inches and had their bones replaced with overboiled spaghetti, he decided that nice, old-fashioned girls were a menace and a hazard to sentient life; what he wanted was a nice modern girl, the sort who carries her own shopping and pays for it with her own money. Anything else belonged on History's scrapheap, along with slavery and dinosaurs.

'There you are,' said a vision of radiant loveliness from behind a pillar. 'I was beginning to wonder where you'd got to.'

David didn't know much about clothes, particularly the female variety, so he couldn't bring to mind any of the technical terms. The net effect, however, was quite simply described: stunning – and horrendously expensive.

'They were awfully sweet about it,' she explained. 'I told them you'd gone off with all the cards and money, and you'd be back soon, and they said go ahead, no need to wait till he gets back. What do you think?'

'It's, um, very nice,' David replied. He knew that wasn't the right answer, but he was too preoccupied with yet another impossible miracle to try very hard. They'd let her walk out of the shop, wearing the clothes, without paying for them? Sure, all the clone stuff and the three identical uncles and all the weird coincidences were enough to stretch his credulity. But this was way beyond stretching: it was industrial-spec extrusion.

'Very nice,' she repeated. 'Oh, well. Come on, I'm starving. Or had you forgotten that?'

After he'd been round and paid for all the clothes (he was very good about it, only sobbed out loud once) he followed her into a small, impractical-looking sort-of-café place, the kind that springs up like skeleton warriors from dragons' teeth and fades away before the mayfly's even started thinking seriously about sensible pension-planning. He made it as far as the corner table before the carrier-bag handles prised apart his cramp-crippled fingers and sunk to the floor. Meanwhile she was at the counter, ordering authentic Moravian cherry torte.

'That's better,' she said a little later, with her mouth full. 'Now then, I almost forgot to mention. Alex is coming over this afternoon to pick me up.'

So what? yelled a small but vocal faction inside his brain, the one he'd started thinking of as the People's Front for the Liberation of David Perkins. In fact, we'll go further. Hooray, yippee and good riddance. Alex can take her away and you can get back to real life. Hey, what the hell are you cribbing about now?

Like most PFLDP statements, it was hard to argue with. After all, hadn't he made a serious error of judgement, and wasn't he, quite suddenly and unexpectedly, being let off the consequences for the laughably cheap price of £12,750 (plus buyer's premium and VAT) and the cost of a few groceries and frocks? It was perfect; not only was she about to walk out of his life for ever, she was also going to visit her unique blend of bewilderment and financial haemorrhage on the person he liked least in the whole world. Couldn't have turned out more pleasingly if he'd written the script himself.

Except that . . . He lifted his head, catching sight of her profile, and realised that he was still in love with her. God alone knew why: force of habit, masochism, a hidden strand of lemming DNA buried deep in his genetic matrix. Whatever it was, the thought of never seeing her again was more than he could bear.

Idiot, screamed the PFLDP, or words to that effect. He thanked them politely for their entirely helpful and sensible suggestions, and dismissed them from his conscious mind. Love, after all, made the world go round;

one of many things it had in common with severe concussion. 'Oh,' he said.

'Anyway,' she went on, 'thanks for all your help. It was very kind of you.'

'Not at all,' David grunted into his torte shrapnel.

'And I think it'd be really, really nice if you'd be Alex's best man at the wedding,' she went on, remorseless as a slender, golden-haired young Sherman tank. 'I'll have a word with him as soon as I see him and remind him to ask you. You will do it, won't you?'

'Oh, sure.'

'That's splendid. Would you mind awfully if we got a taxi back? Only, we might be late for meeting Alex if we wait for the bus.'

Before he could point out that her chances of finding a taxi at this time of day were on a par with stumbling on the secret of the philosophers' stone on a wet Thursday in Stockport, she'd skipped to the door and hailed one, and it was waiting outside, its door obligingly open. There was just enough room for him in it, along with all the shopping.

All this fancy food. The insight came down on PFLDP headed notepaper. The Normandy butter and quails' eggs and ricotta cheese. It's not for her, it's for him. Alex. You know what a pig he is about food. David closed his eyes and managed not to make a groaning noise.

'Would it be all right if I used your kitchen when we get back?' she was saying. 'Only, I did tell Alex I'd fix him some lunch.'

Bloody hell, David thought. 'Fine,' he said. 'Please, go ahead. I won't be joining you, I'm afraid. Got some work I really should be getting on with.'

'All right.'

All right? Is that all you've got to say for yourself, all right? 'That's fine, then,' he said. 'Oh, good, we're here.'

He'd never previously thought of his flat as excessively small; quite the opposite, in fact, since he had to clean it himself. It had a fair-sized bedroom, a modest but adequate living room, more than enough kitchen for someone whose philosophy of cooking was centred around a holy trinity of microwave, tin-opener and electric kettle, and a functional bathroom with deceptively good acoustics. Plenty big enough for one hermit geek; too small to accommodate two people trying to keep out of each other's way (though of course the same could be said of the Albert Hall or the Mojave Desert). All the computer stuff was in the living room, so he couldn't get any work done. He was tempted to go out and not come back till she'd gone, but he couldn't quite bring himself to do that. So he took a laptop into the bedroom, shut the door and played *Blood Frenzy III* in a listless manner, hoping that Alex wouldn't want to see him when he arrived.

So enthralling was the game that he fell asleep. When he woke up, his watch said four-thirty. He closed down the laptop, tiptoed over to the door and opened it cautiously. Nobody to be seen in the living room, just a scatter of dirty plates and glasses on the table. (That figures, he thought bitterly.) He checked the kitchen and, being thorough, the bathroom. Nobody there. She'd gone. No note, or anything like that. Never mind, he said to himself, it's undoubtedly just as well. He made a start on clearing up the abandoned crockery, asking himself as he did so whether his experiences over the last twenty-four hours could be considered as coming under the heading of getting a life, as every-body had kept urging him to do for years and years; if so, at least it had proved to his satisfaction that he was far better off without one, and that at least was a com-fort.

The phone rang as he was carrying plates into the kitchen. He had one of those hands-free phones, the ones you can wedge between collarbone and ear and talk into while walking about and doing useful stuff. 'Hello?' he said.

'David Perkins?'

'That's me.' He dumped one consignment of plates and went back for another. 'Who's this?'

'You don't know me,' said the voice, 'but I believe you've met my brother John. Possibly my brothers Bill and Oliver, too.'

Bloody hell, he thought, *four* of them. 'John as in Honest John?'

'That's right. My name's Arkwright. Jason Arkwright.'

A likely story, David said to himself, lifting a plate and noting with disgust a spreading pool of ketchup on the table top. He'd need to get a wet cloth on that, before it made everything sticky and yuck. 'Fine,' he said. 'So, what can I do for you?'

'Can you tell me, have you by any chance come across a young woman, possibly calling herself Pippa Levens and claiming to be my niece? Or John's niece, or Ollie's, or Bill's?'

'Yes, of course,' David replied, absent-mindedly wiping ketchup off onto his trousers as he lugged the next stackful of china through the doorway. How on earth had two people managed to use so many plates? At the very least, it was a staggering tribute to their ingenuity and resourcefulness. 'She was here earlier, but she's gone.'

'Gone. Damn.' Short pause. 'When was this?'

'Not sure,' David said. 'I was asleep when she left.' A very brief moment later, about as long as it takes light to travel two yards, he realised what that last remark could have sounded like. 'She was having lunch with a friend,' he added quickly. 'I was in the next room, all the time, and I sort of nodded off.'

'A friend.'

'Yes. Well, her fiancé, actually.' As he was saying the words, a thought nudged him. *Possibly* calling herself Pippa Levens. *Claiming* to be my niece. Note the emphases. 'Excuse me, but are you saying—?'

'Fiancé,' the voice repeated, with palpable distaste. 'Sorry to interrupt. Do you happen to know this man's name?'

'Sure,' David replied. 'He's my cousin. Alex Snaithe.'

A sharp intake of breath from the other end of the line, like an imploding heavy breather. 'You're sure about that? The name.'

'Well, yes, of course. I've known him all my life. Is there—?'

The phone went dead. David took it out from under his chin and scowled at it, then turned it off and put it back in its cradle. *Four* of these crazy brothers. Jason Arkwright. Claiming to be my niece.

Ah, well; all gone now, and good riddance. Somehow he had the feeling that once the raucous clatter of the wedding bells had faded away, cousin Alex was going to be getting the kind of family Christmases with the in-laws that he deserved. Best man? Not if he had anything to do with it.

There was a knock at the door, and David winced. Spoke too soon, he muttered to himself; what's the betting that that's Alex and his *bird*, his *paramour*, returned to collect something they'd negligently left behind? That'd be so typical.

As it turned out, he was being unduly pessimistic. It wasn't Alex, or Philippa Levens. Nor was it Uncle Oliver, Uncle Bill or even Uncle Honest John.

It was the police.

CHAPTER FIVE

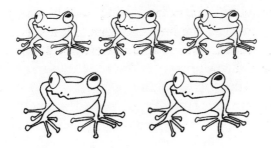

'Honestly,' David said, 'I don't know what you're talking about.'

The policeman leaned back in his chair and looked at him as if he'd just found him crawling about in his salad. 'Really,' he said. 'You know what time it is?'

David looked up at the clock on the wall behind the policeman's head. 'It's a quarter past seven,' he said.

'A quarter past seven,' the policeman repeated. 'In other words, I'm missing the end of the snooker. The final, Wayne Digley versus Snapping Dan Melznic, best of fifteen frames. I've been following it since the start of the tournament. And instead, I'm in here with you. Lucky me.'

David shrugged. 'I'm sorry,' he said.

'You're sorry.' The policeman sighed. 'Of course, I asked her to tape it for me, but will she? Will she hell as like, not if it clashes with her soaps. Obsessed with her bloody soaps, she is. She watches the BBC one and tapes the ITV, so I might as well have saved my breath. What's so bloody fascinating about a load of randy Australian teenagers I really couldn't say. I like *Brookside*, mind. You watch *Brookside*?'

David admitted that he didn't.

'Thought not,' the policeman said. 'All right, let's try again. First, may I remind you that you have a right to have your solicitor present. You have chosen not to avail yourself of that right. Right?'

David nodded. His solicitor was Alex Snaithe.

'Fine,' the policeman went on. 'It's bad enough being stuck in here without one of them sarky buggers looking down his nose and being difficult.' The policeman lit a cigarette. 'Mind if I smoke?'

David coughed. 'Go ahead,' he said.

'Now then,' said the policeman. 'Do you admit that at some time between ten and eleven a.m. yesterday morning, you were in the National Gallery standing looking at a painting, Portrait of Philippa Levens by—' He looked down at his notes. 'By William de Stevens or something like that, can't read my own writing. Anyway, that one.'

'Yes,' David said.

'All right. But you claim that you know nothing about the break-in between one and one-thirty a.m. or the disappearance of the said picture, even though you were stood there like a prune gawping at it and making funny noises for over an hour.'

'That's right.'

'Do you admit that after leaving the gallery you proceeded to meet with one Oliver Dean, a professional criminal with several convictions for fine-art theft, in a pub round the corner?'

David bit his lip. 'I met a man in a pub, yes. And he said his name was Oliver Dean.'

'So you'd never met him before?'

'No.'

'All right. Do you agree that after leaving the pub, you took a train to Ravenscourt Park and visited premises owned by a John Spooner, otherwise known as Honest John, a dealer in stolen artworks well known to the police, and Dean's stepbrother?'

David winced. 'I— Yes, that's right.'

The policeman nodded. 'Fair enough. Furthermore, do you admit that you live in the same block of flats as one William Van Oppen, alias William Oppenheimer, alias Bill the Shiv and something else in German I'm not even going to try and pronounce, also a notorious fine-art thief and Spooner and Dean's stepbrother?'

'I suppose so.'

'Thank you so much.' The policeman sighed. 'Let's just run through all that one more time, shall we? You spent yesterday morning closely examining a certain priceless art object – fifteen photographs of which, by the way, we found in your flat – and the rest of the day hanging out with three brothers who make their living nicking old paintings. Late last night, somebody breaks into the gallery, bypasses all the alarms, steals the price-less art object and buggers off. And you had nothing at all to do with it.'

'That's about the shape of it, yes.'

'Listen, sunbeam.' The policeman leaned across the table at him. 'For two pins I'd arrest you right now on charges of attempting to murder an Old Bailey jury by inducing them to laugh themselves to death.' He shook his head. 'Go on, then,' he said. 'You tell me your version, and we'll see what it sounds like. I mean, maybe you've got a perfectly reasonable explanation, and as soon as I hear it I'll be doing Homer Simpson impressions and wondering why the hell I didn't spot something so pathetically bloody obvious. Try me.'

David took a deep breath. 'Well,' he said.

'Hang on.' The policeman was staring at David's leg. 'What's that on your trousers?'

'Excuse me?'

'There's a sort of reddish-brown mark on your trouser leg, just above the right knee. You care to tell me what it is?'

David glanced down. 'Oh, that,' he said. 'That's just tomato ketchup.'

'You're sure about that?'

'Absolutely. There was some – I mean, I spilled some ketchup and I got a bit on my hands, so I wiped it off on my trouser leg.'

'Fine. It looks more like dried blood to me.'

As the policeman said that, David suddenly remembered that there wasn't any tomato ketchup left in his flat; he'd used up the last dregs of the bottle on Saturday's chips. Nor had anything so mundane as ketchup featured on the list of stuff he'd been given to buy at Sainsbury's. So, if the puddle on the table *was* ketchup, where had it come from?

'Does it?' he mumbled.

The policeman inclined his head gravely. 'And I know what dried blood looks like,' he added. 'It looks like that. As opposed to, say, tomato sauce, which doesn't look like that at all.'

'Oh.'

'But we'll soon know for sure once forensic's taken a

look. Could I trouble you to take off your trousers? I'll get you a receipt for them from the desk sergeant.'

Earlier, David would have defined abject misery as sitting in a police interview room being asked questions to which the only possible answer was yes. After he'd been debagged and issued with his receipt, he made a small but significant amendment to the definition. If ever they send an expedition to Hell, down in the nethermost circle they'll find all the worst evildoers from history, sitting in a police interview room saying yes to awkward questions while wearing nothing below the waist except bright blue boxer shorts and paisley socks. And serve them right for doing all that bad stuff. What David had done to merit such treatment, on the other hand, he had no idea.

'Maybe I forgot to mention,' the policeman went on, 'but about ten minutes after we arrested you, someone fished the dead body of William Van Oppen, alias all those other blokes, out of a skip in Hillingdon. Nasty bash on the head, loads of red stuff down his shirt front – haven't heard back from forensic, but it's probably not tomato ketchup – and a bit of paper in his top pocket with your phone number written on it. Not that I'm suggesting you had anything to do with it. Just making conversation, really.'

Tellingly, the first mental image that flashed across David's synapses when he heard this was the look of utter disdain and contempt on his mother's face as she scowled at him through one of those plate-glass windows they have in prison visiting rooms. It only went to show what he'd always suspected. When the going gets really tough, a boy's worst nightmare is his mother.

'Excuse me,' David said, in a very small voice, 'but could I see my solicitor now, please?'

The policeman shrugged. 'Yeah, why not?' he said. 'I knew it couldn't last. Give me his number and I'll get someone to phone him for you.'

But Alex Snaithe wasn't there; he was out of the office, hadn't said when he'd be back. Would it be all right if they sent his partner, Mr Yaxley, instead?

David had never heard of him, but that was just fine; better, in fact, for obvious reasons. 'That's all right, is it?' he asked. 'You're allowed to have someone who isn't your usual solicitor?'

That was clearly a stupid question, not meriting an answer. 'Better wait till he gets here,' the policeman sighed. 'You stay there. I'm going to see if I can get Sky Sport on the TV upstairs.'

Left alone with a uniformed bogey and his thoughts, David tried to doggy-paddle his way up the rapids of despair. True, the circumstantial evidence against him was so strong that even he was pretty sure he was guilty, but there had to be a simple, reasonable explanation for all this, one that would eventually burst into flower and fill this dismal place with its radiant sweetness. So what if that explanation must inevitably involve a seventeenth-century witch and a backstreet cloning operation in Ravenscourt Park? The truth shall set you free, and all that.

Well, quite. Nothing to worry about, really.

The door opened.

'This is Mr Yaxley,' said the policeman, his tone of voice suggesting that whoever was responsible, it wasn't him. 'He's your solicitor.'

'Hello,' said Mr Yaxley.

Unlike the other three, he had a proper patch over his missing eye; also, his hair was shorter and neater, and his fingernails were clean. Apart from that, he was identical in every respect.

David made a tiny whimpering noise and sagged forward. No, it wasn't polite, in fact it was downright rude; but he couldn't help it. Tucked away in the cupboard under the stairs of his mind, the People's Front for the Liberation of David Perkins asked some very pertinent questions about how come the policeman hadn't noticed the similarity between this Mr Yaxley and the dead body in the skip with the shirt-frontful of not-ketchup, but nobody else seemed particularly interested.

'If I could have five minutes or so alone with my client,' Mr Yaxley was saying (and yes, the voice was a pretty good match, as well). The net result, after a short battle of wills, was that the policeman went away. David wasn't sure this was a good thing.

'Don't tell me,' he said. 'You come from a large family.'

Mr Yaxley nodded and smiled. 'You're obviously very perceptive,' he said.

David frowned. 'Has Van Oppen really been murdered?'

'I believe so,' Mr Yaxley replied, opening his briefcase and taking out a large box file. 'That's what the inspector told me, and I don't think he was lying. Usually you can tell when they're lying. Their ears twitch.'

'And Van Oppen was your brother?'

'Half-brother.'

'Excuse me if this is personal, but you don't seem very upset.'

Mr Yaxley shrugged. 'I'm not,' he said. 'Bill was a

pain in the bum at all times, especially once he'd taken to stealing things. That's the trouble with family, they always expect you to do work for them for free. Anyway, that's enough about me. How about you?'

David closed his eyes. 'I don't think he was your brother.'

'Half-brother.'

For the first time since he was a boy, David was getting angry enough to be rude to a stranger. 'I don't think he was your half-brother or your quarter-brother or your five-eighths brother or anything. I think you're a clone.'

'Ah,' said Mr Yaxley. 'You're thinking of an insanity defence. Imaginative, but I wouldn't advise it, much harder to establish in court than most laymen think. Proof of insanity is governed by what we lawyers call the McNaughten Rules—'

'I think,' David ground on, 'that you're all clones – well, maybe not Honest John, I think he cloned you from himself. Unless he's just another clone and one of you's the real one, I don't know. I don't care, either. I just want to go home.'

'Now we're getting somewhere,' Mr Yaxley said. 'You'd like to get out of here, yes?'

David opened his eyes and nodded. 'I think that would be very nice,' he said.

'Right, then,' replied Mr Yaxley, 'let's have a look at where we are, shall we?' He leaned back in his chair and steepled his fingers. 'I've had a quick glance through the police bumf, and I've got to say, it's not looking desperately wonderful. I mean, if I was on the jury, I'd convict you faster than a Sampras serve. Though, just as an interesting point of law, I could never be on a jury because lawyers aren't allowed, which says something about our legal system, though I'm not entirely sure what. Sorry, where was I?'

'You were saying you think I'm guilty,' David muttered.

'No, I never said that.' Mr Yaxley shook his head. 'Heaven forbid, after all, it's none of my business whether you're guilty or not, I'm only concerned with what the police can prove. And,' he went on, 'not wanting to sound downbeat or anything, but I reckon your spot of bother here pretty well slots into that category. I mean, the blood on the trousers – They've tested it, by the way, and it's definitely Bill's.'

David groaned.

'Awkward,' sighed Mr Yaxley, 'definitely awkward. I'm sorry to say it more or less torpedoes any chance we might have had of getting you out of here by, let's say, conventional means.'

"So,' David said quietly, 'I'm screwed.'

'In a sense,' Mr Yaxley replied. 'At least, that one avenue of approach is probably closed.'

David looked up. 'One avenue of approach,' he repeated. 'You make it sound like I've got another choice.'

Mr Yaxley dipped his head in a neat little bow. 'There are other options available.'

'Such as?'

'You could run away. In fact,' Mr Yaxley went on, 'as your legal adviser, that's the strategy I'd be tempted to recommend.'

'Run away?'

'Figuratively speaking. In practice, of course, running down the corridors of police stations may tend to attract unwelcome attention, particularly if you aren't wearing any trousers. I'd suggest something a bit less energetic; a brisk walk, say.'

'Fine,' David said bitterly, turning his head away. 'And how exactly do you suggest I go about it?'

'Easy,' Mr Yaxley said.

David turned back to stare at him, and saw that he was resting both hands on the box file he'd taken out of his briefcase. 'If it's all right with you,' Mr Yaxley went on, 'I'd prefer it if you didn't make your move, so to speak, until I've gone. Otherwise it could be awkward for me. I'll be waiting for you just round the corner in Acland Street. I'll be in a lime-green Mercedes. Not the colour I'd have chosen,' he added, 'but it was that or a boring old BMW. Best of luck.'

Before David could say anything, Mr Yaxley had opened the door and gone. The uniformed copper came in and sat down by the door.

Well, David said to himself, if I'm going to prison anyway, why not? Very tentatively he opened the box file, expecting to find a gun or a knife, or maybe a can of Mace.

Instead, the box contained a small, round Black Forest gateau.

David snapped the lid shut, closed his eyes and swore softly. A file with a cake in it, he said to himself; suddenly everybody's a comedian.

'Here,' said the policeman, standing up, 'what've you got there, then?'

'Nothing,' David replied automatically.

'Yeah, right.' The policeman was coming towards him. Without stopping to think, David ripped open the box file, snatched up the cake and threw it as hard as he could. Miraculously, it caught the policeman full in the face, with the result that he crashed into the table, fell over it, bumped his head and went to sleep.

For a full five seconds, all David could do was stand very still with his mouth open, like a goldfish trapped in amber. Then, with considerable effort, he rolled the unconscious policeman over and (hoping very earnestly indeed that nobody would choose that moment to come into the room) set about removing the man's trousers. It wasn't nearly as easy as they made it look in the films, and the trousers, once acquired, turned out to be three inches too long and far too wide round the waist; nevertheless, they had to be an improvement on nothing at all. As an afterthought, he hauled off the copper's jacket and put that on as well. He didn't expect it would fool anybody, but at least he'd shown willing and done his best.

The corridor was empty. He took a deep breath and walked out, trying to remember which direction he'd come in.

Although getting from the interview room to the street was the most terrifying thing he'd ever had to do in his life, he got through the ordeal with no difficulties at all. Two policemen he passed on the stairs said hello to him, and a clerk in one of the offices he went through looked twice at him (probably because, as he later discovered, his fly had come undone) but that was it. He lunged through the main door, trotted awkwardly down the front steps (stairs can be a problem when the bones in your legs have melted to the consistency of junket) and tottered round the corner. As promised, there was a lime-green Mercedes parked about twenty yards down.

'What kept you?' said Mr Yaxley, opening the passenger door for him.

'Drive,' he replied.

So Mr Yaxley drove; and, since he seemed to know where he was going, David didn't raise the subject. In any case, he was too busy trembling and hyperventilating to give directions. Instead, he told Mr Yaxley what had happened.

'I told you it wouldn't be a problem,' Mr Yaxley said.

'Mmm.'

'Piece of cake, in fact.'

Not for the first time, David found himself wondering about Mr Yaxley; but wondering required thought, and his brains were too frazzled for that. He stuck a bookmark in the place, and got on with his backlog of post-traumatic shock. 'That was your idea of an escape plan, was it?' he asked shakily.

'It worked, didn't it? Yes, on balance an Uzi would've been preferable, but I'd never have got it past the metal detectors. And here you are, which is the main thing. Why the fancy dress, by the way? Going on somewhere afterwards?'

Ah yes, David thought, that reminds me. 'I need clothes,' he mumbled. 'Proper clothes, I mean, not these things. Oh God, now I'm an escaped murderer, what the hell—?'

'Escaped murder *suspect*, please,' Mr Yaxley pointed out, 'though it must be said, assaulting a police officer and escaping from custody doesn't really gel with the innocent-bystander, pure-as-the-driven-snow image you need to cultivate if you're serious about being innocent. It's all a matter of emphasis, really. Still, there's one good thing. With all the trouble you're in already, a little police-bashing and uniform-stealing's really neither here nor there. Wonderfully liberating feeling, I should imagine, knowing that there isn't really anything you could possibly do that'd make things worse than they already are.'

For some reason, David didn't feel inclined to reply to that. It was hard enough trying to keep his head above the meniscus of the rising tide of terror with only the rubber ring of fortitude and the polystyrene float of hope to keep him from going under. So he wriggled his chin down into the collar of the policeman's jacket, shut his eyes and tried very hard to think about nothing at all.

'If I were in your shoes,' said Mr Yaxley, 'I'd want to know where we're going.'

David shrugged. 'All right,' he said, 'where are we going?'

Mr Yaxley changed gear abruptly and overtook a van. His driving would have interested Einstein, on the grounds that anybody who travelled that fast ought to arrive ten minutes before he left. 'While I was waiting for you,' he said, 'I gave my brother a ring. He'll put you up for a day or two, until things have settled down a bit.'

'Your brother.'

'My brother George.'

Now that David came to think about it, he'd been quite happy and contented in his snug little interview room, with that nice policeman for company. 'Which one is your brother George?'

Mr Yaxley shrugged. 'He's my brother,' he replied. 'His name's George. I don't know what else you want me to tell you.'

'You're right,' David murmured. 'Best not to know, really.'

'Sorry, what did you say?'

'Nothing.'

David looked out of the window, but he didn't know where he was. He tried very hard not to let it bother him, and, inevitably, the harder he tried, the more impossible the task became. 'All right,' he said eventually, 'please tell me where we're going.'

'I just did,' Mr Yaxley replied, braking sharply to avoid a lorry. 'We're going to George's place.'

'Yes, I got that part. Where is George's place?'

'Where we're going.'

David gave up and leaned back against the headrest. Of course, sleep would be out of the question, with his mind churning away like it was, but closing his eyes might have a soothing effect—

He woke up, and realised that the car had stopped. It was dark.

'We're here,' said Mr Yaxley's voice beside him. 'Now then: no offence, but I'd rather not get out here, just in case someone sees us together. I expect George'll lend you some clothes if you ask him nicely.'

That, apparently, was Mr Yaxley's way of saying *Get lost*. David opened his door, then hesitated.

'Thanks,' he said. 'For rescuing me, and arranging all this, and the lift.'

'My pleasure. Any friend of my brother's is a friend of mine.'

David closed the door and the car drove off, spraying his legs with gravel. He looked round and saw a light, a hundred yards or so away. There were no other signs of life, and it was as dark as the dreams of lawyers. It was also unnervingly quiet, no comforting growl of ambient traffic, implying he was in the country somewhere. He sighed, and started walking.

He hadn't gone more than five yards or so when he

heard a noise, and thought: Yes, it's about time one of them showed up. After all, every other horrible thing I could possibly think of has happened to me today, so it's inevitable there'd have to be big dogs sooner or later. He held perfectly still and listened to the growling, trying to figure out where it was coming from.

Although he tended to be open-minded on most issues (to the point where, if asked how many sugars he wanted in his tea, he'd reply that it was something of a grey area and called for a flexible, non-judgemental approach) he was absolutely certain about where he stood in relation to dogs, namely as far away from them as possible, preferably on a tall stepladder. The only good dog, in his view, was the long brown kind you find swamped in mustard inside a finger-roll, and even they gave him wind. On balance, he hated big, snarling dogs more than small, yapping dogs, but there wasn't much in it either way. This one, as far as he could establish, was a big, snarling dog. Very big, now with twenty-five per cent added snarls.

He stood still for a very long time and, as he had nothing else to do, he made use of the opportunity to reflect on the events of the last couple of days, focusing on how he'd managed to go from being a moderately happy computer wizard to a desperate dog-cornered fugitive without doing anything particularly bad. He didn't dare move, and in any case his body appeared to have been frozen solid by fear, so he couldn't get out a pencil and paper and formulate his data scientifically in a pie chart, graph or Venn diagram, but it was all quite straightforward to visualise: a straight line, representing his fortunes, slanting steeply downhill.

It would, of course, all come out right in the end.

The police would catch the real murderer, or Mr Yaxley would find the crucial evidence that would prove his innocence, or three samite-clad women in a white-draped barge would pull up alongside and offer him a lift as far as Avalon. It never crossed his mind for an instant that it wouldn't all sort itself out eventually. After all, he wasn't guilty, he hadn't done anything wrong . . .

Suddenly, for some reason he couldn't figure out, the dog stopped growling and started barking furiously. Terror, like tea spilled on a document-strewn desk, flooded his mind and soaked into his instincts and reactions, reducing them to soggy impotence. He tried to say, 'There now, good boy,' but nothing came out except *Ggg*. He tried to breathe, but it was like inhaling custard.

Then the barking stopped, and something started licking his ankle.

'Ggg,' he reiterated. By way of reply, he heard the soft slap of tongue on leg and various nuisance-phone-call noises. It's possible, he caught himself daring to think, that maybe I'm not going to die after all.

Very slowly and tentatively, keeping his legs straight, he reached down with his fingertips until they made contact with fur. Then he checked his position and general status; he was leaning so far back that his balance was nearly compromised, suggesting that the dog (assuming it actually was a dog, rather than, say, an amorous orc or a really big earwig) stood no higher than eighteen inches off the ground, if that. 'Nice doggie,' he whimpered, and something like warm, wet sandpaper flicked across his knuckles.

At this point the People's Front for the Liberation of David Perkins issued a statement. This development, they felt, was interesting and possibly significant, in that something that had promised to be unspeakably awful had turned out not to be so bad after all. Did this, they asked themselves, suggest a new trend? Would future historians of David Perkins look back at this moment and identify it as the point at which the tide of misfortune ebbed, turned and went out? It was, they concluded, still too early to make any firm predictions; but they were encouraged and optimistic, and maybe it might be an idea to quit standing in the middle of some stranger's lawn and go and find Brother George.

He took a step towards the light. The dog bit him.

The yowl of pain was, of course, entirely instinctive. It also must've unnerved the dog almost as much as it startled David; the jaw pressure tightened, even as David instinctively tried to snatch his hand away, with the result that as he raised his arm, he could feel the weight of a squirming, kicking animal dangling from his hand. Just then, a powerful light came on, and he saw a small Dalmatian puppy swinging in the air like an old-fashioned pub sign.

'Here,' yelled a voice, 'you leave that dog alone.'

'Get it off me,' David shouted, as the dog tried to swim in thin air. Every jerk and wriggle transmitted itself directly through the puppy's teeth into the bitten part of his hand, making him feel as if he was being torn apart by teams of wild My Little Ponies, or eaten alive by Disney characters.

'Put that dog down *now*,' the voice continued, 'or I'll smash your face in.'

(At this point the PFLDP was unavailable for comment.)

A torch blazed in his eyes, and a hand clamped down on his shoulder and started shaking him about. Each

CHAPTER SIX

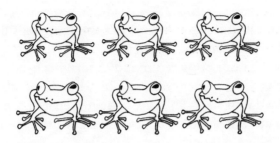

'You were teasing him,' said a voice on the edge of David's consciousness. 'Stands to reason: if you tease a young dog, it'll bite you. Besides, he was only being friendly.'

When he opened his eyes, the first thing that struck him was the ferocious whiteness of the light. It was Super Persil, fresh-snow-in-Antarctica, processed-bread white, and it dug into his optic nerve like a needle.

'Poor thing was frightened out of his wits, getting shaken about like that,' the voice continued. 'What you should've done was keep perfectly still and said something nice and reassuring to him. He really picks up on tone of voice.'

David's first assessment of his surroundings suggested that he was in a hospital: clean, sterile white plastic surfaces, the steel-framed bed he was lying on, the soft hum of the unfamiliar machines surrounding him. But it wasn't a hospital. He had no idea how he knew that, but he knew.

'Where am I?' he asked.

Sound of a tongue being clicked. 'Yes, Max is fine, thank you so much for asking, he's running about quite happily and playing with his little rubber bone. Sorry, did you say something?'

'Yes,' David replied. 'Where am I?'

'Ah,' said the voice. 'No, don't try to move, I'll come round where you can see me.'

David hadn't bothered trying to turn his head to look at the voice's owner, because he knew perfectly well what he'd look like. This one had an eyepatch too, but it was made out of some kind of shiny white metal, with two blinking red lights in the middle.

'You're George,' David said.

'That's right,' said George. 'How are you feeling?'

'More or less all right,' David replied. He traced the source of the pain that was making its presence felt up and down his nervous system, and found it was coming from his heavily bandaged right hand.

'It's all right,' George went on, 'it'll heal up just fine in a week or so once we've taken the stitches out. Which is more than could've been said for poor Max if you'd fallen on him, like you did your best to do. Can't have missed him by more than a couple of inches, poor little mite.'

'I'm sorry,' David lied unconvincingly. 'Was it you who hit me?'

George nodded. 'That's all right, too,' he said. 'Mild concussion, a scalp cut; of course, it bled a lot, scalp wounds always do, but it's no big deal. You'll be fine. You'd better get some rest now. I'll bring Max in to say hello when he's feeling a little stronger.'

George stood up.

'Excuse me,' David asked, 'but you didn't tell me where this is.'

'Later. When you're up to it.'

This time, George got away before David could ask another question. An automatic door purred open and shut somewhere out of his line of sight. The machines carried on humming, presumably because they couldn't remember the words. David thought about sitting up and looking round, to see if there were any clues that might tell him where he was, but decided to postpone the investigation till later, when he wasn't feeling quite so woozy.

Anyway, he thought, I'm not in prison. I'm in a plain white room on my own and I don't think I'm allowed to leave, but I'm not in prison. Always best to look on the bright side.

He lay back and closed his eyes (just to rest them, of course). Something about the gentle vibrations coming up through the bedframe made him think that if he didn't know better, he could easily believe he was moving. He emptied his mind (he found it strangely easy to do; just pull the plug and let the jumbled, disorderly thoughts gurgle away) and—

—Woke up sharply out of a horrible dream: a thoroughbred nightmare, not just the usual going-up-to-do-the-reading-at-morning-assembly-with-no-clothes-on thing but something truly twisted and horrible. For a moment there (in his dream) he'd managed to convince himself that he was a seriously wounded fugitive from justice, tied down on a bed in the belly of a flying saucer that was whisking him away to some totally alien world. Hairy stuff.

'Hello?' he called out.

One of the machines beeped, and some fitment or other swivelled round on its mounting, levelling an array of flashing lights at his head. He wasn't sure he liked the way it was looking at him, as if it was trying to decide between mint sauce, mustard and horseradish.

'Hello?' he repeated. 'George, are you there?'

No reply; but two more machines pointed things at him, and a third made a high-pitch modem-squeal noise. At some level, its tone of voice reminded him of his mother.

This is silly, he thought. Admittedly, he wasn't feeling at his best and brightest, but he was pretty sure he could stand up. He slid to the side of the bed and swung his feet towards the floor. It was a surprisingly long way down before his soles made contact with the steel plating of the deck.

(Steel plating? Deck? Geography wasn't his strong suit, but as far as he could remember, Mr Yaxley had been driving west, along the A4. True, he didn't know *exactly* where he was, but he was prepared to bet a fiver he wasn't more than six miles from Slough. Wonderful place, Slough, it holds the gorgeous West in fee and the man who's tired of it is tired of life, but it's not a seaport. What *was* this place, anyway?)

'It's all right,' he said to the machines, 'I'm just going to stretch my legs.'

One of the machines started barking at him.

He stopped dead in his tracks. In the fallout shelter at the back of his mind, the PFLDP reassured him that it wasn't really a dog, it was just an electronic gadget pro-grammed to make a noise like a dog – a very accurate reproduction, admittedly, close your eyes and you'd swear you were being pinned down by an enormous bull terrier with red eyes and white frothy drool dribbling down its jowls – and although there were any number of things in his immediate environment to be afraid of, this wasn't one of them. On an intellectual level, he accepted that this view was perfectly logical and his fear was irrational. On an intuitive level, he nearly wet himself.

'Now what?' George's voice, somewhere behind a partition or bulkhead. 'All right, all right, I'm coming.'

A door whirred open. 'Over here,' David shouted, over the woofling noises. 'Help. Please.'

'Oh, for crying out loud,' said George. 'All right, Fang, that'll do.' The machine immediately fell silent, twinkled some lights and printed out a sheet of clear plastic embossed with unfamiliar symbols. 'What are you doing out of bed?'

'I was just . . .'

'Well, don't.' George picked up the sheet of plastic, glanced at it and clicked his tongue. 'That's no good,' he said, 'we'll have to do them all over again. All right, back on the bed.'

David did as he was told. 'Will you please tell me where I am?' he asked. 'That's not unreasonable, is it?'

George sighed. 'If you insist,' he said. 'You're on board the survey ship *Uuuuurk*.' He looked at his watch. 'By now, we're probably a few hundred *uurk* from the outer spine of the Casserole nebula.' He grinned. 'Bet you wish you hadn't asked.'

Although David had had his suspicions, he'd dismissed them as the after-effects of concussion or latent insanity. 'We're on a spaceship,' he said.

'That's right, yes.' George frowned. 'You mean Humphrey didn't tell you?'

'Humphrey?'

'My brother, Humphrey Yaxley. He sent you. Didn't he?'

David nodded. 'He said he was taking me somewhere I'd be safe,' he added quietly.

'Safe.'

'From the police.'

George nodded slowly, twice. 'Well, he was right about that,' he said. 'Absolutely no danger of running into the fuzz where we're going, so I guess you could say it was safe. In a sense. I mean, it all comes down to priorities, really, and what you're most afraid of.'

David realised that he couldn't move his toes. 'How do you mean,' he said, '"in a sense"?'

George looked away. 'I'm afraid it sounds to me like my brother wasn't entirely straight with you,' he said. 'Well,' he added, 'he's a lawyer, asking him to be straight with anybody's like trying to get a nuclear bomb to join CND. Anyway, I asked him to find me someone – a volunteer, naturally, and someone with no close family . . . So you're on the run from the police, are you?'

David nodded.

'Shrewd thinking,' George said, chewing his lower lip. 'I mean, the best way to make sure somebody's not going to be missed is to choose a subject who's known to be doing his best not to be found. What was it you're supposed to have done?'

'They think I killed your brother William.'

'Oh. Bill's dead, is he?'

'Apparently.'

George shrugged. 'Plenty more where he came from,' he said. 'Now, would you mind lying a bit straighter? Thanks.'

Strange family, David thought, as George tapped a

few keys on a pad. He'd known stranger, mind, including his own. 'I didn't do it,' he added.

'Sorry, do what?'

'I didn't kill your brother.'

'Ah. That's all right, then. Now, this won't hurt a bit.'

A machine whirred and something on a folding metal arm, like a self-propelled dentist's drill, started to move towards him. David jumped up like a startled rabbit and huddled on the far edge of the bed.

'Calm down,' George said crossly. 'It's just going to scan you, that's all. It's done it once already, while you were asleep.'

The arm jerked a little closer, and stopped. George muttered something under his breath and tapped some more keys.

'You're examining me,' David said.

'That's right. Don't worry,' George added reassuringly, 'you won't feel a thing.'

'I won't?'

'Of course not, we aren't butchers. All the intrusive procedures and amputations and stuff are done under anaesthetic.'

For some reason, David didn't find this quite as reassuring as presumably he was supposed to. 'Mr Yaxley never said anything about this,' he muttered. 'What're you going to do to me?'

'Ah.' George looked uncomfortable, as if he'd just discovered a hedgehog in his trousers. 'Well, that's why I distinctly told Humphrey I wanted a volunteer. I'm going to have to explain that volunteer doesn't just mean not-dragged-on-board-kicking-and-screaming. He sometimes has difficulty with the finer shades of meaning. Professional hazard, I guess.'

The metal arm pounced like a cat and stopped an inch above the top of David's head. He found that he couldn't move at all. 'Answer the bloody question,' he whispered.

'Do I have to? It'll only make you miserable.'

'I can live with that.'

'Oh, you won't have to. Not for very long, anyhow. Really, I'd rather not say; you see, panic and fear and anger and all that sort of stuff, they all have quite marked effects on the chemistry of the brain, and that really screws up the accuracy of the data. The same goes for elation and euphoria, of course, though I can't see that being too much of a problem.' He sighed. 'I'm going to be so cross with Humphrey next time I see him.'

David could feel his eyelids drooping, and remembered what George had said about anaesthetics. 'That's enough,' he said. 'I'm not a volunteer, so leave me alone and turn this thing round immediately.'

George raised an eyebrow. 'So you can go back to Earth, you mean?'

'Too bloody right.'

'Would that be such a good idea?' George said, shaking his head. 'I mean, if the police are after you—'

'Doesn't matter. I want to go home, now.'

'Sorry.' George pulled a stern face, though it was pretty obvious he wasn't happy with the situation. 'I really wish I could help you, but it's out of the question. You've got no idea how rigid the Uuuurk are when it comes to paperwork.'

'Who the hell are the – what you just said.'

'The Uuuurk,' George repeated. 'My bosses, the people who built this ship. You see, I've already filed a requisition order, so as far as they're concerned the experiment's already been done. If I abort it now, I can't go back to them for any more funding. This is all Humphrey's fault,' he went on, scowling horribly. 'I suppose he thought he was being clever, but if he'd just stuck to doing as he was told—'

'I couldn't give a toss about your funding.' David meant it to be a shout, but it came out as a comic little squeak, Donald Duck doing a Bugs Bunny impersonation. 'You can't just kill me for the sake of some rotten science project. I'm a human being.'

George nodded. 'That's precisely why I can,' he said. 'Of course there are safeguards, pages and pages of them. You thought *Homo sapiens* was anal about rules and regulations, you should see the Uuuurk directives governing the humane treatment of lab specimens. Every time I try and deal with all that stuff, I end up wishing I was the one in the tank . . . Buggery,' he added, 'look at these endorphin readings. You've gone and got yourself all worked up and upset, I won't be able to get anything useful out of you for at least six hours. Are you feeling hungry? I can get you a sandwich.'

It occurred to David that if he were to say yes, the best possible outcome would be that George would go away and fetch it, affording him an opportunity to escape, and the worst possible outcome would be that he'd get a sandwich. 'Thanks,' he said. 'What've you got?'

'Ham,' George replied. 'Cheese and pickle. Or I could do you toasted cheese, if you'd rather.'

'That'd be great. Thanks.'

'Don't mention it,' George said. 'Least I can do, really; and it's sort of traditional, the hearty breakfast and all. Meanwhile, you lie back and take it easy, try and think pleasant, calming thoughts. Summer meadows, stuff like that. I won't be long.'

'Please don't rush on my account,' David replied. 'Really.'

George nodded. 'Remember,' he said, pausing in the doorway, 'summer meadows.'

'Summer meadows,' David said. 'With buttercups and cowslips.'

'Whatever works best for you.'

David waited a while after he'd gone, remembering what had happened the last time he'd tried to get off the bed. He thought about George and his apparent fondness for dogs, which had led him to program Fang. He thought about that a lot; then, in as gentle and friendly a voice as he could manage under the circumstances, he cooed, 'Here boy. Good dog. Nice biscuit.'

The machine called Fang blinked some lights at him. An aerial at the back waggled backwards and forwards.

'Good boy,' David said. 'Nice biscuit. Come and get it.'

With a whirr of servos the machine called Fang turned through ninety degrees and rolled across the floor towards him, aerial vibrating. David waited till it was nicely within arm's length, then grabbed hold of the dentist's-drill thing, jerked it sideways till it snapped off and smashed it into Fang's console. The machine stopped dead and rocked from side to side for a couple of seconds; then all its cute little lights went out.

David wasn't particularly happy about that. He'd never knowingly killed anything in his life, and in his mind's eye he could see a translucent cartoon version of the machine, complete with wings and halo, slowly ascending to heaven. He shook himself, urged himself to get a grip and headed for the door.

He'd gone about five paces when something hit him in the small of the back, decking him. Once the shock had cleared from his mind, he realised that whatever it was had four feet and was breathing heavily down the back of his neck.

'Rivet,' said a voice behind his head. 'Where do you think you're going, pal?'

It was a very odd voice indeed. The words were English, the accent sounded vaguely transatlantic but somehow not human. It sounded, in fact, like the synthesised voice that came out of his Korean-made digital answering machine.

'Hello?' he said.

'Hello yourself,' the voice replied. 'My name's Uuuurk. Actually, my regular name is U'uuurqqqk but you humans, your throats are the wrong shape for pronouncing our language. I could care less, it's no big deal.'

Uuuurk? 'This is your spaceship?'

'Yeah.' Something odd and wet flicked his ear. 'And I gotta tell you, you ain't got no right to go trashing it like you did. That multiplanar scanning module you beat up on just now, you got any idea how much that sucker cost me? More'n your whole damn planet, I'm telling ya. But it's OK,' the voice went on, calming down a little, 'you weren't to know that. We'll say no more about it.'

David concentrated very hard. 'You're an alien,' he said.

The voice laughed; rivet, rivet, uuuuurk. 'You could say that,' it replied. 'Like, my people and some amphibious raniforms on your planet share a very remote common ancestor, hundreds of generations ago, but so far back it don't matter any. You wanna make something of it?'

'No, of course not,' David said quickly. 'I was just – raniforms?'

'Scientific word. Technical term. It's just a fancy way of saying frog.'

'Frog?'

'Yeah, frog. Can't say I like your tone of voice, buster.'

'George said you were—'

'George? Who's this George?'

'The other human. The one who brought me here.'

'Ah, right, yes. So that's his human name, is it? Come to think of it, he did tell me once, and I guess I forgot. Like, he answers OK to Uuuurk, so why bother? What about him?'

'He said he was running this project.'

'Hah! Like a human could run this project. Gimme a break, will ya?'

'Sorry,' David said quickly.' It's just— Well, if this is your ship and you're some kind of really advanced alien civilisation—'

The voice croaked. 'We are. That's what being really advanced means, we get plenty of quality leisure time. It's very important when you're a high-profile scientist to stay in touch with your inner tadpole, you know?'

'Ah.' Cautiously, David tried to move. A paw pressed on the back of his neck, paralysing him. Presumably that was just a friendly overture, as well.

'You probably figured it all out already,' the voice went on, 'but I'll explain anyhow, so we all know where we stand. My people are the Uuuurk—'

'I thought you said Uuuurk was your name.'

'It is. Damn.' The alien sighed. 'Shoulda known, you guys just haven't got the brainpower to understand. Yes, my name is Uuuurk. My people are called the Uuuurk. Each one of my people is also called Uuuurk. *Uuuurk* is also the only word in our language – apart from *rivet*, of course, but that just means *rivet*. OK?'

'No.'

'Shit. All right, listen up. It's all in how you pronounce it, see? Like there's *uuuuurk*, meaning a muddy pool; *uuuuurk*, meaning the fourteenth month of the year; *uuuuurk*, to slide quickly off a floating log into the water; *uuuuurk*, the pleasure you feel on a close friend's birthday; *uuuuurk*, an equilateral triangle; *uuuuurk*, the colour of ripe pomegranites; *uuuuurk*, the square root of 1,067—'

'All the same word?'

'But pronounced differently. You could hear the difference, couldn't you?'

'Oh yes,' David lied. 'Clear as a bell.'

'A what?'

David guessed. 'An *uuuuurk*?'

'Clear as the scent of the blossom of a late-flowering *uuuuurk*?' A slight pressure against David's spine suggested that the frog was shrugging its shoulders. 'Hey, you guys, you're something else. Anyhow, we're from a planet in what you call the Sirius system.'

'The Dog Star,' David remembered.

'Dog Star? With a "D"? Must be a typo. Anyhow, we've been watching this Earth of yours.' The voice pronounced it 'Oyth'. 'Been keeping an eye on it for a couple hundred years and I gotta tell you, you guys are weird. Completely nuts. But that's OK, live and let live.

You don't bug us, we don't bug you. Though there is one thing I gotta ask. About the worms.'

'Worms?'

'Yeah. What is it with that thing where you get a worm and you stick a big sharp hook through it and tie it to a rope and *then* you throw it in a pond and drown it. We seen you guys do it, most every pond we stayed at. What the hell did worms ever do to you?'

David thought for a moment. 'It's fishing,' he said. 'You know, catching fish. The fish swims along, sees the worm . . .'

There was a long silence.

'OK,' said the voice, 'forget the worms. There's obviously some really deep-rooted cultural issues here, and we ain't got time to go into all that stuff right now. What you want to know is, what are you doing here? Am I right?'

'Yes,' David replied.

'It's very simple. And before I start I want you to know, there's nothing personal, OK? We like humans. A whole lot of people back home keep humans, they're like a sort of – what's that thing they're called, fashion statement. They're crazy about them. We even got a saying, a human is for life, not just for Planetary Equinox.' The voice sighed. 'If there was any other way – but hey, you know how it goes. What can I say? Anyhow, the straight deal is, we're invading your planet. We need the space. Back home it's getting so crowded we're three, four to a lily pad. And your planet – it's got the atmosphere, it's got the climate, it's got the ecosystem and the mineral resources. You get the idea.'

'I suppose so,' David said.

'Too damn' right you suppose so,' the voice said. 'That's why we chose you for this research project. Like, you're one of them, but also one of us. We take you to bits and figure out what makes you run, I guess you can see where that'd make conquering your world a whole lot easier.'

It was the way the voice said it as much as the words themselves: the eagerness, the enthusiasm, the joy . . . For God's sake, screamed the embattled PFLDP, frogs are going to kill you and take over the Earth, and you're starting to *like* them?

'Are you sure you want to do this?' David asked.

'Sure? Sure we're sure.'

'But . . .' David searched his mind, digging deep into the compost heap of cultural programming, and found what he'd been searching for. 'But animals don't do that sort of thing. Animals don't invade each others' territory or wantonly kill each other or oppress the weak and helpless. Animals are better than we are, that's why we like them so much.'

Silence – stunned silence – David could almost feel the disbelief resonating through the webbing between the Uuuurk's fingers – followed by frantic croaking, which he eventually figured out was laughter.

'Oh boy,' the voice eventually said. 'Have you guys even *heard* of evolution? But that's OK. I'll be straight with you, it's this kinda soft-hearted dipshit naivety you guys have that makes us like you so much. You're *cute*. Listening to some of the garbage you guys come out with sometimes, it makes a person just want to reach out and cuddle you to death.'

David thought for a moment. 'All right,' he said. 'Now, would you mind very much getting off me, because I'm having trouble breathing. I promise I won't be any trouble.'

'Hey, I don't know about that. You done enough damage already.'

'You have my word of honour,' David said gravely. 'As a human.'

'Yeah, OK, what the hell. Hold still, I'll jump off you.'

There was a soft thump, as of four paws landing lightly on the deck plating, and David began to feel sensation returning to his body, along with enough pins and needles to fit out an international voodoo convention. He got up slowly and shakily, and looked round until he saw a large green frog, about the size of an adult chimp. It had huge round yellow eyes, and it blinked at him like a civil servant on being asked exactly why the form had to be signed in triplicate . . . 'Bastard!' David yelled, and kicked the alien so hard it flew through the air and bounced off two walls before landing in a tangled hammock of wires behind some machine. 'Hey,' he added, as a vast wave of euphoria swept over him. 'You know what? All my life I've really wanted to kick a frog, and I never dared, because I thought it was cruel, or someone would see me. What I've been missing all these years!'

Croaking frantically, the alien scrambled out of the wire cradle and hopped across the floor, narrowly avoiding the nondescript metal object David had just thrown at it. 'You gone crazy or something?' it whined. 'What the hell do you think you're doing?'

David grinned and picked up a small console. 'Not allowed to be cruel to animals,' he said, breathing heavily. 'Can't pick on small, helpless, defenceless animals, it's not right. Doesn't say anything in the rules about not picking on small, sadistic, hyper-evolved superbeings, though. Now hold still while I smash your head in.'

While he was saying this the alien must've found some way to trigger the alarm system. Red lights flashed, a siren started blaring *uuurk-uuurk-uuurk*, and something like yellow smoke billowed out of vents in the walls. David said something uncharacteristically vulgar and hurled the console; he missed, but hit the door panel just as it was sliding shut. It stuck half-open, and David made for it as quickly as he could.

Outside, he found himself in a corridor – a round brushed-stainless steel tunnel that clanged alarmingly underfoot. It had an oddly unfinished look, which he might have investigated further if he hadn't been preoccupied with running for his life.

Silly, he told himself as he ran. You're on a spaceship, billions of miles from home, there's no way in hell you'll escape, and all you've done is give them grounds for being extremely upset with you. This time it's definitely the end of the line.

He turned a corner, only to find that he was facing a dead end. The tunnel just stopped, in a seamless cul-desac (as if he was a fugitive cartoon and he'd just reached the edge of the page). He spun round, and saw that he wasn't alone.

'You idiot,' said George.

David sagged. He was bigger and stronger than the alien, but George was bigger and stronger than him, so trying to fight his way through was out of the question. There wasn't enough room to squeeze past, even if he was quick enough. This was it, then: the process that had started when he'd bought the lock of hair had finally reached its conclusion. All this time, he'd been falling down a long, dark hole (which had been bad) and now he was about to stop falling (which would be worse; worse even than going to prison or getting eaten by tigers or being told his job was being relocated to Merseyside—)

'Just tell me one thing,' David asked quietly. 'What did I do wrong?'

George looked at him, puzzled. 'You mean, apart from smashing up expensive equipment and assaulting a Uuuurk citizen?'

'Yes. Why me? What harm did I ever do anybody?'

This time, George looked away. 'It's just one of those things,' he said, in an odd tone of voice. 'It's one of life's minor tragedies that the eggs never get to see the omelette. Next time, we'll try and make it a bit easier, I promise.'

'Next time?' David started to say; but he couldn't make himself heard. The tunnel was reverberating with the deafening sounds of gunfire, klaxons, sledge-hammers and desperate barking.

'Bugger,' said George.

Something exploded or fell over or got dropped from a great height, just around the corner. George swung round; and David, seeing a tiny skylight of opportunity, hurled himself across the tunnel at him in a flying tackle, as seen on TV. Of course he missed – he'd never done this sort of stuff before – and hit the wall (which hurt his shoulder rather a lot) and slithered along the almost fric-tionless tunnel floor on his bum, like someone on a fairground ride. Trying to grab him as he sailed past, George slipped, fell on his nose and knocked himself silly. Never in the field of human conflict had the physi-cal incompetence of the two participants been so perfectly symmetrical.

'Bloody hell,' David muttered, scrabbling to his feet.

Another ear-splitting noise just round the corner. A moment ago the noise had been a good thing, because it had given him a chance to escape. Now, however, it seemed rather more ambiguous. If George had still been conscious, he could've asked him what was going on; but that was out of the question, thanks to his possibly ill-advised Bruce Lee impression. Those surviving remnants of the PFLDP that hadn't already given up on him as his own worst enemy were howling at him to consider the trend. Back when being in prison had been the worst fate he could possible imagine, he'd taken his chances and escaped (and look where that had got him). Before that, he'd been sure that all his troubles would be over if only he could get the unconscious body of the newly hatched clone up the stairs and inside his flat. Before that, he'd honestly believed that recreating Philippa Levens in the flesh was his only chance at true happiness.

Pillock.

On the other hand, how could things possibly get worse? If he stayed put, a load of frogs were going to dice him like pepperoni as a prelude to taking over the planet. If he walked round the corner slap bang into a death ray or a laser beam, it could only be an improvement. Couldn't it?

Well, what the hell. If there was one lesson to be learned from the trend, it was that whatever he did only made things worse. Therefore, if he sat down in the corridor and stayed put, the trend dictated that that would prove to be the wrong decision and the course of action most likely to bury him in the deepest-ranging stratum of trouble. He shook his head, sighed and strolled down the corridor. No point hurrying, after all.

As he turned the corner, someone jumped out from behind him (naturally; big deal) and clamped his shoulder in a bone-crunching grip.

'You're nicked,' said a voice.

A familiar voice; a blessed, wonderful, heavenly voice, like a choir of angels ringing you up to tell you that you've just won a brand new Seat Ibiza. It was the policeman.

'All right,' the voice went on. (Down the corridor, something else blew up, making the floor shake.) 'You have the right to remain silent, though anything you do say will be taken down in writing—'

'Is that really you?' he interrupted. 'Really?'

'Shut up,' the policeman replied. 'You are entitled to have a lawyer present—'

Another explosion; this time only a few yards away, round the next corner, because the shock wave from the blast picked him up and slammed him against the wall like a naan bread being slapped on a tandoor. The grip on his shoulder immediately relaxed; and as soon as he'd picked himself up off the floor and looked round and down, he saw the policeman lying in a heap. Damn, he thought. Really, this isn't fair.

'Are you all right?' he asked.

'Does it look like I'm bloody all right?' the policeman groaned. 'No, I'm not all right, my left arm's definitely bust and probably my left leg as well. And don't think you're going to get away with this, because sooner or later—'

'I don't want to get away with it,' David howled. 'I want to be arrested, you stupid little man. Now get up and get on with it, before that bloody frog shows up.'

'What frog?'

'What frog?' The Uuurk, of course.'

'Uuuurk? Frog?' The policeman drowned in deep bewilderment. 'Are you talking about a French person here, or . . . ?'

'No, you fool, the *Uuuurk*! The aliens whose ship we're on.'

The policeman looked up at him with a very strange expression on his face. 'What the hell are you talking about, aliens?' he said feebly, before passing out from the pain.

Policemen, David thought bitterly. There's never one conscious when you need one.

CHAPTER SEVEN

The choice, it seemed, was his. Either he could stand there like the last cocktail-stick-impaled sausage on the plate at a stand-up buffet and wait for the war to come to him, or he could go to meet it. He felt in his trouser pocket for a coin to flip, but there didn't seem to be one there. It was hours and hours since he'd had anything to eat. I'd probably be a good idea to find a lavatory before too long, as well.

Hands still in pockets, he walked round the corner.

He saw the policemen at exactly the same moment that they saw him. They weren't your ordinary, mildly annoying, excuse-me-sir-but-did-you-know-your-off-side-brake-light-is-defective bluebottles; they were the kevlar-plated, massively armed, dark-blue-pullover-clad types, the sort who'd all had Lewis Collins posters on their bedroom walls when they were kids. They pointed their machine guns at him and yelled, though he couldn't make out what they were saying; the visors of their helmets muffled the words, making them sound unnervingly like yapping dogs.

Ho hum, David thought, as he slowly raised his hands. Hyper-evolved frogs that speak English and Imperial Stormtroopers who don't. Alien is as alien does.

They jumped on him and searched him carefully to make sure he didn't have an anti-tank rifle hidden up his nose; then they charged him with being an accessory. They didn't specify what kind of accessory, but David hazarded a guess that, if anything, he was probably a handbag. When they'd quite finished doing that, they frogmarched him (hah!) out of the door—

—Into bright, dazzling sunlight, and the familiar mean streets of Ravenscourt Park.

'Here,' said one of the policemen, as they shovelled him into a plain black van, 'what're you grinning at?'

'I'm sorry,' David replied. 'It's just so nice to be here, that's all.'

They were about to slam the van doors when a car drew up and two people got out. One of them had an eyepatch and looked distinctly familiar. The other one was Philippa Levens.

'Hold it,' the man said, waving a photograph in a small plastic wallet (either a bus pass, David guessed, or a video library membership card). 'Chief Inspector Urquhart, Serious Crime. Did you get him?'

The Imperial Stormtrooper who'd been about to shut the van door nodded. He was a tall man, well over six feet; if he ever got nits in his hair, they'd need oxygen masks. 'That's him in there,' he said.

'You're sure it's Perkins?'

'Take a look for yourself if you don't believe me.'

Chief Inspector Urquhart (David was inclined to doubt that that was his real name, even if he did have a little plastic card with a photo laminated into it) peered into the van, winked at David, and nodded. 'That's him,' he said. 'Did you get the rest of them?'

The Stormtrooper shook his head. 'Just him,' he replied.

'Not even Honest John?'

'No. It's like they knew we were coming or something.'

'Ah well.' The Chief Inspector shrugged. 'All right,' he said, 'I'll get forensics up here, I expect they'll want to take this place apart brick by brick.' He sighed, turned to go, then turned back. 'You may as well leave this one with me,' he said, in a tone of voice that suggested he was offering to do them a small favour. 'I'm heading back that way myself, I can save you a trip.'

At first the Imperial Stormtrooper looked very suspicious indeed; then, as David watched, suspicion drained from his face like brine from a tin of crab meat. 'All right, thanks,' he said (and there was just the slightest feather of an edge to his voice, suggesting that a tiny part of him couldn't believe what the rest was saying).

The Chief Inspector reached into the van and clamped a hand firmly on David's shoulder. 'He won't be any trouble,' he assured the Stormtroopers. 'Carry on.'

David allowed himself to be herded into the back seat of the Chief Inspector's car and driven off. This time, he made a conscious effort to remember which way they went. After they'd driven in silence for a couple of minutes (due west, David noted) the Chief Inspector cleared his throat in a self-conscious manner and said, 'Sorry.'

David didn't reply immediately. 'Were you talking to me?' he said.

'Yes.'

'Fine. Now stop this car and let me out.'

The Chief Inspector shook his head. 'Don't think so,' he said. 'For one thing, it wouldn't be safe. Once they realise you've escaped again they'll be after you. If you stay out on the streets you won't last five minutes.'

'Doesn't matter. Don't care. Stop the car.'

'Oh, come now,' said the Chief Inspector, and David could see his raised eyebrow reflected in the rear-view mirror. 'You'd rather be arrested and sent to prison for a murder you didn't do than sit in this car with us for half an hour? I don't think so.'

'Half an hour?'

'That's right. And I promise faithfully that as soon as we get there we'll explain everything.'

'Everything?'

'Everything. I swear. On my brother's life.'

Of course, it wasn't as if he had any choice in the matter. From where he sat, most of his forward view consisted of the back of Philippa's neck, her hair-toggle and ponytail. He could reach out, grab her round the throat and threaten to throttle her, but only in the sense that he could also one day be the prime minister of Canada; feasible, in other words, but not very likely.

'It wasn't a real spaceship, was it?'

'No.'

David thought for a minute. 'And you really will explain everything?'

'Yes.'

'Fine. And will the explanation be true?'

'Large parts of it will be, yes.'

It wasn't as if he had anything better to do. 'All right,' he said.

'Splendid. Now, on the seat beside you, there's a big silk handkerchief. If you wouldn't mind tying it round your eyes—'

'Certainly not.'

'I'm afraid I'll have to insist. Otherwise, I'll stop outside the first police station we come to and hand you over.'

David stared. 'You're bluffing.'

'Sorry, but I'm not. For what it's worth, I really am a policeman.'

David breathed in slowly. 'Is that one of the true parts?'

'Yes.'

'Doesn't matter,' he bluffed. 'In fact, it makes it better, because I'll tell them all about you.'

'Fine. Would that be before or after you tell them you were abducted by aliens?'

The silk handkerchief was yellow with big green spots and smelled faintly of peppermint. Tying the knot behind his head in a moving car proved to be annoyingly fiddly. Once secured, it tickled his nose and made him feel extremely silly.

'Here we are,' the Chief Inspector said eventually, after what felt like considerably more than half an hour. (But time behind a yellow silk hankie is flexible and non-relativistic, as any physicist will tell you if you put enough schnapps in his grapefruit juice.) 'You can take the blindfold off now if you like.'

David decided that, on balance, he liked. Unfortunately, he'd managed to get the knot immovably wedged. 'Hold still, I'll do it,' he heard Philippa say; then cool, deft fingers yanked his hair, making him yelp with pain. 'Don't make such a fuss. And hold still. How on earth did you manage to get it this tangled, anyway?'

Bright light flooded in through his eyes, like coffee spilt on a keyboard. Through the car's windscreen, he could see a hedge with a gate in it; through the gate, he could see a field of oilseed rape, glaringly yellow under a pale blue sky. 'Where are we?' he asked, not expecting a sensible answer.

'About three miles west of the M25,' replied the Chief Inspector. 'The nearest town is Beaconsfield. More or less due south of here are the old Denham film studios. I suggest we go indoors and have a drink.'

The house was a flint-faced red-tiled cottage, with genuine organic roses round the door. Inside was like an interior from an American movie set in England: almost authentic in most respects, but overdone. It was the sort of house you could only live in if your complexion and hair colour didn't clash with the curtains.

'Sit down, please,' said the Chief Inspector, waving towards a comfortable-looking armchair with perfectly plumped cushions. 'Drink? Cup of tea? Sandwich?'

There was nothing to be gained by refusing; he could be lied to equally well if he was thirsty, hungry and standing up, but where would be the point? 'Yes, please,' he said. 'Actually,' he added, 'what I'd like most of all is to use your bathroom—'

'Hm? Oh, of course, right.' Sounded as if the Chief Inspector hadn't immediately understood the euphemism. 'Up the stairs, first on the left.'

It was a very nice bathroom. Too nice. Immaculate. The soap, for example, was brand new, straight out of the packet; likewise the toilet roll and the towels. No trace of a tidemark in the bath or the handbasin. There was a window, but it was too small to climb out of.

When he came down again, there was a sandwich and a cup of tea waiting for him (again, mighty curious). He sat down in the armchair, which was every bit as comfortable as it looked. The Chief Inspector was sitting in a matching chair facing him. Philippa was curled up on the sofa, her shoes kicked off and lying on the floor. David considered the scene, and realised that the only thing missing was the Dulux dog.

'This place isn't real either, is it?'

The Chief Inspector smiled. 'Define real,' he replied. 'It's what my brother the lawyer would call a grey area. Consider: you just went upstairs without a nasty fall and bruised shins, so the stairs would seem to be real enough. If you care to bang your head hard against any of the walls . . .'

'All right,' David persisted, 'but they aren't *real*. Like the spaceship wasn't.'

'Actually,' the Chief Inspector said, with a smile, 'the spaceship was real enough. It was an actual, functional spaceship, and for a while there, you'd genuinely gone where no one has gone before. But then the cops showed up, so we brought you back.' He reached for his drink. 'It'd be much easier if I started at the beginning,' he said.

David shrugged. 'Go ahead,' he said.

'Thank you.' The Chief Inspector sipped his drink and swirled the glass round, making the ice tinkle. 'Now then,' he said.

Now then (said the Chief Inspector), long story, so will be as brief as possible.

Once upon a time, and we're going back a few years here, girl met boy, and usual business ensued. She was – well, let's not confuse the issue with culture-specific detail that may have misleading connotations. She came from what you'd call a privileged background. He was . . . Well, he wasn't the out-and-out no-good dirtball her father made him out to be, but he wasn't anything special. Certainly not good enough for daddy's best girl. Query, in this context, whether anybody ever is. I mean, if she were to bring home an incredibly wealthy saint who also happened to be war hero, genius sculptor and Nobel-winning physicist, Mummy and Daddy would still be peering nervously at him over the tea-cups to see if he'd got six fingers or webbed feet. Human nature.

But anyway. Daddy didn't like boy. Girl picked up on this, decided she liked boy even more, precisely because. Became a matter of principle, God help us all. Fingers were wagged, tears shed, words spoken, twenty years of happy family life went down toilet like asteroid down gravity well.

So far, you'll agree, there's nothing much to this story. Happens all the time. All parties probably equally to blame: father obvious villain of the piece, but colour in girl – an Olympic-class emotional blackmailer since she was nine weeks old, will of chrome-molybdenum steel – not to mention boy – healthy twenty-year-old, primary agenda not the most inscrutable thing in Universe – and you begin to get a familiar picture. Faults on all sides. Humans behaving badly.

By this point, everybody heavily into gestures. For girl, mostly limited to slamming doors and unbecoming hairstyles. Daddy – mostly shouting, melodramatic body language. Boy, on other hand, not directly engaged in face-to-face conflict, more scope for grandeur and downright silliness: joins army, goes away. Gets killed. Marvellous.

At this point, I need to fill you in on some background. Bit hesitant about doing this, since it'll require a little suspension of disbelief. In fact, you're going to have to hoist Mr Disbelief higher than a cattle-rustler in old Alabama. Still, we've taken certain steps to loosen up your previously rather rigid views of what is and what isn't possible – it's not all that long ago, for instance, that you were prepared to accept that you were *en route* to a distant solar system to be vivisected by alien frogs. If you could believe that, this ought to be a slice of Victoria sponge.

Daddy, you see— This is embarrassing. I think we can also drop the pretences; you know, like going to the doctor and saying, 'My friend has this really nasty rash right here'. Let's start again.

I did try and make it easier for you; I could've made it a little bit more obvious, but only by recording it on a cybernetic implant and wiring it directly into your brain. Nevertheless, it seems you managed not to get it, which I consider to be quite an achievement. Remind me to get a medal struck, when I've got five minutes.

My name is not important. You can call me Mr Levens if you like. This here – smile for the nice gentleman – is my eldest daughter, Philippa. And maybe I should add that by the time we'd got used to answering to these names, we'd both been around for a good long while. Put it another way: any day now, some coal miner is going to open up a very deep seam somewhere in Silesia, and in that seam, frozen into the coal like the letters in a stick of rock, he'll find a chunk of millions-of-years-old tree with an arrow-pierced heart carved on it. In other words, this mess has been going on for quite some time.

I think it's well enough established that the course of true love couldn't run less smoothly if it was operated by Richard Branson. Even in its most basic form, it tends to snag threads and get wrapped round trees. Add immortality and a few supernatural powers into the mix, and you get a succession of foul-ups that makes the M25 look like something out of Plato.

Think I mentioned a moment ago that my dear daughter here is a strong-willed individual, used to getting her own way. Trivial details tend not to stand in her path if they know what's good for them; and as far as she's concerned, death is a trivial detail. On the cosmic-hassle scale, she rates it somewhere between a broken fingernail and a parking ticket. Accordingly, when her one true love contrived to get himself snuffed in the wars – it's so long ago, can't remember what wars, or who was fighting who, or back then, more properly speaking, what was fighting what; she and I are both old enough for evolution to be something you do your best to keep up with, like fashion – when her sweet-pea got himself killed, she wasn't inclined to view this as anything more than a temporary inconvenience. You're the supreme being, she said to me, with that uniquely contemptuous scowl that can only pass from daughter to father: do something.

Didn't do me much good to explain that I'm not the supreme being, just *a* supreme being, and that whisking someone back from the Hereafter isn't quite as simple as glueing together the sundered fragments of a Barbie hairdryer. She wasn't in the mood for explanations; she wanted action, and she wanted it *then*. I don't think I need point out that this is your essential female, your *ewig-weiblich*; if you haven't figured that out for yourself at your age, I suggest you find a nice lighthouse some-where and arrange for the coastguard to airdrop regular supplies of TV dinners.

Unfortunately, I was in no position to shrug my shoulders and say, 'Sorry, no can do'; because of course I *could* fix things, no question about that. It was just that it was going to take an awful lot of time and effort, and complicate things horribly, to the point where doing the stuff I was supposed to be doing – running an orderly cosmos, superintending the growth of *Homo sapiens* into a good and useful member of society – was going to be seriously prejudiced. Obvious solution in terms of the well-being of all other sentient life was for her to get over it, count up to ten and fall in love with some other schmuck, like normal girls do. Where I made my most serious tactical error, of course, was in trying to explain this. The more I pushed the logic and common sense of this suggestion, the more determined she became, to the point where her heels were dug in so firmly they were practically down to the planetary core. So I did what any loving, caring parent would've done at this juncture. Gave in.

Gave it my best shot; wasn't good enough, of course, still had to put up with decades of moping, sulking, her pretending I wasn't in the room. But it was the best I could come up with, and pretty damn inventive, though I say it myself.

Point is, people can't be returned from the dead, it's not like leaning over the fence, asking, 'Please can we have our ball back, mister?' Different principles at work.

Requires fundamental understanding of what death is: namely, very bad thing, thoroughgoing pain in bum, to be avoided at all costs.

Tried explaining all this to daughter. Needn't have bothered, and breath thereby saved would have cooled an infinite ocean of porridge. Instead, had to find a way of sorting out mess without bending the world too much. Took a while.

Fortunately, we immortals have all the while we can handle, and then some.

Out of the question, as previously stated, to bring back dead person. Like microwaving last night's chips; result never satisfactory, always taste funny. Same with reanimating dead body, because no matter how hard you try, all you ever seem to get is a walking, talking, breathing, living doll. I can tell by your expression and the funny colour you've turned that you've intuitively grasped the point I'm trying to make. So: however you care to approach the problem, you've got to be prepared to accept a certain degree of compromise. This is where daughter and I wasted a lot of time on convoluted and acrimonious discussion. I supported duck principle: if walks and quacks like, is. Daughter maintained that this view not acceptable, suggested uses for duck that even supreme being would have had trouble accommodating. Ultimately, compromised on compromise, basically duck approach but with full spread of supplementary bells and whistles, very awkward to achieve, typical.

What, after all, is a person except the sum of his/her component parts, both physical and mental? Mental stuff we pick up as we go along, like dogshit on boot-heel; physical stuff is genetics, a nose here, a talent for playing violin there, all part of the rich mosaic of DNA.

Mental stuff not too difficult, can program human brain like computer, even get it to do long division and pick nose simultaneously if you take care and use a UNIX shell. Physical aspect is longer term, very hands-on. I had to arrange for someone to be born who exactly resembled daughter's late lamented popsicle in all material respects, down to shoe size and chin dimple.

Took me nine hundred years, during which time I introduced 870,328 men to their future wives, encouraged 269,416 happily married women to run off with dimple-chinned milkmen, spent multiple eternities (or seemed like, at time) in low taverns and hairdressing salons having hearts poured out all over; invented science of genetics, natch; also invented science of mathematics, since back when all this started, limit of mathematical knowledge was eight-nine-ten-*lots*. Been busy bunny, all things considered, and gratitude? Should cocoa.

Anyhow, come end of sixteenth century, all done and dusted, perfect replica of dear-departed born in Cheshire, England. Mental programming now required. Largely piece of cake, since a twenty-year-old man is hardly a complex organism, hasn't had time to develop much complexity, besides which, whole personality so thoroughly marinaded in hormones, hardly any room left for the angst. Should point out that at this stage, I'd been working non-stop for nine centuries while daughter had mostly contributed by way of helpful advice and other comments, so felt it was about time I handed over day-to-day management of project and had a rest. This, in retrospect, a bloody silly mistake, but what can you do?

Daughter proceeded to download relevant personality

data from boot-up disk, saw to it that subject enjoyed/suffered all relevant experiences, was duly attached to pet dog when child, had suitable crush on chambermaid when fourteen, not exactly *difficult*. Only problem was that, in order to reproduce exactly circumstances of original falling-in-love, necessary that she should become appropriate mortal. No problem being born – something any bloody fool can do – but somewhat careless about researching background and cover story, failed to notice salient points about prevailing culture of day – including rising tide of religious fervour. (Admittedly hard to deal with when you're immortal yourself; compare old Chinese proverb about fish not being aware of water. Actually, not proverb, made it up myself, regrettably before concept of copyright properly understood.)

So: daughter was born as daughter of minor nobility, eminently suitable match for subject, families were close neighbours and keen to do major real-estate deal with marriage as pretext. Daughter grew up; but, as mentioned, careless. Remember, age of ignorance and superstition; daughter's scientific activities related to project mistaken by dumb psycho contemporaries for witchcraft. Situation not helped by daughter's rather quick temper and residual supernatural abilities – can't actually turn person into frog, but can make person think is frog, make everybody else in village think same, to all intents and purposes is frog, see above under duck principle. When first wave of witchfinder-general's officers eventually found in pond trying to swallow flies, second wave altered strategy, struck in middle of night, sack over head, no messing.

Thing about immortality is: only ever been two

immortals in history, namely her and me, so a rather limited pool from which to draw information. In early seventeenth century, no reason to suppose that being burned at stake in any way hazardous to health and well-being, as hadn't previously happened. Database rapidly updated in light of findings but, by then, rather too late.

Once I'd got over my general feelings of annoyance and dissatisfaction at this turn of events, decided it wasn't any good crying over spilled milk (another one of mine, by the way: had Berne Convention been around in thirteenth century, would now be richer than Stephen King) and set about finding a way to put things straight. Took a while, but had already gained wide knowledge of most sciences by inventing them, so knew that it was theoretically possible to reconstruct entire human being from small leftover piece, just needed time to figure out the details. Also fully aware that first thing reconstituted daughter would ask me about was whereabouts of heart-throb; wouldn't do at all if I were to answer, terribly sorry but he died of old age in 1672; would inevitably lead to more tears and door-bangings, and after a while that kind of thing gets on your nerves. So, twofold problem to be addressed. Develop science to the point where cloning is possible, and see to it that another identical version of sweetheart is ready and waiting to roll as soon as she hops out of the tank . . .

'Just a minute,' David interrupted. 'All this is really fascinating, and if any of it's true that'd be really amazing, but what's it got to do with me? And why am I being accused of murder? And who are all these brothers of yours?'

The Chief Inspector closed his eyes, making an effort

not to give in to irritation. 'I bet the first thing you do when you buy a detective story is read the ending. Am I right?'

'I don't read detective stories.'

The Chief Inspector shrugged. 'I forgive you,' he said. 'That's one of the perks of being a supreme being, you can forgive people and they actually feel a whole lot better afterwards. Where was I, before you started this red-herringfest?'

'Answer the question.'

This time, the Chief Inspector smiled broadly and benignly, putting David in mind of a pope who, kneeling down to kiss the airport tarmac, finds a ten-pound note. 'You *have* come on in the last day or so, haven't you?' he said. 'When I met you in that pub after the auction—'

'You?'

'—You wouldn't have said boo to the proverbial goose. Now, though—' a faint flush of pride tinged the edges of his smile '—now you'd probably say boo to several geese, if only by e-mail. Of course, you have me to thank for that, but I won't be holding my breath. I try, I really do, and what thanks do I get?'

David frowned. 'Carry on with the story,' he said. 'Maybe you could give me some sort of signal when you get to the mostly true part; lift a finger or waggle your ears, something like that.'

Sticks and stones (said the Chief Inspector). Another one of mine, as you may have guessed, though as it happens I was misquoted. What I really said was, 'Sticks and stones may break my bones, but I have three psychotic brothers who know where you live.' Ah, well.

There I was, with this problem. Daughter to clone,

daughter's honey-muffin to genetically engineer; and to make matters just that tiny bit worse, I'd somehow managed to attract the attention of the Ethics Committee.

Now, I know about you young people. To you, Ethics is a part of East Anglia where the men wear white socks with business suits. To me, as a Supreme Being, it's a painfully real fact of life. It may also have struck you as odd that a being as supreme as I'm cracking on to be should waste time and energy on this incredibly subtle genetic manipulation stuff, when surely all I have to do is stretch forth my hand and say the word. Ain't like that. Got the Ethics Committee to think of.

Of course, there isn't really a committee, in the sense of a dozen old farts sitting round a table criticising the chairman. It's more a sort of tendency. Give you an example. You know that if you're packing for a holiday in the sun, you can bet your life that a suitcase full of nothing but shorts and sleeveless shirts will get you a fortnight of monsoons, whereas throwing in woolly jumpers and a mac guarantees that you'll be frying eggs on your forehead. That's a tendency. Here's a better one: everybody else can park on a double yellow all week and get away with it; you leave a square inch of tyre pressing on yellow paint while you dart across the road for a pint of milk, it's a stone-cold certainty that when you get back, you'll be just in time to see your car getting towed away to the pound.

That's my kind of tendency. There are things I'm allowed to do and things I'm not. Oh sure, I can do the things I'm not allowed to, but the tendency always gets me. Like, if I were to raise someone from the dead, it's better than evens that as soon as he's out of the ground he'll trip over his own headstone and break his neck. If

I stop a famine, nine months later the people I saved will bring in a record harvest and die of cholesterol poisoning. It's just tendencies, but everybody needs somebody to hate very much indeed, so I personify them as the Ethics Committee. Simple things, simple minds. I have no illusions about myself.

Anyway, back to story. Realised that trying to put right daughter's love life was ethical no-no, otherwise wouldn't have gone down pan with such sardonic precision. Therefore, figured out that couldn't act directly to get daughter back; could invent cloning technology, yes, but actual initiative to put bit of hair in tank of green glop couldn't come from me, had to come from someone else. Had to come from you.

'Course, going back four hundred years, no such thing as you then. But since did not exist, was necessary to invent. So did.

'Are you telling me you *programmed* me?' David yelled.

'Hole in one,' the Chief Inspector replied. 'Same way as daughter's replacement sugar-pop. Fourteen generations of your family, lovingly hand-picked and hand-nurtured, shepherded through the maze of history, to produce a young man who'd fall in love with a painting and have the means, the will and the all-enveloping dopiness to clone a copy of the girl in the picture and bring my daughter back to life. You have no idea how difficult it was; no offence, but idiots like you are so complex, so rare, so unique in their multifaceted inscrutability that only a total genius like myself could possibly have managed to pull it off – and there were times when it was touch and go, even then. Your great-great-grandmother, for instance. And your great-uncle

Bill's friend Wesley. Nearly brought the whole magnificent venture crashing to the ground.

'But I did it, just me, sure as God made little green apples (and that was a dirty trick; but no matter). Once again, I can feel the staggering force generated by the vacuum where your gratitude ought to be, but I won't say anything. Not a word about serpents' teeth or anything like that. We'll just let the subject drop and say no more about it.

'Oh, I suppose I'd better clear up the loose ends. For the record, I'm an only child; the various people you've met who look a bit like me aren't my brothers, except in a very general sense. Mostly they're toenail-clippings; Honest John was an accident, when I sneezed into the goo-boiler. Well, had to test cloning process, make sure debugged and up to speed. There's another thirty-two of us you haven't met yet, and of course still have scissors and full set of toenails. Expect tendency will find way to dispose of them all sooner or later, but what hell.'

David tried to get up, but it was one of those really deep, expensive chairs that won't let go of you until it's good and ready. 'All right,' he said, 'but what about the police, and this murder business? Come to that, what about that spaceship?'

'Ah yes,' said the Chief Inspector, looking away. 'Obvious problem with you is, what to do with you after you've done your job? Lesson learned from previous debacle, importance of security and discretion. Can't really have you running about all over the place saying you've been cloning girls; probably nobody would believe you, but can't take risk, not since Dolly the Sheep. Could kill you, of course, but don't really want to, somewhat churlish way of carrying on, and some of us understand the meaning of gratitude, even if others don't. So, plan B, make sure that nobody in their right minds will ever believe anything you say ever again. Turn you into Most Wanted, then have you abducted by aliens. You tell anybody about that, your credibility rating zapped for good, scarcely better than Jeffrey Archer's. Elegant solution, yes?'

'Bastard.'

'You see?' the Chief Inspector sighed. 'Just like I said. To you, grateful is just a unit for measuring coal. Just think: if it wasn't for me, you wouldn't even exist. Oh, there might conceivably be some guy running around calling himself David Perkins, who just happened to have the same parents as you do. But he wouldn't be *you*; he wouldn't have your lucrative talent for computers, your gentle and compassionate soul, your magnificent collection of personality defects and social disabilities. And of course, he'd never have experienced the pure, unsullied, perfect love you feel for my daughter. As I said a while back and never saw a penny in royalties for, it's better to have loved and lost—'

'Bullshit,' David replied. 'What you've done is—' He made himself calm down. 'What you've said you've done,' he went on, 'is obviously not the mostly true part of the story, because for one thing I don't believe it's possible, and for another, nobody could be that *evil*. You're just some nutcase who's latched on to me and decided to play mind games.'

'Perfect,' said the Chief Inspector. 'Much better. Now even *you* don't believe it, which reduces the security risk to nil. I think we can safely say job done and move on. Thanks so much for your help, have a nice life. I'll miss you, of course, but that's all part of being a genetic manipulator. One day you know they'll fly the nest, and—'

'Shut up,' David said. 'Just suppose I did believe it, not that I do. The one thing I can't put down to you playing silly buggers with my mind is, how does my cousin Alex fit into all this? He's a real person – all right, I can't stand the smug little jerk, but I've known him all my life, so you can't have made him up; but *she*—' he pointed without looking round '—she had lunch with him at my flat, and then they went swanning off together. So how does—?'

A puzzled frown crossed the Chief Inspector's face. 'You mean to say you haven't figured that out? Sorry, I assumed you'd have tumbled to that one straight away. He's *him*, or at least Him Mark 2 – I'd done all the groundwork back in the 1580s, so all I had to do was arrange for a throwback four hundred years later. Don't you get it? He's Philippa's boyfriend.'

CHAPTER EIGHT

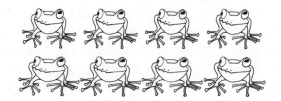

It'll be fine, they'd told him. We'll look after you, don't you worry; everything's been taken care of. Just hang on here for an hour or so, and someone'll be along to pick you up.

It was starting to get dark. David was still sitting where they'd left him, in the carnivorous armchair. As far as he could tell he was alone in the house: there was nobody to stop him getting up or leaving or doing whatever the hell he wanted to do. But what he wanted to do was sit in the chair, so that's what he did.

We've arranged a whole new life for you, they said, in British Columbia. New name, nice house, in the middle of nowhere so nobody'll even know you're there; nice flash computers for you to play with – that's the joy of your line of work, you can do it anywhere. Soon as you've settled in, you'll be as happy as a pig in muck. And it's not as if you had a life here to speak of. In a year or so, you'll be thanking us.

David was no geographer, and wasn't really sure where British Columbia was, though the conflicting resonances within the name itself intrigued him. (*British* Columbia: stronghold of bowler-hatted tea-drinking cocaine barons?) Of course, where it was didn't matter at all, because one place is very much like another once you edit out background trivia such as weather and scenery and which side of the road they drive on. A place is a landscape dotted with people, and all the people he'd met so far in thirty-odd years had sooner or later kicked him in the teeth.

On the wall opposite the chair was a bookshelf, and on the bookshelf was a copy of *The Times Atlas*, and in it was everything there was to know about British Columbia: its mountains and rivers and valleys and cities and principal exports. All he had to do was stand up, walk two yards and pull the book down off the shelf.

Couldn't be bothered.

Instead, he closed his eyes and dropped back into his own mind. The consensus of opinion there was that he should have known, the same way that a rabbit standing in the fast lane of a motorway at night ought to realise that the massive steel object with eyes of fire hurtling towards him isn't an amorous lady rabbit or a self-propelled giant carrot. Damn it, he should have figured it out from the start, because all his life, ever since he'd been old enough to have his own watch, Destiny had been grooming him for the role of servant, straight man and foil to his far-more-interesting-and-talented cousin, why-can't-you-be-more-like-Alex. Therefore it was inevitable, so glaringly obvious that a blindfolded bat in an electric storm would've seen it, that if he were ever to fall in love, it could only possibly be so that Alex's girlfriend could get cloned back into existence. The thought that his own aspirations towards happiness might have something to do with it was so dumb as to be laughable.

Once he'd realised that, everything else slotted into place as neatly as a well-designed modem card into a motherboard – and, of course, it was just plain stupid to resent it. The match doesn't resent the gas ring just because its purpose in life is to have its head ground against an abrasive surface and burnt to a crisp; and the match ends up in the ashtray or the trash, not in a snug little studio apartment in British Columbia. Like the man had said, really he should be grateful.

So: he snuggled his head against the back of the chair and synthesised gratitude. It was all exactly as the nice man had said; there was nothing for him here in England except the small, circumscribed place he'd fenced in for himself, and the prospect of fifty more annual colds. Furthermore, he'd done his job now, served his purpose; the rest of his life was his own. Either his family would believe he was a murderer and turn his picture to the wall, or else Alex would explain it all to them and they'd nod their heads and say that they'd been sure there must have been a good reason for having him, just as well they'd finally found out what it was. Most people don't get to step off the hamster-wheel of responsibilities until they're grey and wrinkly, but he was being turned loose in the prime of life, while he was still young enough to enjoy himself. Nothing more would ever be expected of him, he'd never be a disappointment or a trial to anybody ever again; he could spend the rest of his days unshaven and unironed, eating pizza out of the box, wearing odd socks and watching

Star Trek videos without causing a moment's pain to another living creature. Anybody else would have to spend thirty years sitting cross-legged in an ashram to get where he was going, so what in God's name was he whining about?

And then something happened. It was as dynamic as the division of the first living cell, as subversive as the offer of a half-eaten apple in Eden, and it came prefaced with the fatal words *What if—*

In the back of his wallet was a little plastic envelope, containing the rest of the lock of Philippa Levens's hair. Now then: the policemen had said they were going to take Honest John's lock-up apart brick by brick, so there was Buckley's chance that any of the cloning gear would still be there, just left lying about. But what if they hadn't, and it was? Needless to say, only a highly skilled and knowledgeable cloning technician could carry out the procedure, you couldn't just sprinkle bits of dead person into the green glop like cocoa powder on a cappuccino and expect to fish a live human being out of the tank a few hours later. But what if it really was as easy as that? What if he didn't go to British Columbia after all?

A smile worked its way into his face, like a stray convolvulus seed lodging in a wall. What would she think, Philippa Levens II, on emerging from her tank like a sticky green Aphrodite, when she heard that she wasn't going to get her time-crossed lover after all, because after so many patient, dreary centuries of being dead another Philippa, identical except for being a few days older, had nipped in ahead of her and beaten her to it?

She'd be pissed off.

The smile widened, like a crack in a flyover. If his judgement of Philippa's character had been anything near accurate, she'd be very pissed indeed. She'd also be an extremely powerful supernatural entity, with a temper and a grudge, in the wake of whose wrath small, fragile things like planets might well get dropped on the floor and broken – which (David decided) would suit him just fine.

There was a knock at the door. He ignored it.

More to the point, he reflected, her annoyance would be focused, like as not, on one specific individual, namely the faithless, treacherous lover who'd betrayed her centuries of silent trust by running off with some bimbo who just happened to have identical DNA. David hadn't met many girls, but he'd read a lot of books, and they all said that compared with a woman scorned, an overheated plutonium reactor is a friend indeed. Visions of little bits of Alex drifting down out of the sky like the confetti at God's wedding danced in front of his inner eye, and he grinned till his face hurt.

A key turned in the front door. British Columbia. Buggery.

He jumped up like a jack-in-the-box and looked round for somewhere to hide. Fortunately, the decor left him spoilt for choice. He dived behind a sofa, tucked his feet in, and waited.

'Hello?' someone called out. He recognised the voice; chances were, he knew the owner's brother. 'Dave? Where are you?'

Of course, he particularly hated being called Dave.

Footsteps: in the hall, approaching, getting closer. In the gap between the end of the sofa and the wall he caught sight of a grey-worsted-trousered leg culminating in a mirror-buffed black shoe. Somehow he managed to hold his breath until it went away again.

It's all right, he reassured himself, they won't expect me to be hiding. If they can't find me, they'll assume I've left the house. All I've got to do is hold still and try not to breathe in any dust.

He sneezed.

'Dave? Is that you?' The voice was getting nearer. He peered through the gap between sofa and wall and saw the window. Jump out, sprint, tear open sash, hop out, run: James Bond could have done it, but James Bond always had a director, a writing team, half a dozen stunt-men and the props department in his corner, whereas all David had was a dead spider. Interesting parallel, nonetheless, between himself and Jimbo: two men called into existence to do dirty jobs, face oppressively challenging obstacles; neither of them having any degree of choice in the matter. Neither of them mattering a damn to the people who yanked them into existence. Neither of them real.

'Come on, Dave, we're on a schedule.' And David couldn't help thinking: if this being is as supreme as he says he is, isn't it a bit odd that he can't simply see through the furniture or scan for humanoid life-signs or pick up on noisy emotions such as fear and resentment? If this really was God, David was prepared to bet that on the seventh day the cosmos was still knee-deep in little plastic cones. And if this wasn't God— Quite where all this left him, David wasn't sure. Except that he was: it left him hiding behind a sofa, in very real danger of being found and hauled off to British Columbia. Regardless of the big theological issues, that was something he didn't want to happen.

The footsteps were getting closer again, and instinctively David crawled back a little, until his heels were up against the wall. It was over a second before he realised that he was kneeling on something uncomfortably sharp; unfortunately, he'd backed himself in so tightly that he didn't dare move for fear of giving himself away. Ouch, he thought, loudly.

'Bloody hell,' said the voice; he could picture its owner standing with hands on hips, looking round and scowling. He knew the feeling, the baffled anger when something isn't where it should be. Come on, he urged, figure it out; if I'm not here, I must've gone. The longer you stand there like a prune, the less chance you've got of catching up with me. Go on, shoo—

Abruptly, the door slammed, suggesting that the Voice had left the room, probably in a bad mood. David counted up to a hundred and fifty, just to be on the safe side, and tried to wriggle his way out. It wasn't easy, a bit like trying to get the ship back out of the bottle using only a feather and a stick of boiled spaghetti, and as soon as he put his weight on his left knee—

This time, it had to be admitted, his thoughts were way, way past 'Ouch'. He rocked back on to his heels and scrabbled about until he'd got his fingers round the offending object. Didn't dare drop it, for fear of kneeling on it again, so he folded it into his palm and continued his backing and filing manoeuvres.

It was just as well you didn't have to pass a driving test before you were allowed to take your own body out on the public roads. David was neither built for nor accustomed to squirming around in confined spaces, and it took him far more time, effort and ingenuity to get out than he'd expended getting in. Eventually, however, he scrawled/squeezed/flolloped out on to open carpet, reached back to retrieve his legs (which had been impounded by the frontier guards at the last minute) and lay still and quiet for a moment, catching his breath.

He opened his hand. Almost buried in his palm was a little gold locket, about the size of a tenpenny piece. He frowned; while he'd been talking with the Chief Inspector, Pippa Levens had been sitting on the same sofa, fidgeting with something on a chain round her neck. He felt round the outside for a catch of some sort, and after a moment or so his fingernail brushed against a raised burr and the locket sprang open. Inside was a lock of hair.

Wonderful, David thought. A few hundred more like this and I'll have enough for a cushion. He squeezed the locket shut and dropped it into his top pocket; it might fetch a bob or two, and sooner or later he was going to need money—

He'd been hiding inside his mind from that thought with the curtains drawn, hoping it would assume he wasn't in and pass him by. No money – at least, no cash, and all his other money was on the wrong side of a hole-in-the-wall machine. If he tried getting it out, at the very least his card would be swallowed and a billet-doux sent to the national police computer. In practice, therefore, no money. Also no home, no food, no change of clothes – what the hell was the matter with him, anyway? Right now, he could be sitting in a fast car on his way to British Columbia (delightful place, or so he'd heard: prairies, pine forests, softly crooning moose, maple syrup with everything) and instead he was planning to break into a crime scene and clone more witches, presumably because he believed that it'd somehow make things *better* . . .

Yes, but it didn't matter, because everything was going to work out all right.

Relieved, he stood up and brushed bits of fluff off himself. Now then, he decided, going to have to walk to the nearest railway station, at the very least; once we're there, need to figure out how to stow away aboard a train. Can't be too difficult, people do it all the time, or else why do the railway companies make such a big fuss about it?

He was two-thirds of the way to the door when the PFLDP stopped him dead in his tracks and asked, Everything's going to work out all right, says who? There's absolutely no reason to believe—

The voice in his mind cut out abruptly, as if someone had just pulled a plug out of the wall. For a split second there was a vacuum; then normal service was resumed. Everything was going to work out all right. Impossible to doubt that; it'd be like having doubts about the existence of Loughborough. It wasn't a matter of opinion, it was a *fact*—

Just as well he'd got that sorted out, wasn't it?

As luck would have it, David was able to hitch a lift from a passing frozen-chicken lorry as far as the nearest town. Getting on board the train was much easier than he'd imagined; nobody at the ticket barrier on these funny little rural stations, the poor fools actually trusted you. A guard came round once on the way in to London, but he hid in the toilet with the door ever so slightly ajar, and the guard went away again. From Marylebone he caught a bus as far as Hammersmith; couldn't be bothered to hide from the conductor, just stared at her as if daring her to ask to see his ticket. She went away again, too. Bus from Hammersmith to Ravenscourt Park, same routine. One of these days, he said to himself, it'd be fun to find out just how far you could get without parting with any money. Judging from what he'd seen today, Proxima Centauri.

No sign of any fuzz hanging round Honest John's; oh, they had the place boarded up where they'd smashed the door in, but (typically, he felt sure) the nails they'd used were far too short to be anything more than a mildly amusing exercise in the physics of leverage. Cheapskate, he sighed as he pulled away the last plank. Waste of public money; *my* money, not to beat about the bush. Got a good mind to write to my MP.

They'd turned the power off, but that was all right, because David turned it back on again. At once, something started to hum in the background, and green lights started to glow in the hearts of the glop tanks. He smiled and moved his finger – eeny, meeny, miny . . . Having decided on the second from the right, he took out the little plastic packet of hair he'd bought at the auction and carefully teased loose one strand. Vaguely he remembered Honest John pratting about with various instruments and machines, calibrating the whatever and realigning the whatchamadoodle; but he couldn't be bothered with all that techie stuff right now. Hadn't he felt at the time that it was all voodoo, designed to impress the customer and make him feel more inclined to part with his hard-earned money, when all Honest John was really doing was dropping a bit of body into the Swarfega? The hell with all that; he wasn't after a Rolls-Royce job after all, just something that'd be close enough for jazz. Life was too short for persnicketing about.

He held the hair up in front of his face for a moment, like a conductor confronting an unruly orchestra. Light glinted on it, and he grinned. Then he let go.

He watched it drift down and settle on the meniscus of the glop – waiter, there's a hair in my green jelly; not so loud, sir, or they'll all want one. He smiled. As simple as that. Now all he had to do was wait until she was ready.

If he'd had any sense, of course, he'd have brought a book, or a pocket chess set or something. No good at waiting; he paced up and down for a bit, then decided to explore. But there wasn't anything particularly interesting in the workshop, just a lot of weird-looking microscopes and whirly things and gadgets that looked like old Super-8 projectors after they'd been assimilated into the Borg collective. Techie stuff. Boring. What he really wanted was something like a dart board.

He found a small door in the back wall. An office, he guessed, somewhere Honest John went to have a crafty smoke, fiddle the VAT and ogle the Pirelli calendar. It wasn't locked; a trifle stiff, perhaps, but nothing a smart drop-kick couldn't cure, as he proved by experiment. He groped for the light switch.

As the savage brightness hit him, David realised he'd been here before; not so long ago, either. The last time, of course, he'd been under the mistaken impression that he was on board a flying saucer, being whisked away to some distant star to be puréed by super-intelligent frogs. Amazing, the things you can make yourself believe. But there was the bed he'd been lying on, and the machine that had barked till he trashed it, and all the other bits and pieces. More techie junk; except, of course, that all of this lot was fake, film-prop stuff, made to look impressive but entirely non-functional and inert. It embarrassed him to think that he'd actually been taken in by all this garbage. Anybody with sufficient intellectual standing to aspire to membership of the animal kingdom could tell it was only cardboard boxes covered in Bacofoil. He sighed, reached out and pressed a random button on the nearest console.

All the lights went out, and the floor seemed to surge upwards, tipping David off his feet and slapping him hard on the back, like an over-boisterous friend. He tried to get up but that wasn't possible. Something was pressing down hard on him, giving him a rare insight into how a shirt felt when it was being ironed.

Just when he was wondering whether he'd had a stroke or died or something like that, the lights came back on and the pressure eased off; in fact it eased off so much that David could feel his feet lift off the floor. He tried pushing down with his toes, and suddenly found himself doing a very slow forward somersault – his feet rising up behind his back, his face gradually drifting down towards the floor. Naturally, he reached out with his arms and scrabbled, but that had no perceptible effect whatsoever. A small stainless-steel basin and the crust of a cheese sandwich floated gracefully in front of his nose, like exotic tropical fish in an aquarium.

Zero gravity. Not something you'd instinctively associate with this part of London. I wonder what's going on?

He tried a few swimming strokes, but that only made things worse; by the time he realised that, however, he was hanging upside down like a sleeping bat, watching his house keys drift away and out of his field of vision, like old-fashioned fishing boats in a Mediterranean sunset. Not that it mattered particularly (it wasn't as if he'd have had any use for them, any time soon); but there's a thin, subtle psychological tether joining a man to his keyring at all times (the keys we carry define what we are) and once parted from it he can't help feeling an instinctive pang of emptiness and loss. But going after them was, he decided, out of the question, if he didn't want to end up screwing himself into the wall like a Rawlplug.

'Malfunction,' said a tinny voice somewhere below his left ear. 'Artificial gravity field inoperative.'

Thank you so much, David muttered under his breath as his toes scraped the ceiling Artex, I'd never have guessed. An idea trickled into his mind, but he dismissed it as too silly. The football-sized amorphous transparent blob headed straight for his face turned out to be water.

It was at this point that the locket he'd kneeled on behind the sofa glided gracefully out of his pocket and spiralled slowly upward towards the ceiling. David didn't actually notice, but he was aware of some subtle change; all that confidence he'd somehow acquired (not like him at all) was draining out of him, like crankcase oil from a British motorcycle. Whether this was a good thing or a bad thing remained to be seen.

'Malfunction,' the tinny voice repeated. 'Artificial gravity field has been deactivated. Do you want to deactivate artificial gravity? Reply yes for yes, no for no.'

He hesitated. Too silly, he'd told himself just now, but what was there to lose? 'No,' he said.

Entirely by chance, he landed on a large pile of surgical rubber gloves that had drifted out of an open drawer.

They broke his fall, at least to some extent; and he performed the same function for a number of small metal objects that had drifted as high as the ceiling. Some of them were surprisingly heavy for their size.

'. . . Has been restored,' said the tinny voice, but he'd guessed that already. When he felt up to moving again, he shook off the various bits of junk that were trying to bury him and crawled towards the door he'd come in by. Two filing-cabinet-sized machines had fallen across the doorway, blocking it, and when he tried to shift one of them it spat bright green sparks in his face and started humming. He backed away until he bumped into something else, and looked round for another way out.

'Warning,' announced the tinny voice. 'This program has performed an illegal operation and will shut down in five minutes. You are advised to go immediately to the life pods. Do you want to prepare the life pods for launch? Press any key to continue.'

He spun round – foolhardly, since his sense of balance hadn't quite recovered from the zero-G – and grabbed at a workstation for support. Press any key on *what*, for crying out loud? Sure, he could see a console; any number of consoles, but no way of knowing which one he was supposed to use. On the off chance that they were all networked, he reached for the nearest keyboard and jabbed a key at random. Nothing happened.

He had that silly thought again. Extremely silly: he made his living working with computers, and knew perfectly well that for the foreseeable future, nobody was going to be able to make a computer you could talk to. Shout at, yes; after a dozen years in the industry, he'd learned that computers need constant verbal abuse the way other machines needed oil. But respond to oral commands – no. That was pure science fiction.

'Computer,' he said.

'Standing by,' replied the tinny voice.

Oh well. 'Computer,' he said, 'is there a window or a porthole I can look out of?'

'Lowering blast shield,' chirped the tinny voice. 'Uncovering porthole.'

A panel in the wall behind him shot back, revealing a thick perspex plate. Through it, he could see stars, millions of them, above and below and on both sides. It was like drowning in a screen-saver.

'Thanks,' David muttered in a shaky voice. 'OK, you can shut the window now.'

The panel snapped back. 'Computer,' he said, 'where are we, exactly?'

'Coordinates 345 by 297 by 199 by 26:13:92:07, Homeworld Standard Time.'

Not that that was particularly helpful without any points of reference; it could be a way of saying 'Turnham Green' in base four-and-a-quarter. 'Computer,' he ventured, 'prepare life pods for launch.'

'Please press any key to continue.'

Damn; that old Boolean logic strikes again. 'Computer, which key should I press?'

'Please press any key.'

'Yes, fine, but on which keyboard? Tell me where I can find the keyboard.'

'The keyboard is at coordinates 674 by 185 by 334 by 05:55:92:71 Homeworld Standard Time.'

'Right. Thank you *so* much.'

'You're welcome.'

Ah well. Serves me right for clicking on 'Help'.

'Computer,' he said, trying to sound as if he knew what he was doing (first rule of cybernetics: never let the bastards see you're afraid), 'transfer all functions to the console on my immediate left.'

'Functions transferred.'

He stabbed the keyboard so hard, he nearly broke his finger. At once, another panel (door-sized this time) shot open in the same wall. He took a deep breath and dived through it like a dolphin— And landed in Honest John's workshop, right next to the door he'd gone in by. Before he hit the ground the panel had already snapped shut, and there were no marks on the wall to show where it had been.

'Finally,' said a voice behind him. 'There you are.'

He jumped up like a spring-loaded rabbit and looked round to see where the voice was coming from. Didn't take long.

'You might at least have been here when I woke up,' Philippa Levens continued. 'Simple good manners, if nothing else.' Gobbets of green slime were sliding down her legs and forming a pool on the concrete floor. He tried very hard indeed not to stare, and failed. 'Now then,' she went on, 'where's the shower?'

Was it his imagination, or was there something ever so slightly different about this one? Physically, no; he was in a unique position to confirm that. It was something else, something to do with her manner and tone of voice—

'I said,' she repeated, 'where's the damn' shower? Are you deaf as well as stupid, or just stupid?'

—And on balance, he preferred the Mark One version, even if she had cost him a fortune in delicatessen. 'I'm sorry,' he mumbled, 'I don't know. In fact, I don't think there is one.'

'Oh, for pity's sake. Well, don't just stand there like a fossilised prune. Get me a towel and my clothes, before I freeze to death.'

'Um.'

'I'll try that again without the long words. Towel. Clothes. Now.'

David's mouth opened, but no words came out.

'Forget it.' She pushed past him, smearing green glop down one side of his jacket, and pulled open a cupboard under one of the benches. 'Here,' she said, 'pay attention. This is a *towel*. This is a *shirt*. These are *panties*. Got that, or shall I write it down for you?'

'Sorry,' he mumbled, 'I didn't know they were there.'

'Of course. The elves brought them. Silly me. Now buzz off while I get dressed.'

He turned away. On reflection, he wished he'd stayed where he was. After all, how bad can asphyxiation in the vacuum of space actually be?

'Needless to say,' she went on, 'it'd be too much to expect you to say you're glad to see me after all this time, or you really missed me and you're glad I'm back, or thank you for all the trouble you've been to. Or even,' her voice added, faltering a little, '"I love you". Still, there you are. *You* haven't changed a bit.'

He froze.

It'd be true to say that David understood women the way a seventeenth-century Trobriand Islander would've understood Windows 98. Even so, he instinctively knew that this was one of those situations where there was an infinite choice of things he could say, and every single one of them would be wrong. Once he'd realised that, it all became much clearer and simpler.

'Excuse me,' he said, 'but would you happen to know what's going on in the back room?'

'Nothing,' she replied. 'Unless you've been playing about with the guidance systems. I really hope you haven't,' she added, 'for your sake.'

He turned round slowly. She'd towelled off most of the green glop and put on a shirt; one of Honest John's shirts, by the look of it, since it almost came down to her knees and the collar was frayed past hope of redemption. 'I may have bumped into something,' he mumbled. 'Accidentally.'

She advanced on him like a Napoleonic army, put her arms round his neck and kissed him for a very long time. It was a remarkable experience, a bit like drowning in rose-flavoured fire, even if she did taste quite strongly of green glop. Then she let him go.

'You aren't him,' she said.

'No,' he admitted. 'At least,' he added, 'I don't think I am. But surely you ought to know.'

She scowled at him. 'Give me a break,' she said irritably, 'I'm only fifteen minutes old. What's more,' she went on, 'I'm pretty sure there's some very big holes in my memory. Before you put the tissue sample in the regenerative matrix, are you sure you did the DNA re-sequencing properly?'

Aha, he thought; so that's what Honest John was doing with all those microscopes and soldering irons. 'Possibly not,' he admitted.

Concentrated contempt, point-999 pure, glowed in her deep blue eyes. 'I should have known,' she sighed. 'You've made a mess of things again. Have you got any tissue sample left?'

'You mean the hair? Yes, quite a lot—' He caught his breath.

'That's all right, then.' She was heading for the tank he'd put her in. 'This time, try and get it right, for pity's sake. It's not exactly rocket science, you know.'

She was going to climb back into the tank and . . . He found he couldn't breathe. She was going to climb back in and *recycle* herself, quite calmly, as if she was taking an ill-fitting pair of trousers back to Marks & Spencers. 'No,' he gurgled, 'wait. Please don't do that.'

An impatient click of the tongue. 'Now what?'

'You can't do that,' he said. 'You'll die.'

Tiny shrug of the shoulders. 'Yes. Your point being?'

'I don't want you to die.'

'Oh, come *on*,' she said scornfully. 'There'll be another one of me along in a minute. The real me,' she added, 'at least, assuming you don't screw up the sequencing *again*. True, that's quite an assumption, but what else can I do?'

'But I don't want the real you. I want *you*.'

When he heard himself say that, he hadn't got a clue where it had come from. It sounded very much like the voice of a young man deeply in love. He nearly looked round to see if there was someone standing behind him.

'What did you just say?'

'Nothing. Doesn't matter.'

She turned round slowly and walked back, until she was so close he could feel the warmth of her breath. 'All right,' she said slowly, 'just who the hell are you?'

Tell the truth, said a voice in the back of his mind, and shame the devil. It sounded a lot like his mother's voice; and when the hell had she ever steered him right? Nevertheless—

'I'm David,' he said.

'I didn't ask you what your name was.'

Deep breath. 'I'm nobody, really,' he said. 'There's a painting of you in an art gallery – that's you when you were last alive, four hundred years ago—'

'Four hundred years,' she repeated. 'Thank you so much for breaking the news so gently, by the way. Has anybody ever told you that tact isn't your strongest suit?'

'Sorry.' He looked away. 'Anyhow,' he went on, 'I've been going to look at that painting ever since I was a little kid; I suppose you could say I've been in love with it. You. It. And then there was an auction sale, and there was this lock of hair that was supposed to have come from you; and then I saw this place – you know, clones and everything, and I thought—'

'Yes, yes,' she interrupted impatiently, 'I know all that. Daddy and I set it up when I was – has it really been that long? Four hundred years?'

'Afraid so.'

'Oh well. Can't be helped, I suppose. So you're him, then. The patsy.'

David closed his eyes, breathed in and then out again. 'Yes,' he said. 'That puts it rather nicely.'

She was looking at him, and perhaps her expression had changed just a little. 'It was nothing personal,' she said, in a slightly softer voice. 'Well, it couldn't have been personal, could it? You weren't even born until hundreds of years later.'

'No, that's very true.'

She moved away and sat down on a workbench. 'So, anyway,' she was saying. 'How come you were the one who carried out the procedure? The cloning, I mean. Daddy should've done that.'

'Ah.' It occurred to him that he still had questions of his own that needed to be answered, and that once he'd answered her question, she might not be inclined to answer his. 'Before I tell you that,' he said, 'could you just clear up one small thing for me? That – *thing*, next door. It's not really a spaceship, is it?'

She laughed. 'Don't be silly.'

'Ah.'

'More like a sort of elevator, really.'

That feeling again; rather like being kicked in the stomach by a large horse. 'Elevator.'

'Yes, you know. One terminal here, another terminal back home. You press the button, and there you are. Not at all like a ship. With a ship, you can go anywhere you like.'

'Of course, I can see that. So where's home?'

She shrugged. 'Home. Where we came from. Where we live.'

'I see. Is it far?'

'Well, you wouldn't want to have to walk. About ninety-seven thousand light years, give or take a second.'

'That's a fair old distance,' David conceded. 'And this home of yours. Are there, like, *dogs* there?'

'What on earth are you babbling about?'

'Nothing,' he said, 'that's fine. No dogs?'

'A few, but they're very rare. The cats eat them. Now, will you please answer my question?'

He avoided her eyes. 'Just a moment,' he said. 'If there's no dogs where you come from, why did you program me to be terrified of them?'

She shook her head. 'That wasn't us.'

'Really? You mean that's – well, just me? Something all my own?'

'I suppose so, yes.'

'Ah.' For some reason, knowing that made him feel a

whole lot better; that there was one part of him that hadn't been carefully engineered four centuries ago, even if it was only an embarrassing phobia. 'Sorry,' he continued. 'You were asking me something, and I've forgotten what it was.'

She looked at him, but he was getting used to it. 'Why did you do the cloning?' she asked. 'Why didn't Daddy do it? Nothing's happened to him, has it?'

Well, apparently one of him's been murdered; but the rest of him don't seem particularly bothered, so I suppose it's all right. 'No, he's fine.'

'Ah. So you've met him.'

'Oh, yes.'

She nodded her head: a smooth rhythm, like the ticking of a bomb. 'So how come you're here and he isn't?'

Tell the truth, yelled his mother's voice. Agreed, chipped in the PFLDP, but not all of it. 'Last I heard,' he said, looking at his shoes, 'he was on his way to British Columbia.'

'British Columbia? Where's that?'

'Canada.'

'Where's Canada? Oh, never mind. You mean to tell me that just when everything's ready and I need him here to see to things, he's gone swanning off somewhere and left someone else to do the cloning? *You?*' she added, with wonderful economy of expression.

(Well. Here we are. Wasn't the whole point of this exercise supposed to be revenge? Getting his own back on these insufferably arrogant people who'd ruined his whole life by arranging it centuries in advance? Wasn't it all about stirring up bad feeling and resentment and misunderstandings, throwing a monkey wrench into the works, making them pay for what they'd done?

Somehow, at this moment, when he was so painfully aware of her presence in every cell of his body, that didn't seem quite as important as it had back behind the sofa, with the final indignity of British Columbia breathing down his neck. On the other hand – take that away, and there was no purpose to his life at all. Besides, he'd started the misinformation now. If he changed his story, told her the whole truth, he had a nasty feeling that she might get annoyed with him, and from what he'd seen so far, her annoyance could probably liquefy rock at a mile.)

David shrugged. 'I'm sure it must've been something very important,' he said.

'Important.' She picked up a hammer and hurled it across the workshop. There was no reason to believe she'd aimed it at him and besides, it missed his head by at least two inches. 'Important. Right. Fine. I'll have a word with him about that some other time. Right now, I've got things to do.' She slid down off the bench. 'If Daddy's not here, you'll have to do it.'

'Sure. What?'

'Take me to find Alexander, of course.'

'Um.' Well, go on, now's your chance. Maximum havoc. What're you waiting for? 'There may be a slight problem with that,' he said.

'What are you talking about? He is all right, isn't he?'

'Oh yes, fine.'

'You've seen him? You know where he is? He's not in any kind of trouble?'

Define trouble. 'No, he's perfectly all right. Bright-eyed and bushy-tailed.'

'Then what's this problem you keep jabbering on about?'

CHAPTER NINE

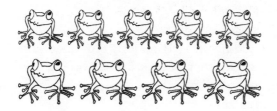

David hadn't expected that.

It was as if he'd planted a bomb in the deepest recesses of the cellar under his enemy's house; and just as he'd set the timer and was getting ready to leave, the bomb had called out to him in a tiny, frightened voice and told him it was afraid of the dark.

He didn't feel wonderfully good about it.

'It's all right,' she sniffled, as he took a tentative step towards her. 'I'll be fine. Here, give me a handkerchief, quick.'

Of course, he didn't have one; or at least, not one he'd ever be prepared to exhibit in public. 'Sorry,' he said.

'Typical,' she said, but he could see that her spleen wasn't in it. 'Doesn't matter,' she added, wiping her eyes on her sleeve and streaking it with residual green goo. 'I'm the one who should be sorry,' she added, turning her face slightly away. 'I'm embarrassing you.'

'That's all right,' he said.

'No, it's not.'

He didn't feel inclined to argue the point; she might be a bomb who was afraid of the dark, but she was still most definitely a bomb. 'Can I get you something?' he said. 'Cup of tea?'

'What's tea?'

He pursed his lips. 'It's a long story,' he said.

'Never mind, then.' She sat down on the bench again. 'So,' she said, 'tell me all about her. This someone else. What's she like?'

Somewhere in the corridors of his mind, he could hear his mother's voice saying, Told you so, but of course you wouldn't listen, always have to know best. 'Oh, you know.' He waved his hands vaguely, as if conducting an orchestra of clouds.

'No, I don't. What's she like?'

'Well.' He scrabbled desperately for some words. 'Actually, she's quite like you. In some respects.'

'Really.'

'Yes.'

'What about the other respects? The ones that aren't a bit like me?'

'She's, um, picky,' David said. 'About her food.'

'So'm I.'

'And she's got expensive tastes. *Very* expensive tastes,' he added, with a slight shudder.

She glowered at him. 'What's wrong with not liking tat?' she demanded.

'Um. Nothing, really.'

'I see. So you like her, too.'

David exhibited more common sense than he'd ever have given himself credit for by not replying to that.

'Oh, well,' she said, staring down at the floor as if hoping it'd open and swallow her up, 'that's that, then. Whole thing's been a waste of time. Needn't have bothered.'

'So . . .' David dug his fingernails into the palm of his right hand. 'So you're not going to, well, do anything about it?'

'Where's the point? If he's forgotten about me and gone off with some slut—'

This wasn't really going the way he'd planned. 'So what are you going to do?' he asked.

She shrugged her slim shoulders. 'Don't know,' she said. 'Don't care, really. Centuries of striving, seeking, aspiring, hoping, dreaming just went down the toilet. Sorry, but I can't just turn round and say, "Oh well, never mind, I'll go and get a job as a barmaid instead".' She shook her head; her hair was caked with drying green glop. 'You're trying to be nice,' she said, 'and I'm making it sound like it's your fault. That's selfish of me, after you went to all this trouble, since my own father couldn't even be bothered to . . .' She turned her head and looked at him. 'That's a point,' she said. 'Why you? I have thought you'd be the last person who'd want to *help* . . .' She frowned, as if doing mental arithmetic. 'Let's just go through this again, shall we?' she said. 'You did what we—' She stopped and started again. 'You saw the painting, had an almighty crush on it, bought the lock of hair, and so on and so forth. But you also know all about the program, and you know Alex has waltzed off with this tart. So why—?' Her frown consolidated into a scowl. 'Oh, I see,' she said icily. 'Waste not, want not, you thought. Alex won't be wanting her, you thought, so why don't I look sharp and nip in there, like a rat up a drain . . .' She sighed, and the hostility evaporated. 'You're wasting your time, too,' she said. 'The whole thing's just one great big exercise in futility, like the Millennium Dome. Did they ever get round to building that, by the way?'

'Yes.' Double take. 'You planned that? Why?'

She grinned lopsidedly. 'Long story,' she said. 'And you probably wouldn't think it was very funny, either.' She cupped her chin in her hands. 'So what are you going to do now?' she said.

'I don't know. I was supposed to go to British Columbia—'

'Isn't that where you told me Daddy's gone?' She lifted her head, then let it drop back into her hands. 'I was going to say, I might as well wait till he gets back, but there isn't much point, really. After all,' she added, 'you've still got plenty of tissue sample there. Best thing would be for him to start again—'

David didn't like the sound of *start again*. Or *wait till he gets back*, either. 'What do you mean?' he said.

'I mean, go back to where we were – what was it, four hundred years ago? He'll just have to engineer another Alex. And another you, presumably. Then, when it's all set up, the next you can buy what's left of the tissue sample and we can give it another go.' She grinned again. 'What you might call a hair-of-the-dog remedy. Or bitch. After all this time, I'm probably not a very nice person.'

'What did you mean,' David said, '"wait till he gets back"?'

She gave him a scornful look. 'Oh, come on,' she said. 'You don't think I'm going to spend the next seventy years moping around this place, do you? Besides, I'm not even properly me – you saw to that,' she added, with a glint of her former edge, 'when you screwed up the resequencing.'

'But you can't—' David could feel panic twitching in the back of his mind. 'I mean, you're here now. You're alive. You can't just say, Oh well, that didn't work out, I guess I'd better stop breathing and die.'

'Why not? Plenty more of me where I came from.'

'Yes, but they wouldn't be you—'

'Just as well.'

At this point, it occurred to David that as far as the moral high ground was concerned, he was in danger of getting a crick in his neck from looking up at it. What he'd just done was, if anything, rather worse than what'd been done to him. After all, he'd been brought into existence to facilitate True Love (which was presumably going on perfectly happily right now over at Alex's place). On the other hand, he had dragged this poor creature into the light simply to use her as a weapon. Not a very nice way to behave, really.

'You could go home' he said.

She looked up. 'Home.'

'In your spaceship. I mean, your elevator. That thing next door. Well, why not? If there's nothing left for you here, that doesn't necessarily mean it'd be the same back on wherever you said it was, all those light years away. For all I know, it might be completely different.'

She smiled. 'It is,' she said. 'We don't have love there.'

David frowned, as if he'd turned over two pages at once. 'How do you mean—?'

'Doesn't exist,' she replied. 'The same way fire-breathing dragons don't exist here. It's something to do with the effect of the high levels of ambient neutranetic radiation in our ozone layer. Either that or we've got more sense. Why else do you think I came to this scruffy little asteroid of yours in the first place?'

He couldn't take all that in at one go, so he nibbled off a corner and digested that. 'So if you were to go back there—'

'I'd be cured, yes. No more love, no more broken heart. I could probably get my old job back at the building society.'

'I see,' David said quietly. 'Then why don't you?'

She looked at him for a very long time. 'You don't get out much, do you?' she said. 'Well, no, of course you don't, we didn't program you to go gallivanting around the place enjoying yourself. I could go back there, yes. Or I could jump off a tall building and get squished into chutney. Nothing much in it either way, really, except I get spacesick in the elevator.'

A little light bulb clicked on inside David's head. He didn't like it much and he wished it would go away, but it wouldn't. He really didn't want to ask. But he did.

'Could I go there?' he asked.

She shrugged. 'Don't see why not,' she replied. 'Of course, a lot of things are very different there.'

'I suppose they would be, yes. Gravity and stuff.'

'No, that's more or less the same. But we drive on the right, and all our plugs are two-pin and, most of our computer systems run on UNIX.' She shook her head. 'And no love, of course. Friendship and camaraderie and a certain level of parental and filial affection, but no love. Mind you, in your case, that probably wouldn't be such a problem. You don't miss what you've never had, right?'

David nodded. 'Right,' he said. Then he added,

'Really? UNIX is your principal operating system? No wonder you beat us to interstellar flight.'

'I suppose it's possible you might like it there,' she said. 'It hadn't occurred to me before, but you might. And what the hell, there's nothing to keep you here.'

He thought about that for five, nearly six seconds. 'And you'd come with me?' he said.

'Why on earth would I want do to that?'

David felt as if he was trying to climb up a greasy rope. 'You said yourself,' he replied, 'going home or suicide, you didn't really mind which. So if it's as broad as it's long—'

'There's the spacesickness,' she pointed out.

'Oh, come on. It can't be that bad.'

She pursed her lips. 'Actually,' she said.

'Never mind. You'll just have to put up with it. You're coming with me.'

That obviously amused her. 'Sure,' she said. 'Just give me a moment to powder my nose. Haven't you been listening to a word I've said? There's no point. If we go there—'

He shook his head. 'I know that,' he replied, 'I'm not stupid. And I didn't mean, Come on, let's ride off together into the sunset—'

'Glad to hear it. First, like I said, it's an elevator, not a ship. But even if it was a ship, if you were to fly it straight into the sun—'

'It's an expression.'

'Oh. Be that as it may,' she said, standing up and stretching, stifling a small yawn, 'there's no point nagging me into going with you. As soon as you get there, you'll find you don't, well, feel anything about me any more, I'll just be somebody you met on a train.'

He nodded. 'Yes. Fine. You'll still be alive, though.'

'Maybe. Big deal.' She moved round to face him. 'Listen,' she said, almost gently, 'it's different for me. I'm only twenty-odd minutes old, I've been trying on this life like a pair of shoes and I've decided it doesn't fit. No problem. No hard feelings. Especially since I know that next time, it can't help being better.' She looked at him for a moment; not quite as if she was thinking of buying him in a shop, more as though he'd come free with something. 'I don't suppose you can understand that, so you'll just have to take my word for it.'

David wanted to shout or jump up and down or bash some furniture. 'Exactly,' he said. 'Twenty minutes. You call that giving it a fair chance? Dammit, how can you judge your life after only twenty minutes? I gave *Farscape* a better chance than that.'

'?'

'It's a television programme,' he explained impatiently. 'What I meant was, at least I did it the courtesy of watching a whole episode before I—'

'You have *television* on this planet?'

David shrugged, as if to say it wasn't his fault.

'That's amazing,' she said, and there was something like light in her eyes. 'Back home we've been experimenting with it for millions of years, and they keep saying it simply can't be done. Have you really got it to work here?'

'Well, yes. Had it for years. Look—'

'That's extraordinary. You know, whole chunks of our culture are based around the myth of the quest for television: novels, plays, puppet shows, the lot, all about a bright and wonderful future where we've finally cracked the enigma of the cathode ray tube and brought about a

golden age of peace, tolerance and prosperity.' She studied the expression on his face. 'It isn't like that here, is
it?' she said.

'Um. Not really, no.'

'Even though you've got television?'

'There's some who reckon it's *because* . . . Look, no
offence, but aren't we getting sidetracked here?'

She laughed quietly. 'Actually,' she said, 'I'd say it's
pretty relevant. Isn't it all about planning and working
and dreaming for something, and when it actually happens it's not what it was supposed to be? In fact,' she
added, brushing a speck of dust out of her eye, 'how relevant can you get?'

David had the feeling he wasn't really getting anywhere. 'If you went home,' he said, 'you could sell the
technology. You'd be rich and famous.'

'Can't be bothered. *You* could, though, assuming it'll
work on our planet. There, you see, I've solved all your
problems for you. You go to Homeworld and make a
fortune, I'll kill myself, and that way everyone's a winner.'

Just for a moment, he was tempted; rich and famous
in a brave new world full of unimaginably different and
startling wonders and no Australian soap operas. And a
place where he'd never fall in love again, or feel the need
to do so.

Forty-eight hours ago . . . Forty-eight hours ago, all
anybody would have seen was a vague blur, as he
sprinted across the workshop and hurled himself
through the door. By the same token, forty-eight hours
ago he'd probably have been delighted at the prospect of
emigrating to British Columbia. 'I'm not going if you're
not,' he said decisively. 'And if I'm staying, so are you.
You *owe* me that.'

She looked up sharply. 'I owe you a kick in the head for bringing me here,' she said. 'That's about it as far as moral obligations go, I reckon.'

'Yes, but you brought me here. And you did it first. You started it.'

'Whatever.' She sounded bored, as if she'd lost interest in the debate.

'Besides,' David said desperately, 'I can't work that thing. It's got lots of different controls, and it keeps barking at me. You'd have to come along and fly it.'

'No.'

'All right.' He took a deep breath, and tried to think, but his brain had more or less boiled dry. 'You aren't coming.'

'I'm not coming. In fact,' she added, 'I'm staying right here. In case you didn't quite get that, I don't ever intend to leave this building alive. Is that absolutely clear?'

That was when the door flew open, and about a dozen men in ski masks grabbed them and hauled them out into the street.

'Mmmm,' she told him. 'Mmmmmm.'

David wasn't fluent in sticky-tape-over-the-mouth, but he could understand *This is all your fault* easily enough when he heard it. 'Mmm,' he replied, trying to sound sincere.

They were bouncing around in the back of a van, blindfolded and trussed up with gaffer tape. No idea where they were going, or who was taking them there, or why. As far as David was concerned, it was a fine allegory for his life so far. At least this time there weren't any dogs.

'Mmmm,' she said; and although he'd have liked to attribute it entirely to stress and the heat of the moment, he had an unpleasant feeling she meant it. But then, he'd probably have said the same in her position.

Time works differently in the dark, so he couldn't really form an accurate assessment of how long the journey lasted. Eventually, however, the van stopped and he heard the door creak open. Someone grabbed him by the elbows and pulled, and his feet jarred on what was probably concrete. Someone told someone else to get a move on. The voice sounded familiar.

'Mmmm,' said the girl, and his intuitive linguistics program translated, *You told me he was in British Columbia*. Well, he should have known he'd be found out sooner or later. Fortuitously, it looked like it wasn't going to matter terribly much. Masked thugs don't bundle people into the backs of vans and drive them to out-of-the-way places in the middle of the night just to ask their opinion of fabric swatches, and he was fairly sure he hadn't achieved enough in his three-and-a-bit decades of existence to merit an appearance on *This Is Your Life*.

(So. This is it, then. Very soon now, I'm going to die. I suppose I ought to be terrified – it's only polite, after all, when they've gone to so much trouble – but I'm not. I suppose that comes later, when they make you dig your own grave, or whatever the procedure is in these situations. I suppose Mum'll be quite upset, but she gets upset about so many things – traffic jams, the poor starving donkeys in Ibiza, rain during Wimbledon, the government, soccer hooligans . . . What I'd really like now, though, is a nice fat cheeseburger with mayonnaise, ketchup and gherkins.)

He stumbled and tripped along until a hand on his shoulder stopped him and collapsed him down into a chair (like folding up the legs of a camera tripod). Behind him, a screech of metal, some kind of steel door being pulled to; that'd be right, he decided – whenever they killed someone in *The Sweeney*, didn't they always take them to an abandoned warehouse with a door that sounded just like that? Always the same warehouse, week after week, like all the planets in *Doctor Who* were always the same disused gravel pit near Berkhamstead.

'Right,' said the voice, as fingers tugged at the tape gag and the knot of the blindfold. (Well, here we go; awfully big adventure; just as well your past life doesn't flash in front of your eyes after all, would hate to think the last thing I'd ever see was a repeat of Deborah Fingest's eighth birthday party—.) Light poured in all around him, flooding and spurting like water from a cracked pipe. 'Now then,' said the voice, 'I expect you could both do with something to eat.'

He was sitting on a chair in – yes, *exactly* the same warehouse – and she was sitting on an identical chair next to him, and they were in the middle of a ring of about a dozen—

'Hey,' she said. 'He told me you were in—' And then she noticed something, and started to count. There were, in fact, thirteen of them (or one and his twelve brothers).

'There's sandwiches,' one of them was saying, 'we've got ham, cheese, ham and cheese, egg and watercress, prawn cocktail, BLT or chicken tikka; or if you'd rather have something hot there's pot noodles—'

'You aren't my father,' she said. 'Any of you.'

'—Or there's some tomato soup in the thermos. No, we aren't. How about you? Can I tempt you with a tuna-and-sweetcorn pasty?'

She made a suggestion involving tuna-and-sweetcorn pasties, which was ignored. For his part, David wished she hadn't interrupted like that, just when it was getting interesting. He hadn't had anything to eat for a long time. Neither, of course, had she – four hundred years, assuming her predecessor had had the traditional hearty breakfast before the bonfire party. Unless you counted green glop, of course; he didn't know enough about the basic science involved to hazard a guess.

'I'll have the chicken tikka, please,' he ventured. All thirteen of his captors turned and looked at him. 'And the prawn cocktail too, if that's all right.'

They turned out to be those Marks & Spencers sandwiches that come in the dinky little plastic boxes, with the peel-off lids that make safecracking look like a kids' game. Worth the effort, though.

'And now,' one of the thirteen was saying, 'I suppose you'll want all the gory details. No problem, we've got plenty of time and not much else to do.' He looked at the girl, who stuck her tongue out at him; he seemed somewhat disconcerted by that, but made a fairly smooth recovery. 'Just as you said, none of us is your father. Not the original, anyway. We're like you: replicants, clones, the boys from the green stuff. Only,' he went on, frowning a little, 'there's a slight difference. We're what you might call unofficial. Accidental, even.'

David looked up. 'Accidental?' he said, with his mouth full.

The speaker sighed. 'That's right,' he said. 'The fact of the matter is,' he went on, glowering at the girl, 'your father— Well, there isn't a tactful way of saying it. He has dandruff.'

'Dan—'

'That's right. *Bad* dandruff. Not good if you're prone to wearing grey or dark blue. Not good at all if you spend time bending over cloning tanks. Of course, I don't need to point out to you guys the fact that, being a bit impromptu, as it were, our bits of tissue sample didn't get the proper resequencing treatment before we hit the green. As a result, a few data errors and deviations from the pattern are only to be expected.'

Both David and the girl looked away when he said that. If he noticed, he didn't refer to it.

'Of course,' he continued, 'because we've got these gaps in our matrices, we don't actually know which aspects we differ in; but we reckon you don't have to be Mensa material to figure it out. Now, we're all ever so slightly different, all thirteen of us, but two things we do have in common: total lack of scruple, ditto of meaning and purpose in our sad, unnatural lives. So we had a brood meeting and talked it through rationally, like sensible almost-human beings, and we decided to devote all our time and energy to doing as much harm to our creator as we possibly can. We figured: we didn't ask to be alive, we certainly didn't ask to be pre-programmed utilities – *duff* pre-programmed utilities, which just rubs that extra few grains of salt into the wound – so the least we can do is try and get even. Puerile,' he added shaking his head, 'and pointless and pretty unpleasant behaviour all round, but apparently it's in our nature, so there it is.'

David felt as if he'd just swallowed a brick.

'All right,' the girl said. 'But what do you want us for?'

'Don't give me that,' the clone replied. 'You're *them*; the lovebirds, the time-crossed sweethearts, you're the reason why all of us got in this mess to begin with. And now, damn it, here you are—'

'Excuse me,' David said.

'Here you are,' the clone went on, 'the culmination of the program, journey's end is lovers' meeting, all ready and poised to live happily ever after like a pair of crazed weasels—'

'Actually,' David said, 'that's not us.'

'And we're not going to— What did you say?'

'That's not us. We're not the, um, time-crossed sweethearts; you're thinking of the other one of her, and my cousin Alex Snaithe.'

The words 'the other one of her' weren't lost on the girl, the way a lighted match isn't lost on a trail of gunpowder running under the door of a fireworks factory. She didn't say anything, though, just listened.

'Don't give me that,' the clone said doubtfully. 'We weren't born yesterday, you know.' One of his colleagues tried to interrupt, but he shushed him before he could speak. 'You're just saying that so we'll give up and let you go.'

'No, really,' David replied. 'I mean, do I look like someone a girl'd go to all that trouble for? Be reasonable.'

The clone thought about that for a moment. 'So who the bloody hell is she, then?'

'Ah.'

Now there were fourteen of them looking at him.

'She's another one of her,' he said eventually. 'It's all my fault, you see. I don't suppose you remember me—'

'Oh yes, we do. You're the patsy.'

'Absolutely right, yes,' David said, with just the tiniest fleck of bitterness tingeing his voice. 'Well, I fell in love with the painting, like you wanted me to – you remember that bit?'

'Of course. Nice touch, we always thought. Go on.'

'I, um, wanted one of her for myself. And there was all this hair left over—'

The clone looked at him for a moment; then he started to laugh. 'Oh, that's wonderful,' he said (with difficulty, because of the laughter). 'Amazing. You see,' he went on, turning to the girl, 'when we were doing the equations for him, no matter how many times we checked the figures, over and over and over again, there was always this pesky little 1.475 per cent asymmetrical variance, but none of us had the faintest idea what it could possibly be. And now,' he concluded with a huge smirk, 'we know. It was a minute residual capacity for doing really amazingly stupid things as romantic gestures. Bingo!'

David looked at him. Now that he'd had something to eat, his number one priority had changed. Now, what he wanted to do most in all the world was pull one of these bastards inside out and scoop out his brains with his own tibia. He didn't mind which one – good or bad, old batch or new – so long as he could do substantial damage in an imaginative way. Of course, that agenda rang a bell too.

'You,' the girl said sharply. 'Make him say what he meant just now about the other one of me.'

The clone grinned. 'I was just about to ask him the same question. Mind you, I can probably guess. My theory is, once he'd done what he was produced to do – bought the hair, ordered the you-clone from Honest John, seen to it that she got her man and all that – he realised he'd still got a nice fat hunk of hair left and decided to help himself. I mean, he's virtually admitted as much already. Haven't you?'

David thought quickly. It was close enough to the truth for government work, and they'd probably believe it; all right, it might get him killed if they left him and the girl alone together for more than fifteen seconds, but it was rather better than the *true* truth. 'Yes,' he said. 'I'm sorry,' he added.

'Sorry.' She tried to get up, but – very kindly, he thought – the clones wouldn't let her. 'You told me he'd gone off with some *bimbo*. And all the time, it was *me*—'

'Well,' said the clone, in a bringing-the-meeting-to-order tone of voice, 'that makes things interesting, doesn't it? Bearing in mind our own agenda, I mean. Seems to me that what we've got here is a fully-charged weapons-grade woman scorned. Seems to me that now she knows the score, all we've got to do is turn her loose with a street map and a baseball bat; fire and forget, as they say in the Air Force.'

'Get knotted,' she interrupted (or words to that effect). 'I'm damned if I'm going to do your dirty work for you. Besides, the only person around here I want to get my hands on is *him*.'

The clone looked surprised. 'Are you sure about that?' he said. 'What about your faithless lover? Not to mention your hated rival? Don't you think both of 'em would look better with two-way kneecaps?'

'No.' She treated all thirteen clones to a scowl that'd have stripped chrome off steel. 'For one thing he's not a faithless lover, he's waited for me and now he's got me. One of me, anyway. It's the principle that's important. And it's not her fault, just because she was there first.

Now, if only a certain selfish, meddling bastard had left well alone—'

Strange how one's opinions about people can change. Suddenly, David regarded the thirteen clones, particularly the two holding the girl down in her chair, as his best friends in the entire world. As for the tender, not to mention soppy thoughts he'd been entertaining about her, they seemed to have got lost somewhere, fallen down between the cushions of panic.

'Now then,' the head clone was saying, 'that's quite enough of that. You've got me intrigued, I must say. In your shoes I don't think I'd be anything like as focused. Well, I'm in your shoes, and I'm not.'

'Breeding shows,' she replied icily. 'After all, you're just the bastard offspring of a small flake of diseased skin. *I'm* descended from a strand of hair.'

The clone pulled a face. 'With a split end, probably. Well, if you won't cooperate willingly, we'll just have to find some way of persuading you. How about: you do exactly what we tell you to do, or this one' (indicating David) 'gets it.'

Her brows furrowed. 'Why the hell should that bother me?'

'Because if we waste him, we'll do it humanely; cream doughnut laced with hemlock, something like that. He'll just go to sleep with a big happy smile on his face and never wake up . . .'

'Hey!' objected David, who liked cream doughnuts.

'. . . Thereby cheating you of your only chance of ripping his lungs out and making him swallow them.' He frowned. 'It isn't grabbing you, is it?'

She shook her head. 'Can't be bothered,' she said. 'It's not as if it really matters, in the long run.'

'Of course—' The clone stood up and walked round behind her. 'Of course, there's another way, and we wouldn't need your cooperation at all.' He reached out and tweaked a single hair from the top of her head. 'And if this one doesn't come out right, we just keep going until we get one who sees things our way, or you go bald. One of your daddy's virtues that didn't get screwed up when we were cloned was his effectively infinite patience.'

'That's sick,' she said.

'You think so? Compared to some of the options we've discussed, it's a mild cold. You got any idea how many hairs there are on the average humanoid? Multiply that by thirteen, and that's just the first generation. Just think of what a truly unscrupulous mind could dream up with ten million identical, expendable bald sociopaths at its disposal. Or,' he continued, wreathing his fingers with her hair, 'you could maybe help us out, and the human race would be spared a vast amount of misery, and we wouldn't end up looking like fans at a Yul Brynner convention.'

'What's a yulbrynner?'

He let go and took a step to the right. 'Alternatively,' he went on, 'we could do something really devious.' He was standing directly behind David now. 'You think it's a pain in the bum having just one lovesick twit yearning after you? Now, several thousand of them, with a few subtle genetic tweaks—'

Nobody was bothering to hold David down in his chair, of course; they'd taken one look at him and formed a fairly accurate view of the degree of threat he posed. One of them was standing in front of the chair as a token guard, but he was looking at his tank-brother.

When David suddenly jumped to his feet, the guard reacted far too slowly and got head-butted in the solar plexus for his pains. It was, of course, an accident; David couldn't have pulled off such perfect timing deliberately to save his life.

'Hey,' the lead clone called out, 'where do you think you're going? Well, don't just stand there . . .'

It was twenty-two yards from the chair to the door, and David covered the distance in just over four seconds; not quite Olympic standard, but fairly nippy for someone who spent most of his time sitting in front of a VDU screen. It didn't do him as much good as he'd hoped, however, since someone had locked the door. People do that sort of thing. It's one of the reasons why, all things considered, they're a pain in the bum.

'Fetch him back here, before I get annoyed,' the lead clone said. The other twelve copies advanced on David in a half-moon formation. It was the sort of situation that Hannibal or Robert E. Lee would probably have relished, as a challenge.

'Just a moment,' David said.

They hesitated and looked at him expectantly, like a theatre audience. This was good, up to a point, but he couldn't expect them to stand there all day, and he didn't actually have anything particularly interesting to say to them. Did he?

'All right,' he said, 'I'll make a deal with you.'

Always sounds good in the TV cop shows; and the twelve clones were clearly impressed. 'What sort of a deal?' one of them asked.

Good question; and all he could think of was—

'My cousin Alex. You know, *him*. The boyfriend. I know lots and lots of useful stuff about him, if you want to go after him.' He paused for breath; they were still listening. In fact, they seemed very well taken with the idea.

'What sort of things?' one of them asked.

David made a vague gesture. 'You name it,' he said, 'I know it. Dammit, there's nothing I don't know about him, really. We virtually grew up together.'

The clones looked at each other. 'What do you reckon?' one of them called back to the lead clone. (What was it that made him the natural leader, David wondered, given that the whole baker's dozen of them were supposed to be identical?)

'Might as well,' the lead clone replied. 'It's not as if we'd got anything else planned. All right,' he said, 'come back here, you've got a deal. And you can start by telling us where he lives.'

It would've been different, David assured himself, if it'd been anybody else. Anybody else in the whole wide world, and he wouldn't have sold them out just to save his own skin. It was because it was Alex (his nemesis, his evil spirit, his constant companion since boyhood, probably – hideous thought, this – aside from his mum, the person he was closest to) and this wasn't cowardice, it was a perfectly legitimate and justifiable act of revenge. Which made all the difference, didn't it?

CHAPTER TEN

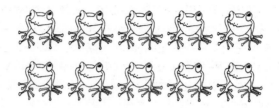

'**B**astard,' she said.

That was probably the mildest epithet she'd thrown at David so far; also, coming as it did from someone who'd been born of the union of a tankful of goo and one of her own hairs, the easiest to shrug off. He still winced.

'In there,' he said. 'Number seventeen, on the fifth floor.'

'Stairs,' sighed a clone, 'always it's got to be up a load of stairs. Just for once, couldn't we get to nobble someone on the ground floor?'

As befitted his new position as ally, David was sitting in the front seat of the van; so he couldn't see her, in the back, looking daggers at him. He could feel her eyes ice-picking the nape of his neck, though, which was almost as bad.

Alex, he reminded himself. These people are going to do something imaginatively horrible to Alex. You don't like him, remember? Never liked him, even when we were kids. Made your life a misery, in fact; damn it, you were bred and born just so he could steal your girl . . . A small ember of hatred glowed; it was enough—

And remember that time, your sixteenth birthday, you'd actually managed to get a date with Sharon Pettingell, you were just getting off the bus outside the pictures, and he just happened to be passing . . . And you ended up sitting in the row behind, because there were only two adjoining seats left for that showing? And what about that time—?

David deliberately throttled back the reminiscences, before flames started shooting out of his nose. He hadn't always wanted to be a shy, reclusive computer nerd; in fact, he'd *never* wanted to be a shy, reclusive computer nerd, but it had come about that way, and there was no doubt in his mind whose fault it was. Besides, it wasn't as if they were going to kill Alex; they'd probably just rough him up a little, trash his DVD player, break the aerial off his mobile phone . . .

Coward. Yes, admitted, guilty as charged; bring on the white feathers by the duvetful. But if it's got to come down to him-or-me, I can't think of anybody on earth I'd rather see playing the part of Him.

'Right,' said the lead clone, 'everybody ready? Seventeen, you said?'

'On the fifth floor, yes.'

'That's fine. You wait here, we won't be long.'

They locked the doors behind them as they went, leaving him alone with her. Of course, they'd taken the precaution of tying her up with washing-line and hand-cuffing him to the steering wheel; and it stood to reason that David wouldn't start yelling for the police.

Apparently they'd gagged her before they left; he didn't suppose they'd done it as an act of kindness towards him, but he was prepared to see it in that light.

'Well,' he said. 'Here we are.'

'Mmm.'

'I suppose we could try to escape,' he said unenthusiastically. 'If I lean back and reach out with my left arm, maybe you could sort of wriggle round so I could untie your hands, then you could climb over the driver's seat, get these cuffs off me somehow and— Oh, I don't suppose you know how to drive, do you?'

'Mmm.'

'Well, at least you could escape; I mean, that'd be better than nothing. And maybe you could go and fetch your dad – your real dad, I mean, or one of him – and maybe then you'd see your way to rescuing me? If it wouldn't be too much trouble?'

'Mmm mmm!'

There are times when inarticulate grunts mumbled through a big hankie are so much more eloquent than mere words. He turned back and sat staring out through the windscreen for a while. At some point he must have closed his eyes because the next thing he was aware of was a thumping noise, as of a gloved fist hammering against the passenger-side window. He jerked his head round. There was indeed a gloved fist, and it belonged to a uniformed policeman, who was alternately bashing the glass and gesturing to him to wind the window down.

It was an old van, without electric windows. David turned the handle with his free hand.

'Right, sir,' said the policeman. 'Perhaps you'd like to explain what you think you're up to.'

'Oh,' David replied, 'nothing.'

'Just sitting there admiring the view?'

'Something like that, yes.'

'I see. Any particular reason why you've handcuffed yourself to the steering wheel?'

'Oh, that wasn't me.'

'Wasn't you?'

'No.' David shook his head. 'Friends of mine.'

'I see,' the policeman said. 'Anybody else in there with you?'

'Absolutely not,' David replied, just as the girl in the back started mmmm-mming like a passionate chainsaw.

'You're sure about that, are you?' asked the policeman.

'Oh, you mean *her*.' Pretty lame, he knew, but he wasn't at his most creative right then.

'Yes, her. Excuse me. Miss?'

'Mmmmmmmmm!'

'I'm sorry, I didn't quite catch that—' The policeman put his head through the window and looked round. 'Ah,' he said, 'fine. Right, sir, if you'd care to unlock yourself and get out of the van—'

'I'm sorry,' David mumbled. 'I haven't got the keys.'

Something in the policeman's expression told David he wasn't convinced. 'You're sure about that, sir, are you? Only, if I have to get another car out here with bolt-cutters and the keys turn out to have been in your pocket all along, I'm not going to be happy, if you see what I mean.'

'Really,' David said. 'No keys.'

'Fine. And where would the keys be, right now?'

'Um.' David swallowed. 'My friends've got them. It's their van, you see.'

'Your friends. And where are they, then?'

David was just about to say 'Right behind you', because he'd been brought up to tell the truth, when it occurred to him that there are exceptions to every rule. 'I'm not sure,' he said. 'Last time I saw them, they were—'

The policeman vanished.

'Quick,' said a clone – he sounded like the leader, but of course there was no way of knowing. Maybe it was a different one. Maybe they took it in turns. 'Everybody get in the van. Yes, bring the bloody thing, let's be tidy.'

David heard the van being unlocked, the rear door opening, people-getting-in noises. Also, someone or something said 'Rivet!' or words to that effect. 'It was the wrong bloody flat,' growled the presumably-the-lead clone, settling himself in the driving seat and putting on his seat belt. 'I'll be charitable and assume it was a slip of the tongue on your part.'

No matter the cost, David had to know. 'That policeman,' he said. 'What did you do to him?'

The driver didn't answer. Somebody or something in the back said, 'Rivet, rivet, *rurrk*!' David hoped very much that it wasn't intended as an answer to his question.

'Keep your eyes open for a garden with a goldfish pond,' the driver was saying. 'And don't let it hop about back there. Driving this thing's tricky enough as it is.'

David took a deep breath. 'You turned that policeman into a—'

'Don't be bloody stupid.' The driver shook his head. 'That's impossible, just think of the technology involved.

You'd need to be able to do teleportation, matter transmutation, God knows what else. Even if you had the tech, the energy required would be more than the total output of a small star.'

'Ah,' David replied, relieved.

'No, all we've done is make him *think* he's a frog.' The driver leaned across and unlocked the handcuffs. 'It's the basis of all our, or should I say *their* technology: manipulating appearances. The thing stays the same, but everybody sees what we – *they* want them to see. He thinks he's a frog, you think he's a frog, and you can run the whole show off two triple-A batteries.'

'I see. So really, he's perfectly all right.'

'Oh yes. At least, so long as he doesn't try breathing underwater or crossing a road. But that's what free will and freedom of choice is all about. Not our problem, in other words.' The driver laughed, and turned the ignition key. 'Don't look so miserable,' he said. 'You should be pleased. Two minutes later and he'd have hauled you off to jail for the rest of your life.'

There was that, of course. 'Thank you,' David said, but he wasn't sure he meant it.

'My pleasure. Anyway, about that flat. Nobody there. And it was the wrong one. Nothing in it at all, not even any furniture. Just,' the driver added, 'and this is the really weird thing, a bag of sugar.'

'Oh,' David said.

(And he was thinking: the thing stays the same but everybody sees what they're supposed to see. Still, if they hadn't figured it out for themselves, he wasn't going to make it easy for them.)

'Like you said,' the driver replied, 'oh. Now, do you know this Alex character's real address, or do you want to spend the rest of your life chasing flies around a lily pad?'

Awkward. Served him right, presumably, for telling the truth in the first place. 'All right,' he said, and just for once inspiration was there waiting for him when he reached out for it. 'They're over at my place. Do you know the address?'

'Mphm. You're sure about that, are you?'

'Sure I'm sure.'

'Well, that's all right, then. What's the quickest way to get there from here?'

Pretty well everything comes in handy sooner or later, provided that you're prepared to wait; even, as David was able to prove, a profoundly rotten sense of direction. He did his best to navigate. If he'd been trying to get them all lost in the back streets of Chiswick Park, he couldn't have done a better job.

'Here we are,' he announced, nearly two hours later. As he'd expected (and hoped) there were several ominous-looking Big Flash Cars lurking round the kerbside like hungry crocodiles. Fortunately, the clones didn't seem to be able to recognise a stake-out when they saw one. 'I suggest you park here,' David said, 'and walk the rest of the way. Just in case.'

'Just in case of what?'

'Oh, you know.'

The clone glowered quizzically at him but followed the suggestion, dumping the van a hundred yards back from David's front door. He'd have preferred a bit more margin, but it was better than nothing. 'Sorry,' he said, 'but I think I lost my house keys back in the clone workshop, so you'll have to kick down the door. Shouldn't be difficult,' he added, 'it's been practically falling to bits for years, a really good sneeze'd probably blow it into matchwood.'

'What about the neighbours?'

'Oh, they're used to me by now,' David said as blandly as he could manage. 'If I had a fiver for every time I've come home rat-arsed and kicked the door in because I can't find my keys—'

'Really? You don't look the type.'

'It's always the quiet ones,' David replied hopefully. 'Anyhow, you won't get any trouble from them.'

'If you say so,' the clone replied, snapping the handcuffs back round David's wrist. 'But if you're lying, then so help me—'

As they piled out of the van, David racked his brains for the words of the truly appropriate quotation. He was all right as far as *It is a far, far better thing than I have ever done before*, but what came after that he wasn't quite sure.

(And what came after that? Unfortunately, having seen a few prison documentaries, he had a reasonable idea of what came after as far as he was concerned; but they had no reason to hold the girl, sooner or later they'd have to let her go, and she'd be out of it, and safe. Relatively safe, anyway. Safer than she was in this van, surrounded by her father's enemies.)

He watched them down the street and in – noisily – through the front door. He saw the watching bluebottles getting out of their cars; gave them thirty seconds to radio for back-up, and then—

He wound down the window with his free hand. '*HELP!*' he yelled, feeling appallingly self-conscious about making so much noise. 'Excuse me! Over here. Help!'

The bluebottles didn't seem to be taking any notice

(understandable, of course; it takes a very special sort of policeman to be capable of walking and listening at the same time) so he stabbed the horn with his elbow and put his weight on it.

They heard that, all right. One of them broke away from the pack and sprinted over to the van.

'Shut it, you,' he hissed. 'We're trying to do a stake-out here.'

'Yes,' David replied, 'I know. It's me you're—'

'I said shut it,' the policeman interrupted, grabbing David's arm and wrenching it away from the steering column. 'Or I'll do you for obstruction.'

'Yes, but I'm the—'

The policeman slapped the van door with the palm of his hand. 'QUIET!'

'Sorry,' David whispered. 'Look, it's me you want. Really.'

'Yeah, sure. Now piss off and play nicely, I'm busy.'

'Really,' David pleaded. 'And look, I'm handcuffed to the steering wheel. And there's a girl tied up in the back.'

The policeman shook his head. 'Wrong department,' he said, 'we're on a murder case here.'

'But—'

'All right,' the policeman sighed, 'tell you what I'll do. Soon as we're finished here, I'll call the perve squad. Shouldn't be more than an hour. You'll just have to hold out till them.' And he started to walk away.

'Bugger,' David muttered under his breath, and jabbed the horn again.

The policeman turned round and came back.

'You said you'd do me for obstruction,' David said, smiling pleasantly.

'Oh for . . . Look, you're under arrest, right? Now wait there. Don't move and *don't* touch that bloody horn.'

This time, David let him get thirty yards up the street before applying the elbow.

'Right,' the policeman snarled at him, 'that's it. Out of the van.'

'I can't,' David pointed out. 'I'm handcuffed to the steering wheel.'

The policeman pulled a face. 'There's always got to be one, hasn't there? Bloody well unlock yourself, and *then* get out of the—'

'I haven't got the key.'

David could see the policeman counting up to ten. Under other circumstances, he'd have assumed this was just showing off ('Look, no fingers!'). 'Then you won't be going anywhere, will you? Look, I *promise* I'll come back for you in a minute, soon as I've finished arresting this highly dangerous murderer. Just leave the horn *alone*. Or,' he added, 'I won't arrest you at all, and you can just sit here all night and catch pneumonia. Got that? Fine.'

This time, David let him get fifty yards . . .

But this time, the policeman didn't say anything when he returned to the van. Instead, he reached inside the cab, flipped the bonnet catch, opened the bonnet and ripped out some wires. Then he ran back to the house.

'Have you quite finished?'

David spun round, nearly dislocating a vertebra. 'How did you—?'

'It was only rope,' the Philippa clone said scornfully. 'Now, if you're through with teasing that man, I think we should leave. There's some sort of disturbance going on over there, and we don't want to be conspicuous.'

'I'm handcuffed to the—'

She made a rude noise, reached over his shoulder, grabbed the wheel and pulled. A six-inch section broke away in her hand. 'Not now, you aren't,' she said. 'Coming?'

'Just a minute,' David said. (His brain was still trying to process what he'd just seen.) 'Why are you rescuing me? You hate me.'

'True,' she replied. 'But you were trying to give yourself up just so as to rescue me, and that was rather sweet. Stupid and utterly futile, of course, and only you could fail to be caught when there's so many of them out to catch you, but sweet. Come on, last chance.'

Well, he thought, why not? He hopped out of the van, just in time to see her walking away, very quickly. He had to run just to catch up.

'Don't run, idiot,' she said. 'It's a sure way of drawing attention, running away. Just walk fast.'

At another time, in other company, David might have pointed out that his attempts at drawing attention hadn't got him very far. But just for once he got it right and kept his face shut.

'You know the area,' she said. 'Where do we go now?'

He shrugged. 'Depends on where you want to get to,' he replied.

She tutted impatiently. 'The cloning plant, of course. Or, to be precise, the ultraspatial interface matr— The lift,' she amended. 'I've got to get back home as quickly as possible.'

David was surprised, but pleased. He'd been sure she hadn't been listening. 'Great,' he said. 'I'm so pleased you came around to—'

'I've got to notify the authorities,' she went on, 'before

they turn every single soldier on your planet into a frog.'

'They weren't soldiers, they were policemen— Oh,' David said. 'I see what you mean. But they couldn't do that, could they?'

'Bet?' She laughed. 'You're forgetting,' she went on, 'when Daddy and I came here, we were able to pass ourselves off as gods for over two thousand years. And even after that, when they'd seen through us, we made everyone believe we were great and powerful sorcerers. And the frog thing's easy.'

'Really?'

'Piece of cake. And efficient, and totally non-violent, which is good. Also one hundred per cent fatal, of course, but in a non-violent way.'

David looked worried. 'Fatal? I thought you said they weren't actually turned into anything, they just believe—'

'That's right. And guess what happens to a fully grown adult human after a week of trying to live on flies he catches with his tongue. That's assuming he hasn't tried to cross any roads or railway lines in the meantime.' She laughed, though without humour. 'We have this sacred commandment,' she went on. '*You shall not kill*—'

'Mmm,' David interrupted. 'We've got that one, too. But—'

'And we're really good about obeying it,' she went on, ignoring him. 'But there's absolutely nothing in our holy books that says, *You shall force-feed people on totally unsuitable diets*, so that's all right. Where we come from, you see, we don't distinguish between – you've got a neat little phrase for it, let's see – the letter and the spirit of the law. If it's not allowed, you don't do it; if it's allowed, that's fine. So we find allowed ways of doing the things we aren't allowed to do, like killing people, and everybody's happy. We have no crime on our world, none whatsoever. And no love, of course, but I think I mentioned that already.'

At least nobody seemed to be following them; no sirens, running feet or, come to that, little spongy paws floppetting down the pavement. David racked his brains, trying to figure how to get to Ravenscourt Park on foot – he didn't have any money for the bus or the Tube, let alone a taxi, and the Philippa clone was still wearing nothing but Honest John's old shirt. If his luck was running anything like true to form, any minute now they'd run into another policeman who'd arrest them for loitering or indecent exposure. He wondered if he ought to share his concerns with her, since they now seemed to be on the same side. He felt sure it was the sensible thing to do.

'By the way—' he began.

'I don't know about you,' she interrupted, 'but I think we'll get there much faster in one of those horseless carts. And besides, I haven't got any shoes, and these stone slabs are hurting my feet. Can you work the horseless cart things?'

'Sort of – I don't have one of my own. But—'

'Fine.'

They were standing next to a green Nissan. She slid her fingertips into the slight gap between the door and the door frame. There was a sound like a giant steel whelk being scooped out of a cast-iron shell, and the door popped open. The lock mechanism was hopelessly mangled.

'Now,' she said, sliding across into the driver's seat, 'how do you make these things go?'

'You can't. Not unless you've got the key.'

'Don't need a key, the door's open.'

'No.' And to think, before this started he'd never been in any trouble of any kind. 'The key doesn't just open the door, it starts the engine.'

'Oh.' She frowned. 'Are you sure about that? Only I was studying the one we were in earlier, and it seemed to me that if you take this wire here and connect it to this one here—' The engine roared into life.

'You worked that all out from first principles?'

She shrugged. 'Not exactly difficult,' she replied. 'Once you've figured that the power source is a series of controlled explosions, and that logically the ignition system must involve some form of electrical discharge'

'Move over,' he said quietly. 'I need to sit here if I'm going to drive.'

She shook her head. 'It's all right,' she said, 'I think I've figured that out, too. This wheel steers, these pedals are the stop and the go, and this one – I'm guessing, but does it operate some kind of power-transmission ratio-interchange device, when used in connection with this stick with a knob on the top?'

'Fine,' David said. 'You can drive.'

'If you like,' she replied, throwing the car into reverse and backing hard into a parked Sierra. 'Not very robust, these things, are they?'

It was an interesting journey, but nobody died, and they got there eventually. 'This is it,' she said, stamping on the brake and stalling in the middle of the road. 'I can see the sign, look.'

David, who'd spent the whole trip struggling to hold the mangled door shut, opened his eyes. 'You've got a very good sense of direction,' he said.

'Yes,' she replied. 'Well, don't just sit there. We've got work to do.'

As he was climbing out of the car, something small and green moved abruptly, right on the edge of his field of vision. He shuddered, and made a conscious effort to ignore it. 'Maybe we should stay here for a minute or two and watch,' he suggested, 'just in case there's someone in there.'

'Don't be so feeble,' she replied. 'We haven't got time for playing silly games. Are you coming or not?'

Another green shape jumped over his left foot, followed by another one, and another. In fact, there were little green shapes everywhere. For some reason, the phrase 'police frogmen' drifted into his mind, and he grinned crazily. 'Coming,' he said.

The doors were, conveniently, open; after the bad clones' forced entry, it was improbable that they'd ever close again. Inside, the floor was covered with frogs—

'It's probably not as bad as it looks,' she said. 'Think about it.'

'I don't want to think about it, thanks very much. Quite the opposite, in fact.'

'All right, then, just keep quiet and watch. Look, there on the bench.'

She pointed at the row of goo-tanks (her birthplace; if she got famous in years to come, would they hang a little blue plaque over it?) as a small green frog who'd been sitting on the edge of the workbench suddenly flexed its hind legs and jumped neatly into the tank. There was a glopping noise—

'There's the commercial aspect to consider,' she said thoughtfully. 'Tell me, has traditional French cuisine changed a lot over the last four hundred years?'

'No! I mean,' David amended, 'yes. Radically. They're all vegetarians now.'

She raised an eyebrow. 'Vegetarian?'

'Somebody who only eats vegetables.'

'Ah.' She nodded. 'We used to call them "poor people" in my day, but—'

David wished he hadn't started this particular thread. 'Actually,' he said, 'it's mostly people who don't want to eat meat. You know, on ethical grounds.'

'Really? Oh well. So if a vegetarian's someone who only eats vegetables, a humanitarian—'

'Let's go and make sure your machine's working all right, shall we?'

He picked his way carefully through the frogs, trying very hard to bear in mind that each and any of them could be a six-foot, fifteen-stone policeman who *thought* he was a frog, to the door he remembered going through before. It was open, too, which was just as well – the girl could probably open it easily enough, but he wasn't sure his nerves could stand very much more of that sort of thing. Carefully shooing away a cluster of frogs (or policemen) he pulled back the door and poked his head round.

The room was empty.

No, not quite empty. All the machines, consoles and other impressive-looking clutter had gone, but in the very centre of the room there was a bag of sugar.

CHAPTER ELEVEN

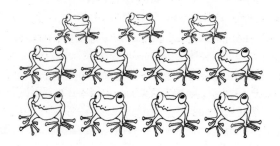

'Would it be all right,' David asked, 'if I burst into tears at this point?'

She was only a few steps behind him. 'Now what's the matter?' she was saying. 'God, you don't half make a fuss.'

He moved aside to let her past.

'Right,' she said, 'I suppose I'd better be getting along.' She hesitated, and frowned, as if making up her mind about something. 'Thanks,' she said. 'For your help, I mean. At least, you didn't *help*, exactly, but I suppose if it wasn't for you I wouldn't be here. Anyway, you turned out to be quite useful in the long run, even if it was by accident. So – well, thanks.'

'Don't mention it.'

She licked her right forefinger and dipped it into the sugar. 'Well,' she said, 'I guess you should leave now. I know I said a lot of stuff about you going to our planet, but I wasn't thinking straight at the time. I wouldn't go there if I were you. They aren't very keen on – well, strangers. At least, not *your* kind of—' She tailed off, sounding rather unhappy. 'Please go away,' she said.

'Oh.' He hadn't expected that. 'But your spaceship.'

'How many times have I got to tell you, it isn't a spaceship, it's a—'

'Whatever the bloody hell it is.' The vehemence of his own words surprised him; he wasn't used to shouting at people, and he was rather pleased to discover that he was actually rather good at it. 'It isn't there any more. It's gone.'

She looked at him. 'No, it hasn't,' she said.

'But . . .' He looked back at her, with fifteen per cent extra, absolutely free. 'All right, then,' he said. 'Where's all the stuff gone? The computers and machines and stuff? It was absolutely jam-packed with them—'

'What? Oh.' And she giggled. He didn't know she could do that. 'Oh, none of that was real,' she said. 'It was, you know, like the frogs.'

He frowned, puzzled. 'Recycled policemen?'

'Optical illusions. Things you thought you could see, but they weren't actually there. I forgot all about it till you mentioned it; standard operating procedure when we let primitives—' She stopped and pretended she hadn't just said the p-word. 'When we let evolutionarily challenged life forms on board our transport platforms. We make them see what they expect to see. It keeps them happy, and it reduces the risk of them figuring out how our technology works.'

'Ah. Fine.' David looked round. 'So that's your technology, is it? A pound of Silver Spoon granulated?'

She shook her head. 'No, silly, that's a bag of sugar.

We always like to suck something sweet during take-off. It helps with the spacesickness.'

'But there's nothing else here!'

'Ah.' She smiled. 'That's what all you pr— emerging species say. And that's why we have to lay on all the imaginary clutter, to stop you panicking.'

He frowned. If this was drivel, at least it was internally consistent drivel, which put it a couple of notches above ninety per cent of what you heard on the television news. 'So what makes it go?' he asked. 'Or are you trying to tell me there's a bloody great big hook screwed into the other side of the ceiling, with a steel cable and a winch?'

'Same principle, actually.' She sounded impressed. 'Slightly more advanced hardware, but the same basic idea. To be honest, I wouldn't have expected you to be able to grasp that.'

'Thank you so much.' He was starting to get very annoyed, to the point where annoyance turned to anger, but it wasn't simply because she was being insufferably patronising about his species. Something else, something major was bothering him, but one part of his mind wouldn't tell the rest what it was. 'Well,' he said, 'you'd better start it up, then.'

'I will. As soon as you get off.'

'No.'

Awkward silence. 'All right,' she said eventually, 'why not?'

'I don't know.' It wasn't the answer he'd intended to give, but for what it was worth, it was true. 'I don't want to stay here,' he ventured. 'Not after what you, well, the other you and your father did to me. And while we're on the subject,' he added, 'why exactly was it necessary to frame me for murder?'

She shrugged. 'Search me,' she said. 'Must've been a reason, I suppose, but I can't remember what it was. But you know that parts of my memory got jumbled. Because you didn't do the resequencing,' she added.

'Must've been a reason,' he repeated. 'Fine. Do you think it might have been to give me an incentive to go along with being shipped off out of the way? Sound plausible?'

'Yes,' she replied. 'Sounds the sort of thing Daddy would've come up with. Attention to detail, and all that.'

'Quite.' He nodded. 'But you're forgetting. The original plan was to ship me back to your rotten planet. That's how I got here in the first place – you know, when there were all those imaginary computers and things in here, and you lot tried to make me think I'd been abducted by frogs.'

She shrugged. 'I can't really help you there,' she said. 'Like I told you, some of it's missing.'

'The point is—' he was almost shouting '—the point is, your precious father was sending me to your precious planet. So why don't you want me going there?'

'You wouldn't like it. And they wouldn't like you. Two good reasons.'

'But not the real reason.'

'All right, it's not the real reason. Now get off my transporter platform, before I throw you off.'

He shook his head. 'No,' he said. And the next thing he saw was the concrete floor, just visible in the gaps between frogs, rushing up to meet him.

David had a dream. In the dream he was Gulliver, lying on his back pegged to the ground by Lilliputians, and there were scores of one-tenth scale policemen in green uniforms bouncing up and down on his chest, snaring passing gnats with their long prehensile tongues.

Fortunately for his peace of mind, the entire dream melted away like a snowman as soon as he opened his eyes again, and saw that he was sprawled on the floor of Honest John's workshop, hemmed in on all sides by a whole lot of frogs. Loads of frogs. An entire green ocean of them.

At another time, under different circumstances, he'd have been seriously freaked out by that. As it was, he found he could take them in his stride, or more accurately in his hop. In fact, he managed to cross the floor as far as the doorway leading to the transporter pad without treading on a single frog, but it was more luck than judgement. Typical, of course; if he'd been worrying himself sick about hurting helpless amphibians and taking special care, he'd probably have flattened half a dozen out of sheer nervous fecklessness.

He pulled open the door. The room was empty, apart from that damned bag of sugar.

She'd gone.

He leaned against the door frame, trying to think. Things were bad, very bad; on top of all his other problems (which he was coping with by ignoring them, the way he dealt with most utility bills and the ruder letters from his bank) it looked like he'd just lost the only girl he'd ever really loved, or at least the only girl he'd ever really loved, version 1.1. For some reason, this seemed to matter more to him than the complete and utter demolition of his life – probably because he hadn't managed to make himself believe in it yet, but never mind. Actually, it felt rather good to be able to say that the greatest sorrow afflicting him was a broken heart, as opposed to, say, a broken thermostat or a crashed hard drive, as would have been the case under normal circumstances . . .

Besides: you don't discover something utterly earth-shattering, like proof of life on other worlds, and then calmly put it out of your mind and go back to fretting about your everyday mundane inconveniences, such as being wanted for murder. You stick with it, press on till you've uncovered the Truth That's Out There – and once you've done that, presumably, the screen flashes 'Game Over' and the reset button solves all the problems you've caused for yourself along the way.

Nothing for it; he'd have to go after her. To Homeworld, or whatever the wretched place was called. That in turn meant figuring out how to work the transport device (and him not even able to replace a broken fuse). Well, he'd faced greater challenges before. He'd installed Windows 2000 without consulting the manual; more impressive still, he'd installed Windows 2000 *with* the assistance of the manual, an achievement comparable to rebuilding a Spitfire engine by following the procedures set out in the Haynes Guide for an Me109.

David walked into the room and shut the door.

It had to have a start button, even if it was nothing more than a glorified lift. The question was, where?

First, start by eliminating the humiliatingly obvious. He picked up the bag of sugar and looked under it. No button.

Next, he inspected every square inch he could reach for signs of hidden panels, concealed monitors or consoles made out of totally transparent plastic. Nothing.

If all else fails, click on 'Help'. 'Help!' he said.

Zzzxt'prt. Sfhds gdsgf qcshxzc. Either the strange noises

inside his head were words, or at some stage he'd swallowed a diehard bee. *Please wait while Wormholes prepares HelpMage to guide you through your enquiry.*

David bit his lip. Getting somewhere, maybe, but he had a bad feeling about this. Meanwhile, the bag of sugar had raised itself eighteen inches off the floor and was pouring sugar into a neat cone, ten inches high. When the bag was empty, it miraculously refilled itself and started all over again.

Definitely a bad feeling.

HelpMage complete. Showing index. Indicate the entry you want, or state search topic.

Now the spilled sugar was rising into the air like sand caught in a whirlwind; swirling a couple of times, then forming itself into shapes that were quite definitely letters, though of course he couldn't read them, not being fluent in Homeworldese. That only left *State topic*, and he knew all about that—

'Um,' he said, 'how about a translation?'

Go to Settings and select language required.

'Fine. How do I go to Settings?'

Go to Start Menu.

'Wonderful. How do I go to Start menu?'

Initiate Start menu sequence.

'Bugger.'

Do you want to initiate Start Menu?

'Yes, please.'

The floating sugar-shapes vanished suddenly, and were replaced by others, equally incomprehensible.

'How do I translate the Start Menu?'

Go to Settings and select language required.

In a way, it was almost reassuring, like coming home after a long journey; the only real difference between this system and the ones he was used to dealing with was that there wasn't anything he could hit, apart from the bag of sugar. Nevertheless; if the people who'd built this thing had managed to leave their planet and head out into the stars, surely it stood to reason that their technology was just a bit more advanced . . . Well, it was worth a try.

'How do I make this thing go to Homeworld?'

Select Operations Menu and indicate Go.

David thought for a moment. 'How do I indicate select the Operations Menu without,' he added quickly, 'using the Start Menu?'

Say 'Select Operations Menu'.

'This is too easy. All right, select Operations Menu.'

Operations Menu selected.

'OK.' He closed his eyes. 'How do I indicate Go?'

Say Go.

'Go.'

That function is not available. You have performed an illegal action—

The bag of sugar hit the floor and exploded, showering him with tiny white crystals. Instinctively he dived towards the doorway and pulled the door open. Only then did he pause.

'Why isn't that function available?'

Device is currently in use. Device will be available for use in 42.774 standard Earth rotational cycles. You have perf—

He jumped through the door and slammed it behind him. A frog hopped on to his foot and tried to jump up his trouser leg. As he bent down to shoo it away, there was a deafening crash just beyond the door, and painfully bright light flooded out through the keyhole.

Just for fun, he tried the door handle (quite gently; he

didn't actually want to open the damn thing). It was stuck, and neglected-saucepan-handle hot. He let go quickly. That, apparently, was that. She'd gone, and taken interstellar travel with her, and left him behind to face a bewildering array of versions of the one-eyed man and the majestic wrath of the law.

Bitch, David thought, but the word wouldn't take in his mind. He wasn't sure why, but he knew she'd left him behind for his own good, or what she perceived as his own good. Probably, deep down, she'd quite liked him. A bit.

Yeah, right.

Not, he decided, that any of that mattered any more, since she'd gone and wasn't coming back until he was either dead or the oldest lag in B wing. 42.774 years, and that was when the lift was working normally. These aliens, he decided, might just be the only sentient beings in the galaxy who could ride on the Bakerloo Line with anything resembling equanimity.

So, now what?

He slumped against the wall and stood for a while, counting frogs in an aimless fashion. Really, if he was going to be sensible about this, the only thing that he could do would be to find that nice man with the missing eye, apologise properly and ask if he could still take him up on his kind offer of a fresh start in beautiful rural Canada. The moral indignation that had put him off that idea originally had evaporated somewhat, ever since he'd caught himself doing exactly the sort of thing they'd been doing to him (only much quicker and far, far less efficiently); and, as befitted a soppy young man who'd just lost The Only Girl in the World (or rather Worlds, plural), he was at that I-don't-really-mind-what-happens-now-so-long-as-I-can-droop-about-sighing phase, and going to British Columbia would probably involve far less effort than living off his wits while evading the combined resources of the State.

So, that's what I'll do. The next question, of course, was how to find the nice one-eyed man. Awkward – but the girl, Philippa Levens #1, would probably know, and he'd be sure to find her at Alex's flat—

Bloody hellfire, he thought.

—Because, of course, the Bad Clones had been to Alex's flat and come out again looking all baffled, since they'd found nothing there but bare walls and a bag of sugar.

'Excuse me,' David said instinctively as he hurried towards the door. Disturbingly, at least some of the frogs got out of the way; but he didn't stop to think about that.

The car she'd stolen was still there. He started it up and drove as quietly and sedately as he could – bloody silly to get done for speeding at a time like this – until he recognised the familiar symptoms of getting lost in west London late at night (primarily, crossing Hammersmith Bridge for the second time, but on this occasion from the other direction). He emptied his mind, trying to think of woodland flowers and village cricket matches and cows being herded down a narrow country lane, and duly found himself outside Alex's flat without really knowing how he'd got there. Amazing, the way it always seemed to work.

As he put the handbrake on, he tried to remember what if any indictable mayhem the Bad Clones had committed last time he'd been there. Tricky: so much had happened that he was running out of RAM to store it in.

He seemed to remember a policeman, and a frog, but nothing that made the area inherently dangerous. Nevertheless, he exercised extreme caution when getting out of the car and approaching Alex's door. Fortunately, nobody could've been watching, since David being deliberately cautious was probably the most sinister and furtive-looking spectacle anybody could ever hope to see.

Now what? Do I ring the bell and wait, or do I break the door down, or what? And how exactly do you break down a door? They stopped using their shoulders in films around the time Technicolor first came in, so presumably it's best if you kick. But where? You could hurt yourself, kicking a big, solid door.

Then he noticed that the door was slightly open, which solved that one. Closer inspection revealed substantial damage to the wood around the lock, presumably caused by thirteen vengeful clones in a hurry. He pushed it with his fingertips until he could squeeze through, and started up the darkened stairs. Luckily, he'd only gone a few steps when the light clicked on, because the shock made him jump and nearly fall over.

'Ah,' said a familiar voice, proceeding from a familiar face, 'there you are. We were wondering where on earth you'd got to.'

David studied him like a cat inspecting another cat across a narrow lawn. 'Do I know you?' he asked.

'Don't be silly,' the man replied. 'We were talking to each other just this afternoon. I was telling you about – well, everything, really, and how we've fixed up a nice new life for you in—'

'British Columbia, yes. So you're him.'

He nodded. 'And then, when we came to give you a lift to the helicopter pad, you'd wandered off somewhere and we couldn't find you. But not to worry, you're here now. And we can sort out some new arrangements for getting you safely away.'

'Wonderful,' David said—

Well, it was. That was why he'd come here, to claim his free prize and his Blankety-Blank chequebook and pen for being a good sport. So why did he feel like his ears should be pressed back against the sides of his skull?

'In fact,' the man went on, 'this is pretty damn convenient, all things considered, because we can actually send you on your way from here, without having to go trekking about the countryside. Just follow me – well, of course, you know the way, don't you?'

David stayed precisely where he was. 'From here?' he repeated, thinking of the bag of sugar.

'Yes, that's right. Bit of a long story to go into, standing on the stairs like this. Let's go up to the flat and talk about it there.'

'No, thanks. I like discussing things on stairs, it reminds me of when I was at college. Are you sure I'll be going to British Columbia?'

The man looked at him with a disturbingly neutral expression. 'What a very strange question,' he said. 'Why, where else were you thinking of? Is there somewhere else you'd rather go?'

David nodded. 'I think so,' he said. 'I think I'd like to go somewhere where I don't keep meeting people who look like you. No offence,' he added, 'but you do seem to make things happen, and I really hate that.'

'Don't be such an old fusspot,' the man replied icily. 'And anyway, wherever you go, you'll need money and documents and all sorts of things like that. We've got everything you'll need waiting for you, upstairs. Just come with me, and everything'll be just fine.'

'No.'

The man was looking at him. He knew that look; it was the old you-don't-want-me-to-have-to-tell-your-father-when-he-gets-home look, the one that's supposed to pin you to the wall like a butterfly. For the first time in his life, it didn't seem to be working.

'No,' he repeated. 'Thanks all the same. If you like, I'll wait here while you just nip up and fetch the stuff. That'd be really kind.'

The man shook his head. 'Don't be so lazy,' he said. 'You've got younger legs than me. Come upstairs.'

David took a deep breath. 'I know what you're up to,' he said. 'I know all about the plain white rooms and the bags of sugar. You're going to send me back to your planet, the one you call Homeworld; and I don't know exactly why you want to do that, but I do know that if you want me to go there, I'm not going.'

The man raised an eyebrow. 'Other planets,' he said. 'Bags of sugar. The other part, the bit about plain white rooms, could well be drawn from recent experience, the way you're talking. Plain white rooms with soft walls, maybe.'

David shook his head. 'Nice try,' he said, 'won't wash. She told me all about it – you know, the girl . . .' He stopped short; of course, this one wouldn't know anything about *his* Philippa Levens replica; nor was it desirable that he should.

He looked at the man, trying to keep the panic out of his face. By the man's expression, he gathered that he'd failed.

'I take it you're referring to the flat above yours,' the man was saying, 'the one I took you up to, when you wanted to borrow some sugar, yes? Nothing sinister about that, I assure you. I think I explained about all that at the time. Didn't I?'

'Did you?' Damnation, he'd forgotten all about that one. In any event, he'd made yet another mistake and made the wretched man extremely suspicious. Time, he felt, to start running away as fast as possible. 'Oh, yes, that's right,' he said, backing down the stairs. 'Sorry, I don't know what could've come over me just then. I really don't rivet rivet rivet—'

CHAPTER TWELVE

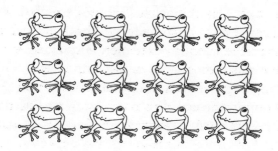

Not rivet, David shouted to himself, as he hung in mid-air above the stairs, not rivet, not rivet. I am not an amphibian, I am a free man—

Out of the corner of his eye, he caught sight of a gnat. His tongue was out and back in his mouth before he even knew what he'd done. Fly; yummy! I mean, yetch.

He tried to jam a wedge under the door of his mind. I know I'm not a frog. I know that they can't really turn people into frogs, they can just make people think people are frogs. I am not a frog. I think, therefore I am not a frog. I think, therefore I don't think I'm a frog. I think, therefore I think I'm not a frog, but so what, there're people out there who think they're Napoleon. I think rivet rivet.

'Here we are,' said a voice far above his head, a voice that was somehow connected to the unbearable heat of the prehensile pink platform he was slumped on. 'In you go, there you are. Nice bowl. Nice water.'

Nice water. Not nice water. Can a human being drown in three inches of water? How the hell can I fit inside this football-sized glass bowl? I can't. I can't, therefore I am a frog. I am not a frog, I'm a person thinking he can fit inside a football-sized glass bowl. This is awful. Is this what they call existential angst? God, I could do with another fly. That's midges for you; eat one and ten seconds later you're hungry again.

There was a rock to sit on, and an interestingly tangled sprig of pondweed, and water to submerge himself in right up to the tip of his nose. It was the earthly paradise; even British Columbia couldn't be a patch on this. And of course it meant the police would never be able to find him, since they weren't looking for a frog. Go on, hissed the tempter in his inner ear, just for once, do the sensible thing. Show some gratitude. Be the frog.

It was almost impossible to figure out what was going on outside the bowl. For one thing, the scale was overwhelming; for another, the optical qualities of the water and the bowl itself meant that he was in the mother of all halls of mirrors. He had no neck to crane, and his eyes were working differently, as well as being where his ears should be.

Not that it matters a damn, whispered the tempter, to a frog. A frog's brain can unscramble all these garbled visual signals. You want to see what's going on? Be the frog.

Sure, he could be the frog; and if he did that, what he saw wouldn't bother him, and he'd probably get to live happily ever after, the term 'ever' in this context being construed in amphibian terms and meaning 'for at least five seconds'. Well, it was a life. From what he could gather, it was better than working for local government.

He reached a decision.

Another difference between frogs and people, aside from the position of the eyes, is the power of the legs. Of course, since he wasn't really a frog he couldn't instinctively calculate the vast array of variables of velocity and trajectory needed to plot an accurate flight plan, so he'd probably end up either overshooting or crashing into the rim of the bowl. Odds against a perfect and accurate landing: pretty damn vast.

He jumped.

—And landed exactly where he'd been figuring to land; landed what was more, without any jarring or slewing, his balance perfect, his legs already cocked for the next jump. Now that was scary.

The voice above him thundered. More scary; it was getting so the words were blurry and indistinct, and he couldn't seem to remember what the few he could make out actually meant. Rivet, he admitted sourly to himself. Rivet rivet rivet, and even if I managed it, rivet riv— Bugger me, I'm starting to think in frog language now. Didn't I read somewhere that once you start thinking in a foreign language, next thing you know, you've become foreign yourself—

The giant pink platform had become a giant five-tined pink scoop, and it was searching for him, relentlessly. It knew where he was, it was only a matter of—

OK, he said to himself, I'm a frog. But I'm a highly imaginative frog. In fact, I'm so imaginative there's probably something wrong with me; always daydreaming, mooning about the lily pad all day, reading frog science fiction, a frog anorak, a frog geek, a freak – I'm so imaginative (desperate hop to avoid the clasp of the killer pink scoop) I'm so imaginative, I can imagine just what it's like to be a human being, about five eight, right arm about two foot four inches long, a human being punching another human being very hard on the nose—

He imagined doing that, vividly; and a moment later, his nearside front forepaw hurt like hell, the thundering voice above him was yelling in pain, and the pink scoop had gone away. Good frog, he thought, clever frog. Now get the hell out of here before—

Instinctively he skittered sharp left, narrowly avoiding a falling black mountain (not a mountain, it's some guy's boot; in my imagination, of course) and hopped as hard as he could for the nearest cover. In fact, it was the only cover in sight; a squat white pillar with blue markings on the face. Either he misjudged the jump through stress, or he wasn't really a frog; he cannoned into the pillar and it fell over, scattering small, sharp-edged white boulders in every direction.

The voice overhead roared some more; as far as he could tell, not being human himself, the burden of the voice had shifted from pain to a mixture of anger and fear – apparently connected to the white column falling over. In any event, the pink scoop was busy lifting up the pillar and trying to sweep up the small white boulders. A good time for a sensible frog to be hopping along.

Hop, hop, hop. Of course, he hadn't a clue where he was headed, or which direction was most likely to lead to safety. He had a vague memory of being on a staircase, but that related back to before he was a frog. What's a staircase, anyhow? Can you eat it?

The black mountain crashed down again, missing him by less than a paw's breadth (but his superior frog reflexes got him out of trouble once again; that's the joy of being small, you're fast. Who'd be a human, huh?)

and he accelerated, heading for a black gap in the whiteness of the horizon. But a noise like the world ending made the floor shake under him, and the gap vanished. He altered course quickly and hurried back the way he'd just come. Every five hops or so the black mountain tried to fall on him, but he didn't have much difficulty in staying clear of it; a mountain is, after all, a clumsy and inefficient weapon to use against a fast, highly manoeuvrable opponent. The word stalemate (or, to be precise, the word *rivet*, in one of its myriad nuances) floated into his mind; he couldn't escape, the human couldn't catch him, it'd come down to who tired out or died first. Hardly an ideal situation, but probably better than holding still.

'All right.' Quite suddenly, the thunder had resolved itself into words; and he wasn't a frog any more, he was a human being, kneeling on the floor with his bum stuck up in the air. 'All right,' the voice repeated, 'that'll do. Be human, see if I care.'

He jumped up (sudden dramatic loss of power to hind legs; he nearly fell over, but fortunately he was close enough to the wall to be able to flop against it and push himself upright) and looked at where the voice was coming from. He saw a human (smaller than he'd expected) with one missing eye and a nosebleed. He was wearing black shoes.

'You bastard,' David said. 'You were trying to kill me.'

'Nonsense.'

'You bloody well were. You were trying to tread on me.'

'I was not. I was just trying to catch you and get you back in your nice bowl, before you did yourself an injury.'

'I don't believe you,' David said.

The man wilted a little. 'All right,' he said, 'I lost my temper, I'm sorry. But you'd just knocked over the navigational computer, and you wouldn't keep still—' He shook his head. 'It was wrong of me, I admit it. I apologise. What more can I say?'

He was, of course, standing between David and the door. 'How about, "You can go now"?'

The man shook his head. 'You don't want to do that,' he said. 'It's dangerous for you out there. Besides, you want to go to British Columbia.' A drop of blood rolled down his chin. 'We agreed, remember?'

That was before you tried to reduce me to two dimensions. 'I've changed my mind,' David said. 'Anyway, I don't think you were ever going to send me there. I think you want to get me into your bloody space-lift and ship me back to your planet.'

'Ah, yes.' The man's expression changed slightly. 'I was going to ask you about that. You do realise that that's all nonsense, don't you? There is no other planet. All that stuff about being abducted by aliens and carried off to the Planet of the Amphibians was just to—' He stopped, perhaps conscious of a tact failure. 'It was all just fun,' he said. 'A bit of a lark, really.'

David took three steps back, and his heel clinked against something. The goldfish bowl.

'I see,' he said. 'And that bag of sugar isn't really the – what did you call it? – navigational computer.'

'No. Yes. Look—'

David knew he wasn't a frog any more, but he still remembered how to hop. He jumped backwards, clearing the bowl and the bag of sugar, then stooped down and grabbed them both. 'I'm wondering,' he said, 'what'd happen if I poured this sugar into this water. Couldn't do any harm, could it?'

The man suddenly went as pale as a black-and-white photograph of Antarctica. 'Put them down, for God's sake,' he muttered. 'Carefully.'

'Why? What'd happen if I put—?'

'Asteroids,' the man said. 'Lots of small asteroids where this planet used to be. Look, perhaps it would be a good idea if you were to leave now.'

David thought about that. 'Yes,' he said, 'I think I'll do that. What is this stuff in the bag, anyway?'

'Sugar. Like it says on the label.'

David raised an eyebrow and tilted the bag very slightly.

'But the stuff in the bowl isn't water,' the man added quickly. 'I'd be delighted to tell you what it is, but your brain's at the wrong angle to understand. Let's just say you don't have anything like it on this planet.'

'Fine. So you dunked me in it.'

'For your own good,' the man said. 'Otherwise you'd never survive the journey. We'd get home, and we'd be hard put to it to salvage enough of you to smear on a microscope slide.' He shook his head. 'I'm afraid these elevators weren't designed with humans in mind,' he went on. 'It's a simple matter of different gravities. Imagine a ripe tomato in a hydraulic press.'

The shock was disconcerting, to say the least. True, the man could easily be lying, though there was no reason why he should lie about this. If he was telling the truth, it meant that using the elevator and going to Homeworld (following *her* to Homeworld – no, yes, dammit . . .) was out of the question, unless he agreed to become a frog once again; and he didn't really want to do that, thanks so much for the kind offer. Yet another thing to hope for, reason for living, alternative to holding still and letting the police arrest him had evaporated into a cloud of twinkly dust. He was getting sick of it.

'Well,' David said, 'thanks for the tip. I'll be moving along now.'

'Maybe not.'

'I really wish you'd make up your mind.'

The man stared at him like a wolf in the hamster department of a large pet-shop but didn't move. This was presumably something to do with the fact that David was still holding the sugar and the goldfish bowl. Mental arithmetic, starting from a total lack of hard data: if a packetful of sugar added to the stuff in the bowl was enough to turn the Earth into gravel, how much damage would just one single grain do? David didn't want to blow up the planet if he could help it, but if he was going to bluff, it'd help to make his bluff as convincing as possible.

'Put the sugar down,' the man said, 'carefully, like I said, and we can discuss this like rational sentient beings.'

At least the one-eyed man's extreme anxiety looked like it was genuine. 'Tell you what,' David said. 'I'll put these things down if you'll stand away from the door. Can't say fairer than that,' he lied.

The one-eyed man stayed where he was. 'I wish you'd just calm down and stop being so hostile,' he said. 'After all, I'm on your side, whether you believe me or not. Dammit, we're practically family.'

David thought about that for a moment. 'You're right,' he said, 'you remind me a lot of several of my relatives. That's probably why I wouldn't trust you if we were standing under Big Ben and you told me the correct time.'

'All right.' The man's sigh seemed to come up through the soles of his feet from the flat below. 'If you want to go, go. No skin off my nose if you get caught by the police; after all, they're never going to believe you, and besides, I don't think I've actually done anything they can arrest me for.' He shrugged, and stepped a yard to his left. 'Off you go, then.'

'Just like that?'

'What do you want me to do now, tie myself up and lie down in a corner? Either stay or push off, doesn't matter to me.'

'Oh.' David took a step towards the door. The man didn't move. 'Out of interest,' David said, 'what happened to Alex? And, um, her?'

The man looked down at his watch. 'Should be nearly there by now,' he said. 'Unless they get held up in the docking queue, of course.'

'They've gone to your planet? Homeworld?'

'That's right.'

'But why would they want to do that? There's no such thing as love there.'

The man nodded, and stepped back in front of the door. 'True,' he said. 'Now, how about telling me how you know that?'

Oops, David thought. 'Someone told me,' he said. 'One of you people. Truth is,' he added with a grin, 'I try to be open-minded, but you all look the same to me.'

'Very smart, yes,' the man said. 'Please answer the question.'

David shook his head. 'Here's another one for you. Alex is human, right? So how could he go to

Homeworld on this elevator thing of yours without getting squashed flat?'

The man smiled. 'You humans have a fairy tale,' he replied, 'about the beautiful princess who kisses a frog?' He shrugged. 'Seven hundred years' worth of back royalties that I don't suppose I'll ever see. Never mind, it's only money. All right,' he went on, 'they haven't gone to Homeworld. It and Earth aren't the only inhabited planets, you know. As you'd have found out,' he added, 'if only you weren't so damned bolshy.'

'Oh.' David's arms were beginning to get tired, holding the fishbowl and the sugar. 'They've gone somewhere else.'

'Yes.'

'Right. What's it like?'

The one-eyed man grinned. 'Actually,' he said, 'it's a lot like British Columbia. Only, in some important respects, better.'

'Really? Less mountains? Better climate?'

'No Canadians. It's not too late, you know,' he added. 'Think about it. If I'm prepared to send my own daughter there, it can't be all that bad, can it?'

If he'd heard it from anyone else, even from a different clone of the same original, David might well have been convinced. 'I'll pass on that, thanks,' he said, carefully putting the fishbowl down on the floor. 'But if it's all the same to you, I'll go now.' He folded over the top flap of the sugar packet, tightly, twice. 'Give Alex my regards if you ever see him again,' he added, with a very slight twinge of guilt. 'He may be a total bastard, but he's my cousin.'

'Sorry.' The man folded his arms. 'I can't let you go. You seem to have found out rather more than you were supposed to do, and it's a matter of planetary security—'

David nodded. 'I thought you'd say that,' he said. 'Catch!' he added, lobbing the packet of sugar into the air.

From the fact that there was still a world at the bottom of the stairs by the time he reached it, he deduced that the one-eyed man had indeed managed to catch the sugar in time. Not that he'd been in the slightest doubt about that, naturally. Every confidence, and so forth.

Still there, that faithful old stolen car of his. He was getting so used to it that he was able to find the wires that went together to start it entirely by feel, without having to crane his neck down to see the colours. Of course, he didn't know where he was going – all part and parcel, he guessed, of having nowhere to go.

Eventually, without ever having formed the intention of going there, he found himself parked outside Honest John's. He wasn't able to get very close to the building, for fear of running over a hundred or so of the vast army of frogs that were hoppiting about all over the pavement and the road, like the lava flow from a green-and-yellow volcano. And somebody's got to notice that, he told himself, sooner or later. Like the plague of frogs in the Bible— He chewed his lip thoughtfully, thinking over what the one-eyed man had said about a certain fairy story, and other stuff he'd heard about this being the second time they'd been through this whole procedure. What a busy fellow that man seemed to have been, to be sure.

If it'd been spiders, nothing would have persuaded him to get out of the car. But he was OK with frogs – didn't like them, but wasn't bothered by them – and found he was able to pick a way through the rivetting, shifting carpet without flinching or feeling sick. Of course, he had a pretty good idea what they must be thinking right now – looming presence, black mountains falling from the sky – and in a sense he felt a degree of empathy towards them. Mostly, though, it was like having to talk to his less attractive relatives – just because they're your own flesh and blood doesn't mean to say you've got to like them. He tried taking big steps and making shooing noises.

'Shoo yourself, asshole,' said a voice behind him.

For about half a second, he was sure he was going to lose his balance and fall over, which would've meant a nasty fall for him and the end of the line for at least a dozen frogs. Luckily, he was able to pull himself back into equilibrium by waving his hands about ferociously.

'Yeah,' said another voice. 'Go jump off a lily pad, tall bastard!'

Very cautiously, he looked over his shoulder but he couldn't see anyone. Nobody here but us frogs.

'Yeah,' said a third voice. 'Drop dead, spawn for brains.'

David took a deep breath. 'Hello?' he said.

'Screw you, scumbag with very big feet!'

Oh God, David asked of the universe at large, have I really got to do this? I can put up with most things turning out to be true, but talking frogs— 'Excuse me,' he said, 'but who am I talking to, please?'

Strange, hoarse laughter, like the creaking of five thousand floorboards. 'Guy wants to know who he's talking to,' said a voice; and try as he might, David had to face the fact that the voice came from somewhere in the bobbling carpet of frogs. Not fair, he muttered to himself, just not fair.

'Excuse me—' he began.

'No!' from the frog-mob, followed by more laughter. 'Go on, get out of here. And take your big stinking feet with you.'

Suddenly, in a moment of appalling clarity, David realised what it must be like to be a teacher teaching a class of thirteen-year-olds. Then it occurred to him that if the comparison was at all valid, he had a superb model to work from. He closed his eyes, turned back his mental clock twenty-one years and visualised Mrs Parfitt, standing in front of the blackboard. Five feet dead in her Clarks sensible shoes, and beyond question the single most terrifying life form he'd ever encountered.

'Quiet!' he snapped.

Quite suddenly the frogs stopped croaking. He had their attention.

Of course, he remembered, it hadn't been so much what Mrs Parfitt said as the way she said it. She could make *I wandered lonely as a cloud* sound like a Mafia ultimatum. 'That's better,' he continued, digging under the scar tissue of his memory for the classic Parfitt intonations. 'Now then. You. Frog. Yes, you in the front row.'

A smallish olive-green frog shuffled slightly. The rest were motionless. 'What, me? said the frog.

'What, me, *sir*,' David amended. 'Yes, you. What's your name?'

'Krdgdt, sir.'

'See me afterwards. Right, then. Somebody'd better explain what you think you're doing. Otherwise,' he added, 'I'll keep the whole lot of you in. Is that understood?'

A low, subdued rumble of 'Yes, sir' from countless

frog throats. 'Please, sir,' said a frog. 'We're here to inherit the Earth.'

All David could do was repeat the last three words.

'Yes, sir. That man promised us we could, if we were good, and got on with our evolution.'

'Ah right. And, um, have you?'

'Oh yes, sir,' said another frog somewhere in the middle. 'When we left our home planet, we were still just amoebas. We evolved on the way here.'

'I see. And how long did that take you?'

'Sixteen million years,' the frog replied. ''Course, we should've been here earlier, only we got held up.'

David had a shrewd idea of who 'that man' was. For one thing, the *modus operandi* was essentially the same; not to mention the unusual level of patience. The one-eyed man might be a nuisance and a hazard to navigation, but he didn't rush into things; the sort of man who, having decided he fancied a ham sandwich, started off with a pair of newly snared wild boar and a single grain of emmer wheat. 'That's a long time,' he said.

The frog nodded. 'Well, you see, sir, faster-than-light travel wasn't invented then. And where we come from's rather a long way away.'

There wasn't much he could do except nod, in as close a facsimile as he could manage of Mrs Parfitt's very best 'all-right-but-don't-do-it-again' manner. 'When you say inherit the Earth,' he said, 'what exactly do you mean by that?' A score of offside front paws immediately shot up. 'You, at the back there,' David selected. 'No, not you, you. Well?'

The frog in question sat up very straight, its throat bobbing in and out like a power-driven bellows. 'Please sir,' the frog said, 'the man told us, at least he told the amoebas we evolved off of, and they told their kids, and their kids told—'

'Yes, I see,' David snapped. 'What did he tell them?'

The frog thought for a moment. 'Please, sir, he said that if we were really good and hard-working and, you know, meek—'

'Meek,' repeated the other frogs. 'Meek. Meek-meek, meek-meek . . .'

'Then,' the frog went on, 'we'd get to go to a planet of our very own where there's no storks or crocodiles or great big fish with loads of teeth, and there's just tons and tons of water and miles and miles of rivers and great big ponds with really cool islands and stuff in them, and there'd be nobody to eat us or push us around or tell us what to do. Is that right, sir? Is that what it's like here?'

'In a sense,' David replied. The frog's eyes were so big and shiny and trusting that he couldn't really bring himself to go into any further details. 'Um,' he went on, 'did the man say why he was doing all this? I mean, was it just out of the kindness of his heart, or was there something he wanted you to do for him?'

The frog looked startled. 'Oh, 'course we've got to work. Everybody's got to work, or they go to the bottom of the Pond.' Judging by the expression in the frog's eyes, it seemed rather taken aback to discover that David didn't know that. 'That's why we got evolved, so's we'd be able to do the work that's ordained for us. Isn't that right, sir?'

'Quite right,' David replied, 'good answer, well done.' The frog swelled a little with pride. 'All right, you can sit down now. You, middle of the fifth row. What's the work you're supposed to do when you get here?'

Some frog who apparently assumed he was the one being addressed hung his head. 'Sorry, sir. Forgotten, sir.'

'Stay in afterwards and clean the, um, lily pads. You in the front row, tell him the answer.'

'Yes, sir.' The reply came from a small, fat, smug-looking frog with a light brown streak running down its back. 'We've got to do exactly what we're told to do once we get here, sir. Is that the right answer, sir?'

David hesitated, to the point where he was in danger of communicating uncertainty and weakness. 'That's about the strength of it,' he said. 'More or less. Of course, it's a bit more complicated than that, but we won't go into the details now. All right, you're dismissed.'

The frogs stayed exactly where they were, apart from two who hopped apprehensively towards him, stopped a few inches from his toecaps and sat there staring up at him. Creepy, to say the least.

'Well?' David snapped, edging away a little. 'What do you want?'

'Please, sir,' said one of them, 'you said to see you afterwards.'

'Oh. Right. Um, I've decided to let you off with a warning this time, but don't let it happen again. You got that?'

'Yes, sir.' They hopped back into the crowd, much to David's relief. He took a deep breath and picked his way across to the workshop doors. They were still open. What the hell, he thought, and went inside.

No frogs in the workshop, which was a definite improvement as far as he was concerned. As far as the weird things they'd told him, and the implications thereof, were concerned, he was rapidly reaching the point where he could take that kind of thing at face value and believe it, while simultaneously believing something else he'd been told by some other version of the one-eyed man or his daughter, simply because it was easier to believe than to think. The one-eyed man could turn people into frogs? No problem. Frogs are in fact *gastarbeiter* shipped in by the one-eyed man to be used as cheap labour on some unthinkably obscure secret project? Yeah, why not? No skin off his nose whether or not frogs are recycled coppers or illegal aliens or both, just so long as he didn't have to do anything about it.

He sat down on the workbench and turned his head in the direction of the door that led out back, behind which was the gadget he truly believed to be an inter-stellar lift (non-functional, needless to say; interstellar or not, the natural default state of all elevators is bust mode). Well, he told himself, here we are. No options left: no British Columbia, no escape to the alien Homeworld. There were policemen staking out his home and at least two bunches of identical clones out to catch him and do him no good at all. Not only had he lost the only girl he'd ever loved, he'd lost her in dupli-cate, like some heartbroken but highly efficient civil servant. He hadn't slept for what seemed like a very long time, and he was seriously hungry. He couldn't help remembering that in prison they feed you and let you snatch a few hours' sleep now and then.

Indeed. Logic dictates that when getting caught is better in pretty well every respect than carrying on run-ning, the very least a sensible person can do is slow down a little.

He looked round. If he'd had the energy, he could

have cooked up a nice little theory about how having briefly been a frog himself had left him with the ability to speak their language. (Of course, he hadn't actually been a frog, just a human being intermittently convinced he was a frog; in that case, shouldn't he only be able to manage pidgin frog?) Another line of enquiry he could've followed up: maybe some of the frogs out here were froggified peelers, and the rest were strange visitors from the planet of the duckpond-divers. And of course there was always the question of whether people who believed they were frogs reverted to their human shape when they died, or whether they'd carry on being rani-form for ever and ever. All fascinating stuff; and when the day came when humans and aliens were able to live together and get along with each other, somebody was going to be able to stiff the worlds' universities for enough research funding to last a lifetime.

David stood up—

(Do what they're told, yes, but what on earth could frogs do that'd justify bringing them all this way, taking millions of years? Why frogs, for crying out loud?)

—And wandered over to the bank of goo tanks against the wall. The glare of the strip lights overhead silvered the meniscus of the glop like the back of a mirror, and in it he could see his face . . .

Another him, identical in every superficial respect; but not him, not him at all. Slowly he reached up and teased out a single hair from the top of his head.

Well, it would solve one fairly major problem; it would give the police someone to arrest. If he remembered how these things worked, there'd be plenty of time to fish his alter ego out and tie him up securely before he woke up for the first time. Then all it'd take would be one anonymous phone call; he could be miles away before the squad cars arrived. Of course, the clone would go to prison for something he hadn't done, it'd be monstrously unfair, but if there was a terrible injustice wandering about looking for someone to happen to, that wasn't his fault; effectively, it would be self-defence. Well, no, of course it wouldn't be, but it was the only chance of wriggling off the hook that he was likely to get. He looked at the hair: you or me, he thought, and I haven't done anything wrong, so why should it be me? Whereupon the hair seemed to look back at him, as if to say that he hadn't done anything wrong *yet*.

David sighed. It'd be so easy to let go, watch the little brown wire flop onto the green goo like a hair from a paintbrush. His decision; for once in his life, he had a genuine choice.

No, he decided, I can't. I couldn't live with myself. Either of me.

And that was the moment when someone slapped him cheerfully and hard between the shoulder blades, making him let go of the hair.

CHAPTER THIRTEEN

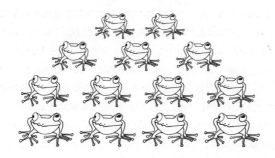

The hair seemed to take a very long time to fall.

'Hello there,' said a voice in his ear. 'What the bloody hell are you doing here?'

David recognised the voice, and the minute part of him that wasn't busy watching the hair fall riffled through the necessary card indices and identified it as Honest John's. The hair landed.

'Fuck,' David said.

'What's the matter with you?' asked Honest John. 'Lost a contact lens, or something?'

'Something like that.'

John laughed. 'Just as well it didn't go in the tank, then,' he said. 'Otherwise—' He stopped. 'It went in the tank.'

'Yes.'

'Fuck.' John sighed. 'By the way,' he added, 'are those your frogs out there?'

'What? Oh, no, they're nothing to do with me. At

least, I don't think so.' He turned round. 'What do you mean, my frogs? I thought they were yours.'

John frowned. 'What the hell would I want with a thousand frogs?' he asked.

'But—' David bit off the question. Right now, frogs weren't the issue. In fact, things had gone way, way beyond frogs. 'One of my hairs just fell in the goo,' he said. 'Can we stop it?'

'From growing, you mean?' John shrugged. ''Course we can. Just flip the mains switch, that's that. Of course,' he added, 'it'd be murder. If you look at it that way, I mean.'

'Murder?'

John nodded. 'Maybe not in law,' he said, 'it's what you might call a grey area. And it wouldn't bother me, I couldn't give a toss. *You* might, though.'

'You're right, I probably would.' David closed his eyes. 'The bloody stupid, *annoying* thing is, I came this close to putting the damn hair in there on purpose. It'd get me out of a hole, you see, it'd be really convenient not to have to go to jail for the rest of my life. But I decided not to.'

'Ah, well, then,' John said. 'Maybe you were meant to drop that hair in that tank after all. Makes you think, really.'

'Actually, thinking's never been a problem as far as I'm concerned. It's the not thinking that gives me trouble.' He looked away from the tank. 'What are you doing here?'

'Me?' John laughed. 'I'm getting as much of my kit out of here as I can before the next load of coppers shows up, that's what. It's extremely expensive, delicate equipment, this is. I can't afford to go buying it all again.'

David pursed his lips. 'John, can I ask you a question?'

'You just did.'

'All right, can I ask you a different question? Like, what's behind that door back there?'

John raised an eyebrow. 'Nothing,' he said.

'Nothing?'

'Nothing,' John replied. 'Oh, except for a bag of sugar.'

'Bag of sugar.'

'That's right. I like two in tea and three in coffee. Why?'

David looked closely at John's one remaining eye. 'Just a bag of sugar, nothing else,' he said. 'Nothing like, say, an interstellar elevator or anything like that?'

'What's an interstellar elevator when it's at home?'

David nodded, very slowly. 'All right,' he said. 'Where are you from, originally?'

John did a mild double take. 'Basildon,' he said. 'What about it?'

'Nothing.' David took a deep breath, and let it out slowly. 'So, have you got somewhere to take all this stuff?'

'Sure,' John said. 'I got a unit on an estate up Watford way.'

'Watford.' David thought for a moment. 'That's quite a way from here, isn't it?'

'Doesn't take long on the motorway.'

'Yes, but it's not *close*.' David smiled. 'Do you need a hand shifting the stuff?' he asked.

'Wouldn't mind.'

'Fine. So, what's first?'

The cloning equipment was heavier than it looked,

but with two of them on the job it only took a couple of hours. For some reason, the frogs kept well back as they carried things out to the van; they stood in rows, like kids at school assembly, and made soft rumbling noises. Eventually, there was nothing left in the workshop except one glowing tank.

'So what do you want to do?' John asked.

'Don't ask me,' David replied. 'It's your tank.'

'Yeah, but it's your clone.'

David shook his head. 'No,' he replied. 'He'll be his own clone, when he wakes up. Poor bastard,' he added with feeling. 'Right. Before we go—'

'Oh,' John said. 'You're coming too, then?'

'Well, you'll need someone to help you unload, won't you?'

'It'd be a help,' John admitted.

'There you are, then. But first,' David said, 'I'd just like to use your phone. Quick call,' he added.

'Help yourself,' John told him. 'I'll wait in the van.'

David dialled 999. 'Police,' he said. He rang off when they asked for his name.

'All done?' John asked him, as he slammed the van door shut.

'All done,' David replied. 'You know, it's a funny thing, but I've never been to Watford.'

John started the engine. 'Haven't missed much.'

'Maybe not. But I'm sure it's better than, say, British Columbia.'

'That's in Canada, isn't it?'

David looked out of the side window. 'I believe so,' he replied. 'Though I've heard different.'

'I think it's in Canada,' John replied. 'Dunno. I always liked the sound of Canada, myself. Pretty sure it's got to be better than Watford. But then, all depends on what you want out of life, doesn't it?'

As they waited at a T-junction, they saw a fleet of police cars with their sirens blazing, going in the direction they'd just come from. 'Bloody hell,' John said. 'Just as well we got out of there when we did.'

'Isn't it?'

David fell asleep shortly after the Hillingdon roundabout. He was woken up by the sound of a door slamming. It was dark outside. He wound down his window. 'Are we here?' he asked.

'Yup. You go round the back, I'm just opening the doors.'

Light flared up on the other side of the windscreen, revealing an empty building with whitewashed walls. David grunted and got out of the van. It took rather less time and effort to unload the gear than it had to cram it all in.

'Good job,' John said. 'Right, I think we've earned a cup of tea.'

David nodded. 'Thanks.'

''S all right. Got the kettle,' John went on, 'and tea bags, should be a tin of powdered milk somewhere. No sugar, though, must've left it behind, sorry.'

David lifted his head. 'You're sure about that?' he asked.

'Yeah. Might be some of them sweetener things in that small tea chest.'

'You're sure,' David asked, 'that there wasn't another bag of sugar here when we arrived?'

'Didn't see one.'

'Ah.' David breathed a long sigh. 'It's all right,' he said. 'I'm trying to cut down on sugar. It can be really bad for you, I'm told.'

'Yeah, well, they say that about everything, don't they?'

Honest John made the tea. It came out dark and strong and fairly horrible, with just a faint savour of cloning goo. It was the first cup of tea David had had in a very long time. He enjoyed it. 'Want a biscuit?' John asked.

'Yes.'

John rootled about in one of the tea chests and produced an elderly packet of digestives. They were soft and chipped and crumbly. David ate them all.

'Excuse me if this is a bad thing to ask,' David said eventually, his mouth still full of mashed crumbs, 'and please just say no if you like, but would there happen to be any jobs going around here?'

Honest John looked at him. 'Around here?'

'In Watford. In the cloning industry.'

John shrugged. 'Could be,' he said. 'You think you know someone who'd be interested?'

'Yes. Me.'

'You?' John scratched the back of his head. 'But I thought you'd got a job,' he said.

'Not any more,' David replied.

John nodded thoughtfully. 'It's a long way to come each morning, though, from where you live to here.'

'I don't live there any more,' David replied. 'In fact, I was wondering if you'd mind if I sort of camped out here for the night. If that's no trouble, I mean.'

Suddenly, John laughed. 'I think I know what's going on,' he said. 'That bird I done for you; the snotty one, with the big—'

'I know who you mean.'

John nodded again. 'Your wife found out what you've

been up to, and now she's slung you out on your ear. Something like that, is it?'

'Something like that,' David replied.

'Serves you right,' John said, but not entirely uncharitably. 'You ought to have thought about that before you started cloning birds all over the shop. Always ends in tears, that kind of caper. Still,' he continued, wiping his mouth on the back of his hand, 'that's none of my business, what you get up to. So what makes you think you'd be any good to me?'

David looked at him. 'Oh, it's just a feeling,' he said. 'I have an idea that you, or someone like you, could find me very useful under certain circumstances.'

John raised an eyebrow. 'What line are you in, then?'

'Computers.' David looked away. To his surprise, he hadn't seen anything in John's face that shouldn't have been there. Maybe, he wondered, maybe he's called Honest John because he's honest. Then he thought: Nah, because they call New York new, but it's been there for ages. It's probably just a nickname, like Chalky or Ginger.

'Never got the hang of them bloody things,' John sighed. 'Got to use 'em, mind. Couldn't do all the calculations by hand when you're configuring, it'd take years. Hundreds of years, even.'

David nodded. 'And that'd be a problem for you, would it?'

''Course it would. I mean, it's not like I'm going to live for ever.' John laughed. 'Oh, I can see what you're thinking. You're thinking, why bother when I could just clone up half a dozen of myself and make them do the maths.' He shook his head. 'Wouldn't work. At least, *they* wouldn't work. More likely to start a fight with each other, or try and clone a whole army and take over the world. They're like that, see, multiples, once they get together. That's why it's so important not to have two copies of the same original at the same time. If they ever run into each other, you're in trouble.'

'Ah,' David said; and he thought of the two Philippa Levenses, both *en route* to Homeworld.

'Oh yes,' John said. 'It's like when you got an original and a clone and they get together. Real trouble. That's why I try and only do dead people. Too risky else.'

This time, David thought of the other David, the one he'd left semi-alive, floating in green slime, for the police to arrest. 'I can see the logic there,' he said. 'Tricky business you're in, really.'

'Not half.' John sighed. ''Course, my dad wanted me to be a fireman, same as him. Can't go wrong being a fireman, he told me, people'll always be setting fire to things. Had to know better, didn't I?'

'Children always do, don't they?'

'Don't they just.' Honest John frowned, his thoughts clearly elsewhere. 'You do your best for them, try and stop 'em making a fuck-up of their lives, and the more you try, the worse it gets. Playing God, see, trying to make people do what you want, not what they want. Never works out. Same with clones, of course.'

For some reason, David looked up sharply when he said that. There was something in the voice. Before he could follow up on the lead, however, John stood up and yawned. 'Yeah, sure,' he said, 'you can come and work for me if you want to. Hours are terrible, money's worse and it makes your hair smell. But if you know about computer stuff—'

'Oh, I do. Believe me.'

John shrugged. 'That's all right, then. And if you want to doss down in here for the night, be my guest. Wouldn't suit me, mind, but you're welcome. You can make yourself useful while you're here, keep the spiders out of the tanks, stuff like that.'

'Thank you,' David replied. 'I'll see about finding a place to stay tomorrow. In my lunch break,' he added quickly.

'Lunch break?' John grinned. 'You'll be lucky. But you can use the phone if you want to ring round. I'll stop the cost of the calls out of your money.'

'Right,' David said. 'Thank you.'

''S all right,' John yawned. 'I'm off home. Don't leave the lights on late, for crying out loud. I'm not made of money.'

He wandered out, shutting the door behind him, and left David wondering; sure, John wasn't made out of money, else he'd be a sort of blue papier-mâché statue. But if he wasn't made of money, it raised the question, what *was* he made of? The usual slug/snail/puppy-dog-tail gumbo that our flesh is heir to, or something greener, slimier and less vexingly random? Bottom line was, this one didn't seem to know; that, or he was one hell of an actor. The resequencing faults, now: they seemed to banjax the memory, sealing off whole chunks, so maybe Honest John really didn't know anything, and genuinely believed that David was there because he had a wife who objected to beautiful girls wearing nothing but green slime being smuggled into the matrimonial home. It was possible. It had to be, or else why did David instinctively trust him?

The fact remained that he did; and that was about as odd as you could get outside of a picket line in front of an integer factory. Quite possibly it was simply because he'd turned up at such a useful moment and helped David so much with his getaway – very helpful he'd been, extremely helpful, suspiciously helpful . . . And all this business about going to work in the clone factory; where the hell had all that come from? Stood to reason: if David had any sense, he'd be keeping a whole lot of distance between himself and anybody with a case of bad conjunctivitis, let alone a missing eye.

But here he was; here and, for the moment, by the looks of things, dry, fed and safe. Yeah, what about that? There was something wonderfully old-fashioned and wholesome about starting over sweeping floors and making tea and scrubbing out the tanks and all the stuff he'd just signed on to do; a new day dawning, a new door opening as the old one slammed, the perfect fresh start.

In the clone trade. In Watford. Well, perhaps not *perfect*.

David found a heap of sacks to lie down on, turned off the lights and closed his eyes.

'Something you said yesterday,' Honest John said, his eye fixed on the machine he was wiring up. 'About how it'd be nice not to go to prison for the rest of your life. You in trouble or something?'

Up till that point, it had all been going rather well. Mostly they'd worked together in silence, John fiddling round the backs of grey steel boxes with a screwdriver, David locked in the archetypal light/darkness struggle with Windows 98.

'Yes,' David said, and waited.

'Oh.' Pause. 'Anything to do with that clone? You know, the one I did for you?'

'In a way,' David replied. 'No, I didn't kill her or anything like that, if that's what you're thinking.'

'Isn't, actually. Can you pass me a seven-mill socket?'

'What's a seven-mill socket?'

John got up off his knees and walked over to the workbench. 'One of these,' he said.

'Ah, right. Small cylindrical metal thing. I'll remember that.'

Silence, apart from John ratcheting and David typing.

'So what did you do?' John asked.

'Nothing.'

'Ah.' John sighed. 'That's all right, then. Only, if it was thieving or something – well, you know what I mean. There's valuable stuff here.'

David half-turned in his swivel chair. 'In 1981,' he said, 'either late July or early August, I can't remember exactly, I stole a Mars bar from the Woolworth's on Ealing Broadway. They never did get me for it, though I guess they stopped trying to track down the perp some time ago. Apart from that—'

'Yes, all right, fair enough. Can't blame me for asking. I mean, I only met you a couple of times.'

'True. And you didn't have to give me this job, I appreciate that.' He tapped a few more keys. *Please wait,* the screen told him, *while Windows compiles the appropriate wizard.* He hummed a few topical bars from 'The Wizard of Oz', and turned away again. 'Out of interest,' he said, 'why did you give me this job?'

'Because I can't do computers.' He grunted, putting his weight behind his spanner. 'Never did understand the poxy things, never will. Don't even have them where—'

'Where you come from,' David said evenly. 'Where was that again? Basildon?'

'Weren't any computers in Basildon when I was growing up there,' John replied; and to his credit, he handled it very well, with just the right lack of concern. But not well enough. 'Managed perfectly well without 'em, too, with just a slide rule and a pencil. People nowadays though—'

They looked at each other, and a kind of understanding passed between them: specialised, though not particularly rare. It was a sensible compromise in bad circumstances – you know I know you're lying, but it's all right, I'll pretend I don't. You can see it any day of the week in the eyes of long and wearily married couples when they say, 'I love you'.

But that was all right, David assured himself as he swivelled back to work, because I knew all this already. What matters is that, for reasons best known to himself, he *rescued* me. Which is good, surely?

'I know what you're going to say,' he interrupted, with forced cheerfulness. 'If the abacus was good enough for the Ancient Egyptians, it's good enough for you, right?'

'Never could get on with them things,' John replied. 'Like I said, give me a slide rule any day.'

'Sure. What's a slide rule?'

Apparently, wiring up and adjusting the machines was a much longer job than pulling them out, because it took the whole working day. 'Half five,' John called out at one stage. 'Knocking-off time.'

'All right,' David called back. He was genuinely intrigued by the Byzantine complexity of the snarl-up in John's Internet software; it was as if the programs had come alive and been struck stupid at exactly the same moment, and in their panic had tried to dig their way out of the system, burrowing frantically clean through anything that had got in their way. 'Just give me a few minutes, will you? I've almost got this thing fixed— Oh, scrod.'

'I don't pay overtime,' John warned.

'What? Oh, I see what you mean. Sorry, I'm so used to working for myself, I forgot that time has a value. Don't worry about it. If I can just get it sorted tonight, it means I won't have to start from scratch first thing tomorrow.'

'Please yourself,' John said. 'Here, you had anything to eat since this morning?'

At 8.20 a.m., John had swooshed open the shed's sliding door and marched in with two styrofoam cups and a big, partly transparent brown paper bag containing two jumbo bacon rolls. David had eaten and drunk his share ravenously, anxious to get as much of it down his neck as he could before the other 4,999 disciples showed up. 'It's OK,' he said, 'I'm not hungry right now. Could do with a coffee, though, as and when you're making one.'

'Sure.'

John put down his spanner and pottered away. David tapped a few keys in a desultory manner, but the thread had escaped him and slithered away, like a slow-worm escaping into long grass. You need to have a clear head and supple mental joints if you're going to go crawling about in the maze of tunnels that honeycomb the mind of a computer; if your concentration's impaired in any way, stay well clear, go and find something else to do. He sat back and closed his eyes to clear them of little flickering dots.

Well, David thought, here I am; and I'm sitting in

front of a totally screwed-up computer, trying to figure out how it possibly got that way, which is, of course, my default setting. A little sliver of normality. Hooray. I can focus on that like mad, and that'll help me keep my mind off the small matter of how I came to be here and what the hell is going on. Sure, I feel like I'm a small child who's been given a comic to read while its parents hack at each other with big knives, but at least it implies that somebody's thinking of me. That makes a pleasant change, and of course I'm pathetically grateful.

But . . . He wound back various things Honest John had said, the expression on his face while he'd been saying them. Unless Honest John was Olivier and Gielgud and Dustin Hoffman with a side salad of De Niro and a cocktail olive, when he'd said or implied that he didn't know anything about interstellar lifts or murdered clones or duplicate Philippa Levenses, he'd been telling the truth – in which case, he wasn't the Good Cop in this scenario, and his motivation was either much simpler or vastly more complex than David had assumed. Really, it had only been that one stray remark about there being no computers where he came from that had put a dent in his credibility; and there were plenty of good explanations for it that didn't involve superbeings from alien worlds or centuries-old conspiracies to make a fool out of David Perkins. Maybe Honest John had grown up on a remote Scottish island or a coral reef in the South Pacific. Why he'd choose to lie about something like that wasn't immediately obvious, but people do strange things for strange (but entirely terrestrial) reasons. Perhaps he really was on the level, after all.

(Fine. In which case, why are there two dozen men

who look just like him running around out there trying to get me locked up or lure me onto spacecraft?)

After he'd thought through a couple of alternative explanations, debugged them for continuity errors and assessed them for viability, he reached one inescapable conclusion; namely, that there really are things in the universe even more bafflingly incomprehensible than a fucked-over Microsoft product. That being the case, he resolved to rest his brain by getting back to work. The rest and the confrontation with a far nastier problem had done him some good, and he was just starting to make some progress when Honest John came in with the coffee.

'There you go,' he said.

'Thanks.'

''S all right. Did you say two sugars?'

David nodded.

'That's all right, then, 'cos I put two sugars in there.'

David was so wrapped up in the computer problem that it took several seconds for the implications of that last remark to sink in. 'John.'

'Hm?'

David asked the question very calmly. 'Did you, um, nip out and get some sugar, then? Only there wasn't any, if you remember.'

John shook his head. 'Well, there's plenty there now,' he replied. 'Whole new packet. But I didn't—'

He didn't get to finish the sentence; he was too busy sidestepping to avoid being crashed into, as David sprang up out of his chair and sprinted across the workshop towards the back office. John called out some mildly bewildered enquiry after him as he grabbed the handle and tore open the door.

The room on the other side of the door was (surprise, surprise) completely bare and painted a blinding shade of white. There was no trace whatsoever of a bag of sugar. But the room wasn't completely empty.

Standing in the exact centre of the floor was Philippa Levens.

CHAPTER FOURTEEN

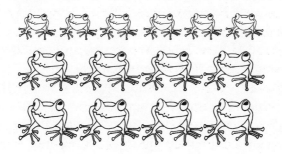

'Oh,' she said. 'It's you.'

—Which saved him having to ask, 'Excuse me, but which one are you?' On the other hand, it went some way towards answering the question, 'Why did you come back?' by ruling out the one answer he'd have liked to hear.

'Yes,' he replied, 'it's me. What are you doing here? I thought you were going home.'

'I was.' She looked past him, presumably searching for the door. 'I changed my mind.'

'Oh. Why?'

'None of your business. Where is this?'

Well, he guessed she wanted something a bit more specific than 'Earth'. 'Watford,' he said.

'Never heard of it. Why am I here?'

Neither the time nor the place for a facetious answer. 'This is the, um, cloning place. Only it's moved. We packed everything up and brought it here to get away from the police.'

She nodded, dismissing the explanation as both sufficient and irrelevant. Marvellous command of body language and facial expression; she could probably do the whole of *Peer Gynt* just with eyebrow movements. 'Who's "we"?' she said.

'Me and Honest John. You know, the man who does the cloning. Your dad. One of him.'

She shrugged, as if sliding out of a wet bathrobe. 'Don't think I've met that one.'

'He's different from the others,' David said. 'Actually, I can't figure him out at all. But I trust him.'

'Good for you,' she replied, yawning. 'Well, I'd better go and talk to him.'

'All right.'

She frowned. 'I'll find it much easier to do that if you shift your fat bum from in front of the door.'

Actually, it wasn't fat; even David, who'd always had the self-esteem of a soggy cardboard box, knew that. In which case, if the comment wasn't factually accurate, it was an attempt to be deliberately offensive. Another less than optimistic sign. Without a word, he got out of the way.

'Well, don't just stand there,' she called out over her shoulder. He followed.

Honest John had gone back to tinkering with his machine. He was lying under it, with only his legs sticking out. She attracted his attention by kicking his ankle.

'Mind what you're bloody well— Oh.' John looked at her. 'I know you,' he said, getting up.

'John,' David called out, 'this is—'

'Of course you know me,' she said wearily. 'And can

we do without the small talk, please? I've had a thoroughly horrible journey and I'm not in the mood.'

John looked straight past her. 'This is the one I did for you, isn't it?' he said.

David chewed his lower lip. 'Sort of,' he said. 'In a sense.'

'Bloody awful attitude she's got,' John went on. 'Maybe I didn't set the jumpers right when I reconfigured. Sorry about that.'

'Not your fault,' David said. 'In fact—'

'Hey. I'm still here, you know.'

'In fact,' David went on, 'my fault. All my fault. You see—'

'Not a lot I can do about it now, of course,' Honest John said, shrugging his shoulders. (Though not nearly as elegantly as she'd done it: imagine the 'Dying Swan' performed by (a) Pavlova (b) Mo Mowlem; that degree of difference.) 'Least, not from the technical side. A good clip round the ear's about all I can suggest.'

She gave John a look you could have cached a mammoth in. 'Whoever this person is,' she said, 'he's not my father. Looks a little like him, I suppose, but that's all.'

David took a step back, scrutinising each of them in turn. One or both of them was pretending, but so far he hadn't seen anything to indicate which one it was.

'What's she on about now?' John asked.

'Nothing,' David said. 'At least—'

'You.' She pushed past him and planted herself about eighteen inches from Honest John. 'You set all this up, didn't you? All the cloning stuff.'

John nodded. 'What's it to you?' he said.

'And you cloned someone just like me? From a bit of old hair?'

'Dave.' John was frowning. It was a rather ominous sight. 'What did she mean by that, someone just like her? Isn't this the one I did for you?'

'Not really.' David had a very strong urge to be some-where or someone or even some*thing* else. 'Same pattern, but not the same, um, individual.'

'Bloody hell. So where'd she come from, then? Jump out of a birthday cake or something?'

'I, um.' They were both looking at him. 'Well, you weren't there, and I was feeling thoroughly pissed off, and—'

'She's not the one I did?'

'No.'

'Then who did her?'

What's the single most embarrassing word in the English language? At that moment, David knew exactly what it was. 'Me.'

'But you don't know how,' John said. 'You don't know how to do the settings or compensate for drift or any of that stuff. You can't just go dropping things in tanks, it's asking for a bloody disaster.'

'You know,' said the Philippa clone, dangerously sweetly, 'you're wasted in this line of work, you should have been a diplomat. Just think of all the fascinating wars you could've started.'

'I know,' David replied. 'At least, I know now. I didn't then. It, um, seemed like a good idea at the—'

'Oh, for crying out loud.' John shook his head, as if this was the most terrible thing he could possibly imag-ine. 'You don't set the jumpers right, you get corrupt data paths, random meme fluxes, personality disorders like you wouldn't believe—' He sighed, like the wind whispering through the ribcage of a buffalo skeleton on the open prairie. 'Bloody hell,' he said, 'people are fucked up enough as it is without that kind of stuff as well. I wouldn't do what you just did to a frog.'

Interesting example to choose, David couldn't help thinking, but that wasn't really the point at issue; at that precise moment, frogs were so far down the agenda you'd need a spade to reach them. 'All right,' he said, 'I'm sorry. Like I said, I didn't know.'

'Just a minute!' The Philippa clone had a surprisingly loud voice for someone of her size and build. 'There you two are, talking about me as if I was Chernobyl or something. I hate to contradict you gentlemen, but I'm not actually as bad as all that.' She glared at them both. 'One of you agree with me quick, or I'm going to start breaking bones.'

'Oh.' David's face turned the colour of raw steak. 'I didn't mean it like that, there's nothing really the matter with you—'

The clone made a noise like a suspension bridge in the last throes of metal fatigue. 'Thank you so much,' she snarled. 'Nothing really the matter with me. I'll say this for you, you don't muck about with all that compare-thee-to-a-summer's-day palaver. Nothing really the matter, for God's sake!'

'See?' Honest John said sadly. 'Skip the set-up procedures and this is what you get. Hysterical outbursts. Yelling and stamping and chucking things about—' He ducked, just in time, as a medium adjustable wrench whizzed through the space his head had been occupying. 'Not to mention bloody awful hand-eye coordination,' he added, rather unfairly.

David scuttled across and stood in front of Honest John. 'Really,' he said, 'it's all my fault.'

'Oh, shut up and get out of the way,' the clone replied. 'You're not to blame, you're just an idiot. But he shouldn't have left all this stuff lying about in the first place.'

'You should have told me,' John went on, 'really you should. This is delicate scientific equipment, you could've screwed up all the default settings. Why the hell people can't just leave well alone . . .'

'Yes,' David interrupted, 'all right.' He faced the clone squarely. 'You didn't say why you came back,' he said.

'None of your business,' she replied. 'Oh, all right, then, just so long as you stop staring at me like that. It's enough to make me want to throw up.'

'The question,' David reminded her.

'All right, all right, I'm just getting to it. I came back to warn you.'

David did a double take. 'Me? That is, warn me about what?'

She tried to point round him. 'Them,' she said. 'Or him. That's where it gets confusing. Particularly,' she added, 'since you made such a mess of my memory. There's great big bits missing, and so the people I was talking to—'

'Who?' John interrupted.

'Back home. And I'm not talking to you, so shut up. The people at Immigration. At first they were going to arrest me, because they thought I was her.'

'You are her,' John put in.

'Did someone just say something?' she asked. 'Or is there an echo in here? They thought,' she went on, 'that I was – what was the charming way they put it? They thought that I was an illegal alien called Philippa Levens. But then I told them about how I'd been made out of slimy green goo a few hours earlier, and that got them interested right away.'

'When she says "back home",' John said, 'what the bloody hell is she talking about?'

'Quiet!' David commanded. 'When you told them you're a clone—'

She nodded. 'They've got another term for it,' she said, 'but it isn't very nice. The point is, back home – and I would have known this, if I didn't have a half-eaten plate of alphabet soup where my memory should be – back home, this cloning stuff is very, very illegal. They go berserk if you even mention it. So they said I couldn't stay, I had to come back. So I did.'

'Oh.' David's face fell like one of Galileo's experiments. 'You said you came to warn me.'

'That's what I'm doing, idiot. At least, if you give me half a chance, that's what I'm going to do. What they told me was that at some stage, he – the original, I mean – he did a copy of himself, but he got it wrong, and it turned out bad. Really, really bad. Not just scrambled-eggs-for-brains, like me, but nasty and horrible and vicious—'

'Like I told you,' John muttered, peering over David's shoulder, 'if you don't set those jumpers – I mean, you can see for yourself. Look at that face she's pulling.'

'Vicious,' the clone repeated, 'and also vindictive and very, very cunning. And as soon as it found out what it was, and that it'd been called into existence just because its creator was too bone idle to wash his own socks and keep the workshop tidy, it decided to get its own back. And you know how it did that?'

'I can guess,' David said quietly.

'Handful of hairs in the cloning tank,' she said, 'when

the boss wasn't looking. So, to cut a long story short, there's one genuine one of him, and all the rest are just out to make trouble.'

'Where did you say all this happened?' John asked. They ignored him.

'All right,' David said. 'Now, is there any way of knowing which one's the original?'

The clone nodded. 'Apparently,' she said. 'Didn't sound very convincing to me, but they're sure it'll work. Worth a try, anyhow.'

'So?' David demanded. 'What is it?'

She shook her head. 'Don't be a complete idiot,' she said. 'I can hardly tell you with him standing right there earwigging, now can I?'

'But—' What David didn't say was that if what she'd said was true, he was ninety-nine per cent sure that Honest John had to be original, because he was *nice*. In a sense. Nice as far as miserable old gits go. But she was glowering past him at Honest John with an expression on her face that you could have dissolved iron in, so instead he said, 'Well, I suppose you can't be too careful. And if something's worth doing—'

'She's off her rocker,' John said. 'Next off, she'll be telling you she's really from another planet, or something.'

David shook his head. 'No, I know that already. Anyway, you be quiet.' He looked back at the clone. 'Come outside and you can tell me—'

The clone scowled at him. 'What, and leave him here on his own, with all these tools and equipment? I'm not turning my back on any of 'em, at least not till we've igured out which is which.'

John pushed past David and stood looking at her for a

moment. 'Get real, son, will you?' he said. 'You don't want to go believing anything she tells you. God's sake, she's a bad clone, the jumpers weren't set, like I told you. Chances are she's all those things she said, you know, vicious and vindictive and cunning, and she's out to get her own back on you for making her in the first place. Who are you going to believe, Dave? Her or me?'

'Why can't I believe both of you?'

'You just can't, that's all.' Honest John looked away. 'Go on, you tell him. I'm right, aren't I?'

'He's right,' the clone said, nodding assertively. 'Bizarrely enough, I agree with him. Which of us is it going to be?'

Actually, the question was pretty straightforward and didn't require any thought. 'Her,' said David, hoping they wouldn't ask why. (Because he's more likely to be telling the truth, but she's the one I'm in love with. Or words – desperately embarrassing words – to that effect.)

'Bloody marvellous,' John said. 'All right, what do you want me to do? Wait outside?'

The Philippa clone shook her head. 'And give you a chance to make a run for it? Not likely.'

'But hang on,' David interrupted. 'If we can't go outside, and *he* can't go outside, and you can't tell me while he's listening—'

'Who says I've got to tell you anyhow? Just so long as I know and you believe me.'

This was getting silly. 'Come over here,' David said firmly – apparently he could do that, though he couldn't remember learning how – 'and whisper. All right?'

She scowled at him, but by now he was moderately scowlproof. 'Oh, all right,' she said. 'But if he hears, it'll spoil everything.'

'Fine,' John grunted. 'And while you're doing that, I can be getting on with some work. You know, work, the stuff I'm paying you to do.'

David walked over to the opposite corner of the workshop. 'All right,' he whispered. 'So what's this special secret clue of yours? If it's something like not being able to see his reflection in a mirror . . .'

'Don't be silly,' she whispered back, 'it's nothing like that. But all clones have got a mark on the backs of their heads. Look,' she added, quickly glancing across at Honest John, to make sure he wasn't watching. 'There, see?' She lifted her hair away from her neck. Sure enough, there was a little mark, a star-shaped twist of scar tissue.

David nodded. He found it completely unconvincing, for some reason, which was awkward, since of course he had to believe her, on political grounds. 'All right,' he said. 'Stay there, I'll go and check.'

'I'm coming too.'

'No, you aren't. Stay there.'

Remarkably, she stayed. No earthly reason why she should have.

'Hello,' muttered Honest John, without looking up from what he was doing. Of course, he had shoulder-length hair, just like all the other versions of himself. That made it impossible to see the back of his neck. Surprise, surprise.

'John,' David asked, keeping his voice down, 'you know all about clones.'

'Not all. Most.'

'Whatever. Is there really a way of telling them apart from, um, real people, just by looking at them?'

'Yeah.' John picked up a spanner – a big, ugly spanner

that'd make a pretty effective weapon. 'Several, actually. But the one your bird over there's probably thinking of is the scar on the back of the neck. Here,' he added, and swept his hair out of the way. There was nothing to be seen. ''Course, that's easy as anything to fake. Any plastic surgeon worth spit'd have that off in ten minutes with a Stanley knife, and you'd never know it'd ever been there.'

'Ah,' David said. 'Well, thanks, anyway.'

'You're welcome.' John tightened something with the spanner and put it down again. 'You want to know a really good way of telling the difference?'

'Well . . .'

'It's easy. All to do with loss of definition in the nerve endings. Clones aren't ticklish.'

All David could think of to say was, 'What?'

'Ticklish. You know, if you tickle them, they don't laugh. Absolutely foolproof test, that is.' David nodded. 'Except,' he said, 'if you happen to know about it. Then, if someone tickles you, all you have to do is pretend to be laughing.'

John nodded. 'There's that, of course.'

'Thanks, anyway.'

'You're welcome. And of course,' he added, 'there's a third way you couldn't fake even if you did know.'

'Ah,' David said. 'And what's that?'

'Distinctive elongation of the heart ventricles,' John replied. 'One quick shufti through a microscope puts it completely beyond doubt. Of course, you'd have to open the subject up and cut his heart out before you could look.'

'Thanks,' David replied. 'That's quite indescribably useful.'

He walked back across the workshop. 'Well?' she demanded.

'No sign of any mark,' he told her.

'Oh. Right. So he must be the original, then.' David dipped his head as a sign of agreement. 'So what are you going to do now?' he asked.

'Simple. They told me back on Homeworld that if I bring him back so they can put him on trial and lock him up, they'll let me stay there even if I am a clone. So that's what I'm going to do.' She looked round, then picked up an eighteen-inch length of steel pipe. Judging by the gleam in her eye, David guessed she wasn't choosing materials for an improvised flute.

'Of course,' he said quickly, 'just because he hasn't got the mark doesn't mean to say it's him.'

'What do you mean?'

'Think about it,' he said. 'Mark like that, any competent plastic surgeon could take it off in, um, ten minutes with a Stanley knife.'

'Plastic surgeon? You mean, like a robot?'

Did he want to try explaining? No, he didn't. 'That's right,' he said. 'Very efficient they are, too. Just stick your credit card in the slot, dial in the operation you want and hold still. And they can say, "How are we feeling today, then?" while looking out of the window just like the real thing.'

'Oh.' She appeared to be thinking it over, then shrugged. 'Well, that's a bloody nuisance. Means I'm wasting my time. And if I can't find the criminal and bring him in, they won't let me live on their planet.'

From what he'd gathered about the place, David couldn't really imagine wanting to, if he had any choice at all. 'Oh well,' he said, rather more cheerfully than he'd meant to. 'I suppose that means you're stuck here with us. Just have to make the best of a bad job, I suppose.'

'Apparently.' She narrowed her eyes and looked at him. 'And we both know whose fault that is, don't we? Talking of which,' she went on – she was still holding the pipe – 'when I was on the Homeworld, I got the impression that they're really, *really* anti this whole cloning business.'

'Oh yes?' David took a step back.

'They really hate the whole idea,' she said. 'Which makes me wonder. True, I can't bring back the cloner they specially want, but they might be interested in – well, second-best. A consolation prize.'

'You think so?' The back of his heel touched the wall. 'I don't think so. I mean, like you said, they did specify this one particular clone-artist—'

'Yes, but they didn't know there were others. It's worth a try,' she added. 'I mean, what harm could it do?'

'Plenty.'

'Only to you.'

The words *vicious vindictive and very, very cunning* – all the Vs, if you stretched a point for *very cunning* – floated into his mind; likewise the slogan, *Honest John, the man you can trust.* Query: would true love be able to overlook a bash on the head, followed by being abducted by aliens and probably executed in an unspeakably horrible way?

'Alternatively,' he suggested, making sure he maintained eye contact, 'you could just settle down here and get a job. All sorts of things you could do.'

'Such as?'

Assassin. Vivisectionist. Chief of Security for a

discerning Latin American dictator. 'Oh, loads of things—' He caught sight of the movement and flinched away. The sound of metal on bone was loud and unmistakable; the curious thing, though, was that he was still standing up, and it didn't seem to hurt.

'Told you,' said Honest John. He was looking to see if he'd bent his spanner. 'You had to know best, of course.'

He looked down at the clone, sprawled on the floor. There didn't seem to be any blood.

'She'll be all right,' John said. 'Probably just a headache. That's another thing about clones, actually; their bones are a bit tougher than ours.'

Manners, he remembered. 'Thanks,' he said.

''S all right,' John replied. 'You haven't been around clones as long as I have, you don't know what they're like. Besides,' he added with a grin, 'you're soft on her. Go on, admit it.'

David smiled weakly. 'You guessed.'

'It wasn't all that difficult,' John replied. 'In fact, it was pretty obvious. Actually, a blind, deaf man with a sack over his head—'

'Yes, right,' David said. 'I get the point. Mind you, it's just possible I might revise my opinion.' He looked down at the sprawled clone. 'She was going to kidnap me and take me to this planet . . .'

'Yeah,' John said, 'right. You don't believe all that stuff, do you?'

David shook his head. 'God only knows,' he replied. 'I don't see why not, all things considered. Seems to me like I can believe almost anything these days. I suppose it means I'm growing, as a person. Does it matter whether I believe in things or not? It doesn't seem to make any difference. Although,' he added, 'I didn't believe in British Columbia, and on balance it looks like I made the right call there.'

'British Columbia?' John frowned. 'You're a funny bugger, you are. You stand there telling me you're pre-pared to believe in little green men from another planet, but you aren't having any truck with Canada. What do you need, a sworn statement from the Royal Geographical Society? Or will a satellite photo do?'

'I didn't mean it like that. Doesn't matter, anyway. What are we going to do about her, then?'

'Up to you, she's your sweetie-pie. I reckon she'll be really pissed off when she wakes up.'

David sighed. 'I wouldn't be at all surprised,' he said. 'I mean, her attitude isn't all that wonderful when she *hasn't* just been bashed on the head with a spanner. What would you suggest?'

'Chuck her in the back of the van, dump her in Epping Forest, get the hell out of the way before she wakes up. Easier all round that way, I reckon.'

'It'd be the sensible thing to do,' David admitted. 'But I don't want to be sensible. All right, here's a compro-mise for you. We could put her in the van, drive her to the nearest hospital— Why are you shaking your head like that?'

'Doctors,' John replied. 'And the off chance she might get examined by some vet with slightly more imagina-tion than the average small rock. Wouldn't take a doctor long to figure out that there's something bloody odd about her. And if he goes taking blood samples and wee samples and x-rays and God knows what else all—'

David hadn't thought of that. 'They'd be able to spot that she's a clone?'

'With their eyes shut, probably. And that wouldn't be

good. Forget how much trouble that could get me in; do you really think she'd want to spend the rest of her days in a research lab, getting prodded with glass rods and having bits scraped off her?'

'All right,' David said. 'Suggest something else.'

John thought for a moment. 'You're going to be all picky and say it's got to be non-lethal, aren't you? Thought so. Well, that rules out my only suggestion, which was weighting her down with bricks and dropping her in the reservoir. Your problem, sunshine. And don't take all day about it, you've got work to do.'

And that, David reflected, was probably John's idea of going out of his way to be helpful. He took a couple of steps back, as if being further away from her was going to make the problem any easier to get a handle on.

Curiously enough, it did; because stepping back allowed him to catch sight of the door to the back office, a room entirely devoid of windows or doors other than the one he was looking at, which she'd somehow or other managed to find her way into without first going past him through the workshop. It was all very well for Honest John to pull faces and say, 'You don't believe in all that stuff, do you?' without even trying to put up a rational explanation of how she'd got there. Not good enough, David decided; and, since he'd somehow managed to bring himself to believe in all that stuff before John tried to put him off the idea, he could see no reason why he shouldn't go back to believing it again.

(And that's supposed to be a logical argument? Sure. On a par with concluding that the atomic number of beryllium is 46 because 7 out of 10 *Daily Mirror* readers think it ought to be.)

Nevertheless.

He bent down and tried to figure out how to get her back into the interstellar lift without violating her person or doing in his back. In the end he opted for grabbing her wrists and dragging (but carefully, and with total respect), a policy that seemed to be working out just fine until her feet got wedged in the door frame. He got her there in the end, though, and she didn't wake up even when he accidentally clouted her head while closing the door.

Now, then. It was all very well deciding to send her back to the aliens' homeworld, but exactly how was he supposed to go about it? Empty room, whitewashed walls, nothing in there at all except the two of them and a bag of sugar; and something told him that the fine print on the back of the bag probably wasn't *Interstellar Elevator Operating Procedures for Dummies*.

But David read it all the same, just to make sure. Or, at least, he tried to. It turned out not to be possible, because the writing was in some kind of strange, otherworldly script that was either interstellar alien or Burmese. He said something uncharacteristically vulgar and put the packet down hard; whereupon a voice said 'Please wait.'

That would've been a good time to leave. But he didn't.

'Transliteration and translation complete,' said the voice; and now the writing on the packet was in proper letters, and it said—

CONGRATULATIONS! on your purchase of a General Utilities SKZZ889 Litespeed. Properly cared for and serviced by your local GU agent using only genuine GU replacement parts . . .

There was quite a lot more in that vein, and David skipped down until it started to get interesting.

Operating your SKZZ889, he read; and then there was a little logo, and *Where do you want to go today?* in bright red letters and a different font. Under that, it said—

First, input your departure coordinates using the plotting numerator and simply follow the on-line instructions. If your SKZZ889 is not fitted with a raniform numerator, use the back-up glyceroballistic system, taking care to avoid exposure to naked moisture. Next, input your arrival coordinates—

Of course, he was used to this kind of thing; indeed, following the call of duty, he'd once or twice climbed into the cage with Hewlett-Packard On-line Help, alone and armed with nothing more than the traditional upturned chair and whip. But that didn't make it any less frustrating. What, for example, was a raniform numerator? And if he didn't have one (he was prepared to bet lots of money that he didn't have one, because the ones he got of anything never had the optional helpful bits referred to in the manual) what in buggery was a back-up glyceroballistic system? He read on; and as he worked his way down the back of the packet, he tilted it so as to be able to see the words – and a few grains of sugar spilled out of the top and touched the floor—

'Departure coordinates set. Stated departure coordinates do not agree with coordinates in system memory. Replace or cancel?'

Ah, David said to himself, so that's what it means: from 'glycero', meaning 'sweet stuff', and 'ballistic', meaning 'to throw'. He frowned; twenty to one in fivers that the beta version of this contraption used salt instead of sugar, hence the superstition.

Anyway, that could wait. 'Cancel,' he said.

'Operation cancelled. Please input departure coordinates.'

Oh for pity's sake, he thought, not again—

—And while he was thinking that, a tiny speck of fluff that must've got into the room when he opened the door flew up his nose and started tickling unbearably—

Now would be a very bad time to sneeze; a very bad time inde— inDEEshoo!

There was a brief, rather lovely snowstorm of floating sugar, like the snow scenes in those old-fashioned shake-'em-up paperweights; and even before all the sugar had settled, the voice was saying, 'Coordinates set, departure initiation sequence completed, departure in five, four, three, two—'

On *two*, he had his hand on the door handle. On *one*, he'd started turning it. On the *dep* of *departure completed*, he'd turned it as far as it would go – and found out that it wasn't nearly far enough.

CHAPTER FIFTEEN

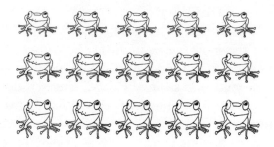

If there was any movement, David didn't feel it. As far as he was concerned, there was a period of about five seconds when the door handle wouldn't turn; then the door opened and he nearly fell through it.

'Hey.' The voice came from somewhere around floor level. 'So where do you think you're going in such a goddamn hurry?'

He didn't recognise the voice, as such, but it gave him a clue as to what to look for and, come to that, where to look for it. He redirected his attention to toecap level, and sure enough . . .

'Hello, frog,' he replied. 'I, um, come in peace. Take me to your—'

'Not so fast,' snarled the frog; one of the frogs, he couldn't tell which. He hoped it was safe to assume that the speaker was the slightly larger frog at the head of the military-looking formation of about two dozen raniforms, though he realised he was extrapolating from his knowledge of human hierarchies, which wasn't very scientific of him. The main justification for his assumption lay in the fact that the front frog was wearing some sort of headgear and managing to grip a small metallic object in its offside front paw. 'Stay exactly where you are, nice and easy, and nobody's gonna get hurt. Copy?'

Not just gripping a small metallic object; pointing it, too. Remembering how important it is not to let them see you're afraid (a principle he'd absorbed from a TV series about dog training), David managed to restrict himself to a slight frown. 'Fair enough,' he said. 'I can quite understand why you're worried, and I promise I'll be careful.'

The frog looked up at him, and David could almost feel it frantically flipping through its mental card index of clichés to find an appropriate response. 'Worried?' it said, eventually. 'Who're you calling worried, big guy?'

'Well, you,' David replied kindly, 'obviously. You're afraid I might tread on you. I can see your point, of course. After all, I'm so much bigger than you are.'

'Hey!' The frog's throat swelled to hen's-egg size. 'I ain't scared of you, buster. I ain't scared of *nothing*.'

'Really? Splendid.' David smiled. 'Then it stands to reason that you aren't afraid of me, and you won't mind if I move. Thanks – I was getting cramp.'

The frog didn't answer, but it was still pointing the metallic thing. Of course, it could just be some harmless artefact, like a fountain pen or a tyre-pressure gauge, that it had picked out of the pondside mud on its way here. Or it might not be; and if the hypothesis forming in David's mind was correct, it almost certainly wasn't. He stayed put.

'Did I mention that I come in peace?' he asked politely.

'Sez you,' croaked the frog. 'Me, I ain't so sure. Who's the dame?'

Interesting: the frog's entire repertoire of Human seemed to have been gleaned from gangster movies and war films. David had once met a man who'd learned German from opera libretti, which meant he could chatter away all day about swords and dragons and magic rings, but couldn't order a cup of coffee or ask the way to the bus station without florid arm gestures and a phrase book. In the frog's case, he suspected it was something to do with the old (therefore cheap) films that satellite TV companies bounce off their orbiting hardware. On balance, George Raft movies were probably a better paradigm of human culture and society than the Aussie soaps, but there wasn't a great deal in it; it was still a bit like the UK government sending Basil Brush to represent British interests at the United Nations.

'The dame?' He looked round, and realised that the frog had been talking about the girl, still blissfully asleep on the floor. For one moment, he'd assumed Judi Dench or Peggy Ashcroft had managed to sneak in while his back had been turned. 'Um, she's with me.'

'Oh yeah?' The frog didn't seem to know what to make of that. 'Then the two of you better stay right where you are.'

'Oh well,' David said. 'So what do you suggest we do now?'

'Shuddup,' replied the frog. 'I'm thinkin'.'

'Think away,' David said, with the very slightest trace of a yawn. 'Of course, in your position I'd take me to your leader, I mean your superior officer, and let him deal with it. Then anything that went wrong would be his fault, not yours. But if you feel confident that you can handle this situation yourself, that's absolutely fine. Wonderful, in fact, that your society's armed forces are so keen to encourage individual initiative.'

The frog glowered at him.

'Also,' David went on, 'in your position I'd be asking myself how come a Hideous Tall Bastard can understand what I'm saying, and talk back to me in words I can understand. I'd be really concerned about that, personally.'

Frogs don't have facial expressions the way humans do; even so, David could recognise Extremely Worried when he saw it. Something to do with the slight sideways twist of the neck, a definite tensing-up of the main hind-leg muscles. 'Yeah,' said the frog, 'what about that? You gotta come and explain that to the Chief.'

'Delighted,' David replied. 'Which way?'

A rhetorical question. The room he'd found himself in was, of course, empty and whitewashed, though almost the first thing he'd noticed was the absence of bags of sugar. But of course there wouldn't be any, would there? Not when there was a perfectly good raniform numerator instead.

(A living, breathing computer; a computer made up of several dozen frogs, instead of chips and little bits of wire. The idea appealed to him strongly in his professional capacity; all his working life, he'd wanted to find a computer that actually felt pain when you belted it.)

'Oh no you don't, wise guy,' snapped the frog. 'You stay there. I go fetch.'

There was, of course, a single door in the opposite

wall; the question was how the frog was going to reach the door handle. In the event, however, there was no need; the frog croaked twice, the door opened. Should've seen that one coming, David rebuked himself.

The Chief, when he hopped in, turned out to be slightly larger and a slightly deeper shade of green, but otherwise identical. 'OK, sergeant,' it said briskly, 'I'll take it from here. While I'm talking to the prisoner, you and your men go implement first-contact protocol seven. You got that?'

'Right on it, boss.'

Pause. 'You know what first-contact protocol seven is, do you?'

'No, boss.'

'Look it up. Copy?'

'Copy, boss.'

'They're all right, really,' said the Chief in a hopeful tone, once the other frogs had hopped away, almost but not quite in step, like Mr Jones the butcher. 'Enthusiastic. Try hard. Persistent. Frogged. Once they've shrugged off this annoying habit of getting everything they do wrong, they'll be good soldiers.' The Chief hopped a pace closer and studied David's shoes for a while, as if trying to figure out if they were in charge of the enormous thing resting on them. 'So,' it said. 'You can understand every word I ark ark rivet?'

David nodded. 'I've been wondering about that,' he replied. 'Look, you may find this a bit hard to believe, but a while back, somebody actually managed to turn me into a fr— into, um, one of you gentlemen. At least, he made me think I was—'

The frog shook its head vigorously. 'No,' it said, 'not possible. Least, you've got it the wrong way round.' Brief silence, as the frog thought hard. 'I'll try to explain,' it said. 'You see, whoever this person was, he didn't turn you *into* a frog. He turned you—'

'Back.' David nodded. 'You have no idea how relieved I am to hear you say that. I'd pretty much convinced myself I was going crazy.' He looked away, gathering his thoughts. 'I knew there was something fishy going on at the time,' he continued. 'Like, I'd seen some other people – *human* people – turned into frogs and I'll swear they didn't realise what was going on; one minute human, bang, next minute frog, the whole frog, nothing but the frog. But when it happened to me—'

'You remembered.' The frog nodded. 'You remembered being human. You remembered who you were. You knew what had happened to you. Am I right?'

'Exactly. And I couldn't have done that—'

'—If you were really one of them.' The frog hopped round in a small, tight circle. 'Actually, it's pretty simple. This turning-into-things, it's all based on belief; on what you truly believe you are. You take one of those Ugly Tall Bastards—'

'Humans,' David amended reproachfully.

'Whatever,' said the frog equably. 'What's in a name, after all? You take one of those *humans*, all you gotta do is sorta reach into his mind and turn the dial ninety degrees; suddenly he believes he's a frog. You know why? Because he's never had to think, what am I, which species am I being today, he's always just got on with being what he is. But you, of course—'

'Different.' David rubbed his chin, and noticed that his throat was bobbing froggishly. 'Because although I was turned into a human at a really early age and never consciously knew any different—'

'Subconsciously—' The frog took up the train of thought like a relay racer's torch: quick, efficient, no fumble. 'Subconsciously, you still know you were once something else; so all the time your mind's running spot checks – what am I right now, have I turned back, have I reverted to my proper shape? And, when the moment comes and suddenly there's this huge big clue bearing down on you—'

'I remember,' David said. 'I panicked. Suddenly I didn't know what or who I was, and instinctively I grabbed out for the default setting.' He shook his head slowly from side to side. 'And ever since then,' he went on, 'I've been wondering . . . And there was something else,' he added. 'I was in front of this workshop sort of place, and there was a whole load of fr— of *us*, standing out in the road. And I could talk to them.'

'A whole load,' the frog repeated. 'Interesting.'

David shrugged. 'So that's it, then. All these years I've been kidding myself I'm a human, when really I'm—'

'Quite. Now, what I want to know is, who turned you into an Ugly Tall— a human; and why? Fact is,' it went on, 'around here, turning someone into a human, no offence, it's a really horrible, terrible thing to do, even to your worst enemy.'

'You've got humans here too?'

'Of course.' The frog laughed – and David knew it was a laugh, not just a slightly different kind of croak. 'For pity's sake. I mean, where did you think they – sorry, this is getting awkward, and if I'm not careful I might offend you without meaning to; where did you think *humans* came from?'

'Actually, we rather thought we evolved. Out of apes.'

'Quite right.' The frog's throat bobbed, and David could almost understand the body language; almost, but not quite. 'They did. They evolved from desert-dwelling chimps living in the equatorial regions of our third biggest land mass. Smart critters, we were able to tame them, train them to do useful work, fetch and carry stuff for us. Got quite attached to them. Frog's best friend is his human, and all that. So, when we colonised that planet of yours—'

'Earth.'

'Naturally, we took a bunch of humans along with us, for transport in mountain regions where scudders couldn't go; or as pets, even. And sure, some of them escaped into the wild – these things happen – and sure, it didn't do the ecological balance a whole lot of good—'

'Like rabbits in Australia.'

'What?'

'Nothing,' David said. 'Go on with what you were saying.'

The frog hopped a couple of short hops, signifying a folk memory of mild guilt. 'It was some time before we realised how much damage we'd actually done, letting them get established like that; but of course, the conditions on the planet were absolutely tailor-made for them – climate, vegetation, abundant food sources, no major predators they couldn't handle – while we quickly found we couldn't hack it at all. All that salt water. Fact is, our initial surveys screwed up, and nobody owned up because they were afraid of the consequences. Very immature behaviour; but we were still capable of that sort of thing two million years ago. We're better now. We hope.' The frog thought about that for a while before continuing. 'Anyway, eventually the message sort of burrowed its way through our thick skulls that we'd made a mistake and the planet wasn't for us, so we cut our losses and came home. And left the humans to it, of course.' David identified the faint gleam in the frog's eye as sardonic humour. 'My, haven't you grown,' it said.

'Thank you,' David replied awkwardly. 'All right,' he went on, 'let me try this one on you. Shortly after you people abandoned Earth, a couple of you figured that if they went back there, in human shape but with, um, frog powers and—'

'Frog intelligence.'

David hesitated, then nodded. 'Frog intelligence, yes; and all the advanced technology and stuff they could carry with them. They figured that on Earth, among humans, they could pretend to be gods—'

'Not so much of the pretend, either,' the frog pointed out. 'Like we say here, if it walks like a human and talks like a human, it probably is a human. So, if they could do all the things gods can do, like work miracles and live so long they're practically immortal, who's to say they aren't gods? In human terms, I mean. Of course,' the frog added, 'we have laws about that sort of thing. Big, heavy laws you really don't want to find yourself under. Yes, I'm well aware of the case you're talking about. Caused an almighty scandal at the time; but he was from a noble family, connections in high places, right up to the Golden Lily Pad itself, so nothing could be done. Still can't, for that matter, unless he's stupid enough to come back of his own accord. Which he won't be.'

A picture of Honest John, patiently tinkering with a recalcitrant machine, drifted into David's mind. Honest John as a wanted criminal. Honest John as an amoral aristocratic empire-builder. Come to that, Honest John as a *frog* . . .

'I suppose not,' he said. 'But you're saying there was just one of him? Not two?'

'Him and his son. But the boy was just small, can't really blame him.'

'Son.' David turned his head a little. Out of the corner of his eye he could see the girl, still sleeping on the floor. 'You mean daughter.'

'I don't think so,' the frog replied. 'Of course, it's been a while, and I never actually knew him, it was before I was even born. But I'm pretty sure it was his son he took with him.' Then something clicked inside the frog's mind, and it looked up. 'Just a minute,' it said.

'Hey,' David said nervously. 'What're you looking at me like that for?'

The frog was crouching a little more than usual. 'You,' it said. 'You're one of us, we've already established that. So—'

'Yes, but—' David shook his head. 'Absolutely not. No way. You ask my mother. I mean, she may not be the sharpest knife in the drawer, but even she'd have noticed something like *that* . . .'

'Maybe,' the frog said. 'Maybe not. More to the point, what about your father?'

David frowned. 'My parents split up,' he said, 'when I was just a kid—'

The frog shook its head. 'Kids is goats,' it pointed out. 'The correct word in this context is "tadpole".'

'But that's . . .' David started to back away. 'That's nonsense,' he said. 'My mother would never have—'

The frog's throat bobbled reassuringly. 'Actually,' he said, 'it's not nearly as bizarre as you think. Let's see: on your planet, do you have a fairy tale about a beautiful princess who kisses a human – no, scratch that, on your world it'd be kisses a frog—'

'Yes, but—' David hesitated. 'Really?' he said. 'That's disgusting.'

'We think so, too,' the frog replied. 'But *we*'re broad-minded. Besides, she probably didn't realise. I mean, you're a frog, but members of the opposite sex don't run away screaming as soon as you ask them out for dinner. Or at least,' it added, 'not for that reason.'

David thought for a moment, then realised that thinking in this context was probably a bad idea. 'I've had enough of this,' he said. 'You going to take me to your leader, or what?'

The frog opened and shut its mouth in a manner that could be construed as laughter. 'You want our leader,' it said, 'you're talking to him. Sorry. If I'd known you were coming I'd have hired a band or something. We aren't very keen on hierarchies here, I'm afraid. They don't seem to work very well in a telepathic society.'

'Telepathic?' David looked up sharply. 'You mean you can read my—?'

'I could,' the frog admitted, 'but it'd be terribly bad manners. And besides, it'd probably give me a headache, no offence intended, like – well, in your case, like trying to cram your head into a very small steel helmet. Like I said, I haven't been eavesdropping, but the noise coming out of your head was audible back in the ward room.'

'Oh,' David said, turning crimson.

'Sorry, I thought you must've figured that out for yourself by now. Otherwise, how would you have accounted for the fact that we can chat to and fro like this?'

David shrugged. 'I hadn't given it any thought,' he said. 'Back home, we have stories about magical talking animals, so I assumed—'

'How very strange. The things you can make yourselves believe, I mean, just like that. We can't do that; it's half a strength, I suppose, and half a weakness. No, if I were in your shoes, I'd be asking myself, how come we seem to be speaking the same language, when a frog's tongue and palate couldn't make human speech noises, and the frog language consists of ark, erk and rivet.'

'I see,' David said. 'And, um, if you asked yourself that, what would the answer be?'

'Oh, simple,' replied the frog. 'You think you can hear words, but in fact we're sending direct into each others' minds, and I suppose your brain's interpreting it as heard speech because that's the only concept it can accept without completely freaking out. That's another advantage you've got over us: your brains protect you from stuff you can't handle. Basically, by lying.'

David closed his eyes. Perversely, he seemed to imagine that shutting his eyes in what surely had to be some kind of bad dream would help him open them in real life and make him wake up. He wanted to wake up very much indeed. 'So,' he said. 'I'm a frog, Honest John's my dad, and this is the frog homeworld. You know what? I don't think you need to be a telepath to figure out what I'm thinking right now.'

The frog gazed at him for a moment out of the depths of its yellow-and-black eyes. 'Maybe,' it said, 'you're thinking that all through your life you've had a suspicion that every time you walk into a room, everybody immediately stops talking for a split second and then carries on deliberately trying to act normal, so you won't suspect. Maybe you're thinking that thirty-odd years of taking things on trust and believing the first thing you're told just because it seems to fit the facts has got you to a point in your life where you're prepared to believe in magic talking animals simply because it's less hassle than trying to work out the truth. Maybe you've grasped the very important fact that none of the stuff they taught you in school is necessarily the truth just because they said it was, and that none of the rules that you always felt you had to obey even apply to you, because super-advanced frogs from Gamma Orionis Four don't have to take that kind of crap from anybody. Or maybe you're just wondering if there's anything to eat on this planet other than honey-roast fly.'

David frowned. 'I swallowed a fly once,' he remembered. 'By accident. I nearly threw up.'

'I don't suppose you're very fond of live prawns, either.' The yellow in the frog's eyes glowed warm. 'Look,' it said, 'you can't be expected to take all this in at one gulp, you need time to mull it over, come to terms with it all. So here's what I'd suggest. Go back to your planet and your ape-descended friends, sort out all your problems and your unfinished business there, so you aren't trailing round a whole bundle of guilt and remorse wherever you go; then, when you've got your head straight, come back and we'll talk about it. How does that sound?'

'Oh, fine,' David said. 'That's assuming I can get all these simple chores done without having my head knocked off by a low-flying pig. You don't even know what kind of godawful mess I've made for myself back there.'

'You didn't do anything,' the frog told him. 'Oh, sure,'

it went on, as David opened his mouth to protest, 'you did a couple of things that *you* aren't very happy about – cloning the girl, yes? And then the other clone, the one of you that you left to take the blame for everything. Now then: how'd you feel if I told you that where I come from – where *you* come from – that sort of thing's entirely legitimate, not to mention praiseworthy, as constituting quick thinking in a crisis?'

'Doesn't matter,' David replied. 'You can tell me I've just been chosen Frog of the Year, it still wouldn't make me feel any better. I know what I did. I'm still me.'

'Fair enough,' the frog said pleasantly. 'If it matters to you, then you'd better go back and sort it all out, otherwise you'll only fret and make yourself wretched. Fortunately, I can help you with that.'

'Really?' David grinned sardonically. 'I don't think so.'

'Straight up,' the frog replied. 'You're a frog, remember? You can do anything you want to. It's all a matter of belief, you see. For pity's sake, if you can spend thirty-two years believing you're human, kidding other humans into believing you're human, a little tidying-up's going to be a slice of cherry bakewell. All you need to do is unlock your latent potential. Get in touch with your inner frog.'

David scowled suspiciously. 'If this all turns out to be some kind of Scientology thing,' he said, 'you're going to get two-dimensional very, very quickly.'

'What's Scientology?' the frog asked, sounding puzzled.

David relaxed. 'Sorry,' he said. 'Doesn't matter, forget I mentioned it. Are you telling me I can have the same sort of, um, super-powers as the rest of them? You know, making people believe things, and all that stuff?'

'Of course.' The frog was laughing at him, but in a kind way. 'You can do all sorts of things you never knew you could. You can swim underwater, but you never tried it because you were convinced you'd drown. You can jump forty-six times your own body-length, but you never tried that either, because *people* can't. You can read minds and hear thoughts. And you can make any human believe anything you want him to, just by putting the idea in his mind and telling him, *Hey, this'd be really, really cool if it was true.* It's like with the language business we were talking about just now, how your brain makes the best of things to spare you the shock of the truth. Same principle; all you have to do is put a thought in a human's mind and he won't be able to resist, because his brain'll tell him it's one of his own thoughts. And a bloody good one, too.' The frog hopped round in a small, tight circle. 'Now can you see how easy it was for your dad to pass himself off as a god?'

David was silently thoughtful for a moment. 'About my—' he began. 'About Honest John. Sounds like he's in a lot of trouble with your lot. What's going to happen to him?'

'If you mean what are we going to do to him, the answer's nothing. He's on your planet, deeply disguised as one of you, I mean them. Grabbing him and bringing him back here would be like busting him out of one jail just to lock him up in another one. He'll stay where he is. If we need him, we can find him. Till then – well, it may be cruel and unusual, but at least our taxpayers aren't having to pay for it. But be honest: it's not him you're really thinking about. Is it?'

'No,' David admitted.

'Well, there you are. Piece of gnat.' The frog hopped

sideways a step or two, so that it could peek between David's shoes and see the sleeping girl. 'If you want her to fall in love with you, all you've got to do is reach inside her head and click on *Start program*.'

David threw that idea out of his mind like a nightclub bouncer ejecting a teenage drunk. 'Another thing,' he said. 'We've got frogs on Earth. Are they—?'

The frog huddled down a little. 'You mean the indigenous raniforms?' It hopped round in a tight clockwise circle until it was back in exactly the same place. 'Not a subject we're very comfortable with, I'm afraid. Long story short: we went to Earth because we thought there were frogs there – long-lost cousins, basically. When we got there, all we found were these dumb green things that ate flies and sat on logs. Their minds just didn't seem to want to switch on, if you see what I mean. Hell of a shock; we'd gone there expecting to find people like us – you know, people we could have a meaningful cultural dialogue with and sell things to – and instead we got the planet of the zombies. Another reason why we decided not to hang around.' The expression in the yellow-and-black eyes wasn't hard to interpret. 'It's a nice enough place to visit, so they tell me, but you really wouldn't want to live there.'

'So they tell you.'

'So they tell me, yes; but they were right about fire being hot and getting trodden on by elephants being bad for you, so I'm inclined to believe them. No offence intended.'

'None taken.' David shifted his weight off his left leg, which had gone to sleep. 'I couldn't do it, you know.'

'Sorry, do what?'

'Fiddle about with her mind to make her like me

better. I just couldn't bring myself to do something like that.'

'Really? Why not?'

'Well . . .' David thought for a moment. Yeah, *why* not, exactly? 'Because it'd be wrong,' he said.

'Immoral?'

'Immoral. Wicked. Bad.'

'I see. Tell me, is it true that on your planet, your species have these things where every so often you – sorry *they*, pronouns can be a real pain in the bum when you aren't used to them – *they* line up in two rows facing each other and start fighting and bashing and kicking until one side runs away or they're all dead?'

David bit his lip. 'You mean war,' he said.

'That too,' said the frog, 'though actually what I had in mind, I think it's called something like *rugbyfootball*. But either of those'll do. The point is, they can shoehorn something like that into their ethical system, but gently tweaking a few brainwaves in a good cause, that's unthinkable and beyond the pale. Interesting. It's a mammal thing, I guess.'

'Yes,' David said. 'Well. It is. Anyway, I can't do it, and that's that.'

'Your decision,' the frog replied, demonstrating that a shrug meant the same thing in both human and frog body language. 'In that case, you'll just have to work that one out the best you can, and the very best of luck to you. Though even if you will insist on playing by primate rules, it ought to be a foregone conclusion. I mean, when all's said and done, if it's just a simple matter of persuading her to see it your way, you don't need telepathy, you just use your vastly superior intelligence. Five-minute job, ten at the outside.'

David's leg had just shifted from numb to pins-and-needles. 'Vastly superior intelligence,' he repeated.

'Well, of course. You're one of us, she's one of them. No contest.'

'You know,' David said thoughtfully, 'you'll tell me it's because I never knew or I never tried, but I've never felt like I've got a vastly superior intelligence compared with other people. In fact, I can barely cook a jam omelette, and when the car I had once broke down I was as helpless as a newly hatched starling. I always assumed I was fairly dim.'

'Really,' the frog said. 'Well, now you know better, so that's all right. Look, I certainly don't want to seem rude, especially to such an interesting and unique visitor, but I do actually have other things I ought to be getting on with – governing the planet and so on – so I'm going to have to hop off now. Do you know how to program the elevator so it'll take you where you want to go?'

David admitted that he didn't.

'Ah. Well, in that case—'

The knowledge, all of it sealed up in a neat package, landed in David's brain like a cricket ball sailing through a greenhouse window. As a method of assimilating information it was quicker and more efficient than three hours with a Haynes manual, but it made the insides of his eyes hurt. Nevertheless, it did no harm to be polite. 'Thanks,' he said. 'So, that was telepathy, was it?'

'A mild dose, yes.'

'I can see why they call it a marriage of minds,' David said. 'Well, you've been a great help. I think. For what it's worth, I also think I probably believe quite a lot of what you've told me.'

'I'll take that as a compliment,' the frog replied. 'Well, so long, and don't swallow any wasps.'

'I'll do my very best,' David promised. The door opened and closed again, and he was alone in the room. A bag of sugar had appeared out of what he'd thought was thin air. Now, of course, he knew what to do.

Map, he thought; and a black circle, like a negative spotlight, appeared on the floor. He opened the bag and spilled a little sugar into the palm of his hand, as he downloaded the necessary data from his newly installed files. When he had a clear picture of what he wanted in his mind, he started laying out single grains of sugar on the black circle, each one representing the position of a given star, as seen from the exact point he wished to go to. When the map was complete he thought go.

If there was any movement, he didn't feel it.

And here we apparently are, he told himself. His left leg was better now, the pins and needles suddenly gone – a collateral benefit, he assumed, of instantaneous travel halfway across the galaxy. Cautiously, he opened the door. Beyond it, Honest John's workshop. Watford. Real life.

The girl grunted and stirred a little; and that was the moment at which the shiny new penny dropped and started rolling down the ramps in David's mind—

(She'd been there, hadn't she? To the frog home-world, the place he'd just come back from. And hadn't they told her about the ferocious anti-clone taboo, and other stuff like that? But she wasn't a frog, apparently – not even a clone of a frog – so why had that bunch of human-hating xenophobics even deigned to talk to her? Come to that, how had they been *able* to talk to her, since she was only a human? Likewise, how had she

come by the frog-magic powers she'd demonstrated earlier, if she was nothing but the great-lots-of-times-grand-
daughter of some transported bipedal *gastarbeiter*? And
why, most of all – why in hell's name had he brought her
back with him, when the whole point of going there in
the first place was to take her home and leave her there?)

While David was hunting around for something that
would do until a real explanation happened to come
along, she woke up.

She seemed upset about something.

CHAPTER SIXTEEN

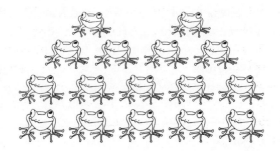

'Y̲ou hit me,' she said.
      'Well, actually—'
'You *hit* me.' There was more incredulous disbelief than anger in her voice, but that still left room for an awful lot of anger; more than you'd want to share a small, confined space like a galaxy with. 'You bastard. How could you?'

Another step back, matched by a step forward from her. 'Be fair,' he said, 'you were going to take me to the planet of the fr— back to the, um, alien homeworld, so they could execute me or something. Besides, it wasn't me that hit you.'

'Wasn't you?' He could see her doing the arithmetic. 'You mean him? The clonemaker?' She shook her head. 'He wouldn't do a thing like that, hit a woman. You would, though.'

'Me? No fear. Well, a small one, maybe, but only if I absolutely had to.'

She sneered. 'Chivalry?'

'Cowardice,' David replied. 'And when you're short and weedy like me, cowardice is an extremely valuable survival skill. Rule one, don't pick a fight with anybody who's bigger than you. Rule two, don't pick a fight with anybody smaller than you but who might have a big brother or similar relative. Rule three, when picking fights with very small siblingless orphans, wear shin-guards. Besides, you were hit from behind, and I don't have abnormally long arms.'

She frowned. 'Well, all right, then, you didn't hit me, I apologise for slandering you. Now, are you going to come quietly or do I have to drag you?'

'Come quietly where?'

'To the Homeworld, silly. You're my ticket home, remember.'

'Ah.' David pulled a wry face. 'It's not as straightforward as that, I'm afraid. You see, I've been there already, and it's not—'

'Rubbish.'

'It's not quite the way they led you to believe,' David continued firmly. 'In fact, it would appear that they were using you to get me to go there.'

'I know. That's what I just said.'

David held up his hand. 'Not quite. You see,' he went on, wondering how the hell he was going to put this, 'you aren't actually who you think you are. Neither am I. It's, um, complicated.'

'I'm sure it is. Get in the lift, or I'll thump you.'

'They wanted you to take me there,' David ground on, 'because, you see, I'm one of them.'

'One of who?'

'The fr— the aliens. Apparently, I'm one of them because Honest John – you know, the clone guy—'

'The one you say bashed me.'

'Him, yes, that's right. Apparently, Honest John's my father.'

She stared at him as if he had something growing out of his ear. 'Don't be ridiculous,' she said. 'That'd make you my brother—'

'Actually,' David said, wincing in anticipation, 'no. You see, he's my father but not yours. Or so they told me.'

'The aliens told you that?'

David nodded.

'Fine. No doubt they spoke to you through your microwave. Well, why don't we go and ask them if they'd like to confirm that?'

'I—' He took another step back, and found the wall was in the way. Awkward. Deep inside his mind, a small voice said rivet rivet.

(No, he replied, I won't do it, not under any circumstances. It's wrong.

Rivet. Rivet rivet.

I said no. My mind's made up. I'd rather go back to the planet.

Rivet rivet. Ark.

Put like that, the logic was hard to resist; and she was closing on him fast, and he really didn't want to have to go back to the planet and explain about, or to, the frogs. So instead he tried to pinpoint in his mind's eye the exact centre of her head.)

'Thought not,' she said. 'Very well, if you insist on doing this the hard way—'

There it was, the place he'd been looking for. He visualised it as a sort of control room, with workstations and screens (and in her case, armed guards on all the doors) but when he got there it wasn't like that at all. Instead it

was just a place in the middle of someone else's head
where there was a great big lever you could sort of put
your weight against—

(I really don't want to do this, he objected. Because
once I start, there's really no going back. And besides,
it's not one of those things you remember fondly when
you've been married for forty years, and she says, Hey,
do you remember that time you burgled my mind and
made me do stuff I didn't want to do, and then you
both laugh and think, how sweet we both were in those
days. And the little voice heard him and said 'Rivet ark
urk rivet', and although he hated it for being right all the
time, what else could he do?)

—So he put his weight against it, more to see what
would happen than anything else, and at first it didn't
want to budge, and then it budged a whole lot—

'Oh,' she said.

She'd stopped advancing on him, anyhow; that had to
be a good thing, because otherwise either he'd have had
to fight her (which he probably couldn't have done,
because he loved her, not to mention Rules One to
Three inclusive) or he'd have been, please excuse the
expression, frogmarched back to the alien planet; and
they'd have croaked at him as if to say, 'Oh, you again;
we thought we'd told you to go away and sort your life
out, what's *she* doing here?' And then she'd have learned
the stuff he'd been trying to tell her about, no question
about that; but in a way that would have squashed her
up like a Coke can. Somehow he figured that finding out
that she was just someone else's easily solved problem
wasn't something she'd be able to handle very easily,
especially if the truth fell on her like a bag of flour mis-
chievously balanced on the top of a door. That's what

came of being big and fierce and vibrant and passionate and alive enough to have a functional sense of self-worth; if it got bent, you were stuffed. Not a handicap he'd ever suffered from; but in her case, the damage would be hard to fix.

'Oh,' she repeated.

Cautiously, he slipped back in under the cat-flap of her mind. This time, he saw a plain white-emulsioned wall; and someone had spray-painted on it the words:

[DON'T TAKE DAVID TO THE PLANET]

– no explanations or cissy stuff like that, just a command. In his notional hand he found a pencil, so he chose a corner of the wall and started to write:

It's all right.

(That was, of course, the most important part.)

Really, he wrote on a new line, *it's no big deal, but oddly enough the aliens on the other planet look remarkably like what we call frogs. And you aren't one of them, you'll be delighted to hear. No, you're perfectly normal, apart from the being-cloned thing, and of course that's no big deal either, because you're just as real as if you've come into the world the messy, old-fashioned way and had to do all that tedious potty training and adolescence and stuff. Nor, you'll be glad to discover, are you related in any way to that tiresome Honest John character. You're not his daughter, or even an artificially generated copy of his daughter. You're you, and—*

He stopped. There were so many things he wanted to write next, things that she wonderfully was, as opposed to all the things she mercifully wasn't, but if he allowed himself to write them, he'd be crossing the line, from self-defence into interference and manipulation. Sneak in, do just enough to keep from being shoved into the elevator, sneak out again. No more; not even a doodle of a heart with an arrow through it, right up in the top left-hand corner.

'Oh,' she said; and this time, he felt confident, she meant it. 'I see,' she added.

He stared at her for two seconds. 'Good,' he said.

'Except,' she added, 'there's just one thing. If I'm not his daughter – and I can see now, I couldn't possibly be his daughter, absolutely no way; but why do I keep *thinking* I'm his daughter, and that we came to this planet yonks ago to rip off the natives? It's such a strange thing to believe, if you see what I mean.'

David nodded. 'All right,' he said, 'let's do a test. Think back. Can you remember what it was like when you were a kid?'

She frowned. ''Course not,' she said. 'I wasn't a kid, ever. I was born in a glass tank full of mutant tarka dall a couple of days ago, and before that I was a single strand of some dead person's hair.'

'Yes, but—' He slowed himself down. 'But you've got some memories, haven't you, carried over in the hair's DNA—'

'Does Not Apply?'

'You know. The gene stuff.'

'Denim? I carry other people's memories around in my trousers?'

'In the hair's genetic matrix,' he said severely. 'You said so yourself. Only some of them got a bit scrambled—'

'Because you couldn't be bothered to set the jumpers when you cloned me. I can remember *that* bit all right.'

'I'm sure you can.' He scowled at her; she stuck her

tongue out at him. It was that gesture that reminded him: a small boy dragged unwillingly to an art gallery on his birthday, a painting that had caught his eye, a trick of his imagination. 'Do you have any childhood memories?' he said.

'No.'

'Now we're getting somewhere. What's the earliest thing you can actually remember?'

'Tricky.' She furrowed her brow thoughtfully. 'Waking up in a tank full of goo, I think.'

That took David a little by surprise. 'Are you sure?'

'No, I'm lying. Of course I'm sure, you idiot.'

'Oh. But all the other stuff; about coming to this planet and—'

'It's all stuff I just seem to know,' she replied, in a distinctly thoughtful voice. 'In the same way as I know that John Whatsisname isn't my father. Only, before I knew that I knew for a fact that he was. That's – odd,' she concluded. 'Isn't it?'

But David was way ahead of her; he was back inside her mind, beside the plain white wall, and this time he knew what to look for. Didn't take him long; it was scrawled in green chalk down in the bottom left-hand corner:

[HONEST JOHN SPOONER WAS HERE]

– and under that, in smaller letters,

[What kept you?]

What the hell? he thought; but there wasn't time to hang about there, so he jumped out again. He was just wondering how on earth he was supposed to explain about frogs and telepathy when she smacked him hard across the face.

'Ouch,' he said, not unreasonably.

'Bastard!' she explained, kicking him on the left shin. He did what any well-brought-up young man would do in the circumstances, and fell over.

'Bastard!' she pointed out, kicking him on the right shoulder where he lay. 'That's for sneaking about inside my mind, you horrible creep!'

He looked up at her in amazement. 'But how did you—?'

'You told me. Just now. While you were in my head.' Her foot lashed out again, but this time he managed to wriggle out of the way. 'At least, you didn't mean to tell me, but you're so damn' noisy I couldn't help overhearing. You're a telepath, and you've been putting stuff into my mind. Like the stuff about Daddy not being—'

'Yes, but Daddy isn't. I mean,' he added, by now anticipating the speed and direction of her foot and taking the necessary evasive action, 'Honest John's a telepath, too, and he put the stuff about you being his daughter into your head. But it's not true.'

'Why should I believe you?'

'I don't know,' David admitted. 'It's just true, that's—' He stopped short, suddenly realising that he'd instinctively nipped back inside her mind. This time, however, in front of the wall there was a large, angry-looking Dobermann on a long, flimsy-looking chain. He left, very quickly.

'You don't like dogs, either,' she said smugly. 'So I imagined one. Just one, because really I'm just an old softie. Next time, it'll be like Crufts in Hell.'

'Yes, all right,' he said, cringing. 'And I'm sorry, I didn't mean to do that, it just sort of happened.'

'Well, it had bloody well better not just-sort-of-happen again.' She looked at him for a while, with anger and something else burning in her eyes. 'But I believe you,' she said.

That surprised him more than anything else. 'You do?'

She nodded. 'What you said about no childhood memories and everything,' she replied. 'It makes more sense than the alternatives. Which means,' she added, as much to herself as to him, 'that this John person's been playing games with me. With both of us, I guess.'

'That's right,' David said. 'You know, I think it's been him all along. Just him,' he added grimly.

'Just him all along what?'

He stood up. 'Come on,' he said, 'let's go and ask him.'

'Ask him what, for crying out loud?'

But – surprise, surprise – John wasn't there. No sign of him in the workshop, outside the workshop or in the street. 'He's gone,' David said.

'Good Lord, I wonder why,' she said. 'Really, you'd almost think he knew we were going to come looking for him with a view to kicking his head in. Like he's – oh, telepathic, or something.'

'And the van's gone, too.'

'I don't think the van's telepathic as well. More likely, he got into it and drove it away. There, how's that for an imaginative hypothesis?'

He turned round and scowled at her. 'And another thing,' he said. 'Will you please stop taking the mickey out of me all the time? It's starting to get on my nerves. She looked a little uncomfortable. 'Well,' she grumbled, 'at least you've got nerves to get on. More than I have, thanks to someone not a million billion light years away, who forgot to—'

'Yes, all right.' His scowl deepened. 'All right,' he said, 'you were an accident. No, worse than that, you were a mistake. An error of judgement, even. So are thousands and thousands of people. The only difference is, the way you were born.'

'But I wasn't,' she said. 'Born, I mean. Instead I came out of a tank of green glop, like Botticelli with mushy peas. And that—'

'That,' he interrupted, 'doesn't matter at all. You know your trouble? You think of yourself as a clone instead of a person. Which means you can't take yourself seriously, even when you want to.'

'What do you expect?' she snapped at him, with a catch in her voice. 'I'm not a human being, I'm a hi-tech sock puppet. I'm only here because you wanted to make some silly gesture.'

The last dribble of his patience leaked away and evaporated. 'Fine,' he growled. 'You're a puppet, so bloody what? You think you've got problems? I'm not even semi-human, I'm a *frog*. You can't possibly begin to understand – what the hell are you laughing at?'

She pressed her lips together tightly, but it didn't help. She giggled again. 'You,' she said.

'Me?'

'Yes, you. You just said you're a—'

'Frog.' He folded his arms. 'Come on, then,' he said. 'Frog jokes, let's get them over with. All right, then, I'll start. Waiter, have you got frogs' legs? No, monsieur, I always walk like this. There was an Englishman, a Lithuanian and a frog, and the Lithuanian said—'

She was laughing even more, though presumably not at the joke. (Defective memory, yes; feeble-minded, no.) 'I wasn't laughing about that,' she said, 'it was something else.'

'Was it really? Such as?'

'I was just wondering,' she told him, 'if you're really a frog, what'd happen when I did this.' And she kissed him.

It wasn't one of your great kisses. Hardly surprising, when you think about it, since all she knew about the subject was what had filtered through from the residual memories of a four-hundred-year-old strand of hair. But as far as David was concerned, it was good enough for jazz.

'And now, you see,' she was saying, grinning like an idiot, 'you're supposed to turn into something. You know, like in the fairy story?'

He looked at her. 'You're strange,' he said, 'did you know that?'

She shrugged. 'Hardly surprising, really,' she said. 'So what did the Lithuanian say?'

'What?'

'You said there was an Englishman, a Lithuanian and a frog, and the Lithuanian was about to say something. So what was it?'

'I can't remember,' David admitted. 'You still haven't told me why you did that.'

She grinned. 'To shut you up, primarily,' she said. 'You talk an awful lot, you know, and you were starting to get all stuffy and boring. And because you said you're a frog. Gives us something in common, you see.'

That one jumped right out at him like a stepped-on rake lurking in the grass. 'It what?'

'Oh, come on,' she said scornfully. 'That green goo in the cloning tanks. You do know what it is, don't you?'

'Well,' he admitted, 'no.'

'You idiot,' she said fondly – yes, genuine affection there, though he was almost too preoccupied to notice. 'It's frogspawn.'

It was one of those infuriating moments when everything feels like it ought to make sense, but it doesn't, quite. 'Frogspawn,' he said.

'Yes, you know. Where baby frogs come from. Or were you under the impression that the stork brings them? Because if that's what you were thinking, I've got to tell you, that's *not* the reason why storks are so unpopular among the frog community—'

He frowned, having noticed something unusual. 'You're babbling,' he said.

'I am not.'

'Yes, you are. All this stuff about frogs and storks. People only babble when they're embarrassed about something. What are you—?'

'Three guesses,' she snapped irritably, and kissed him again. 'Although,' she went on, disentangling herself, 'why I'm doing this, I really haven't got a clue. I guess I must like you or something.'

'It'd certainly fit the available data.'

'Maybe,' she replied, 'but it's pretty unlikely, all the same. I mean, look at you.'

'I'd rather not,' David replied, looking at her instead.

She scowled at him. 'Look,' she said, 'we've got to be sensible about this. Because, you see, chances are we're only feeling this strange, inexplicable mutual attraction because somebody's manipulated us into it, the same way they've been manipulating us both all along.'

'Good for them,' David replied. 'I definitely prefer this kind of being manipulated to the getting-framed-for-murder sort. And on balance I'd say it's probably got the edge over the being-held-hostage-by-deranged-clones variety as well.'

'Yes, but it's still not *right*.' Her scowl deepened, and she turned away. 'We can't let them get away with it, you know.'

'Really? I mean, after they've been to all this trouble.' He took a step closer; she stayed where she was. 'And for all we know, maybe the whole point behind all the being manipulated was to bring us together. In which case—'

'No,' she said firmly, 'not until we've sorted this out. Sorry, but it's really starting to bug me.'

Oh, for crying out loud, David thought. But what he said was, 'Right. In that case, let's start by finding Honest John.'

'I suppose so,' she said. She didn't seem keen. 'Did he say where he was going?'

'No.'

'Well, that pretty well blows that idea out of the water, then. Unless you were thinking of roaming around the streets of wherever this is on the off chance of catching sight of him.'

I love you with all my heart, he thought, but at times you can be so annoying . . . 'All right, then,' he said, 'so what do you suggest?'

'I don't know, do I?' She clicked her tongue. 'You're the one who wants to go charging off on a quest. That's typical male behaviour, that is, always trying to find solutions to things, like the whole of life's some kind of intelligence test. I suppose that's why men are so difficult to talk to.'

He decided he didn't want to go anywhere near that one. Instead: 'How do you know it's frogspawn?' he asked.

'Frogspawn?'

'In the tanks.'

She shot him a look you could've made yoghurt with. 'Here's me,' she said, 'practically throwing myself at you, and all you want to talk about is bloody frogspawn. Oh, thank you very much.'

He froze. 'I'm very sorry,' he said.

'Well, don't be,' she snapped. 'I don't want you to be *sorry*, that isn't going to help. I want to know what's going on.'

'Maybe we could help.'

Both of them spun round like the *Position Open* notice on a post office counter, just as you finally grind your way to the front of the queue. Standing in the doorway was someone who looked exactly like Honest John. Behind him, they could just see a whole lot of other people who looked identical, apart from a few very minor variations in shoe type.

'It's you, isn't it?' David said, realising as the words passed the gate of his teeth that even by his standards, that was a stunningly unhelpful thing to say, in the circumstances. But the man in the doorway seemed to catch his drift, because he said, 'Yes, it's me. Us.'

David tried to get between them and the girl without breaking eye contact. He succeeded in treading on her foot. 'What do you want?' he growled.

'John asked us to drop by,' the man said. 'Can we come in?'

'No.'

'Fair enough.' The man shrugged. 'I suppose I can

explain just as well standing out here in the road as indoors. I mean, it's no skin off my nose if the spectacle of a dozen identical men queuing up outside a lock-up workshop attracts a huge crowd of curious bystanders.'

'I don't believe John asked you to come here,' David maintained.

'Well, of course you don't.' The man smiled in a singularly patronising and offensive way. 'You believe we're the bad guys. Naturally. It's what you were meant to believe.'

'Meant to believe?'

The man nodded. 'To be precise, what John wanted you to believe. So of course, being a dutiful son, you believe it.'

That one hit him in the solar plexus. It was a while before he'd recovered enough to ask, 'How the hell do you know—?'

'Oh, we've known all along, silly,' the man replied. (And, yes, contrary to all expectations and probabilities, he managed to sound even more annoying than he had the last time he said anything. An amazing natural gift, wasted on a mere henchman-grade clone. With a facility for nasal intrusion like that, at the very least he should've been chairing *University Challenge*.) 'Look,' he went on, 'not wanting to harp on about it, but standing in line like this, we're obstructing the highway, and it's only a matter of time before some twat calls the police. Can we come in now, please?'

There didn't seem to be much point refusing. If they meant harm, with odds of six to one in their favour, there wasn't any real chance of keeping them out. 'All right,' David said. 'But no—'

'Funny business, I know.' The man stepped aside, and

a short column of identical versions of himself trooped in. 'Weird, really. I mean, I thought your species *like* comedy even if they're not too smart at it sometimes. But it's all right, we promise to behave. And if you do catch us telling jokes or doing extracts from Molière and Congreve, you can jolly well throw us all out again. Can't say fairer than that, now, can I?'

So they came in; and a truly bizarre sight they proved to be, too. It was like watching a bunch of Elvis impersonators lining up for an audition, except that none of them looked like Elvis. When they were all crowded inside, making the workshop feel like the Bakerloo Line hall of mirrors, their spokesclone (who was sitting on the edge of a bench, wedged in between two carbon copies of himself) cleared his throat, and said: 'Now then, would you like me to explain?'

The girl nodded. 'Yes,' she said. 'But I expect I'll be disappointed.'

'Really? Why?' replied the spokesclone, a born straight man.

'Because all you're going to do is tell us a whole load more lies,' the girl said. 'Come on, I'm not stupid, even if he is. Last time I saw you lot, you had me tied up in the back of a van.'

'True,' the clone conceded. 'But that was a necessary part of the process, as you'll see as soon as I start explaining. That's if you'll let me start, that is.'

David sighed. 'Oh, go on,' he said. 'We might as well hear him out. Not like we've got anything better to do,' he added, with a slight edge to his voice.

Either she didn't take the point or she ignored it. 'And another thing,' she said. 'Talk about your coincidences. There's me saying I want an explanation, and the words are hardly out of my mouth when you pop up to provide one. Coincidence?'

'Certainly not. More like superb timing. But then, this whole operation's worked like the proverbial well-oiled machine, though I say so myself as shouldn't. Look,' the clone went on, 'if you want us all to go away, you just say the word; we're only here for your benefit, after all. And if we push off now, we could all be home in time for the motor racing on *Grandstand*.'

'It's all right,' David said firmly. 'You say what you've got to say, and we'll form our own opinions. How about that?'

'I'm impressed,' the clone said. 'But that's the difference between you two, no offence intended; you're a frog, she isn't. Now then—'

David jumped up, inadvertently elbowing a clone in the face as he did so. 'How did you know that?' he said. 'And is it *really* true?'

'To the second question, yes. To the first question, shut up and listen, and you might just find out.' The clone sighed. 'You've changed in the last few days,' he said. 'It was a damn sight easier getting a word in edgeways the last time we did this. But now you're all self-confident and cocky – as it should be, of course, but makes my job harder.' He smiled. 'Now, then. Are we all sitting comfortably? Well, tough, because I'm beginning anyway.'

CHAPTER SEVENTEEN

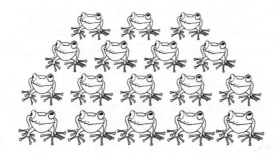

In the beginning (said the spokesclone) the world was without form and . . .

You want the short version. Okay, then: shit happens. Does that answer all your questions? Thought not. Now, if you'll shut your face and let me tell this my way, we might actually get somewhere. Thank you.

In the beginning, the world was without form and void. Worse still, it was just sitting in its orbit doing nothing except growing a bit of coal here and there: a bit like a human being first thing in the morning, really. Certainly, it wasn't making any money for anybody.

Then we came along. By we, of course, I mean someone who looks just like me – my brother, if you like – and you. Don't suppose you remember, you were only, what, three thousand, six hundred and eight at the time, barely out of nappies.

What do you mean, which one of you? Him, of course. My son, or should that be nephew? Look, this is going to get pretty convoluted in a minute or so, unless we fix this pronouns thing straight off the bat. Just assume that I'm him, all right? Which I am, of course, in many respects.

We were sent here – well, you know all that, I think, they told you when you went to Homeworld just now, I can see it in your head. The colonisation project was one of those good-idea-at-the-time things that miraculously crop up just before general elections. A bit like mushrooms, really; in fact, quite a lot like mushrooms, if you care to consider precisely what *they* crop up out of.

Well, the project failed, as I think you already know, and all the colonists packed up and came home, leaving the domesticated humans we'd brought with us to inherit the Earth, and welcome to it. And, as you also already know, you and I sneaked back here a few hundred thousand years later to do highly unethical and profoundly illegal god impersonations with a view to kidding the monkey people into providing for us in our old age.

Now, what they didn't tell you was the real reason why the project went pear-shaped. I expect they fobbed you off with a load of old socks about the water being salt or the glaciers being too slow or the sea being the wrong colour to go with the curtains. Forget all that – I mean, it's true enough, but nothing our people couldn't fix in an afternoon. No, it was something far worse than that; something we'd never even heard of before, which of course is why it didn't show up on our preliminary surveys, because it'd have been like asking a blind man to scan for paisley.

I'm referring, of course, to love.

You're damned right we don't have it back home, not

in any shape, size or form, notsoever. Think about it for a moment, will you? We're amphibians. What the humans call love is basically a by-product of their mammalian reproductive cycle, more or less in the same way that lethally toxic nuclear waste is a by-product of electricity. Think, if you will, of all the really shitty stuff mammals have got to do in order for there to be more mammals. For a start, the female mammals spend months on end waddling around as a combination mobile incubator and crèche. Hastily drawing a veil over the really gross way the little mammals actually come out into the world, let's consider the months – years, even – that lady mammals have to spend waiting on the wee horrors, wiping their little bottoms and putting up with their intolerable behaviour without strangling them or feeding them to the alligators. Let's also consider that in quite a lot of mammal species the females insist on making the males hang around while all this is going on, sending them out to do the hunting and gathering for the reproductive unit when they'd far rather be doing something else. It's a pretty tall order, if you ask me; and when you think that in our society it's as simple and straightforward as boink, lay eggs, bugger off and get on with something useful, you can see precisely why we're so much more advanced than you are. We've got the time and the vigour to invent faster-than-light travel and matter-energy conversion, because we don't devote two-thirds of our gross racial product to the spawning process.

But to get back to you poor suckers: you've got all this horrible stuff to get through somehow so obviously there's got to be an incentive, or at least some kind of fix for you to get addicted to. That's love: possibly the sneakiest trick ever played on any variety of life form by a notoriously conniving Universe. You do all these dismal, soul-destroying things because you get attached to each other.

Well, you can imagine – *maybe* you can imagine what it was like for a bunch of rational, liberated, progressive amphibians like us suddenly to find ourselves plagued by these entirely new and incomprehensible emotions. Total and absolute chaos. Nothing got done, of course; we were all too busy staring longingly into each others' eyes and going for romantic moonlit hops and sitting uncomfortably on park benches trying to tell each other about our feelings, to the point where nobody noticed that the generators had stopped working and nobody had bothered to do any building or produce any food. Luckily, when mission control back on Homeworld realised that we hadn't reported in for some time and all the transmitters seemed to be down, they got worried and sent a rescue mission to see what the matter was. As soon as they got here and figured out what was happening, they evacuated the entire colony and shipped us back home, where we spent several thousand years in isolation hospitals having our heads sorted out. Fortunately, the love thing stopped working once we'd been home for a while, and virtually all the colonists were cured and went on to lead happy, productive lives as useful members of society.

Virtually all. All minus, in fact, one. Me. And this is where it gets really rather embarrassing.

If you're considerably more perceptive than you look – and let's fact it, a small rock's more perceptive than *you* look, no offence intended – you may have noticed that earlier on I referred to you as my son. Now, consider my recent eulogy about amphibian life, with particular reference to the spawning process as practised by grown-up life forms. Hubba-hubba-hubba, eggs are produced, eggs hatch, thousands of tiny amphibians start out on life's journey. Mummy and daddy, meanwhile, are miles away lounging beside the pool, probably aren't even aware that the brood's hatched out. Once they're up and hopping, of course, you've got Buckley's chance of knowing if a particular tadpole's yours or someone else's. So, that being the case, how the hell would I know you're my son; more relevantly still, why the hell would I care?

Answer: you were conceived, tadpole mine, on this godforsaken planet, when the love thing was in full spate. Your mother – well, she was the most amazingly stunning opaque shade of greenish khaki, and she had a tongue that could nip a gnat out of the air at four centimetres. We were utterly devoted to each other – at least, we were until the rescue team got us back to Homeworld and started shining lights in our eyes. After that, she went off and left me and the last I heard of her, she was the director of some quantum physics institute somewhere, developing a whole new method of interstellar communications. More fool her, huh? Well, quite.

But – I don't know, maybe I spent more time on the planet's surface than most, or maybe I'm just more susceptible to the love stuff than regular folks; anyway, they really tried their best to cure me, but they couldn't. In the end they gave up and decided that they were going to ship me off to a remote province where I couldn't do any harm. Not this frog, they weren't; I waited till they weren't looking, and hopped it. And I took you with me.

Just you; there were six thousand, four hundred and thirty-nine tadpoles in your brood, but you were the only one I could get to in the short time available. I had to leave the rest of 'em behind; and you know, it's a funny thing but every night, when I'm trying to get to sleep, when I close my eyes I find I can see all their little faces looking up at me, like they're saying, 'Daddy, why did you go away?' Really bugs you, that kind of thing, after a few hundred thousand years.

But I'd got you; and – please excuse me if this is embarrassing for you – and I guess that because I missed your brothers and sisters so very much, all the love that should've been shared round between the whole six and a half thousand sort of got dumped on you. Sorry about that, but these things happen.

Anyway: I hotwired an elevator and brought us back here, and pretty soon I had the whole god scam running beautifully. Of course, it was an utter pain having to pretend to be humanoid all the time. (I have no idea why, but no matter how hard I tried, I just couldn't get the idea of a frog-shaped god to catch on with these people. Gods with wings, yes; gods with horns, gods with crocodile heads and cat heads and thirty-seven different heads all arguing with each other; gods in the shape of every other kind of critter that walks the face of the Earth, in fact, not to mention burning bushes and pillars of fire, but not frogs. As far as humanity is concerned, God may move in mysterious ways, but He doesn't hop.) But after a while, you can get used to practically anything, and as long as I stayed away from mirrors and pools of water, there were times when I forgot I was condemned to a lifetime in fancy dress. And as for you – well, you'd only been a frog for a tiny short time, so you never missed it at all. As far as you were concerned, the monkey suit's what you really look like. Which was fine by me, so long as you were happy; and you were. We both were, for ages and ages and ages. Until, of course, you died—

'I died,' David interrupted. 'No, sorry, that wasn't me. Something like that, even I'd remember . . .'

The clone shook his head. 'My fault,' he said. 'Trying to introduce a hint of melodrama into the narrative. Won't bother in future. Let me put it another way. No, of course *you* didn't die. You weren't even born yet. *He* died. My son.'

David frowned. 'Your other son? One of the six and a half thousand?'

'No.' The clone looked upset. 'Obviously you haven't been paying attention. It was just us two on this whole planet, us and the ape people. And we were chugging along so nicely, too. Of course, by that stage we'd more or less given up on the god thing. As scams go, it's one of the very best, but every now and again you've got to stand back and let them cool off, before things get out of control and they start having religious wars and stuff. On that occasion – well, with hindsight I'd have to say we pressed on a bit too long before stopping for a rest. Simple as that.

'At the time, though, it didn't look that bad until it was too late – and then, bingo, there we all were in the early seventeenth century, with Catholics and Protestants hating each other to bits wherever you cared to look, and the whole witchcraft thing getting horribly out of hand almost overnight; well, in our terms, anyhow.

'A bad time, then, and certainly a point where both of us needed to keep a cool head. Instead, what do you go and do? You fall in love.

'Well, yes. Who am I to talk, because it was me falling for the whole love thing that caused the problem in the first place. I accept that now, but back then I just couldn't see it. After all, she was a human, this Philippa Levens person you were suddenly besotted with. As far as I was concerned, it wasn't just inappropriate and inconvenient, it was downright obscene. But you wouldn't see that, or couldn't; of course not – as far as you were concerned, you were as human as she was, and so was I, and all these objections I kept raising didn't make sense. I was just being difficult, a spoilsport. So, understandably enough, you didn't listen to anything I told you, even the bits that actually made a whole lot of sense, like: whatever you do, don't go teaching this chickadee of yours anything even remotely resembling magic powers; not when there're nasty men in black hats wandering around the place calling themselves witchfinders-general and what have you.'

The clone was crying.

'Which is odd,' he said, fumbling a handkerchief out of his pocket, 'when you consider that the sad bit, which is coming up right after this break, isn't actually *my* sad bit, because of course I wasn't there at the time. None of us were, the tanks we came from hadn't even been designed back then, so really there's no call for me to get all upset like this, is there? Oh, sure, I've got exactly the same memories as he has, right down to the last heart-breakingly pathetic detail, but I wasn't actually involved, you aren't actually my son. I mean,' he added, sniffing ferociously, 'even if you were actually him – which you aren't, of course – you wouldn't be my son.' He dabbed at his one eye. 'So, either I'm crying because it's just a very, very sad story and anybody would be moved to tears by it – no frog is an island, and all that – or else it's some kind of genetically coded reaction, I don't know. But then, we're all coded, aren't we? Coded to buggery . . . All of us, we've all got his memories and his brainwave patterns locked away in our heads; she's the same, she came loaded with Philippa Levens, like a new PC with its operating system already installed; and she's a mammal as well, so she's got all that emotional-instinctive stuff clogging up her hard drive. And as for you – well, I'm coming to that.'

'Good,' David replied.

All the other clones were snuffling now: David noticed that eight of them went for their handkerchieves at exactly the same moment, in precisely the same way. Now *that* was unnerving.

Anyway, continued the clone, where was I? Oh yes.

You see, you fell in love with this girl. We were in England at the time (well, everybody's got to be somewhere), we were playing at being country squires, keeping our heads down, just pottering quietly along, seeing what it was like to be normal and ordinary, just for a lark. That big house in Buckinghamshire, where we had our previous little talk: that was where we were living at the time. You might say it's been in the family for generations, or at least generation.

Details; let's see. She was the niece of the next squire along, she'd come to pay a visit. She was riding in the deer park when her horse stubbed its hoof on a molehill and catapulted her into a small pond. When you came by, she was sitting in the water with pondweed in her hair – it's only just occurred to me but maybe that's what attracted you to her in the first place. No? Well, that's exactly what your mother was doing when I first set eyes on her.

Anyway. You fished her out and took her home to dry off, and one thing led to another; and right from the start I was thinking, no good'll come of this, it'll all end in tears, but I ignored all that because you were obviously dotty about this mammal person, and I knew that if I made you choose between her and me— Well, there you are. Nothing like that ever happens on Homeworld, which is why we have particle sublimation technology and humans have Mills & Boon. Did you know, by the way, that if humanity put the same level of resources into biopolymer research that they currently devote to growing long-stemmed red roses, by now you could've invented plastic steel? Just a thought.

So there you were, courting away like a little peacock; and, needless to say, you were showing off, because that's what mammals do, they can't resist it when the female gazes at them with big round eyes and says, Gosh, you're so clever . . . Crazy thing is, nine times out of ten the female isn't impressed at all: she's just saying to herself, being able to do this matters a lot to him, obviously, so I'd better pretend I'm interested. Well, there you are. And you were showing off, like I said, and you were telling her you could do magic. And of course she's saying, Go on, don't be silly, you can't really do magic, cue big round eyes and smouldering glance, excuse me while I throw up. And you said, I can so do magic, just watch. And I can't remember offhand how it started, but the upshot was that you taught her how to turn people into frogs.

Not that you did, of course; what you taught her was how to make everybody *believe* that some poor fool of a mammal was a frog. Same difference; because when she went home, she couldn't resist trying it out just to see if it really did work, and she'd never much liked her lady's maid anyhow. And she turned her back again immediately, no harm done; except that a couple of the village kids happened to be watching from behind some bushes, and so they ran straight home and told their folks, guess what, the fine lady up the big house is a witch. And the parents clipped them round the ear and said, don't say that kind of thing about your betters, and then went out and told the parson; and the parson told the archdeacon, and the archdeacon wrote a letter to London, and three men in black hats were on the next stagecoach, just in time to see young mistress Levens play the same trick on the innkeeper's son.

We've got to do something, you said; and I told you, too bloody right we've got to do something, we've got to get as far away from here as we can, pretty damn quick. And I explained to you that although our people live so very, very much longer than humans do, this admirable longevity is conditional on our not getting tied to a stake with brushwood piled up round our toes and getting set light to. Getting killed isn't good for us, it's really bad for our health. But you wouldn't listen: we used to be gods, you said, we used to have people worshipping us and asking us as a special favour to bring back the sun every morning, surely we can still do a pathetically simple little thing like rescuing one girl. And I tried to explain – my mistake, I should have known better – I tried to explain that back then, the stuff we did that the humans thought of as magic was good, they liked it when we did it; now, I tried to tell you, magic is bad, and they'll torch us before we can say alacazam! And while I was explaining this very basic truth about human perceptions and the effects of religious fervour on the feeble mammalian brain, you said some very unkind things and went storming off.

I keep asking myself – because I can't actually remember after all this time – did I just sit there sulking because I'd absorbed all these human emotions, or do our people back on Homeworld have huffs and offence and umbrage and all that sort of destructive shit too? If it's a purely human thing – and it's got to be, surely, because our lot are *advanced* – then that's another thing I can wallow in guilt and self-torture about. Me and my stupid addiction to this loathsome little planet: if we'd both stayed home, none of this would've happened.

When you didn't come home, at first I told myself he's still sulking, damned if I'm going to be the one who backs down and apologises, after all, I'm his father, and I'm right. Then, when you still didn't come home, I was thinking, where the bloody hell can he have got to? Then, when you still hadn't come home, I started worrying. Then I thought, screw it, and went looking for you.

It wasn't till quite some time later – years, actually – that I finally managed to piece it all together and figure out what happened to you. I won't bore you with the detective work, I'll just cut to the chase.

You went running off to rescue the girl from the black hats; but by the time you got there, it was all over bar the shouting and the charming local custom of roasting chestnuts in the embers. You were a bit cut up about it all, to say the least. Your first instinct was to turn the whole lot of them into frogs; fortunately for everyone involved, you thought better of that. Instead, you resolved to bring her back to life, or at least the next best thing.

You thought: I think I'm human, but really I'm a frog. But I and they *believe* I'm human, and so does everybody else; doesn't that mean that, for all practical purposes, I'm just as human as anybody else? Fine, you thought: if there was a girl, and she wasn't actually Philippa but I believed she was Philippa, and she believed the same thing, and she was exactly identical to Philippa in mind and body, right down to the mole on her neck and her occasionally infuriating habit of changing the subject in the middle of an argument – well, wouldn't she be Philippa, for all practical purposes?

So that was what you did: you looked round till you found a girl in the village who was Philippa's age, and you turned her into Philippa, using a slight variation on the old frog hex. I can't remember offhand who the poor kid was – some tradesman's daughter, I suppose. Anyway, you went ahead and did it. But – no offence, son, but you never were quite as good at the turning-things-into-things schtick as you thought you were. The Philippa you created looked just like her, but there was a very slight personality drift. Only one character trait was affected: she wasn't in love with you. Instead, she was in love with her cousin, Nathaniel Snaithe, a notary with a thriving practice in Princes Risborough.

When you realised that, you weren't happy. In fact, you were just a little bit upset, which probably goes some way to explain what you did next. Screw the both of them, you exclaimed, and may they be very happy together; you scampered off to the next village down the valley, found another girl of the right age, and tried again.

Well, this time you did slightly better. The girl that resulted from this escapade was in love with you, but there was significant personality drift in other areas: Philippa Levens 1.3 was short-tempered, sarcastic and inclined to be unreasonably miserable, which disappointed you rather. Amazing how stupid young men can be: you actually tried to persuade her to be more cheerful, less of a pain in the bum; and while you were engaged in this utterly idiotic project, somehow or other she figured out what had happened, what you'd done.

Fireworks? Imagine November the Fifth if Guy Fawkes had actually succeeded. Cut a long story short: she told you exactly what she thought of you and stormed off, expressing the wish that she never set eyes on you again, on this or any other planet.

Here the story bifurcates, like a split end. Let's follow up her story first. Having pranced off in a huff, she walked into our village. Bad move, since they'd just finished burning her at the stake. However, they were nothing if not persevering, those black hats. If at first you don't succeed, they told themselves, try, try again. Rough on the girl, of course. Why *do* humans barbecue each other to death in this peculiar manner? Never could figure it out, and I've been on this planet longer than *Homo sapiens* has existed.

Enough about her: exit your second chargrilled baby, back to you. The second girl's parents found out what you'd done, or at least part of it: someone had seen you put the first stage of the hex on her and make her vanish, anyhow. Off they hurtled to get the back hats, who grabbed you before you knew what'd hit you (probably the flat of a shovel, but I wasn't able to get reliable data on that point), tied you up real good, and slung you in jail pending trial and incineration.

Now this brings me to what I've always thought was a flaw in the whole witch-catching business; namely, if someone was really a witch or a wizard, and a bunch of ordinary guys managed to catch this person – well, think about it: the witch or wizard isn't going to hang meekly about while they heap up the firewood. Screw that. Said person'd turn the guards into frogs and run like hell, and if they can't do a simple thing like that, stands to reason they can't do magic, period, and they're not guilty, by definition. Anyhow; you raniformed a couple of warders and hopped away. All fine as far as it went, but there you still were, hunted man with price on head; talk about your dead-end jobs.

Then, purely by coincidence, you stumbled on a little secret. To be precise, my stolen interstellar elevator, which I thought I'd hidden so carefully that nobody would ever find it again. Well, I thought under a church was pretty neat. I've been wrong quite often, over the years.

Needless to say, you were thrilled to bits. Hop on the elevator, you thought, and off you go to Homeworld; not only do you escape the black hats and their lynch mob, you wind up on a planet where love doesn't exist, and where they can cure you of being in love with the late Philippas before you end up hexing every female on Planet Earth. Ideal, yes?

Except for one drawback: you couldn't get the perishing thing to start. All systems were perfectly functional – I'd been very careful about servicing and maintenance over the years – but the central data processing unit was missing, or so you thought. Actually, all you had to do was walk down the churchyard as far as the village pond, carrying a jam jar, and you could've scooped up enough computing power in five minutes to get you to Andromeda. But, of course, you weren't to know that.

You're giving me that totally blank expression again. All right, it's like this. On Homeworld we'd experimented with silicon-based information technology back in our Dark Ages, and given it up as a bad job. Too unpredictable, couldn't be relied on. The plain fact is, any civilisation based on what humans think of as computers is never going to get much further than the evolutionary equivalent of potty training, because the hardware will let them down: it'd be like trying to build a ladder to the stars out of freshly boiled spaghetti. Not to put too fine a point on it, that's the reason why I took it on myself to give mankind silicon-based information technology in the second half of the twentieth century. It was my way of encouraging humanity to develop along the lines I wanted them to go along; or, if you prefer, sabotage.

Our people, by contrast, use *real* computers, ones that work; and what drives them is not tiny quivering rocks, but organic brains.

To begin with, we used bees: a nice, straightforward hive mind that could handle binary code quickly and efficiently (and the honey was a nice bonus, as well). But bees took up a lot of room and had a tiresome habit of stinging you or dying of pique, so we switched to ants instead. Ants were good enough to get us halfway across the galaxy – to here, in fact – but they were still limited. They could do yes/no stuff, run up the left channel or the right, but they couldn't think in more than two dimensions. Then we landed on Earth, and guess what we found. That's right: terrestrial frogs.

Well, it was exactly what we needed. The frogs we found here weren't sentient, like us; we weren't obliged to build schools for them or give them the vote. But their brains were inert microcosms of our own; like ours in the way that a Matchbox toy car is like a real Ferrari. Six Earth frogs could outcompute several million ants, and do things ants never could. So we converted our antiquated, no pun intended, systems to Raniform-Activated Memory, and never looked back.

Anyway, that's what was missing from the elevator when you tried to fire it up. Reasonably enough, you couldn't figure it out from first principles (and of course I'd never actually told you; I didn't want you skipping off and leaving me, which was why I'd hidden the elevator in the first place) so you were stuck here after all, with no way of getting off the planet. Meanwhile, the black hats were closing in. What to do?

You won't like what I'm about to tell you.

As you came out of the church, you saw some guy with a scythe cutting the grass in the churchyard. You walked up to him and hexed him; you turned him into you. Then, while he was still wondering what the hell was going on and why he suddenly felt different, you thumped him on the head and left him sleeping peacefully for the black hats to find. Then you ran away.

I don't know whether you felt bad about it at the time. Me, I'd have felt bad about it and I've never actually liked humans terribly much. Since you were always that much closer to them, I guess you probably felt pretty raw about the deal, but not bad enough to hold still and let the black hats catch you instead. I don't know, and you don't, obviously, so it's not much use speculating, is it?

Looked at objectively as a tactical gambit, though, it was smart. But things didn't pan out the way you'd intended; because as you sprinted away from the churchyard, leaving your scapegoat to his fate, you ran straight into the black hats and the lumpy end of a hay rake. The rest, I'm sorry to say, is pyrotechnics.

As for the little guy in the churchyard: I don't know why it works this way, but if one of us turns someone into something and then dies, the hex goes away and they're back to normal immediately. So the little guy came to no harm, no thanks to you. In human terms, that's a good thing. I didn't see it that way, but I'm biased.

So there I was: my son dead, all my fault. All I could think about was, how am I going to put this right? Because I couldn't just leave it like that, *accept*. It's not the way we do things where you and I come from. We fix.

Now, then. Back home, we'd known for centuries how to synthesise a copy of a living thing from one small sample taken from the original – what you've come to call cloning. But we'd also taken an irrational dislike to it at a similarly early stage. I don't know why; purely a cultural thing, something like some humans not eating pork or wiping their bottoms with their right hands. Anyway, it was taboo, *verboten*, not to be done under any circumstances. But it *could* be done. That, of course, was all I knew about it, since because of this taboo thing the actual technology was kept very quiet indeed, and I'd never come across it.

But I had time; God knows, I had plenty of time. I could figure it out from first principles. Easy. It'd take a few hundred years or so, but I could make another you, not absolutely identical but a damn sight better than nothing, provided I had just a tiny piece of you to start with.

That's the trouble with burning at the stake, though; it's so annoyingly final. Nothing left but ash, with all the genetic codes burned out. I went through your things, looking for a hair or a stray toenail clipping, but that was no good. When you died, you see, all the imaginary human bits fell out from under the hex, and the hair and nails and flakes of skin vanished into thin air. You were gone. Completely.

All I found was a single lock of Philippa's hair. And that gave me an idea. When – not if; when I got you back, I'd clone you a Philippa Levens from the lock of hair, and then everything really would be right again, as if I'd never interfered.

Anyway. I set to, brushed up on my high-school science, figured out what I didn't know. After a century or so I could see it was going to be a long job, so I hit on a short cut.

I caught an Earth frog, and grafted bits of me into the poor little sucker, like grafting apples, to make it a true Homeworld frog. Then I turned it into a human. Sure enough, it believed it was human, and set out to make its way in the world – with a little help from me, of course. From then on, it was a matter of subtle genetic engineering. In each generation, by fiddling about with the lives of innocent humans and badgering them into

forming relationships with other innocent humans, I
bred you, chromosome by weary chromosome, a dash of
spliced-in frog now and again to keep the levels topped
up, personality traits woven in heedless of trouble and
expense. Backwards-calculating the genome was a mammoth task in itself – it took two hundred and
ninety-seven thousand arranged marriages over three
hundred and twenty years just to get the shape of your
nose right. The whole project nearly fell apart in 1782,
when one of your key ancestors somehow managed to
die of cholera in southern India while my back was
turned. I had another nasty turn in 1869, when one
of your however-many-greats-it-is grandmothers in
Andalusia ran off with a handsome but entirely unsched-
uled bullfighter on the eve of her wedding to the
candidate of my choice. But I fixed both of them, and a
score of others besides; and now here you are. Not the
original you, by any means; but close enough for government work, as the saying goes.

That just left the final stage: mental attitude.

Physically and mentally, you were as near as dammit
to completion. The hardware was ready and the operating system was installed, but I still needed to do the last
bit of programming. I needed you to fall in love with
Philippa Levens. And not just any old Philippa Levens;
that would have been too easy. No, it had to be the right
one, the one whose lock of hair I'd managed to get hold
of so I could clone her for you. Philippa Levens 1.3.

Which one was that? Well, not the real one, because I
didn't have any of her to work with. And not the first
pretend-Philippa-Levens, the one who ran off with her
cousin, for the same reason. The lock of hair I had came
from the second pretend-Philippa, the one who stormed

off in a hissy-fit and got caught by the black hats. It'd got snagged on a stray bramble as she ran away from you, and it was pure luck that I was able to bag and tag it at the time.

So: impossible task number two. I had to make you fall in love with a girl you'd never really been in love with, first time around. I'd taken account of this during the centuries of the breeding-you process, making a few tiny tweaks and modifications here and there that would lead to you preferring the foul-tempered, miserable version of Philippa Levens to the sweet, charming Mark I. Astoundingly, I managed to lay the genetic and behavioural groundwork, so to speak, but even I couldn't crack it so it'd be love at first sight. In order to achieve that result, I had to recreate a substantial part of the experiences that led up to Philippa 1.3 coming into existence. To be precise, you had to create your own Philippa 1.2, selfishly and without really considering anybody's feelings but your own, only to lose her to someone else, just as happened the first time. Then you had to create your Philippa 1.3 as an even worse act of selfishness, and she had to find out at least part of what you'd done; then you had to seem to lose her for ever, *and* find yourself in such desperate, life-threatening schtuck that you'd go even further and create the scapegoat version of you to throw to the wolves, just exactly like the first time. And you did, just as I was sure you would. I managed it all by running off a bunch of clones of myself, partly because I can't be in twelve places at once, partly so you'd be kept confused and terrified and thoroughly off-guard at all material times, therefore unable to put two and two together until it was time to send you to the Homeworld for a short interim briefing, using one of the spare elevators I've built over the years. To get you to the precisely calibrated pitch of panic I needed, I had my alter egos pretend to be evil clones gone astray and meaning me harm; and to help you grow the necessary degree of backbone, I put you through various unsettling hassles that I knew you'd be able to get yourself out of once you'd built up the necessary emotional muscle. Every step along the way, every single thing that's happened has been in the script since the early seventeenth century; and, to my total astonishment and overwhelming relief, it's all worked out just right, to the millimetre, to the half-second. I am, of course, the original me, the one you've been thinking of as Honest John, though my given name is, in fact, Rivet. It's now (he glanced at his watch) 23:42:16 precisely, which is two seconds ahead of the schedule I wrote in 1619, but in the circumstances I think I'm entitled to say, So Fucking What? I've finished now. The rest is up to you.

CHAPTER EIGHTEEN

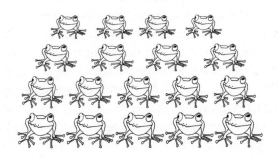

David stared at him for four seconds. Then he swung as hard as he could with his right fist and knocked him off his chair on to the ground.

'Bastard!' he pointed out.

Honest John sat up, wiped blood from his nose and glanced at his watch again. '23:43 precisely,' he said. 'I'm delighted to say we're exactly back on schedule. Ouch,' he added, with feeling.

David stepped back and tapped the girl lightly on the arm. 'Your turn,' he said.

'What?' She looked round distractedly. 'Don't understand.'

'Your turn to bash him,' David explained. 'You *do* want to bash him, don't you?'

To his surprise, she shrugged. 'Not really,' she said. 'What good would it do?'

'But . . .' He wasn't quite sure how to put something so blindingly obvious into words. 'But you heard what he said. He admitted it, it's all his fault. He arranged *everything*—'

'So?'

David's jaw dropped. 'Oh . . .' he said in an anguished voice. 'Oh well, guess I'll just have to take your turn.' He lashed out again, this time connecting with Honest John's chin.

'Hey!' John said, picking himself up again.

'Well?'

John's voice was rich with awe and wonder. 'I didn't expect that,' he said.

'It's your own fault, you brought it on yourself . . .'

'I didn't *expect* that. Don't you get it? Four hundred years,' John went on. 'That's the first genuine surprise I've had in four hundred years. *Thank* you,' he added, smiling warmly, if a little lopsidedly.

A look of intense pain crossed David's face; then he shook his head and turned to the girl. 'I'm sorry—' he began.

'Don't be. Not your fault.' Her voice was as cold as last night's take-out korma. 'Blaming you would be a bit like blaming the stone rather than the small boy for breaking the window, don't you think? And before you say anything, don't blame him either. He was really only trying to be helpful, in his own misguided way.' She smiled bleakly. 'You know the funny thing about this? I'd actually managed to forgive you for creating me when I thought you'd done it of your own free will. Now, though, I can't forgive where forgiveness isn't needed; and since it wasn't you who fell in love with me, it was a dead Jacobean frog of which you're an authentic modern replica, polite term for "fake" – well, no feelings are called for in this matter, and accordingly I have no feelings. That pretty well covers everything, wouldn't you say?' She laughed bitterly, and turned to look at Honest John. 'Did I get that right, or did I leave anything out? And from now on, wouldn't it all be much simpler and tidier if we had scripts?'

John shook his head. 'None of my business any more,' he said. 'I've done my part. From now on, you're on your own.' He frowned, and asked David, 'What's so funny?'

'You,' David replied. 'You said that like you expected us to believe it. But how the hell are we expected to believe anything you tell us?'

'Simple,' John replied, looking just a little confused. 'You're one of Us, remember? Just take a look inside my head and see for yourself. I was assuming you'd been doing that while I was explaining everything just now; from that expression on your face, I take it you didn't.'

'No.' David shook his head. 'And if you think I'm climbing inside your mind, you're mistaken. I wouldn't go in there if you paid me.'

John laughed. 'You make it sound like it's full of spiders.'

'I have the feeling that what's inside your head is way, way beyond spiders,' David replied. 'Besides, even if I did crawl in there and poke about, that'd prove nothing. For all I know, you can lie just as easily with your mouth shut as open.'

'Please yourself,' John said, apparently unconcerned. 'But as far as I'm concerned, I've done what I set out to do, and flawlessly, and bang on time. Dammit, when you consider that your human pals can't even do something as simple as build a road without it dragging on endlessly and costing twice as much as they thought it

would, I think a pat on the back might be in order.
Maybe even just possibly a word or two of thanks—'

'Drop dead.'

'Leave him alone,' the girl sighed. 'Or, if you insist on
fighting, do it outside. You're giving me a headache.'

Instinctively, John and David looked at each other; for
a split second, you could have imagined they were father
and son . . . 'I think I'll go outside for a walk,' John
announced. 'And you lot,' he said to the twelve carbon
copies of himself, 'stop gawping and come with me. If
you've got nothing better to do, you can go for a walk.
Like the old proverb says, a strolling clone gathers no
moss.'

After they'd all trooped outside, neither David nor
the girl (and what the hell am I supposed to call her?
David asked himself. Philippa? Philippa #3? Clone Girl?
Ms Levens? Sweetheart . . . ?) said anything for some
time. Eventually—

'All those frogs,' David said. 'Wonder what he wanted
them for.'

She looked up at him. 'Frogs?'

He nodded. 'One time when I went to his workshop,
the whole place was seething with frogs. The building
was full of 'em, and they'd spilled out into the road.'

'Sounds like he was building a computer.'

'Must've been a biggie, then. Didn't he say it only
took a dozen or so?'

'Can't remember. Wasn't listening particularly.'

He got the impression that she didn't really want to
talk about frogs. 'You know,' he said, 'if I'd done philosophy instead of computer science, I could really hurt my
head thinking about this. I mean to say: I'm ambling
peacefully along, minding my own business, I've

managed to reach the age of thirty-two without having had to get a life – no small achievement, if you ask me – when suddenly God pops up out of a propane-fuelled burning bush and says, Guess what; your whole life's been mapped out for you, and you've had no free will whatsoever. And I say, Right, fine, we covered that possibility in year two, I can handle it. And then God says, Ah, but from now on, you're on your own, and all the consequences of the mess I got you into will be your fault entirely.' He shrugged. 'It'd explain a few things about God,' he said. 'All that moving in mysterious ways is just ducking to avoid things thrown at Him.'

'You're weird,' she observed. 'Did you know that?'

David shrugged again. 'Don't blame me,' he replied, 'I only work here. You got any complaints, take them up with the designer.'

'Ah.' She smiled thinly. 'Excuses. Always useful to have a good excuse or two by you, in case of emergencies. You know what? I don't believe in all this product-liability stuff. It's like suing the rope manufacturer because a century ago your great-grandfather hanged himself.'

'They'd do that in America,' David pointed out. 'Normal business practice over there.'

'Only goes to show,' she replied listlessly. 'There's creatures even more alien than frogs, if you know where to look.'

Something about the way she said it led him to believe it wasn't only Americans she had in mind.

'Meaning me?' he asked.

'Oh, I don't know,' she said impatiently, 'does it matter? It's all pointless anyhow.' She sat down on a workbench. 'Your father,' she went on, 'your father and his clones, I should say, they've tactfully gone away so you can talk to me, sort out whatever nonsense it is that I'm fretting about in this silly little head of mine.' She snarled. 'When he comes back,' she went on, 'I've a good mind to make him drink his cloning tanks. One by one,' she added savagely, 'if necessary, intravenously.'

'I see. Just now, you were saying hitting him was pointless.'

'Changed my mind.'

'It was just an observation, not a criticism.'

'Good.' She picked up an adjustable wrench and threw it across the room. 'Well,' she said, 'you'd better get on with it.'

'With what?'

'Persuading me of the error of my ways.'

David shook his head. 'I wasn't planning on doing that, if it's all the same to you,' he said. 'I figure that how you feel is how you feel. When you've got that figured out, maybe you'll tell me and then at least I'll know.'

She shrugged. 'I could do.'

'For what it's worth,' he went on, 'I'm pretty sure I still love you.'

She looked round. 'Pretty sure?'

'I'd say about seventy per cent certain. Of course, it's a bit early yet to say for sure. I've only been master of my fate and captain of my soul for about three minutes, and this feeling I'm assuming is love may turn out to be indigestion.'

'Fine.' She turned her head and looked round the workshop. 'Talking of which,' she said, 'I'm hungry.'

'Me too.'

'In fact,' she went on, 'I'm starving. Do you think there's anything to eat?'

David shook his head. 'There were biscuits,' he said, 'but I think John and I ate them all.'

'Selfish pigs. Besides, I want something a bit more substantial than a couple of Rich Teas.'

'I won't argue with that,' David said. 'Tell you what: how about going and finding something to eat? After all, this is Watford, the Constantinople of the Home Counties. At the very least there's got to be a fish-and-chips place around here somewhere.'

'I like fish and chips.'

'There you are, then.'

A thoughtful look crossed her face. 'I wonder why,' she said. 'I mean, what subtle purpose in your dad's grand design is served by having me like cod in crispy golden batter? Knowing him, there must be a purpose.'

David considered that for a moment. 'Perhaps our mutual fondness for cod and chips is what brings us closer together,' he said. 'You know, shared interests, all that stuff.'

'Actually, my favourite is rock salmon.' She paused, frowning. 'And that's odd, because I'm prepared to bet good money they hadn't invented fish and chips when I was alive. Come to think of it, by the time I died, Sir Walter Raleigh had only just discovered the potato.'

'Good point. So it must be deeply rooted programming after all. Have you got any money?'

'No, of course, not. Have you?'

'No. But that's all right,' he added. 'I know where John keeps the petty cash tin.'

She looked at him for quite some time. 'In other words,' she said, 'you're suggesting that if we ignore all this stuff – everything that's been done to us, basically – it'll just go away and we can live happily ever after.'

David shook his head. 'Not really,' he said. 'In fact, if we're going to have any kind of lasting relationship, I can see that fairly soon we'll need to have a whole series of long, dreary, horribly embarrassing conversations about it, of the kind that can only end in tears, recriminations, slammed doors and mutually assured sulking. What I'm hoping is that after a while, we'll both get so sick and tired of the subject that we'll leave it alone. Unlikely, though. You can't have serious relationships where you only talk about nice stuff; that'd be like skipping the main course and having a triple serving of ice cream. It specifically says in the Rules you can't do that.'

She frowned. 'Just as well,' she said.

'Oh, I agree. It also says we've got to have lots of those conversations where you keep trying to make me understand how you feel, and I keep agreeing with you and saying, Yes, you're exactly right about that, and still you won't shut up. But that's OK, because I'll be expecting them.'

She was still frowning. 'Tell me,' she said. 'Do you happen to know offhand what we saw in each other, four hundred years ago?'

David shrugged. 'Sorry,' he said, 'no idea. I don't have any memories from my previous life, I'm afraid. How about you?'

She shook her head. 'The same,' she replied. 'I mean, there must've been something.'

'Obviously, I must've been absolutely crazy about you, or else John wouldn't have gone to all that trouble just to make sure we got back together again.'

'Stands to reason,' she agreed. 'And I must've had it really bad to go and get myself burned as a witch.

Twice,' she added. 'Wonder what on earth it could've been.'

'Search me.'

'Oh, come on.' She scowled at him. 'In your case, I'd have thought it's fairly obvious.'

'Really?'

'Sure. Straightforward physical attraction, nothing more complicated than that.'

'Oh.' He raised an eyebrow. 'You find me physically attractive?'

'Not you, idiot. I mean what you saw in me. You probably took one look and started drooling.'

'You think so?'

'A born drooler if ever I saw one. No, what I can't begin to figure is what the attraction was from my point of view. Could be you originally had nice eyes or something, and John wasn't able to reproduce them exactly with his selective breeding stuff. Or maybe I just had a soft spot for short, annoying men. Obviously some women must like them, or the strain would've died out thousands of years ago. Where are you going?'

David kneeled down and fished about under the bench. 'Somewhere,' he said, 'around here. Ah, yes, got it.' He pulled out a battered grey cash box and opened it. 'We're in luck,' he said. 'Two ten-pound notes and some copper. Well, are you hungry or aren't you?'

She pulled a face, one he couldn't immediately classify or interpret. 'I don't know,' she said.

'You don't know if you're hungry?'

She nodded. 'And that's not all,' she said. 'Truth is, I'm not sure I know *anything*.'

'Really?' David chewed his lower lip thoughtfully. He'd had conversations like this before, ten years ago, when he was a student; conversations so like this one, in fact, that he was prepared to bet that the next line would be—

'I suppose,' she said, 'it all depends on how you define *know*.'

Exactly right. Spot on, even down to the tone of voice. There's depressing for you. 'Well, quite,' he said, 'definitely one of your all-time top five grey areas. Meanwhile, if you want to go and get something to eat . . .'

'Mostly what I don't know,' she went on, as if he hadn't said anything, 'is how much of me is *me*, and how much is just Personality Traits for Windows 3.1.' She picked up a St Bruno tin full of small drills and threw it at the opposite wall. 'You want to know if I'm hungry? How the hell should I know? Maybe I'm hungry, maybe a dead Jacobean witch used to feel a bit peckish around this time of day, or maybe my CPU clock has just triggered the rumble subroutine in my stomach. I'm supposed to be in love with you; when I close my eyes and ask myself if this is true, everything seems to say yes; but when I ask myself *why*, nobody seems to know, or if they do they aren't telling. Whose favourite colour is red, hers or mine?' (A tack hammer and a ratchet screwdriver went hurtling after the box of drills.) 'Did *she* throw things when *she* got angry and upset, or is this destructive streak all pure me? Or is it because you made a mess of cloning me and forgot to set the jumpers?' She hefted a cordless drill, searching the opposite wall for an appropriate aiming mark. 'And you have the boneheaded insensitivity to stand there asking me if I want to go out and get *food*.'

'Sorry,' David muttered.

She threw the drill at him. Fortunately he'd anticipated

that possibility, and ducked just in time. 'Don't be *sorry*,' she screeched, 'it's not your *fault*. It's not anybody's fault. That's why it's so bloody *annoying*.'

David counted up to ten under his breath. 'Have you stopped throwing things?' he asked.

'For now,' she replied. 'I reserve the right to throw some more stuff later, if the situation calls for it.' She shook her head. 'Tell me,' she said, 'the other people who love you, did any of them ever say why? I'd just like a starting point, is all.'

David shrugged. 'My mum loves me because I'm her son,' he replied. 'Which is another way of saying she doesn't know why, either. Just – well, just Because, I guess.'

'Others?'

'Not that I'm aware of. Unless you count John, bearing in mind what he said.'

She shook her head. 'Leave him out of this. Just your mother, then. You're sure?'

'Pretty sure.'

'Oh.' She frowned. 'That's odd. I mean, you aren't *that* bad.'

'Thank you.'

'You're welcome.' She looked round, scanning the workbench. David stepped forward and handed her a cold chisel. 'Try this,' he suggested.

'Thanks.' It took quite a chip out of the opposite wall. 'I didn't see that there.'

'It was half buried under a pile of old newspapers,' David explained. 'What'd you like to try next? There's a nice steel set-square under the bench here.'

'I'll pass for now, thanks. Actually, I feel a bit better already.'

'My mother used to throw things when I was small,' David said. 'Teddy bears and scatter cushions, mostly. She had a foul temper but she was always practical.'

'Very sensible woman, obviously. After all, you don't want broken china and glass everywhere if you're the one who'll have to clear up the mess.'

'Some things did get broken,' David admitted, 'but usually they were things we'd been given as Christmas presents by Mum's aunts; you know, limited-edition plates and little statues of wizards holding cut-glass jewels. Usually by New Year's Day there was nothing left but porcelain dust and a few stray shards of commemorative shrapnel. Like I said,' he added, 'practical.'

'Sure. I mean, why smash something you like?'

David nodded. 'So you don't much care for cordless drills, then?'

'Actually, I try and keep an open mind where power tools are concerned.'

'That's good.' David took a couple of steps towards the door. 'I'm going to get something to eat,' he said, 'because I'm hungry. You don't have to come with me if you don't want to.'

She looked at him. 'Actually,' she said, 'I might just stay here quietly for a bit. You know, think about things.'

'Fair enough.' Three more steps towards the door. 'I could bring you something back; a sandwich, maybe—'

'Thanks, but I'll be fine.'

'If you're sure.'

Two more steps. 'I'm sure,' she said.

'Right.' There was only about a yard to go before he reached the door, and he couldn't think of anything to say that might generate a pretext for not covering the distance. 'Be seeing you, then.'

'Be seeing you.'

He closed his eyes as he turned his back on her, and waited half a second before opening them again. But nothing changed. He reached for the door, turned back the Yale lock latch, and opened it.

'Bastard!' somebody snarled in his face, and pushed him back inside.

The next three or four seconds were largely taken up with stumbling, sailing through the air, landing painfully on his back on the concrete floor, and various related issues. When he'd dealt with these aspects of the situation and had a chance to open his eyes and look up, he saw (in the order in which they impressed themselves on his attention) a large gun – and a carbon copy of himself.

'Bastard,' the carbon copy repeated.

On balance, the sudden appearance of a doppelgänger had to be the most important consideration, though the big scary-looking gun clearly was no trifling matter; and even if it was a trifle, it was an assault trifle, and very much pointed at him—

'You must think you're really clever,' said his mirror image.

'No,' David replied truthfully. 'Who are you?'

The doppelgänger made a vulgar noise. 'I'm David Perkins,' it said. 'And you're the evil, sadistic little bastard who took my place and left me to be arrested for a crime I didn't do. A crime *you* did, more to the bloody point.' The doppelgänger clicked one of the many levers on the side of the rifle, presumably to demonstrate hostile intent. David didn't actually know what it did – for all he knew it could have been an immersion heater – but he got the message. 'I'm going to kill you,' the doppelgänger added, just to hammer the point home.

'Oh,' David said; then he frowned, and added, 'Just a moment.'

'No.'

'Please. There's just one thing I want to clear up first.'

'Oh, for crying out— All right then, what?'

David marshalled his thoughts. 'What he said,' he said. 'It all figures – because, yes, I did clone you and I did leave you for the police to find and, yes, it was very wrong of me. But what did you mean by "took your place"?'

The doppelgänger now looked puzzled as well as very, very angry. 'Took my place is what I meant,' he said. 'Let me spell it out for you. My name is David Perkins. You're a filthy little clone who turned me in to the police and stole my life. Which is why—'

'Hold it.' David's brows furrowed like stormclouds. 'Are you saying you're the *real* David Perkins?'

Even more puzzled, and definitely even more angry. 'Don't mess with me, frogspawn,' the mirror image snapped. 'I'm a real, live, flesh-and-blood human being. You're a gallon of green slime with ideas above its station. Prepare to die.'

'Excuse me,' David said, 'but are you sure about that?'

'Of course I'm bloody well sure.'

'May I ask why?'

The doppelgänger grinned. 'Well, for one thing,' he said, 'I can see it in your mind.'

David hadn't been expecting that. 'You can read my . . . ?'

"'Course I can. You know I can, because of those crackerjack Homeworld superhuman powers that come from being a wonderfrog. I know you know all about them, so it's no good playing dumb with me.' He seemed to hesitate, and a slight frown crossed his face. 'Now there's a funny thing,' he said.

'What, in my mind?'

The double nodded. 'Seems like I owe you a very small apology,' he said. 'Not that it means you aren't a bastard after all, and I'm almost certainly still going to kill you, but according to what I can see inside your skull, you've forgotten all about it. The fact that you're the clone, I mean, and I'm the genuine article. For some reason, you've blotted all that part of it out and spliced in some garbage where you created me, and then left me for the cops.' He rubbed his chin thoughtfully with his spare hand. 'Bloody strange thing to do, if you ask me; after all, why would you deliberately invent a version of the story where you come out of it an even bigger arsehole than you already are?'

David couldn't think of an answer to that; not that it was at the very top of his mental agenda. A bit prosaic, perhaps, not to mention self-centred and probably shallow, but he was more concerned with the 'almost certainly going to kill you' part. His best chance of short-circuiting that, however, appeared to lie in keeping the other him distracted. Accordingly:

'I don't know,' he said. 'But can we just get this whole thing straightened out, please? You're saying you're really David Perkins—'

'Correct. And you're a copy of me, inadvertently generated when a stray flake of skin or a loose hair or something floated off me and into the cloning tank. At least I assume that's what happened; first I knew about it was when you jumped up out of the green soup and tried to strangle me.'

'I did that?'

'Quite,' the doppelgänger agreed. 'Not the sort of behaviour I'd expect from me. But then, if you were an accident, nobody would've set the jumpers or checked your input stream for corrupt data; hence you're me, but a thoroughly screwed-up, fucked-over version of me with severe personality disorders. And, apparently, a selective memory.'

'Oh,' David said; and although it really was neither the time nor the place, he started wondering. After all, it was far-fetched but by no means impossible, by the rather idiosyncratic rules of possibility that seemed to operate in these parts. 'Would it be all right,' he asked, 'if I took a peek inside your head, just to compare? It'd save you a lot of time and effort explaining.'

The doppelgänger thought about it for a moment. 'Don't see why not,' he said. 'If you like, we'll make that your last request, shall we?'

David nodded. 'That's very kind of you.'

'No problem. Any friend of me is a friend of mine, and all that. Help yourself. Oh, and if you were thinking any silly thoughts about bunging up my head while you make a grab for the gun, forget it right now. I want shooting you to be a solemn, dignified moment, not something out of a Marx Brothers film.'

Carefully, so as not to make his alter ego nervous, David slipped inside the doppelgänger's head and started to look around. The first thing he saw was a very large, solid, inflexible Purpose, of which the main feature was his own execution. Quickly sidestepping round it, he found himself in Memories. There was this other him, tied to a chair the way he'd been left in Honest John's workshop, the night he and John had made their epic escape to Watford, leaving the scapeclone behind.

As he watched, the door flew open and a mob of police-men in Darth Vader costumes burst in, brandishing machine guns. A split second later, after an exquisitely brief but quite distinct moment during which they wob-bled and warped like a TV picture in a thunderstorm, they'd gone and a large number of frogs were skittering around the floor, hopping in and out of the armholes of the suddenly empty flak jackets that lay strewn on the ground. He watched as the alternative David Perkins wriggled free from the chair, grabbed one of the police-men's guns and ducked out through the back door, the one that ought to lead to the interstellar elevator pad. He didn't get any further than that, because at that precise moment the girl (who'd been sneaking up behind the doppelgänger while all his attention was focused on keeping the gun pointed straight) clonked him very hard on the head with a Stilson wrench.

'Actually,' she said, 'even though it wasn't really you, that was *fun*.'

'Thanks,' he replied thoughtfully. 'Here, do you think there might be any truth in what he was saying?'

'About you being the fake and him being the real milk chocolate? Wouldn't have thought so. Why, do you?'

'I'm not sure,' he admitted. 'I looked in his mind like he said I could, but I hadn't found the relevant bit by the time you socked him, and now I can't see in there at all.'

The girl gave him a filthy look. 'All my fault, needless to say. Look, if you like I can wake him up and we can run through that scene again, complete with him stick-ing that gun up your nose.'

'It's all right,' David replied absently, 'it isn't actually loaded.' He looked up sharply. 'How do I know that?

Suppose I must've seen it in there. Anyhow, there aren't any bullets in the bullet-holder thing.'

'Want to bet?' She reached over, picked the gun up and broke out the clip 'Nor there are,' she said, sounding rather bemused. 'Why's that, do you think?'

David shrugged. 'Don't ask me,' he said. 'Either he didn't want to risk accidentally blowing me away if his hand slipped, or when he was escaping he happened to pick up an empty gun. The first alternative's more charitable, and since in both versions of the story I haven't been very nice to him, I think I owe it to him to assume the best, don't you think?'

'I think you're an idiot,' she replied. 'But fortunately, I'm here to bash up your enemies, so it's not as much of a problem as it might otherwise be.'

'Gosh,' he said. 'That sounded almost affectionate.'

'Really? Like I keep telling you, you're weird.'

He looked down at the doppelgänger, who was sleeping loggishly in a crumpled heap at his feet. Odd to think that for a while there he'd been scared stiff by an exact facsimile of himself; scary was the last term he'd ever have thought to apply to himself, with or without a machine gun. Seeing himself like this, he couldn't help wondering yet again what she saw in him, assuming she did see anything and wasn't just being polite, or the sum of her programming.

'What're you going to do with him?' she asked.

'God only knows,' he replied. 'I can't just tie him up and call the fuzz; not again. It'd be so much worse, second time around.'

'True,' she admitted. 'But you can't turn him loose, either. I don't want to sound gloomy or anything, but I don't think he likes you very much.'

'I don't blame him,' David said. 'And let's face it, what if he *is* telling the truth? If he's the real me, I mean. What the hell am I supposed to do then?'

She pulled a face. 'If you stop and think about the implications of that remark,' she said, 'you'll see why I find them very offensive. I'm not the real me either, remember.'

'But that's not—' He stopped, recognising that she had a point. 'What do you suggest?' he asked her.

'What we should do with Sleeping Beauty there, you mean? Sorry, haven't got a clue.' She grinned. 'Turn him into a frog, maybe.'

David looked at her. 'Say that again,' he said.

'Why? You heard me all right the first—'

'Say it again.'

'All right. You could turn him into a frog.'

David punched his fist into his palm. 'And send him back to the Homeworld,' he said. 'Ideal solution, thank you.'

'It is?' She wrinkled her nose. 'Can't actually see what's so good about it, myself.'

'Think about it. If he's me, or a copy of me, whichever; either way, he's bound to share my strongest and most intense characteristic.'

'Stupidity?'

'Loving you,' David replied. 'And I don't care how hard done by he's been, I'm not having that. Back Home, of course, there's no such thing as love, so he'll be fine.'

'And that's your idea of solving a problem, is it? Thank God you never became a doctor.' She frowned, started to say something, stopped, then started again. 'Actually,' she said, 'I'm pretty well certain he's the clone and you're the real one.'

'Oh?'

'Yes, actually.'

'No, I meant, what makes you say that?'

'Simple.' She shrugged. 'I don't love *him*. And you may be so dim you can't tell the difference, but—'

'Meaning,' he interrupted, 'that if you don't love him . . .'

'All right, yes,' she snarled irritably. 'Though I still can't think of a single thing about you that's even remotely attractive, so it's got to be programming and stupid DNA tricks. Sort of like soya-bean-substitute veal.'

'You do love me.'

'Yes. For crying out loud, don't go on about it.'

David didn't know what to say. In fact, he was so caught up in the ensuing maelstrom of strong emotions that he almost failed to notice the door flying open and the place suddenly filling up with massively armed and armoured policemen.

CHAPTER NINETEEN

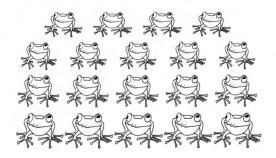

Bloody hell, David thought, as they slammed him up against the wall and cuffed his hands behind his back, she really does love me! Who'd have thought it?

His feelings must have seeped through onto his face, because one of the policemen demanded to know what he was smirking about.

'She loves me,' David replied. 'Isn't that amazing?'

'No accounting for taste,' the policeman replied. 'Now shut your face and keep still, or I'll blow your head off.'

'What? Oh, right. Sorry.'

Me, he thought, as they dragged him backwards through the door, she actually loves *me*, not just the face or the voice or even the whole ensemble put together. Otherwise she'd have loved that other me, too; but she didn't. That's so incredibly wonderful . . .

Then he surfaced; just in time to notice that they were about to throw him into a black van with no windows, along with the girl of his dreams and the other him. He frowned. If he allowed himself to be carted off and locked up in some cell, it could seriously disrupt his plans. 'Hang on,' he said, 'what do you think you're doing?'

'Shut up and get in the ark ark rivet.'

He hadn't actually meant to do it. Instinct must've grabbed the wheel and taken control. Terribly sweet of instinct to be so concerned on his behalf, but he had the feeling that it'd just made things significantly worse—

Thunk. He heard the noise of the rifle butt hitting the back of his head, even had time to identify it before the Sandman grabbed him by the hair and swept him away to Dreamland—

(He'd never quite trusted sleep, even when he was quite small; indeed, his childhood had been populated by nightmare monsters who snatched teeth from under his very pillow or scriggled down his chimney clutching sinister sacks and laughing like maniacs. Always at the back of his mind there'd been this feeling that sleep was out to get him; and now he knew why—)

'Turn them back!'

His eyes snapped open, and showed him a huge purple face, only an inch or so from his own. It was frightened and very, very angry, both at the same time. David sensed that this was probably a highly dangerous combination.

'Did you hear me?' the face snarled at him. 'Turn them back. Now.'

Behind the face, he saw plain brick walls painted government light blue. Recent experience told him exactly where he was. Stone walls do not a prison make, nor iron bars a cage; but when you wake up in a room painted that particular shade of blue from floor to ceiling, it's a safe bet that you're in the shit again.

'Are you a policeman?' he asked.

'Yes,' the face growled. 'And don't try it. Just don't. This room is under *total surveillance*.' He was right; the face was extremely frightened. 'You even think about turning me into anything, we'll flood the room with knockout gas and bash you to a pulp while you're asleep. You got that?'

Curious sensations these. Not so long ago, he'd learned that someone really loved him. Now here was someone who was actually afraid of him. Remarkable. He raised an eyebrow.

'What on earth are you talking about?' he said.

The face drew back and scowled at him. 'Don't you come that with me,' it said. 'We know all about you, what you did. We got it on video.'

'Got what on video?'

'You,' the policeman hissed, 'turning them other officers into frogs. In this very bloody room. So don't you—'

'But that's impossible. You can't turn people into frogs.'

The policeman shot him a look of pure hatred. 'No,' he said. 'I can't, but you can. And if you do—'

'No, I can't.'

'Yes, you *can*.' He could almost hear the click as the policeman clawed back his self-control from the edge. 'Like you did to Sergeant Hoskins when he arrested you. We got that on video, an' all.'

David shook his head. 'I'm sorry,' he said, 'but there

must've been a mistake somewhere. Changing people's shape just isn't possible. It'd be – well, magic.'

'So you can do magic,' the policeman roared at him. 'Big fucking deal. Now turn them back.'

'No, I can't.'

'Yes, you *can*!'

David smiled placidly. 'Prove it,' he said.

The policeman's face turned the colour of a choice Victoria plum. 'Didn't you hear me?' he said furiously. 'We got it all on video.'

David nodded. 'And George Lucas has got miles and miles of film of space battles,' he replied. 'Somehow, I don't think it'd stand up in court, though. Sorry, but you're going to have to do better than that.'

'All right.' The click he thought he'd heard earlier was replaced by the most deafening creaking sound made by the tension-strain of the end of the policeman's rope. 'All right, let's make a deal. What'll it take to get you to turn them back? I can talk to the judge.'

'I bet you can,' David replied. 'And when you start trying to prove I can do magic, I expect *he*'ll want to talk to *you*. Can I see my lawyer now, please?'

The policeman stood up sharply, turned away and walked to the door. David couldn't see his face, but he was sure he heard a distinct sniffle. It made him feel a trifle guilty. After all, the man was only doing his job; or, to put it another way, obeying orders.

Carefully, so as not to startle him, David reached out into his mind and made a few delicate adjustments. He didn't change much: a few misapprehensions about frogs, a few strange beliefs about so-called magic powers, a fresh perspective on the Van Oppen murder, which hadn't in fact taken place. Nothing major.

The policeman turned round and stared at him.

'Can I go now, please?' David asked.

'Huh?' The policeman frowned, reaching for a memory that wasn't there any more, like someone trying to scratch an itch in a missing limb. 'Yes, I suppose so. In fact, come to think of it, I don't know what you're doing here in the first place. You haven't done anything wrong, have you?'

'Me?' David shrugged. 'Don't think so.'

'Thought not. Right,' the policeman went on, 'you can be on your way, sorry to have troubled you.'

'No problem. And the others—'

'Others. Oh, you mean the young lady.' The policeman's forehead wrinkled like folded corduroy as he scrabbled desperately for a whole bunch of stuff that wasn't there any more. 'And the bloke who looks like you. Yeah, they can go too. I'll tell the sergeant.'

'Thanks,' David replied. 'Have a nice day.'

Outside the police station, it was chilly and fresh, with a hint of rain in the air. David and his mirror image looked at each other for a moment in silence. Then David said, 'You aren't really me, are you? You're the clone.'

The other him shrugged. 'Yes, well,' it said. 'You stitched me up, I thought I'd do the same for you. I'm sorry.'

'It's all right,' David replied. 'I asked for it.'

'Thanks. And thanks for getting me off the hook with them. You could've left me there.'

David shook his head. 'We David Perkinses must stick together,' he said, with a slightly forced smile. 'So, what're you going to do now?'

'Emigrate,' the other him said forcefully. 'I was thinking of British Columbia.'

366 • Tom Holt

'I've heard it's nice there,' David replied neutrally. 'Or there's another possibility you might consider.'

'Oh?'

David nodded. 'Nice place,' he said, 'so I've heard. You'd like it there, I'm sure.'

'Why are you sure?'

'Well.' David thought before answering. 'If I were you – and I am, almost – I'd like it. I'd like it a lot. Really.'

'Fine. So why don't *you* go there, and *I'll* stay here. With,' the doppelgänger added, 'that absolutely stunning girl I saw you with, just before we got arrested. Is that the famous Philippa Levens, by any chance?'

David smiled at his double, thinking all the while that, if anything, British Columbia was too good for him. 'Sort of,' he replied.

'Sort of? Oh, you mean she's a clone, too? Ah well, that's all right, then. Plenty to go round.'

David's smile broadened, revealing more of his teeth. 'Nicely put,' he said. 'Actually,' he went on, 'that's one of the great attractions of this place I was telling you about.'

'Really?'

'Oh yes. They're absolute wizards at cloning; run you up anybody you like; exact copy, molecule-perfect, while you wait. Don't even need to have a DNA sample, they've got a bit of pretty well everybody on file, it's sort of like the British Library, only with people. All you've got to do is go up to a government official and ask.'

'Is that right?'

'Would I lie to you?' David asked. 'Come to that, *could* I lie to you? After all, you're me.'

The doppelgänger reflected for a moment. 'So

basically I could go there and order anybody I liked, just like a drive-through McDonald's.'

'Exactly,' David replied, 'only with less waiting, and no compulsory free soft furry toy. Try it and see.'

'All right,' the doppelgänger said confidently. 'After all, no disrespect to Ms Levens, but if I could have an exact replica of any girl in the history of the world . . . Helen of Troy,' he added. 'Marilyn Monroe. Liz Hurley. Cleopatra. You do see my point, don't you?'

'Absolutely. Why settle for time-crossed true love when you can have really hot chicks?'

The other him looked at him oddly, like a paranoid mirror. 'I can't read your mind any more,' he said. 'What're you doing?'

'Oh, nothing. I think I may have a bad cold coming on, that's all. So, do you want to try this place I've been telling you about?'

'You seem very keen indeed to get me to go,' the other him said suspiciously.

'Of course. I want the very best for clones of me; you know, give 'em the start in life I never had, and all that.'

The copy thought for a moment. 'I believe us,' he replied. 'We have an honest face.'

'Honest Dave,' David said. 'It must run in the family. I should get some cards printed.'

'Hm? Oh, I see. Don't give up our day job. Well, if this mysterious place of yours is so absolutely wonderful, why are we hanging about? Let's go there at once.'

'Sure.' David hesitated. 'How are we going to do that, exactly? Have you got any money?'

'What? No.'

'Neither have I,' David said. 'And that's a bit

awkward, this being Hammersmith and the, um, the way of getting to this other place being in Watford—'

'Watford? Where we just were, in John's shed?'

'That's right. Rather a long walk, I'm afraid.'

The other him scowled. 'Bugger that,' he said. 'I say we go right back in there and demand a ride home in a police car. After all, they brought us out here, they should damn well see to it that we get back.'

David shook his head. 'There's a certain degree of logic in that,' he said. 'But if you think I'm going back in there of my own free will, you're dozier than we look.'

'All right,' grumbled the doppelgänger, 'so what do you suggest?'

'I haven't the faintest—' David started to say; then something caught his eye. A beat-up old yellow van had drawn up on the opposite side of the road, and the driver was waving at him. 'Why don't we cadge a lift?' he said.

'A lift? Who the hell with?'

David smiled. 'Honest John.'

Of course, there was no way of knowing whether the driver of the van was John himself in person or one of his duplicates. But it was John's van, and the driver was wearing John's old warehouse coat and scuffed-up brown lace-up shoes, and John's deceptively vacant-looking grin; and when he said 'Hello', he sounded pretty much like him. Close enough for jazz, David decided. 'What are you doing here?' he demanded.

'Philippa sent me to get you out,' John replied. 'I told her not to be so daft, you'd get yourself out in your own good time. But she insisted.'

David raised an eyebrow. 'Pretty confident, weren't you?' he said. 'More confident than I was, anyway.'

John laughed. 'Oh, I knew you'd be able to cope. If I wasn't sure, I wouldn't have called them in the first place.'

Here we go again, muttered a large part of David's instincts. He managed to ignore them. 'You called the police?'

''Course. After all, had to get all that stuff sorted out, otherwise they'd have been after you the rest of your life. Whole bloody country would've been overrun with frogs.' He paused. 'You *did* get it sorted out, didn't you?'

'Well, yes,' David admitted. 'But it was a close shave at times. Next time you feel like solving my problems, tell me first.'

'Close shave be buggered,' John replied scornfully. 'Can't have taken you more than two minutes to get yourselves out of there.' His grin widened, to the point where his face was in danger of unzipping at the back. 'Anyhow,' he said, 'nice to see you two getting on so well together.'

'Oh, I see,' said the doppelgänger, 'you turned us in to the Filth so we'd bond in adversity, like a quality epoxy resin. Very smart, if a trifle transparent.'

'Ah,' John replied. 'Someone's got to think of these things.'

Only it hasn't worked, David thought to himself, as quietly as he could so John wouldn't hear. Because I don't like him very much, which is why I'm trying to fool him into going to the Homeworld. And just because he likes me – talk about your major universal truths – just because he likes me, I don't actually *have* to like him . . .

Well done, son, said a voice in David's head. Took your time, but you got there in the end.

'What are you two grinning at each other for?' the doppelgänger asked suspiciously. 'And why can't I see inside your heads?'

'Can't you? I mean,' David quickly amended, 'it's nothing, I'm just, um, smiling.' Am I? Apparently I am. Why, for God's sake? Nothing to smile about here, is there?

You were grinning like a dog, replied the voice between his ears, because you thought you'd got one over on me. I'm grinning 'cos that's what you were meant to think. I win. Again.

But suddenly David knew that it wasn't so; that John was just trying to make him think that, by way of damage limitation. And, at the same moment, he knew that where he was savouring this wonderful insight was a place in his head where John couldn't go, a place he didn't even know about—

—Or was he supposed to think that, too?

'Don't believe you,' growled the doppelgänger. 'You're up to something, both of you.'

'All right,' John said. 'We were just thinking, you'll really like it back on the – where you're going. We were thinking, you've had the rough end of the stick all this time, you deserve to get the happy ending. Earned it.'

'Oh.' The doppelgänger's brow tightened so much that a fly perched between his eyes would've been squashed flat. 'Really?'

'Would I lie to you?' John replied. 'My own son's replica's clone?'

The doppelgänger looked away, slightly ashamed. 'I suppose not,' he said. 'Sorry.'

''S all right,' John conceded magnanimously. 'Just

want what's best for you, that's all. You getting in, or do I drive off without you?'

So they both got in the van; and in the back there was nothing except the plain white-painted sides, and a bag of sugar.

'Just a minute—' the doppelgänger began to say. Then both John and David threw open their respective doors and jumped clear, landing awkwardly on the pavement. They stayed where they'd pitched for five whole seconds.

'He'll be better off there,' John said eventually.

'You reckon?'

John nodded. 'Well, he'd only've been miserable here,' he said. 'Think about it: he's only been alive a few days and already he's been lied to and generally shafted by every single person he's ever met. Most humans don't get to that stage till they're at least fifteen.'

'Even so.' David picked himself up and, very cautiously, stuck his nose round the back door sill of the van. No sign of anybody or anything, apart from a bag of sugar and a few stray grains on the van floor. 'He really did get a raw deal, you know.'

John shrugged. 'And he really will be better off at Home. All his personality disorders basically came from being in love with your Philippa, only sort of once removed. Two weeks back home, you ask him what love means, he'll shrug and say, Don't ask me, I don't know anything about tennis.'

'And that'll make him happy?'

John pursed his lips. 'Can't really say anybody's *happy* on the Homeworld, it's not a concept they're good at. But he won't be nearly so miserable, that's for sure. Got to be better that way.'

David thought for a long time. 'And what about me?' he asked. 'Would I be happier there? Or less miserable, if you'd rather.'

'No idea,' John replied. 'But *I* wouldn't be happy if you were on Homeworld. So that settles it, really. And anyway,' he continued, before David could object, 'Homeworld's the last place in the Universe *you'd* ever want to go. Specially now you've finally got the girl, right?'

'But if I went there, I wouldn't want her any more; and maybe that'd be the best thing for me in the long—'

'Oh, shut up,' John said, 'for crying out loud.'

For some reason he couldn't fathom, David felt he was entitled to score that one as a win for him.

John drove for a very long time. After a while, David fell asleep in the passenger seat, only waking up when John elbowed him in the ribs and said, 'We're here.'

'Are we?' David yawned. 'Where's here?'

'You know,' John chided him, 'here. The workshop. Home.'

'Oh, right,' David replied. 'Watford.'

'Like hell it's Watford,' John said, with another of those enormous grins wrapped round his face, like a hyperactive puppy's lead round a tree. 'You may have been to Watford at some time for all I know, but this ain't it.'

'But—' First, David looked out of the window; then he opened the door, got out and took a few steps. 'How do you mean, this isn't Watford? It's the same place you brought me to the last time. I've been living here, for pity's sake, of course I can recognise it.'

'Sure. It's just not Watford, that's all.'

'Not— All right,' David growled. 'If it's not Watford, then where the hell—?'

'Ah.' John smiled sweetly at him. 'That'd be telling.' He got out of the van and slammed the door. 'Remember the first time I drove you here? Don't suppose you do, but you fell asleep on the way then, an' all.'

'So? I often go to sleep in cars. And the M25 isn't exactly the most enthralling experience of my entire life.'

'Did you notice what I've got in the back of the van?'

David frowned. 'A bag of sugar,' he said. 'But not the first time,' he remembered. 'It was all full of your cloning gear, machines and tools and big glass tanks—'

John was shaking his head. 'Use your brains, son. Or didn't you wonder how the hell we got a whole laboratory full of bulky stuff into a small yellow van?'

That needed some careful thought. 'You were hexing me?'

'Bad choice of words. I made you believe the van was full of gear, yes.'

'Too right you did. I nearly killed myself helping you load it.'

'You *thought* you nearly killed yourself.' He laughed. 'What you thought was a bloody great cast-iron drill stand was—'

'Let me guess,' David said icily. 'A bag of sugar.'

'Got there in the end.' John shrugged. 'What put you to sleep both times was neural shock caused by the infraspatial shift. Zonk, like you'd been bashed over the head with a brick. But of course, you didn't see it that way, so you didn't mind.'

'Fine.' David breathed out slowly through his nose. 'So where *are* we, then? Not—' He scowled horribly. 'Please,' he said, 'don't tell me this is—'

'British Columbia?' John laughed. 'Nah. Actually, British Columbia isn't British Columbia; 'least, the one I take people to isn't the one that's shown on the maps. Bit further afield, actually.'

'Further? How *much* further?'

'Since you ask, about two hundred light years, give or take a mile. Too far for you to walk home, anyway.'

David shivered involuntarily. 'Homeworld?'

'No.' John shook his head. 'Wouldn't catch me going back there. Matter of fact, getting caught's why you wouldn't catch me going there, if you get my drift. Luckily, there's other places.'

'Other planets, you mean?'

'Don't look at me like that.'

'An alien world in a distant star system, with a breathable atmosphere, that just happens to look exactly like downtown Watford?'

'Yeah, well,' John replied, shifting his feet a little. 'Eye of the beholder, really, if you see what I mean.'

David didn't answer. He saw what John meant. He had an awkward feeling he'd been seeing all sorts of things that John meant for quite some time, and had never realised it. Instead, he concentrated; and as he did so, quite suddenly he realised that he knew how to do what he wanted to do here. Just a matter of closing the eyes, clearing the floor of his mind, and *looking*—

What he saw was a flat, dreary tundra sheeted over with red ice under a pale green sky. It was savagely cold, and a gust of high wind blew a pinch of snow in his face, leaving him spluttering and fumbling for the collar of his shirt. Here and there, small tufts of wiry purple grass stood up through the snow. Overhead, a big, weak blue sun shimmered hazily, sandwiched between two small yellow suns that could have been tugs towing a crippled warship. If there was anything alive here, other than John, the grass and himself, he couldn't see it. No birdsong or buzz of insects interrupted the shrill nagging of the wind. The air stank of sulphur and iron.

'I see what you mean,' David said, though without having to bother with words or sound. 'You're right. On balance, Watford's an improvement.'

'It's not all bad,' John replied. 'There's some really cute pink glaciers on the eastern continent. Tricky to get to, though, since all the oceans are sulphuric acid. You can fly, but for crying out loud don't go too low. If you trail a toe in the water, all I can do for you is imagine you a replacement.'

'Charming,' David said with a shudder. 'And you seriously believe I'd rather live here than on my own dear little blue-green planet—'

He broke off. John's grin might be profoundly annoying, but nine times out of ten it seemed to mean something. In this case, he made a policy decision that if the Earth itself was like this, green-carpeted and blue-watered only through the power of John's imagination, he really didn't want to know.

'Hold on, though,' he said nevertheless. 'If this is another planet, then how did those coppers manage to get here and arrest me?'

'They drove here in a couple of big vans,' John replied. 'Bigger than mine, for sure.'

'But each one with a bag of sugar in the back?'

'Not sugar.' Honest John's breath was freezing into pale pink cloud. 'They had a proper Homeworld computer—'

'Frogs?'

John dipped his head by way of affirmation. 'Thanks to your identical twin getting stroppy with them earlier, one thing they weren't short of was frogs. All I had to do was convince them they were humans, and the whole frog thing never happened.'

'But they *are* human. Well, policemen, actually, but let's not split hairs. They're humans, and he persuaded them to believe they're frogs.'

'And I persuaded 'em to believe they're frogs who believe they're humans. Believe me, it's a damn sight easier just to do it than explain what I'm doing and how.'

David decided not to get too close to that one. 'All right,' he said, 'let's have Watford back. There's not a great deal in it, but I miss the buildings.'

John chuckled. 'Really? You want to carry on living a lie and all that? I thought you didn't hold with it.'

A dark mauve cloud covered two of the suns, casting murky purple shadows. David shivered. 'Warm, sunny lies are an exception,' he said. 'Pack it in, I want to go home.'

'Really? Home, or *home* home? There's one really good thing about this place that maybe you haven't considered, you know.'

'Is there?' David's teeth were chattering. 'What the hell could that possibly be?'

John started to whistle 'If you were the only girl in the world'.

'Oh, right,' David said angrily. 'You think the only way she won't ditch me and run off with someone else is if I'm the only other non-vegetable life form on the planet. Thank you so much. Your confidence in me is little short of overwhelming.'

'Be like that. But there's nothing quite like being *sure . . .*'

'Drop dead. I want to go *really* home. Now.'

Immediately, the pink planet vanished, and was replaced by what David had hitherto assumed was Watford. 'Yeah, right,' he said. 'But I want proof. I don't believe you any more.'

'Fine.' John snapped his fingers. In the sky, in enormous letters of burning gold, appeared the words—

REALLY, THIS *IS* WATFORD.
STRAIGHT UP.
WOULD I LIE TO YOU?
BEST WISHES,
GOD

'Oh, come on,' David sighed. 'If you think I'm going to be fooled by that—'

''Course you aren't,' John replied pleasantly. 'I'm just making a point, aren't I? You can see the writing, clear as day, but you don't believe it. If you can't believe what you see and hear, how can you ever really *know* anything's real? It could just be me, all of it.'

'I see. Please explain how knowing that's supposed to make me feel better.'

''Tisn't. It's just the truth, that's all. Deal with it.'

David looked up. The sky looked very skylike; too skylike to be true, perhaps? He closed his eyes; once you started thinking like that, hopeless insanity was never more than a gentle stroll away. 'Do you promise?' he said slowly. 'Faithfully, on your word of honour?'

'I promise.' John yawned. 'Use your loaf, son. Who in his right mind would create a pocket universe for his only begotten son, and disguise it as this crummy place?'

'Double bluff,' David pointed out. 'As in, that's exactly what you *want* me to think.'

John shrugged. 'Look at it the other way,' he said. 'Even supposing this isn't really Watford; if there's no way in hell anybody could ever tell it from the real thing, what difference would it really make?' He grinned, suddenly and savagely. 'Come to that,' he added, 'what on earth makes you think the *real* Watford is real?'

David sagged. 'Screw it,' he said.

'That's the most sensible thing I've ever heard you say.' John took a long step back and vanished. 'Well,' he said, 'take care of yourself. I think you're about ready now.'

'Ready? Where are you? Stop fooling about and stand up where I can see you.' David looked round, but there was no sign of John, and his weight had lifted from David's mind, so that when he reached out, there was nothing there.

He counted to ten. 'You don't fool me,' he said aloud. 'I know you're still here, somewhere. Look, I'm not in the mood for silly games.'

Nothing. It was only now that John had gone that David realised what his presence had looked and felt like, the landmarks in his mind that had always been so familiar that he only knew they'd ever been there now that they were irrevocably gone. 'John!' he shouted. 'John, Dad, stop it, it isn't *funny*!'

'Hey, that's great. You never called me Dad before.'

He whirled round, but there was nothing there; and when he played back the impression of the words, he realised that he hadn't heard them or even felt them in his mind. The thought had been his alone, and yet it had somehow come from John, transmitted like a recorded message down centuries of selective breeding and genetic manipulation. And then he realised: *bang on schedule, right down to the last half-second.* And now he was on his own – genuinely alone, for the first time ever.

He wasn't sure he liked the feeling very much.

In fact, the more he thought about it, the less it appealed to him. Being on his own like this, he felt— No other words for it: lonely. Lonely, in the way that someone living in a treehouse a hundred feet above the ground might feel if the tree suddenly stopped being there.

Out of the corner of his eye, he noticed a small piece of paper tucked behind the windscreen wiper of the van. It hadn't been there a minute ago. He pulled it out, but the wind teased it out of his fingers for a moment, and he had to snatch if back before he could look at it – two lines, in scruffy, cramped handwriting and thick pencil:

> *And, deeper than did ever plummet sound,*
> *I'll drown my book*

Gosh, David thought. Then on impulse or instinct or both, he turned it over, and saw that the neat, bold handwriting on the other side read—
Dere Warden. Tax disc form in poast. Yores, J Smith.
– And, of course, no way of knowing which way round it had been. (For what it was worth, there was no visible tax disc on the van windscreen.) David looked at it, one side and then the other, for well over a minute, before reaching the only sensible conclusion. Both sides. Simultaneously.

The hell with it, he thought. He didn't like being alone, but fortunately he didn't have to be. Quickly he

CHAPTER TWENTY

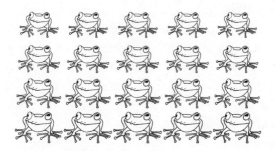

A nd that, David muttered to himself, would've been
a perfect point at which to end the story, with the
main issue sort of resolved, and an implied happy-ever-
after scowling horribly at him across the threshold. But
it doesn't work like that. All that happens when the story
ends is that the film crew packs up its gear, pays its bar
bill and breakages, and moves on to its next assignment.
Life goes on, and happy (whether ever-after or only
from-time-to-time, in spots) is in the eye of the
beholder. Besides, right now he felt that a better analogy
would be two unexploded bombs left over from the war.

'Sorry,' he said meekly. 'I got arrested.'

Some women have the knack of expressing the phrase
Oh-for-crying-out-loud wordlessly, with the tiniest
movement at the corner of the mouth. 'I know,' she said.
'I was here, remember? You *do* remember me, don't
you?'

'Yes, of course I . . .' (Memo to self: get out of the

habit of ducking into the short-pitched delivery) 'I got arrested,' he repeated. 'But it's all sorted out now, there won't be any more trouble. So—'

'It's all sorted out now.' She gave him a milk-curdling glare. 'You couldn't phone, of course, to let me know you were all right.'

He considered pointing out that for most of the time, he *hadn't* been all right. Policemen had been pointing guns at him, and accusing him of serious crimes. Fortunately, he realised in time that the truth is not always a boy's best friend. 'I'm sorry,' he said. 'But I don't know the number.'

'What?'

'John's phone number,' he clarified. 'I don't happen to know it, offhand. That's assuming he's got one here, of course. I don't actually remember seeing—'

She said something extremely vulgar about Honest John's telephone number, followed by something in even worse taste about Honest John himself. 'I was worried sick,' she said. 'But, of course, that never even crossed your mind. Oh no. You were too busy having *adventures*—'

'It won't happen again,' he said, sitting down on a workbench. 'Promise. The police aren't after me any more, the other me's been shipped off to the Homeworld, and John's, um, gone. I don't know about his thirteen clones,' he added, 'but I've sort of got the feeling they've gone too. I have an idea I'd know about it if they were still here – I think it'd be like having an itch in an amputated leg, only the other way round. The other you and my cousin Alex seem to have ridden off into their own private sunset, or at least I haven't seen or heard anything about them, so I'm assuming they've slung their hooks. That just leaves a couple of hundred frogs, you and me.' He took a deep breath. 'I think it's over,' he said. 'And we've won.'

'Won what?'

David shrugged. 'Probably a free radio alarm clock or a weekend for two in Market Harborough,' he said. 'Nothing very exciting, at any rate. What I meant was, they've all gone away and we're still here. In my case,' he added, thinking aloud, 'meekly inheriting the Earth.'

She walked a few steps away and sat down on the single, rather rickety chair. 'Marvellous,' she said. 'You've inherited the Earth. Well, I haven't a clue where you're going to keep it, and you can bloody well dust it yourself.' She made an impatient gesture that ended with a box of small taps spilling all over the floor. 'What the hell do you want with the Earth, anyhow? I didn't think all this was about Earths and stuff, I thought it was about—' She stopped and scowled ferociously at him, presumably for causing her to come perilously close to saying something embarrassing.

He looked at her for a moment, ignoring the scowl. 'That's not the point,' he said. 'The point is, they've *gone*. We're free. From now on, every time we decide to do something, it's really us deciding. Isn't that amazing?'

'No.' She folded her arms across her chest. 'Everybody else in the whole world does that. And I don't know if you've noticed, but most of them seem to be pretty miserable most of the time.' She looked away. 'We're missing something,' she said.

'Really? What?'

'I don't know, do I? You're the one who's just inherited the Earth, you bloody well figure it out.'

'You don't seem—' He stopped without finishing the sentence.

'Don't seem what?'

'You don't seem particularly happy,' he said.

'Of course I'm *happy*,' she spat. 'I'm absolutely bloody delirious with joy. But something isn't right, and it's got to be dealt with.'

He'd seen that look before, several times; usually in the eyes of his mother when, halfway from London to Scarborough, she'd insisted on going back to make sure the gas was turned off. When that look was on the loose, he knew perfectly well, negotiation was utterly pointless. 'All right, then,' he said. 'We'll just have to put everything – the happy ending and the triumph of true love over adversity, all of that – on hold until you've figured out what it is that's bugging you. Is it likely to take long, do you think?'

'How should I know, when I don't even know what it is?'

He shrugged meekly. 'While we're waiting,' he said, 'would you like a cup of coffee?'

'Black, no sugar,' she replied, looking away. 'And unless I get something to eat very, very soon there's going to be real trouble.'

Just as well she didn't take sugar, since there wasn't any. As far as food was concerned— 'All right,' he said, 'let's go and get some food immediately. Any idea what you'd like?'

'Frogs' legs.'

'Apart from frogs' legs.'

'Anything,' she growled, 'I really don't care. Just so long as—'

Abruptly she fell silent, and David realised that she

was staring past him at the doorway. He looked round, and saw a frog. Then loads of frogs, following the first one at a cautious distance. A whole green Sargasso Sea of small, round-eyed frogs was watching them both through the partly open door.

'About what I said I wanted for lunch,' Philippa whispered. 'I didn't mean it, really.'

David ignored her. Instead, he concentrated very hard on a little ridge right between the first frog's eyes, then suddenly (typical Homeworld behaviour, of course) slipped past Philippa's defences and into her mind while the ushers' attention was elsewhere. Once inside he planted the thought he'd come to deliver, and sneaked out again as quickly as he could. The thought was a small, simple one, a mental image of a plate, empty apart from the last smear of gravy and a few minor crumbs, and above it the inscription *Not Hungry Any More*.

He didn't feel very good about doing it, but it was for her own good; better falsely to believe you've been fed than correctly to know you're starving. Or something like that.

(There you go again, he told himself, interfering. Making decisions for people. Playing God.)

'That frog's looking at me,' she said.

'It's all right—'

'No, it bloody well isn't. That frog is *staring*—'

David frowned. 'Actually,' he said, 'I wasn't talking to you. It's all right,' he repeated, pointedly to the frog, 'she does know all about it, really. She just forgets sometimes, that's all.'

The frog hopped forward one step. 'That's rude,' it said.

'Well . . .'

'Staring,' the frog maintained. 'It's rude. And talking about a person as though they aren't there. That's very rude.'

David shrugged appeasingly. 'I know,' he said. 'But you've got to make allowances. I mean to say, she's only human.'

'Then what's she doing talking? They aren't supposed to talk.'

David managed to get up off the workbench and stand blocking Philippa's line of fire before she'd even had time to pick up the heavy spanner that lay conveniently next to her left foot. 'Get out of the way, please,' she said, 'I want to smear that frog over at least three walls.'

'That's *really* rude,' the frog pointed out. 'She really shouldn't ought to be allowed to say that.'

'Hold on.' There was an edge to David's voice that surprised him even more than it surprised Philippa. The frog didn't seem surprised at all, but that's frogs for you: the innate sang-froid of the born diplomat, and they can jump up to fifteen times their own length. 'Hold on,' David repeated, 'and shut up, both of you. Now then,' he continued, after a very brief pause for thought, 'I'm guessing you're local, right?'

'What's "local" mean?' the frog replied.

'From around here.'

'Then you're wrong, Mister Clever,' the frog replied cheerfully, 'because I'm not from here at all. I'm from ever so far away. In fact, I'm from a different *planet*.'

'Are you really?' David said sarcastically. Then the penny dropped, from such a height and with such a terminal velocity on impact that it punched a hole clean through his preconceptions. 'Are you really? From a planet where everybody's like you?'

'Yes,' the frog replied. 'Where everybody's smart and good-looking like me and there aren't any stinky humans, except in the woods and the jungle where they belong. It's much nicer there.'

'I believe you,' David lied. 'So,' he went on, 'how old are you?'

'Me? I'm eight.'

'Eight where you come from?'

'That's what I just said, silly.'

David nodded, ignoring Philippa's what-the-hell-is-all-this-about hand-signals. 'Eight where you come from,' he said. 'And you've been here a while? Or have you only just got here?'

'Been here a few days,' the frog replied. 'That's here days, I mean; they're not like the days back home. The days back home are much better.'

'Of course. Longer, are they?'

'Oh, yes. *Loads* longer.' The frog blinked twice. 'Why are you asking me all these questions?'

'You'll see,' David said softly. 'Now then, are you on your own, or did you come with a lot of other fr— other people from home?'

'I came with everybody else. Lots and lots of us. All my brothers and sisters, for a start.'

'Thought so. And have you ever seen me before?'

''Course I have, silly. Outside Dad's old place, the one you and he left in such a hurry.'

So that was it, then. He was right. 'You're one of the frogs I, er, talked to. There were thousands of you, so many that you couldn't all fit in the workshop, so some of you were outside. Yes?'

'Yes. Why are you asking me if you know the answer already?'

'Just a moment, we're nearly there. So, um, why did you come here? To this planet, I mean?'

'You do ask funny questions. Because Dad sent for us, that's why.'

'Fine. And—' David surreptitiously sneaked a deep breath before asking the question. 'Do you know who I am?'

'Well, naturally. You're David. Our big brother.'

'Yes!' Philippa shouted, before David had a chance to do or say anything. 'I *knew* there was something else, and you wouldn't believe me.' She stopped, and stared. 'This *thing* is your brother?' she asked.

The frog looked up at her and wobbled its throat four times. 'That's her, isn't it? The one you made out of pondslime because all the others got—'

'Yes,' David said quickly. 'Well, sort of. Near as makes no odds.'

'Oh. Don't know why you bothered, really. Don't like her, she's snotty.'

'Tough.' David smiled. 'Because fairly soon now, she's going to be your sister-in-law. And if you don't like it, you can—'

'*What* did you just say?'

The frog ignored her. 'What's a sister-in-law?' it asked.

David turned slowly through ninety degrees and looked Philippa square in the eye. 'That's right, isn't it?' he said.

'But—' There was a short moment of extremely profound silence. 'I suppose so,' she said cagily. 'Presumably. I mean, it's not as if I've got a lot of say in the matter, really—'

'Yes, you do,' David interrupted. 'We're free now, remember? You can do whatever you like.'

'Oh, shut up,' she replied. 'Just because he's gone, that doesn't mean we're free of anything. What I mean is, we aren't free of *ourselves*. And like I said, I don't really have much choice.'

David nodded slowly. 'Breeding always shows, huh?'

'Especially selective breeding,' she answered with a sigh. 'I can't not love you, any more than I can't go and live at the bottom of the sea without an aqualung or a diving bell. The fact that I'd like to live under the sea very much indeed doesn't change anything. I can't, so that's that. And the same in this case, too.' She shook her head. 'Sorry,' she said. 'I'd prefer to be a bit more upbeat about it, but I can't.'

The frog hopped round in a small circle. 'Can we get on with it, please?' it said. 'Only it's boring listening to you two arguing.'

Philippa looked up sharply. 'Get on with what?'

'Hey.' The frog wobbled its throat again. 'Doesn't she know?'

'Doesn't she know what? Oh,' David added, as a complete explanation arrived instantaneously in his brain. 'Bloody hell,' he added.

'Bloody hell *what*?' Philippa demanded. 'Look—'

David pursed his lips. 'I – I mean *we* need to ask you a small favour,' he said.

'Small?'

'Small. Smallish.'

'How small?'

'Oh, quite small. Lots of quite small favours.'

'Lots?'

'Um,' David said.'

'Lots,' Philippa went on, 'as in several thousand?'

David nodded. 'If you don't mind,' he added. 'Only—'

She was glaring at him so ferociously he expected his fillings to melt. 'You want me to kiss several thousand frogs, don't you?' she said. 'To turn them into human beings.'

'*Pretend* human beings,' the frog pointed out vehemently.

No tactful way of answering that David could see. 'Yes,' he replied. 'Dammit, they're my brothers and sisters, and they've come ever such a long way—'

'And it was dangerous,' the frog pointed out. 'Really, really dangerous. First we had to break out of the places we were living; then we had to stow away on elevators to get here. It's taken Dad *years* to set it all up.'

'Homeworld years,' David pointed out. 'I don't know how long a Homeworld year is in Earth terms, but if he's my brother and he's eight—'

'Listen.' You could have sharpened carbon steel on Philippa's tone of voice. 'All right, these frogs aren't ordinary frogs. In fact, they're superfrogs. If Nietzsche had been a frog, he'd have written a book about them. But that doesn't alter the fact that they're *frogs*—'

'Actually—' the frog started to say.

'And that there's *lots and lots and lots* of them,' she continued remorselessly. 'Damn it, even if I could keep up a rate of a hundred kisses an hour, fifteen hours a day, that's still four days of kissing frogs. Screw you, I'm not going to do it.'

'Oh.'

'Don't look like that,' she snarled guiltily. 'It's not fair, even you should be able to see that.'

'Yes. Right.'

Philippa found she couldn't maintain eye contact, so she looked away. 'For one thing,' she went on helplessly, 'what actual hard evidence have you got that kissing the rotten things'll turn them into anything?'

'Well, you could kiss just one, to find out. And then we'd know.'

'Yes, but—' David didn't need to burgle her mind to follow the train of thought: kiss one (successfully) and she'd have to kiss them all, otherwise it'd be bitterly unfair and mean of her. He could see that, just as he could see her point, as clearly as if it was a hundred and fifty feet tall with a big flashing orange light on top to warn passing aircraft. The thought of kissing even one frog was enough to make him feel distinctly unwell.

Nevertheless.

He had two options, he could see that. One was to turn to face her, putting on that I-ask-you-to-do-this-one-little-thing-for-me expression that fulfils the function in a relationship performed in global diplomacy by a flight of a hundred Cruise missiles. The other was to apologise and change the subject very, very quickly. He had no more than a third of a second in which to make up his mind, failing which it'd all be academic anyhow. Piece of cake, really.

'Please?' he said.

She scowled at him for a full five seconds. 'No,' she said. 'Sorry, but I'm not going to do it.'

'You're sure about that?'

'You bet I'm sure. One hundred per cent sure, mind closed like a bank on Sunday. Sorry.'

Yes, but they're your brothers. Well, in a sense they're your brothers. He took a deep breath. 'I'm asking you to do this one little thing for me . . .'

'Excuse me,' said the frog.

'Not now,' David hissed. 'One little thing,' he continued wretchedly, 'and it'd mean so much to them if only . . .'

'It's not a little thing, it's a great big enormous thing.'

'Fine, I'm asking you to do this one great big enormous thing for me, all right? Now if it was the other way round, and I was the one who had the chance to bring—'

'Excuse me . . .'

'I said shut up. Damn, where was— Oh yes, right, bring happiness into the lives of all these thousands of—'

'Hey.' The frog made an enormous jump and landed on David's toe. 'You up there, I think there's one very important point you may have missed.'

'Well? What?'

Instead of replying, the frog made an even more enormous leap, landing on David's shoulder this time. Before David could say 'No, you fool, you're thinking of parrots', the frog had planted a loud, smacking kiss on his cheek and shot into the air like the Space Shuttle leaving Florida. When it landed, it did so on two feet, not four—

'Bloody hell,' David said.

'You were the one who assumed we were all your brothers,' replied the erstwhile frog. 'But we aren't, as you can see. Now . . .'

Apart from the unusually long legs, big hands and bright green hair, the ex-frog looked just like any human female you might happen to run into on, say, the catwalk of a Paris fashion house, or the main lot of a major Hollywood studio. 'You're my sister,' David said slowly.

'That's right.'

'I see. And, um, how many of you are, well, girls?'

The ex-frog smiled. 'All of us,' she replied. 'Just as

well you haven't got anything arranged for the next four days, really.'

'Yes, but—' Part of him wanted to ask Philippa what she thought was so amazingly funny. The rest of him could guess what her reply would be. Damn, he thought; and, Oh, well.

'Also,' the former frog went on, 'while I think of it, you'd better find us all something to wear. It's not just the distinct nip in the air, there's also a small matter of primitive human nudity taboos. And after that, you can fix us something to eat.'

David's mouth was wide open. When he managed to get control of it again, he said, 'Do you mean to tell me I've gone from being an only child to having six thousand sisters?'

'Lucky you,' the frog replied. 'Come on, I'm freezing my curiously shaped human appendage off here.'

'All right,' David groaned, 'all *right*. So what do you want me to do first, clothe and feed you, or kiss a load more frogs?'

'Don't be so brusque. And really, you should be more organised. No offence, but you're going about this whole business in a rather cavalier fashion.'

('Six thousand sisters,' Philippa whispered cruelly. 'That's *wicked*.'

'Six thousand sisters-in-law,' David replied, with extreme venom. 'Hadn't thought of that, had you?'

There was a slight pause before she replied. 'I'll manage,' she said. And that seemed to settle that; which was probably why David suddenly smiled, and actually seemed to relax a little.)

It was Philippa who got things organised, in the end.

Very sensibly, she saw that the logistics of kitting out six thousand new adult human beings and getting them ready to face the world had to be sorted out once and for all before any more sisters could be added to the tally. All she said was, 'Wait there, don't do *anything* till I get back,' and, fortunately, David had the good sense to do as he was told. While she was away, he asked the ex-frog—

'I don't have a name,' she said, in answer to his question, 'or at least, not what you think of as a name. You'd better give me one.'

"Me? Why . . . ?"

'Oh, stop being difficult and give me a name.'

'All right,' David replied. 'Gertrude Ethel.'

'That's two names, isn't it?'

'I'm in a generous mood.'

'Could've fooled me. Are they nice names?'

'Very,' David replied. 'Very fashionable.'

'Fashionable? What is . . . ?'

'Very popular,' David explained. 'And people will admire you and think well of you because your name's so, um, nice.'

'Really? What a strange system. Gertrude – what was the other one again?'

'Ethel.'

'Ethel.' Gertude-Ethel shrugged. 'Oh, well' she said, 'I'm sure I'll get the hang of all this sooner or later.'

Gertrude-Ethel told him every detail of her life on Homeworld. It took her twenty-one seconds, including a digression and a parenthetical criticism of the way he combed his hair. On Homeworld, she told him, they'd sat around all day in a big compound. The authorities felt that since they were the offspring of the notorious anarchist rulebreaker whom nobody ever talked about, it wasn't really safe to let them loose among right-thinking Homeworlders, just in case – they'd calculated that there was a one-in-seventeen-million chance of the criminal's mental deviance having passed on to one of his children; and on Homeworld they practise zero tolerance when it comes to risks to public safety. So they'd spent the last eight Homeworld years (from various clues contained in what she told him, David figured that one Homeworld year was roughly equivalent to two million Earth years) hopping around in a big glass dome, dividing their time between sitting on rocks in the middle of the water and not sitting on rocks in the middle of the water. All in all, Gertrude-Ethel said, they were beginning to ask themselves if there was possibly more to life than this when Father suddenly arrived to lead them to the Promised Land, even though everything they'd been told by the Homeworld Information and Education Service made it sound rather more like the Threatened Land—

'It's supposed to be so hot,' Gertrude-Ethel explained, 'that if you're out of the water for more than fifteen seconds, you shrivel up and die. That's assuming the predators don't get you first – the huge two-legged lizards and the flying ones with the long, pointed beaks . . .' It took David a moment to realise that she was talking about dinosaurs; which gave him an idea of how up-to-date Homeworld's information about his planet was, or had been before his brief trip home. He explained that things had changed a bit since Homeworld did its official surveys of the place: ice ages, the twilight of the great reptiles, the mobile-phone revolution, that sort of thing. Not, he added quickly, that she'd missed anything much.

While he talked to her, he couldn't help but be aware of all the other frogs, the huge sea of them, waiting at a safe distance just inside the door, or sprawled out front in the road. They were bizarrely silent, and he realised that they were listening attentively to every word he said. 'They've never heard an alien before,' Gertrude-Ethel explained, 'or at least, not properly. And they're only eight.' Something in his expression seemed to trouble her, because she suddenly looked very worried and asked, 'You *are* glad to see us, aren't you?' To his everlasting surprise, David didn't have to think at all before answering 'Yes.'

'That's all right, then,' Gertrude-Ethel replied, closing the subject as firmly as a Swiss vault door. 'You know,' she went on, 'this place is so much more fun than home. We're really going to like it here.' At which point the other 5,999 frogs all simultaneously croaked three times, presumably by way of agreement (and if it gets more bizarre than this, David thought, I really don't want to know).

'Really?' he replied. 'But all you've done since you got here is sit about on concrete going rivet rivet—'

'Are you kidding? We've been out in real sunlight. We've been able to hop more than five hops at a time without crashing into each other. We've been for rides in the elevator – one to get here from Homeworld, another from Father's old shed to this shed here, that's two journeys. In less than a year. Amazing. And as soon as you turn us into humans—'

David winced, though he tried to pass it off as cramp. 'Yes,' he said, 'right. As soon as Philippa gets back—'

'Isn't that her now?'

David looked round, and saw Philippa walking

through the door. For a brief instant his newly acquired survival instincts had him go through a mental checklist, to make sure she was wearing the same clothes and shoes, had her hair the same length, and so forth – once upon a time, he could just remember, life had been so simple that there'd been only one of everybody, so that when you saw someone, you could guarantee that it was the real, genuine and original person and not some sixth-generation copy synthesised from genetically modified frogspawn – but he knew almost immediately that it was her, *his* her. He just knew, that was all.

'Right,' she said, wearily brisk. 'All sorted. There should be a big van round in about half an hour with the clothes and shoes and stuff – you lot'd better all be the same size, or there's going to be big trouble. The food's not going to be here for another two hours or so, but you'll just have to be patient. The lorries to take you all to Brize Norton airbase were promised for six-thirty sharp—'

'Philippa,' David interrupted. 'What the bloody hell are you talking about?'

'Arrangements,' she replied irritably. 'The difficult, complicated, exhausting arrangements I've just spent hours and hours and hours making on behalf of you and your family. Not that I'd expect any thanks, God forbid, but you might at least—'

'Philippa. Thank you. Now, what arrangements?'

She sighed. 'Well,' she said, 'there's six thousand aubergine sweatshirts and six thousand pairs of burgundy jogging pants on their way from Redditch – *not* what I'd have chosen personally, but getting anything in that quantity for immediate delivery was a minor miracle, let me tell you. Food: I wasn't at all sure what to get that'd do for frogs *and* people, so I settled on bread and fish . . .'

'Don't tell me,' David interrupted. 'Three loaves, five fish—?'

Philippa looked at him. 'Don't be ridiculous,' she said. 'I ordered seven thousand white medium sliced and six thousand cans of John West tinned salmon. Obviously I'd rather have gone for fresh, but you've got to be realistic, haven't you? I mean, supposing for some reason we don't get this lot transformed in time, six thousand semi-deliquescent smoked-mackerel fillets . . .'

'Quite. But,' David asked, 'where the hell's it all coming from?'

'Marks and Sparks. Which reminds me: underwear—'

'Marks and Sparks,' David repeated. 'I see. Paid for with what?'

'Your Visa card, silly. You don't think I had that sort of money on me in cash, did you?'

David went a rather unique shade of white; almost the same white as the underside of certain kinds of poisonous woodland fungus, but slightly more pastel. 'My— Hold on,' he said, as a small thought patiently battled its way through the rising surf of terror. 'How did you get hold of my Visa card?'

'I didn't. I just gave them the number.'

'Right. And who told you the number?'

'Nobody. It wasn't the real number, anyhow. I just persuaded them it was, and they believed me.'

'They believed—'

Then David understood. Of course.

They hadn't burned the original Philippa Levens at the stake because she wore jet-black proto-Laura Ashley flowing cotton or kept cats. They'd decided she was a witch because, well, she could do magic. To be precise, she could do simple acts of persuasion – making people believe what she told them, or turning them (in their own estimation and that of their peers) into frogs: the basic repertoire of party tricks he'd taught her while he'd been in full showing-off-to-impress mode. Now she was back, and in no immediate danger of getting barbecued, and she still had the knack. Evidently.

'They believed you,' he repeated. 'Um, well done. That was—'

'Extremely clever, verging on quite brilliant. Yes, I know. But positively mediocre compared with the real coup I managed to pull off. But I don't suppose you're interested, so I'll just wrap a tarpaulin round my shoulders and sit in the corner pretending to be a small stack of pallets.'

David counted to five under his mental breath, and asked, 'What coup?'

'Oh, nothing much. I just found us all somewhere to live, that's all. Rent-free, of course, and everything else entirely taken care of. But it's no big deal, really.'

'Philippa. Stop wittering and explain.'

So Philippa explained. With the attitude pared away, the gist of it was that she'd phoned the Prime Minister of Canada—

'Of course, to start with I got put through to some secretary or other,' she said. 'But I explained that I really needed to talk to the Prime Minister himself, and the secretary understood perfectly; but the best she could do was pass me on to some bureaucrat or other, and I had to explain all over again. In the end, it took me nearly twenty minutes before I got through to the man in person.'

David nodded. 'And you explained to him, of course.'

'Well, of course. And he was a bit brighter than the rest of them, I guess, because he came round to my way of thinking in two minutes flat. Couldn't have been more helpful, in fact.'

'Philippa,' David said cautiously, 'what exactly was he helpful about?'

'About giving us somewhere to live,' she answered. 'You should try listening when people tell you things. I know it spoils the surprise, but—'

'Where?'

She yawned. 'British Columbia, of course,' she said. 'Well, not all of it. There's no point being greedy, and of course we'll have to keep the grass cut and generally make the place halfway habitable, so I said we'd be perfectly happy with a town and a couple of hundred square miles. Besides, when you take out the mountains and the bits where it's freezing cold most of the year, there's not a lot left. We've got some lakes, which'll be fun, and a couple of oilfields we can rent to petrol companies, and for proper serious shopping, there's a place called Seattle, apparently, just the other side of the American border. Why are you looking at me like that? You weren't seriously expecting this lot to settle down in west London and get jobs in building societies?'

'I—' David shook his head. 'Why British Columbia?' he asked.

'I thought that's where you'd always wanted to go.'

There was no answer to that: not without the risk of seeming ungrateful. 'Um, yes,' he said.

'So you're pleased, then?'

'What? Oh yes. Thrilled to bits.'

'You don't *sound* very pleased.'

'It's just taking me a moment to get used to the idea, that's all.' He frowned. 'What about the people who live there already?'

She shook her head. 'No problem. I asked them if they wouldn't mind packing up and clearing out—'

'You *asked* them?'

She nodded. 'The Prime Minister had his technical people patch me through into the radio and TV stations,' she explained. 'Really, they can be very clever and resourceful when they want to be, not to mention efficient. I don't know how they did it; he just said, "Hold the line just a moment, will you?" And I waited for a bit, and then he said, "You're on," and I explained.'

'You explained.'

'That's right. And then I had to wait a bit longer, and finally he came back on and said all the people in the bit I'd chosen were loading their stuff into their cars and moving out. Of course, there'll be a few who didn't catch the broadcasts first time round, so he's having Navy helicopters cruise up and down with loudspeakers playing a recording every ten minutes. Means we won't be able to move in for a week or so, but that's fine, because it'll take you that long to kiss your way through all these sisters of yours. They're building a special aquarium thing at Port Moody where we can stay till everything's ready; you can do the kissing there. Oh, and they're sending their air force to pick us up and take us over there. The Prime Minister felt it was the least he could do.'

'Oh,' David said. It seemed to be the only word in any language that came anywhere near expressing what he felt.

Philippa, however, clicked her tongue. 'You haven't got it, have you?'

'Got what?'

'The reason for doing all this.'

David shrugged. 'I can't say I—'

'Typical. All right, think. Remember what John told us, about Homeworld computers?'

'They aren't computers,' David replied. 'At least, not what we think of as computers, little grey tellies that go wrong all the time. Homeworld computers are groups of frogs—'

'Precisely. Ten or twelve frogs; for a really big, powerful mainframe, maybe as many as fifteen; and that'd be powerful enough to run a planet, send ships through interstellar space and maybe even handle *Tomb Raider 2* without freezing solid.' She grinned suddenly. 'So if you had a computer made up of, say, six *thousand* frogs—'

David blinked about five times in a row. 'There's a thought,' he said quietly.

'Quite. And, being one of mine, it's pretty damn' brilliant. Of course, we'd only want to run it part of the time – say, when this lot are asleep, so as not to cut into their free time. Even so, I think it ought to be more than enough to sort out this funny little planet, don't you?'

David thought about that for a moment. 'You want to rule the world?'

'Good heavens, no. If we did that, everything would be our fault. I was thinking more of selling computer time to everyone who needs it. I think the expression I'm groping for is "global monopoly".' She smiled. 'I just thought it'd be a good way to make lots and lots and lots of money, that's all. To keep us and all your relatives here in a modest degree of comfort.' She frowned. 'Just in case the penny's still teetering in the balance rather than actually dropping, you may care to consider the concept of a happy ending. You know, where we can all live happily ever after, doing whatever we want and not having to go to work or do our own laundry. Well?' She challenged him abruptly. 'Isn't it what you've always wanted?'

He opened his mouth; and then he thought: a nice house in the country (and whatever else it may be, Canada's indisputably a country), my own computer business; and when I was a kid I always thought it might be fun to have a brother or a sister . . . And Philippa, of course. She's what I always wanted. It's just that—

(And at the back of his mind, a very familiar voice said, 'Finished. Forty-seven seconds ahead of schedule, what's more. Now, how's that for planning?')

For a split second – about the time it takes to put a pound's worth of petrol into your car, no more – all David wanted to do was grab John firmly by the ears and bounce him off the sides of buildings. Since that wasn't really practical, he did the next best thing and broadcast feelings of hatred and contempt so intense that television viewers in Stevenage called the BBC to complain about signal interference. Pointless, of course; he couldn't feel John's presence anywhere, inside or outside his mind. And if John didn't want to be found, finding him was a bit like trying to swat a flying wasp with a sledgehammer.

Of course, David rationalised, once he'd cooled down enough to be able to think, he only means it for the best. Probably thinks he's helping. Well, obviously he was helping, even after I thought he'd buzzed off for good. That was fine, as long as I didn't know; but no, he had to go and spoil it, because he simply can't help showing off how clever he's been—

And he has been clever, too. Absolutely no doubt whatsoever about that. And here I am, on the verge of becoming Emperor David I of No-Longer-British Columbia *and* Bill Gates, having apparently won the love of the girl of my dreams, not to mention having the useful knack of being able to turn policemen and similar pests into pondlife. It's—

'It's impossible.' Philippa interrupted. 'On the one hand, everything anybody could want. On the other hand, the feeling that you were born with a silver spoon rammed violently up your bum. Oh, and whether having a life partner who can read your mind is a good thing or a bad thing, a blessing or a curse – that's something you'd better not have to think too hard about, if you know what's good for you.'

David shrugged. 'I don't know,' he said. 'I mean, I suppose it's roughly the same for Crown Princes and tsarevitches and all that crowd; yes, they get all the nice things and the big houses and stuff, but from the moment they're born, their lives aren't their own, every last detail's mapped out for them, they're the result of hundreds of generations of careful dynastic planning.' He smiled bleakly. 'Most of them seemed to cope, I guess. But of course they *knew*, and I've only just found out—'

Philippa clicked her tongue. 'You're going to have to sort that one out for yourself,' she said. 'After all, compared to me you're laughing; I'm not even the lead, I'm just the accessory chick. For God's sake, I've been viciously killed at least once.' She yawned, and stretched. 'You know what I'd do, if I was in your shoes?'

David thought for a moment. 'Limp?' he suggested.

'In your shoes metaphorically, cretin. If I was in your

figurative shoes, I'd shut my face and make the most of it. Do what everybody else does. Stop trying to make your life into an ideal home and just camp out in it. I mean, think. Exactly what alternatives have you got, short of hanging yourself?'

It occurred to David that in Philippa's vocabulary, *upbeat* was Newspeak for getting your teeth kicked in. True, if he was only a week or so old and had been born in a tank of green slime—

'—You'd be bloody miserable too. Exactly. And here's me trying to cheer *you* up. I think it ought to be the other way around, don't you?'

David sighed. 'Probably,' he said. 'I just wish—'

Without warning, Philippa smiled. He wasn't sure he'd seen her – this Philippa, at any rate – do a really full-out, fifteen-hundred-amp smile before. It changed a lot of things, somehow. 'Screw what you wish,' she said. 'Face it, this is as good as it's likely to get. And this time the day before yesterday you were a penniless, desperate fugitive cowering in a lock-up industrial unit in Watford. Really, there's no pleasing some people.'

David stood up. 'Oh well,' he said. 'Suppose I'd better go and kiss a few frogs, then.'

'Better had,' Philippa agreed. 'That's the thing about work, it's something you can throw yourself into and not worry any more.'

'Ah. A bit like a combine harvester, then.'

She appeared not to have heard him. 'And in case you were wondering,' she said, 'though if you were, surely you'd have mentioned it just once in all this time—'

'What?'

'This.' She leaned forward and kissed him, with a

certain degree of enthusiasm. For a moment, a voice in his head tried to make the point that it didn't mean a damn thing, any more than a tape recorder talking to you when you hit the play button means that it likes you. And for a moment, David wondered if the voice in his head was his own or someone else's. And for yet another moment, he thought, That reminds me, I've got to kiss six thousand frogs as soon as we reach Canada. And for yet another moment, he reflected on the fact that, to all intents and purposes, he lived in a cosmos where God's name was Honest John. Then, as each of these moments crumpled and burned up like a sheet of paper in a good fire, he realised that he didn't care: it didn't even matter if the kiss lasted exactly to the nanosecond that John had calculated it would back in the early seventeenth century. All that mattered was the fact that he was participating in the kiss, and that somehow, utterly improbable as it might have seemed only a day or so earlier, he had finally managed to reach the end of the story.

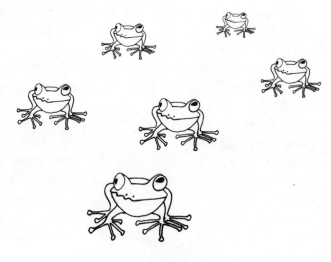

SHETLAND LIBRARY